Oath of Starfire

Rikki Starbuck-Smith

Oath of Starfire

This is a work of fiction. Names, characters, places, and incidents are either the product of the author's imagination or are used fictitiously. Any resemblance to actual persons, living or dead, events, or locales is entirely coincidental.

Cover design by Kaydee Alexander
Kaydeegraphics.com
ISBN: 979-8-9993586-1-5
Fourth Edition: September 2025
Printed in the United States of America

Table of Contents

For the fantasy romance, fairy-smut loving freaks.
We choose morally grey men the way kids pick up feral cats—without hesitation and with zero regrets.

Chapter 1

Everly

The shrill cry of my alarm clock catapulted me from the comforting clutches of sleep, shattering the predawn silence like glass meeting a brick. The sun hadn't even bothered to peek its golden head above the horizon, and here I was, begrudgingly joining the land of the living again. Waking before dawn was a cruelty I endured daily, and no matter how routine it became, it never grew easier. With a grunt of annoyance, I flung the covers aside, a shiver running down my spine as the morning chill gnawed at my bare arms.

Dragging my feet across the cold wooden floor, I trudged to the ensuite bathroom, each board creaking beneath me as if resenting the early hour too. The mirror reflected a woman with fire-red hair erupting wildly around her face, as though she had wrestled a storm instead of slept in a bed. I attacked the unruly mane with a brush, taming it into reluctant waves, then traced my green eyes with eyeliner, hoping to lend at least a semblance of sharpness to my groggy appearance.

My uniform, a plain white tunic and loose cotton trousers, lay folded neatly on a chair, screaming "university student" in its simplicity. Today, though, it felt different. As I slipped it on, the fabric seemed to whisper of changes to come. It was my final year, my twentieth summer, the threshold of the unknown. Today was the day of the Assignment Ceremony. By nightfall, I would know my place in society, the role I was destined or doomed to play. A knot of excitement and anxiety tightened in my stomach as I dressed, the fabric sliding cool against my skin.

The comforting hum of life drifted from the kitchen as I padded down the hall, barefoot to keep my steps silent. The rich, savory scent of sizzling bacon reached me first, curling through the air and tugging me toward its source. My mother stood at the stove, her back to me, a quiet figure of steady industry. Her honey colored braid slipped over one shoulder, swaying slightly as she reached into the fridge for a carton of eggs and a jug of milk. This was unusual. By now, she was normally gone, already at work in the Palace before the sun had even risen.

I paused in the doorway, leaning against the frame. She hadn't noticed me yet. I watched as she cracked eggs into a bowl, her movements precise and practiced. Her brow furrowed faintly, as if her mind was elsewhere, and for a moment, I wondered if she, too, was thinking about today's ceremony.

"You're up early," I said softly, breaking the silence.

She startled slightly before turning, her warm smile spreading when her eyes met mine.

"Big day," she replied, her voice gentle but edged with something I couldn't quite place. "I thought I'd make you a proper breakfast. You'll need your strength."

Her words lingered in the air, heavy with meaning. Today wasn't just a milestone for me, it was a turning point for both of us, a moment that would change everything. I stepped into the kitchen, the cool tiles grounding me as I slid onto a stool by the counter.

As she worked, I studied her carefully: the rhythm of her hands, the faint lines at the corners of her eyes, the way her smile lingered even when she thought I wasn't looking. The smell of bacon mingled with the soft hiss of eggs hitting the pan, weaving a simple, comforting symphony that felt like home.

Yet beneath the ordinary morning, anticipation buzzed in the air. The Assignment Ceremony loomed ahead, its shadow touching every thought, every heartbeat.

What would today bring? Would I be assigned to the Guild of Scholars as a researcher? A healer? Or perhaps a seamstress, like my mother? The possibilities were endless, both thrilling and terrifying.

"Eat up," my mother said, setting a plate in front of me. Her eyes lingered on mine for a moment, as though searching for something. "You'll need your wits about you today."

I nodded, though my appetite was fickle. Today was the day everything changed, and though I could not yet see the path ahead, I could feel its weight pressing against me, waiting to be claimed. I wanted to commit this moment to memory, but then I stopped myself.

It's not like I was going to war. It was just a job assignment. Why was I acting as if I would never see my mother again?

Yes, life would pull us into different rhythms once my role was assigned, but that's the nature of growth, isn't it? Still, the weight of this beginning felt suspiciously like an ending. She felt it too, which I could tell, explaining the impromptu morning together.

Not that I was complaining. On most days, breakfast meant a cereal bar shoved into my pocket as I rushed out the door. I glanced at the newsleaf sitting on the counter in front of her chair. The open page displayed a headline in bold print:

DESOLATION CONTINUES EAST OF ERYNVALE. CASUALTIES UNKNOWN. CITY OF DOREN NO MORE.

"I guess the blight is moving closer to the capital?" I asked around a forkful of eggs as she sat down beside me.

My mother glanced at me, her eyes a striking shade of grey that verged on silver, shimmering with unshed tears.

Those eyes, the same ones I had gazed into every day of my life bore the unmistakable hallmark of her Mystic heritage.

This mystical lineage, marked by its distinctive eye color, was one of the defining traits that set her and, by extension, me apart from others. As the child of a Mystic mother and an Elemental fae father, I embodied a rare first-generation hybrid, though my features leaned more toward my father's Elemental side.

Elementals typically carried darker hair shades of black or brown, yet my own hair was a vivid red, a striking anomaly even among other half-Mystics, half-Elementals I had encountered. Our ears bore the sharp points of Elementals, unlike the softly rounded tips of the Mystic kind.

We were a rarity, especially within the Capital of Verdanis, the jewel of Erynvale where I was born and raised. Most interfae families, those of blended bloodlines, lived in smaller, less prosperous settlements on the fringes of the kingdom. But my mother's prestigious role as Royal Seamstress to Queen Anastasia granted us comfort and privilege in the opulent heart of the city.

Historically, the major territories had been divided with rigid precision, each bound to bloodline alone. Laseel belonged solely to the Elementals, while Verdanis had long served as a haven for Mystics, ruled by Queen Anastasia herself, a Mystic by descent. The city was enclosed on three sides by towering white stone walls, with the Saffron Sea guarding the fourth.

For centuries, these borders were sealed, forbidding mingling between the fae peoples. As a result, mixed-bloods nearly vanished rumors whispered of darker ends they might have met. Only within the past two decades, after the borders reopened, did children like me begin to appear once more.

Even then, within Verdanis, suspicion followed us. Those of blended heritage were regarded with unease, for the magic in our veins did not awaken until the age of twenty.

What form it might take, no one could say. The fusion of distinct bloodlines carried the promise of untold power, but also the shadow of uncertainty. And in Verdanis—its ancient streets steeped in tradition and fear, the unknown was the most dangerous magic of all.

Deep wrinkles etched her forehead, a testament to both concentration and worry. She sighed heavily and sank deeper into her chair.

"I don't know why I cling to hope each day that less of our land will fall and that your father might return," she murmured, her voice thick with longing.

Her yearning for him was an ever-present ache in our home. Our bond was unshakably strong, which wasn't uncommon; many children of mixed heritage like me were often raised by a single parent. My father had been drafted when I was only weeks old, torn from our lives to fight in a mysterious conflict whose details were concealed from all but the highest ranks. The only fact we knew of him since his departure was that he had risen swiftly through the ranks, becoming a highly regarded Supreme Commander in the Empyrean Army. Information like that was known only to someone close to the queen herself like my mother.

"He will return one day. We haven't received the blue box, so hope remains," I reassured her, squeezing her hand. "Even if this war with the Blight drags on another decade, he's due home in two years."

The Imperial Council had set this as the maximum service period for conscripts many of whom, like my father, came from the Elemental bloodline. Notably, a large number of them were parents of the first generation of mixed-lineage children. In the capital, where most Mystics lived, support for the alliance that had unified our lands was lukewarm at best. Families received no news from the front, only the dreaded blue boxes containing uniforms, grim symbols of loved ones who had fallen.

"I know," she sighed, then tried to shift the mood. "Let's focus on something positive like Assignment Ceremony Day!" Her voice carried a note of forced cheerfulness as she tried to smile. "Any guesses where they might place you? Everyone at the palace would be thrilled to have the child of a smart, talented, beautiful royal seamstress on their team. Assuming, of course, you know such a child." She teased, winking over the rim of her coffee cup.

"Given that my last attempt at sewing nearly cost me a finger, I doubt it," I laughed, biting into a piece of bacon. "We'll find out soon enough."

After breakfast, we strolled leisurely toward the University, where the much-anticipated ceremony would take place. The sun had barely risen, yet the streets of Verdanis already buzzed with energy, crowded with families of final year students. It seemed the whole city had paused to celebrate, while non-participating students were confined to their usual classes.

Anxiety churned in my stomach like twisted steel as we climbed the white stone steps of the grand building, which gleamed with the splendor of a small palace. The commons hall, typically quiet, rang with the vibrant chatter and laughter of nearly two hundred attendees. The space was a mosaic of proud parents, doting grandparents, eager siblings, and distinguished fae, all gathered to witness the future unfold for their young ones.

Before joining my peers, I pressed a reassuring kiss to my mother's cheek, promising to reunite after the ceremony.

From childhood, my circle of friends was small, beginning with Peris, whom I met through my mother. Our first encounter was during an early primary school play for which my mother designed the costumes. Peris, assigned the modest role of "tree number four," insisted his costume deserved more flair. By opening night, thanks to my mother's artistry, he stood out as the most splendidly dressed tree ever to grace the Erynvale Primary stage. That memory became the foundation of our lifelong friendship.

Peris was striking, with rich brown hair that swept perfectly into place and eyes of piercing ice blue features rivaled only by his radiant, infectious smile. Despite being half-elemental, a trait that deterred many due to prevailing prejudices, his wit and charm were undeniable.

Then there was Ferra, a fiery sprite whose presence was as commanding as her personality. Petite in stature, she styled her spiky jet-black hair to lend the illusion of height, while her silvery eyes made her appear more Mystic than Elemental.

These two became my refuge through years of bullying and loneliness, harsh consequences of living in a territory still skeptical of the Alliance that reopened our borders. As we neared adulthood, the isolation deepened, worsened by public disdain and the cruel label of abomination.

At last came the Assignment Ceremony, a pivotal event where each student, under the scrutiny of the Imperial Council and before family and peers, was appointed to their future role based on lineage and academic record. Professions often followed family lines: teachers raised teachers, lawyers raised lawyers. In my case, I steeled myself for a menial post, likely something hidden from public view, aligning with society's desire to keep someone like me out of sight.

"Well, if it isn't the little halfling girl. Half ugly, half unwanted. Excited to get your assignment as a toilet scrubber?" Anezka Wilks sneered, her venomous voice dripping spite as I took my seat.

I turned to face her, my lifelong tormentor since primary school. She looked every bit the archetype of privilege and cruelty. Flanking her were her sycophantic shadows, the twins Britonya and Vanna, whose cruelty mirrored each other so completely they might as well have been one person. Anezka smirked, waiting for me to break. Instead, I met her gaze with a cold smile.

"We all know you're better suited for that job. It'll keep you close to the asses you love to kiss," I shot back, my tone sharp and biting. With a dismissive flick of my hair, I turned away, leaving her speechless.

The murmurs of the hall fell away as Queen Anastasia ascended the podium. Her presence commanded instant silence and reverence. Though she stood in her fourth decade, her centuries of life were evident in her aura of timeless grace. Her golden hair flowed like molten sunlight across her shoulders, casting a radiant glow against her flawless skin. Her silver eyes shimmered with the depth of starlight, reflecting wisdom far beyond her youthful appearance.

Her regal attire reflected the hues of our realm, flowing fabrics in the colors of sea and sky, woven from the rarest silks and ethereal threads of the hidden markets. With each graceful movement, the dress shimmered as though spun from the very essence of water and air, shifting from deep ocean blues to the soft pastels of dawn.

Atop her brow rested a diadem of sapphire, each gem cut to perfection, gleaming with the brilliance of the midnight sea. The crown, symbol of her sovereignty, seemed a fragment of the heavens themselves, set in intricate silver thorns that only heightened her otherworldly beauty.

Queen Anastasia embodied the enigmatic allure of the fae—ruling with a gentle hand yet an indomitable presence. Her aura was a seamless fusion of her people's ancient magic and the serene majesty of the natural world she vowed to protect.

The bustling crowd fell silent in reverence.

"Welcome. Today we gather for a momentous occasion. The next class of students stands ready to embark on their journey of service. They have spent years preparing to become productive members of our society. Job assignments are a great honor, and Erynvale would not remain the paradise it is without every individual fulfilling their role.

No matter how small the task, each contributes to the greater whole. Thank you for your dedication. We will now call each fae forward to receive their new titles."

The air thickened with anticipation. Some shuffled anxiously in their seats; others froze, holding their breath. I caught Ferra's worried expression, her brows knit in silent hope that she would join the educational guild like her mother.

Peris, by contrast, dreamed of a more social calling perhaps working in a salon where gossip flowed as freely as tea while he styled hair or polished nails. The idea repelled me, but it delighted him.

The queen's voice carried across the hall:

"Janis Asher, law. Muriel Bennet, baker. Charlie Birch, guard."

Each student, upon being named, stepped aside to receive a handbook outlining their mentor and training schedule.

"Ferra Handson, education."

Ferra's expression was unreadable as she crossed the stage. Whether pleased or not, I could not tell, but I clapped softly all the same.

"Peris Kennedy, seamster."

Not his first choice, yet fitting for someone with such flair for fashion likely sparked by his early role as tree number four. His gleeful skip to collect the handbook betrayed his satisfaction.

As the uncalled grew fewer, my heart pounded, each thud echoing in my ears.

"Everly Walker…"

The rest of the world faded beneath the drum of my pulse.

"…royal guard," the queen declared.

Gasps rippled through the hall. My blood seemed to freeze, my vision narrowed. A royal guard? Such a post was reserved for the most exceptional, not for someone of mixed heritage.

I moved as if in a dream, accepting the handbook. My fingers lingered on the embossed title, Royal Guard Handbook, disbelieving.

Back in my seat, Peris's chatter washed over me unheard. I sat in stunned silence, the weight of my new future settling over me. A royal guard, protector of the queen and her council. Impossible. Yet real.

The queen's voice rang out once more:

"Anezka Wilks, sanitation."

The hall erupted in murmurs and stifled gasps. From Anezka's family came audible protests. I bit back a laugh, though amusement tugged at the corners of my lips. Soon, whispers and speculation replaced the shock.

Clearly, I would not be the only subject of gossip weaving its way through the capital's corridors. The council, no doubt, would face sharp inquiries as to why someone branded an "abomination" by traditionalists had been granted such a prestigious position. The mere thought of the coming scrutiny sent a nervous shiver down my spine, and the weight of expectation coiled in my stomach like a knotted serpent.

As the ceremony drew to a close, the final remarks slipped past me, drowned by the tide of my spiraling thoughts. Yet the last words must have been a cue, for the entire graduating class rose in unison, their applause rolling like a sudden storm.

Only then, amid the clamor and ovations, did I allow myself to scan the crowd. My gaze found my mother in the fourth row, her beauty timeless, her smile reaching her eyes in a way that only genuine joy can. Our eyes met, and I saw tears glistening there, a silent testament to her tangled emotions about the day's proceedings.

Navigating the throng of the commons was no easy feat. I wove through clusters of celebratory embraces until I reached her side. Her arms enveloped me, her voice warm with pride.

"Oh, honey. Congratulations! Royal Guard, that's a big deal." Her eyes sparkled with unshed tears of joy. I mustered a smile, my heart a chaotic swirl of pride and apprehension.

"Far better than kitchen or bathroom duty," I joked, trying to lighten the weight of the moment.

"You were always destined for greatness, my love. Your father would be proud," she murmured, brushing my bangs aside. "Let's go home and celebrate. I picked up a pie from the bakery perfect for today."

Her eyes flicked to the packet in my hand, one I had nearly forgotten. Flipping it open, I skimmed through the standard congratulations and job description until my gaze landed on the section about mentorship:

You will report to your mentor on the first day of training. This person will serve as both your superior and your guide.

My mentor was listed as Cain, a name that made my mother nod with immediate approval.

"He's remarkable. The youngest head guard in history, and very handsome," she added after reading over my shoulder. "Quite the heartbreaker, though he seems curiously immune to the swoons of admirers."

"Maybe he's not into girls," I blurted, the words tumbling free before I could stop them a rogue thought escaping unchecked.

On another day, such a comment might have earned me a sharp look. But the joy of the moment seemed to shield me. My mother only raised a single eyebrow, her mood far too buoyant to be unsettled by my cheek.

Outside, I spotted Ferra and Peris not far off, their figures partially hidden by the dispersing crowd. Standing with them was Ferra's father. Tall and stately, his black hair fell in sleek strands over his shoulders, nearly brushing against his sharp, dark wings. His attire was a pale blue shirt paired with crisp white slacks contrasted strikingly with his commanding features. One glance at Ferra beside him made it clear where she had inherited her strong bone structure and striking presence. Seeing them together stirred a pang in me, a reminder of what might have been when my father's own service ended.

"There you are! Thought we'd be stuck listening to our parents talk about the weather until we keeled over," Peris teased as I reached them.

"We're immortal, Peris. We don't keel over from boredom, we just grow duller," Ferra shot back, her outfit now a bold ensemble of a deep purple tank top and black jeans. It was a daring choice in Erynvale, though styles like hers were slowly gaining acceptance with the city's growing diversity.

"I'm actually heading home to celebrate with Mom," I admitted, a touch of guilt in my voice as I declined their company. "Training starts in two days, and we want a little time together before it all begins."

Ferra's face flickered with disappointment but softened with understanding. Everyone knew trainees endured grueling schedules, and early bonding with family often mattered most.

As we returned home, the city streets hummed with the echoes of countless other stories unfolding beneath the same sunlit sky. I couldn't help but wonder about the paths untaken, the lives unlived. But for now, my road had been set before me.

"What is it, my love?" my mother pressed gently, her voice both firm and tender.

"I'm just nervous," I confessed.

I didn't tell her of the scrutiny I feared, the target I already felt painted across my back because of my controversial assignment. She only hugged me tighter, her familiar scent of pine and vanilla wrapping around me like a shield.

"It's been a long day," she said softly. "How about we share some of that pie and get some rest?"

When dawn broke, its light slipped between the curtains, pulling me into the quiet rhythm of morning. My mother sat in the main living space, reclining against the cushions of a chaise while cradling a steaming cup of coffee. I poured one for myself and joined her in the chair opposite.

"No work today?" I asked, raising a brow at her uncharacteristically relaxed posture.

"I managed to take the day off to be with you," she replied warmly. "I thought we could head into town and pick up everything on your supply list before your assignment begins tomorrow."

The reminder jolted me back into the weight of reality. For a moment, I had almost forgotten what awaited me. I plucked a sugar cube from the small dish on the table, dropping it into my cup to blunt the bitterness I had never learned to enjoy.

As I stirred, my mother continued.

"I was reviewing your list. It isn't long, so we should finish by the afternoon. Mostly uniforms and books. But what caught my eye is that you'll be issued a Starfire sword after completing your training. That's quite exciting!"

Starfire weapons were legendary, infused with the blood of the council members themselves. This sacred ritual, performed in close collaboration with Queen Anastasia, bestowed upon these weapons unmatched power. The Mystic blood fused with the wielder's own, ensuring the sword could only be wielded by its rightful owner.

Lost in thought, my mother's gaze drifted. The room fell silent, broken only by the soft clink of my spoon against the cup. I lifted the handbook from the table, feigning interest in its contents while quietly studying her distant expression.

Clearing her throat, she snapped back to the present.

"Are you planning to see Ferra and Peris later this evening?" she asked, her voice distant despite her effort to engage.

"Yes, after we finish in town," I replied, setting my cup down. "It'll be good to catch up before everything… changes. Mother, are you alright?"

I shifted slightly, angling myself to catch her gaze. She blinked, refocusing.

"Yes, love. Why do you ask?" Her tone contradicted her words, tinged with something unspoken.

Taking a deep breath, I decided to confront the question that had gnawed at me all morning.

"Why do you think I received this assignment? Was it because of your ties to the queen, or did they weigh my father's rank as well?"

The words escaped sharper than I intended, sharpened by nerves and frustration.

She hesitated, her expression taut as though balancing her response. Finally, her features softened into resignation.

"Honestly, it's very possible. I'd like to believe they chose you for your merits and your excellent test scores, but your father's stature as Supreme Commander and his decorations could have swayed their decision. They see potential in you akin to his. My relationship with the queen may have had some influence, too, but I had no direct hand in it."

Her candor startled me. I sat in silence, turning over her words. Asking had not eased my anxiety; if anything, it deepened it.

After breakfast, we tidied up and ventured into town. Shopping, once a delight I relished, felt strangely different today. Our destination was a boutique renowned for its chic and sumptuous fashion. Through the display window, my heart leapt at the sight of a mannequin draped in a pink dress that flowed like a dream, the fabric whispering luxury and leisure. Beside it, another mannequin stood in a sharply tailored tunic and trousers, both ensembles designed to dazzle the boutique's affluent patrons.

The usual buzz of excitement that shopping stirred within me was muted, overshadowed by the weight of tomorrow's looming responsibilities. Even as I admired the elegant displays, the reality of why we were here tempered any flicker of enthusiasm.

As we entered the boutique, the bell chimed crisply overhead, cutting cleanly through my muddled thoughts. The shopkeeper, a woman with her hair neatly braided down her back, looked up and fixed us with a gaze that lingered briefly on me. Her smile, though polite, carried a formality that never quite reached her eyes.

Was it my appearance that gave her pause, or the influence of my mother's well-known connections?

Her greeting was courteous yet restrained. Even in moments meant for pleasure, the shadow of my family's legacy stretched long, reminding me that not every door opened with a genuine welcome.

"We're here to pick up a uniform I ordered for my daughter under the name Magda," my mother informed her.

"Ah, yes, the royal guard uniforms," the woman replied, her gaze flickering with something like disbelief. "I'll fetch it from the back."

While she disappeared, I wandered the small establishment, admiring the contrast between the sumptuous gowns and the sturdier, more practical attire. When she returned, she unveiled the uniform. The gold button-down shirt, trimmed with white embroidery and adorned with epaulets, was flamboyantly regal. Its matching trousers carried the same embellishments. The royal crest was stitched over the left breast: a shield bearing a crown of thorns at its center, pierced by two crossing swords.

"How lovely, isn't it, Everly?" my mother prompted, her eyes sharp on my expression.

"Yes. Quite lovely," I replied, my tone dipped in irony subtle enough, I hoped, to escape the shopkeeper's notice, but not my mother's. I forced a smile, more for the sake of politeness than admiration.

"Now, do you recommend a place where we can find her boots and scabbard? I know about Nico's down the lane, but I heard there's a newer boutique with more variety for women."

As my mother and the shopkeeper discussed local options, I slipped outside, desperate for air. The gaudiness of the uniform and the weight of the future it symbolized pressed heavily on me. I drew in a few deep breaths, but the doubts clung stubbornly. Could I truly live up to such an esteemed role? The gold-embroidered crest seemed almost to mock my uncertainty.

Lost in thought, I picked up my pace. Just a few steps from the boutique, my reverie ended in disaster. I collided with a stranger stepping onto the walk, sending his freshly purchased books scattering across the pavement. My foot caught awkwardly, and I stumbled, ending us both into a graceless heap.

"What the..." a gruff voice growled from beneath me.

I scrambled upright, brushing myself off more from irritation than actual need.

"Look, I wasn't trying to audition as your personal hurdle," I shot back before I could stop myself, my words carrying a mix of sass and embarrassment. "I was just... caught up in my own world. Didn't exactly plan to take you down with me."

Even as I spoke, my hands moved instinctively, gathering his books.

When I finally took a moment to look at him, the man I'd literally fallen for was brushing off his clothes. He was young, only a few years my senior, with sandy blonde hair that contrasted with the golden hues common in our region. His skin was deeply tanned, and his eyes, captivating pools of molten metal streaked with blue, seemed to swirl like tiny storms.

What truly set him apart, however, was his attire and the magnificent black wings unfurling behind him, larger and more breathtaking than any I had ever seen. They shimmered with a vitality all their own, so unlike my mother's more subdued, grey-blue wings.

"Is there a problem?" he asked, his voice edged with impatience as I realized I had been staring.

"Nope, no problem at all," I quipped, handing him a book while masking my awe with forced nonchalance.

My gaze flicked down to the cover of Royal Guard Training Protocol. Recognition jolted through me, and my eyes shot back up to his.

"You're Cain," I blurted, more statement than question.

"Who wants to know? I don't have time for this," he snapped, snatching the book from my grasp before turning away, his retreat as sharp and brisk as a gust of wind.

Great. My first run-in with my mentor, and I'd probably left a memorable impression for all the wrong reasons.

His striking features, especially those unforgettable wings, ensured he wouldn't easily fade from memory. Shaking my head at my clumsiness, I turned back to find my mother still inside the boutique, blissfully unaware of my little disaster outside.

The rest of the day passed uneventfully, mercifully without another sighting of Cain. While my mother busied herself with uniforms and meal plans for the hectic weeks ahead, I tried to shove the awkward encounter to the back of my mind. It wasn't until dinner that I remembered she'd also been assigned a new trainee during the ceremony.

"We've been so wrapped up in me, I completely forgot to ask who's the lucky victim you're mentoring this term?" I teased as we cleared the dishes.

"Peris, of course," she replied, her lips curving into a wry smile.

I wasn't surprised. It was hardly a coincidence. My mother, after all, wielded her position as the royal dressmaker with a subtle influence capable of swaying even the queen's choices.

"He's going to love that. You've always been his guiding star, though I do feel for whoever's stuck mentoring that nightmare, Anezka."

At the mention of Anezka, her left eyebrow twitched the familiar sign that she was either stressed or sitting on a juicy piece of gossip.

"What's going on?" I pressed, leaning in with a grin that mirrored hers, sensing she was about to burst with gossip.

Her eyes sparkled mischievously as she met my gaze, lips curving into a sly smile.

"Well, I may have mentioned once or twice how poorly Ms. Wilkes treats those she considers beneath her. With Queen Anastasia championing the Alliance and dismantling territory barriers, such behavior hardly goes unnoticed."

My jaw nearly hit the floor. "You sabotaged Anezka's assignment?"

"Not directly," she admitted. "I simply pointed out her family's lackluster support for the queen's policies. And perhaps hinted that the Selection Committee should take a closer look at her academic record. Anezka assumed her family's legacy would carry her; she never bothered to study. In the end, she sabotaged herself. And her mentor? Mrs. Norris will be... an interesting challenge for her."

Mrs. Norris was infamous for her iron-fisted management of the palace's lower ranks, from kitchen maids to gardeners. I stifled a laugh, savoring the thought of Anezka trying to slip past her strict oversight.

"Every assignment holds importance," Mom reminded me firmly, though her tone softened as she spoke of the palace hierarchy. "Her family may have hoped for something more prestigious, but she's still earning a respectable wage. Do you think my role is any less significant than yours?"

That struck a chord. I had never doubted my mother's importance; she was a master of her craft, respected and admired in her own right.

"It's not really about importance. It's just... oddly satisfying to imagine Miss High-and-Mighty scrubbing latrines," I admitted, a sheepish grin tugging at my lips.

At this, even Mom giggled, sharing in the release of old frustrations Anezka had caused me as a child.

"We both have an early start tomorrow. Let's get some rest," she said, placing the last dish on the drying rack before kissing my forehead. I watched her retreat down the corridor, her footsteps soft against the silence.

Too restless to sleep, I slipped into the bathroom for a long, steamy shower. As the room fogged, I studied my reflection in the briefly clear mirror before it clouded again, forest-green eyes in a face framed by blood-red hair and pointed ears. A stark reminder of the heritage that set me apart and made me a target for scrutiny. How was I, with all my quirks and fire, supposed to fit inside the gilded cage of my new role?

Afterward, I padded quietly back to my room, the floor cool beneath my feet. My mind buzzed with possibilities and looming challenges. Curling up under the covers, I let the day's events tumble through my thoughts, chasing the elusive pull of sleep as moonlight cast a pale glow through the window.

Chapter 2

Everly

My morning ritual now echoed the rhythm of my old school days. The familiarity was oddly comforting, though shadowed by new anxieties. I was jolted awake by my mother's stern warning that if I didn't hurry, I'd be walking to the palace. The reality of our new shared workplace lingered in the air, a constant reminder of our intertwined destinies.

I reluctantly slipped into the uniform laid out for me, its appearance every bit as dreadful as I had imagined. The gold accents, meant to convey regality, only exaggerated the ghostly pallor of my alabaster skin. My fiery red hair clashed violently with the yellow tones. Altogether, the ensemble looked like a garishly painted sunset by an overzealous toddler.

As I stepped out of my room, my mother's eyes swept over my attire. Her fingers fussed at the jacket's lapels as if she could coax something redeeming out of it.

"This color! It brings out the… well, it looks…" Her voice faltered, reaching for a compliment that refused to surface.

"It's hideous. We can say it's fine, Mom. At least it's temporary. Once I finish training, I'll get the black suit." I forced a grin, already bracing myself for the day I could cast off the golden monstrosity.

With a reassuring smile, she handed me a paper bag lunch, and together we set off for the train. Walking to the palace was possible, but the heavy fabric of our uniforms trapped the morning heat. The summer air felt oppressive, especially under the shadow of the Blight. Though today's skies were kept clear by the weather Mystics, their moods were fickle. One sour disposition could summon a storm. Now more than ever, rainfall was a choreographed event for ecological preservation.

Throughout Verdanis, the old wove seamlessly with the new, crafting a life both simple and enriched by innovation. Enchanted trains glided through the city's heart, powered by fae magic harnessed by the Power Division. Our homes glowed with faerie lights, while modern conveniences, such as plumbing, transport, and more, surpassed anything found in the outlying territories.

Yet, even as enterprising fae devised new contraptions to ease daily burdens, such innovations underwent strict scrutiny to ensure they didn't breed complacency. Our society prized diligence. Every garment was still meticulously hand-stitched, not only to preserve craftsmanship but also to sustain local shops and livelihoods.

Expertise and training are revered, a stark contrast to the forgotten era chronicled in our history books, an age when technology once dominated our sister realm, reducing interactions to cold exchanges behind screens, breeding anonymity and cruelty. Yet, amidst this intricate tapestry, I find solace in the simplicity of our trains: efficient, unassuming, and reliably effective.

The train was usually a sanctuary of silence for me. Today, however, it buzzed with the nervous energy of new fae recruits, all clad in varying shades of yellow and gold that marked them as trainees. The incessant chatter and occasional squeals to my left came from a group of fledgling healers in their scrub-like attire.

When they disembarked near the hospital, confirming my suspicions, I turned my gaze away from the remaining passengers. Still, I felt the weight of their stares. Whispers about the "little halfling who landed a Palace Guard position" buzzed around me like invisible wasps. Lost in my observations, a familiar voice suddenly cut through the hum of the crowd.

"Eww, what in the realm did they make you wear?" Peris grimaced, his nose wrinkling in distaste. Without missing a beat, I pulled Ferra into our group hug, her laughter blending with mine.

"Just when I thought my day couldn't get any worse, you two show up to remind me how truly ridiculous I look," I said.

Our laughter drew a few raised eyebrows from other passengers. Catching my mom's eye across the car, I saw her wave and smile reassuringly as she chatted with a group of palace workers. I flashed her a quick 'see you later' gesture before ushering my friends toward the back of the train for some privacy.

Once we settled, I turned my attention to Ferra, concern edging into my voice.

"So, how's the future educator feeling about shaping young minds?"

She exhaled sharply, her expression caught between resignation and frustration.

"Oh, it's fine, I guess. There's no real action, which thrills my mother to no end. Dad's another story he just grunted twice over his newspaper this morning when Mom mentioned my assignment. He hasn't spoken to me since the ceremony. I love the idea of molding the next generation, but I think they're worried about how people will feel about a mixed fae teaching their children."

Ferra slumped into her seat, as though releasing the weight of her worries. Peris cast her a sympathetic glance, clearly feeling the tension as much as I did. Then, perhaps to lighten the mood, he turned to me.

"I'm actually optimistic about my assignment. Considering seamsters are in charge of designing and making the uniforms, I think my talents will be put to good use. Maybe I'll even start by redesigning these monstrosities."

He gestured disdainfully at my uniform, then at Ferra's, which, though similar to mine, was styled slightly more casually with flowy pants and a loose-fitting tunic.

"Who decided all trainees should wear yellow and gold? So uncouth."

Ferra and I couldn't help but laugh at his obvious disgust for our garb.

"Yellow is bright and lets everyone know we're still learning the ropes. It's meant to make it easy for others to offer help if we seem lost," I explained.

"I get that, but as halflings, we already stand out enough. These colors do us no favors," Peris retorted his tone light, but his point clear.

Their conversation drifted on as my gaze turned toward the window. The landscape of Erynvale blurred past, a swift panorama of green and gold. After what felt like an eternity, the train slowed, finally pulling into the depot nearest the palace.

My legs felt heavy as I made my way to the doors, each step sluggish, as though wading through jelly. With a quick wave and a couple of whispered good wishes to my friends, I disembarked.

A short walk brought me to the palace's impressive façade. The vast white building, trimmed with gold and framed by a majestic wrought-iron gate, was as imposing as it was beautiful. Stairs cascaded down on either side of a central fountain, with beds of vibrant flowers dotting the landscape. Their sweet fragrances perfumed the air, lifting my spirits as I prepared to step inside.

I clutched my bag heavy with books and the lunch my mother had lovingly prepared and edged toward the palace. Having grown up in the shadow of its grandeur, with my mother a lifelong servant to the royal court, I had long since learned to navigate its intricate corridors with ease. Yet the hall I sought today lay deeper within its bowels, a place less familiar.

The palace was a labyrinth of beauty and mystery, its halls thronged with guards at every turn. The air buzzed with the vibrant flashes of teleporting fairies, a whirl of colors marking their brisk passage. Others flickered in and out of existence, mastering the art of spatial leaps. Some, blessed only with the simplest magic, opted instead for the elegance of flight.

The Hall of Guards was an oasis of silence amidst the surrounding cacophony. My footsteps resounded with a hollow echo as I pushed open the colossal double doors.

Inside, the lobby sprawled vast and opulent. Couches dotted the space, flanked by rows of desks and chairs. The back wall bore an impressive tapestry of maps detailing the Forest of Fae, with territories both named and unnamed. To one side, a library ascended, its shelves climbing toward a ceiling lost to shadow. The books grown over centuries by the quiet magic that permeated these walls stood as a trove of endless knowledge.

A petite woman with grey hair, her eyes a striking shade of violet, sat at a desk near the library's entrance. As I approached, the terse click of her typewriter paused.

"Excuse me, I'm looking for my mentor… Cain, is it?" I managed to keep my voice steady, despite the butterflies performing a chaotic ballet in my stomach.

She peered over her glasses, her gaze assessing. "You? You're the new guard trainee?" Her tone, steeped in disbelief, nudged my anxiety higher.

"Yes, I am here for training. I'm looking for my mentor, Cain," I replied, my voice firmer though a tremor edged at its corners.

Before she could respond, a deep voice rolled over my shoulder. "That would be me."

The presence behind me was undeniable as he spoke to the woman, thanking her. "If you'll come with me, Miss… err…"

As I turned to face him fully, I was struck by the impeccable cut of his black suit, tailored not merely to contain but to emphasize the power of his physique. The gold buttons and epaulets on his shoulders caught the flicker of the lobby's lights, casting a warm glow that contrasted with the cool intensity of his stare.

His eyes, sharp and unyielding, held mine in a gaze that felt as though it could pierce straight through to my core the core currently heating under that scrutiny.

The first few buttons of his shirt were undone, revealing a glimpse of an intricate tattoo that hinted at stories yet to be told. Each line and curve of his frame pressed against the tight fabric, suggesting a deliberate choice whether to showcase his strength or issue a subtle challenge.

His commanding presence left no doubt he was Cain, my mentor, and, more intriguingly, my newest trial. In that moment, the air between us was charged with disdain and something unfamiliar.

"Everly Walker, but just Everly will do. We can skip the formalities," I quipped, hoping a touch of sass might lighten the mood. He paused, his gaze sliding past me, distant as if distracted or simply uninterested.

"Fine. Come with me," he said at last, his voice clipped. "Guard training doesn't afford us the luxury of time." With that, he spun on his heel and strode away. I hurried after him, my thoughts tumbling over themselves.

Had he not recognized me from yesterday's awkward encounter? The uneasy knot in my stomach eased slightly.

"And try not to bump into me this time," Cain called back over his shoulder, shattering my brief sense of relief.

I quickened my pace to match his. We climbed two flights of iron spiral stairs and passed through a narrow hallway before reaching a space that felt forgotten by time.

The office, though clearly Cain's professional domain, carried the warmth of a private study, something you might expect in the residence of a high-ranking official's heir. It was the size of a large boutique, with a loft overlooking the main area, hinting at private quarters or a secluded workspace.

The walls were a bibliophile's paradise, lined from floor to ceiling with books. More shelves crowded the room, leaving space only for a couple of low lounges and a modest coffee table. At the far end, a small hallway led to what seemed to be a compact apartment.

The décor spoke of military heritage memorabilia hung alongside shelves of books. This was more than an office; it was a command center, a library, and a home all in one. Cain sank into his chair.

"This is my office," he said, his tone firm yet instructive, gesturing to the ordered chaos around us.

"Here, you'll master the knowledge essential to our cause: the history and geography of our territories. The practical side of your training in combat basics will take place in the gym. But above all, our duty is to safeguard the queen and the Imperial Court whenever they step beyond the palace walls."

He paused, his gaze sharpening.

"Occasionally, the elite among us are assigned special missions. If one arises during your training, you'll join me. Do you have all your books?"

"Yep. All right here," I said, lifting my bag slightly to prove my readiness.

"Good. Start with Origins of Fae, Volume One, and notify me once you're finished," he instructed, turning his focus back to a stack of folders, dismissing any chance of further conversation.

With a sigh, I retreated to a less cluttered table and began setting up my workspace. Despite the initial thrill of entering this new chapter, a tinge of disappointment crept in. Hadn't I moved beyond the stage of simple textbook learning?

I arranged my notebook and books, my gaze drifting to a nearby shelf that housed titles like Dark Magic and Dangerous Beasts and The Wings of Soldiers. Their spines hinted at a collection organized by Elemental themes, a familiar system from my earlier studies.

Driven by a mix of curiosity and a need to break the suffocating silence, I asked, "Are these books organized by Elemental themes?"

Without lifting his eyes, Cain made a sharp shushing sound, his voice low and edged with irritation. "Studying does not require talking, Miss Walker."

His dismissive tone grated on me. Though close in age, Cain carried himself with an air of superiority, no doubt shaped by his lineage. His father, a celebrated war general of the Empyrean Army, was a man both revered and criticized. Renowned for his military exploits, he had remained in service well beyond his obligation, returning only sporadically to update the Defense Counsel in Verdanis on strategic matters.

Rumors swirled that he had abandoned his family, a claim that gained weight after he allegedly disowned Cain following a childhood accident that left the boy with permanent damage to his leg. Many believed the general saw no future in a son maimed so young an assumption that seemed to fuel Cain's relentless drive to prove his worth beyond his physical limitations.

As I studied, fatigue began to dull my focus. I startled myself awake when my head slipped forward, striking the table with a jolt. Glancing toward Cain's desk, relief washed over me he wasn't there to witness my lapse.

Where could he have gone? I wondered.

Stiff from hours of sitting, I rose, stretching until my joints snapped back to life. A walk seemed necessary, partly to shake off the drowsiness and partly to find the bathroom. As I wandered through the desolate office, the maze-like corridors felt even more daunting. Rounding a corner, I collided head-on with a solid, unexpected obstacle. We both stumbled, the moment breaking into a blur of surprise and clumsy chaos.

This time, when his hands gripped my arm to steady me, a vivid image flickered across the canvas of my mind, like a scene from a forgotten dream. In the vision, I was alone with Cain in a dimly lit room, the walls draped in shadows that shifted with the flicker of candlelight. Our gazes locked intense, unyielding a silent conversation flowed between us.

Slowly, as though drawn by a force greater than either of us could resist, we leaned toward one another. The distance dissolved until I could feel the warmth of his breath mingling with mine. Time itself seemed to hold still as we inched closer, eyes reflecting a storm of emotions just before our lips brushed in a tentative, yet inevitable kiss. The fleeting premonition left me breathless, excitement and confusion swirling within me as the boundary between dream and reality blurred.

"Again? Really? Do I need to put a bell on you, Miss Walker?" Cain's voice, gravelly and faintly amused, snapped me out of the haze.

As I steadied myself and pushed aside my wild imagination, I noticed he had changed clothes. My eyes betrayed me, tracing his frame before I could stop them. The plain black shirt hugged his torso, every line and muscle sharply defined beneath the fabric. A sudden tightness seized my chest, my breath faltering as though his presence alone commanded the rhythm of my body.

“I… uh… sorry. I was just looking for the… uh… bathroom. Needed a break,” I stammered, tripping over my words.

Why am I so flustered?

Heat crept across my cheeks in a rising blush.

“Across the lobby, next to the bookshelves,” he said, pointing back the way I had come, his voice a low rumble that seemed to reverberate straight through me.

My fingers trembled slightly as I bent to gather the papers that had spilled from the folder he carried. Curiosity overrode restraint, and I couldn’t help but glance at the pages before handing them back.

My breath caught. It was a meticulously detailed roster of the Elysian Army names, birthplaces, family ties all laid out in precise order. Information like this was far beyond the scope of any ordinary palace guard.

“Planning your own invasion?” I quipped lightly, trying to mask my unease with humor as I handed the list back.

For an instant, something fierce flashed in his eyes, then vanished. His expression hardened; lips pressed into a thin line as he snatched the document from my hand with a sharp, almost brusque motion.

“Nothing for you to concern yourself with, Miss Walker,” he said firmly.

“Please, just Everly,” I countered, irritation pricking my voice. “Miss Walker makes me sound decades older. No offense to my mom.”

Without waiting for his reply, I turned sharply, retreating to my table with the weight of his stare heavy on my back.

But the implications of the list gnawed at me. Those weren’t random names, they were all Elemental soldiers, each tied to the ancient forces of nature. And that realization only deepened my suspicion: Cain’s reluctance to train a hybrid fae like me was far more than simple prejudice.

I unpacked the lunch my mother had lovingly prepared, laying out the contents with a small smile. She had included a meat pot pie, a handful of crisp carrot sticks, and a square of lemon cake, a comfort from home meant to bolster my spirits on this daunting first day.

Tucked beneath the meal was a note in her familiar scrawl: Have a wonderful first day! I knew such notes would become rarer as palace life grew busier, but for now, it felt like a hug from home. I slipped it into my bag and began to eat.

Halfway through the pie, a prickling sensation ran along the back of my neck the weight of a gaze. Looking up, I caught Cain watching me with an unnervingly sharp intensity.

"What?" I asked, my fork frozen mid-air.

"Your mother packed your lunch?" His tone carried both curiosity and something I couldn't quite place.

"Yes. She wanted to make sure I had a good first day," I replied, trying to keep things light.

"Interesting," he murmured, his stare lingering a moment too long.

"Why is that interesting? Doesn't your mother cook for you?"

"Not anymore," he said curtly, turning back to his papers.

Clearly, I had touched a raw nerve.

I finished my meal as the room shifted hues through the tall windows, the gold tint giving way to crimson, then violet, before fading into black as night settled in. Just as I opened my mouth to ask if the day was over, Cain stood abruptly.

"We are done. Hopefully, you made it through volume one. I will have a test ready first thing in the morning. Tomorrow, you will also join the other trainees in combat class. Come prepared."

With that, he strode toward the door.

"So this is it? Just me reading and taking tests like I have for the last ten years? I thought you were meant to mentor me, not supervise another round of self-study," I blurted, my frustration spilling over, tinged with embarrassment for speaking so boldly.

Cain stopped, though he didn't turn. "You will do as I say, and that is final," he said, his voice iron-hard.

"Is there a reason you're so cold with me? Does it have anything to do with your lists of Elementals in the army?" I pressed.

He spun around, his eyes like flint.

"If truth is what you want, then truth is what you'll get. The fact that someone of your background was placed in a role others consider more deserving hasn't made my job any easier. Many believe I should have rejected the assignment and believe me, I tried. Unfortunately, Queen Anastasia seems to think you have potential. The list you saw is none of your concern. Now, I suggest we both leave and rest, so we can continue this absurdity in the morning. Good night, Miss Walker."

He didn't wait for a response; his figure already dissolving into the shadows as he left.

Stunned, I stood frozen, the cold truth settling in, he resented me not only for who I was, but for the lineage I represented. I had hoped his harshness was simply his nature, but this personal disdain cut much deeper.

Gathering my belongings, I hurried out of the building. The night air was brisk, a sharp contrast to the storm of emotions swirling inside me as I pushed forward into the quiet streets. The train station felt deserted at this late hour. I slid into a seat in a nearly empty car. The rhythmic clatter of the rails beneath the train offered a faint comfort, though it couldn't quite drown out the occasional sniffles and muffled sobs that escaped me.

When I arrived home, the familiar embrace of the house surrounded me. My mother was waiting, as if she had sensed my need for comfort. Concern filled her eyes, and without a word, she gathered me into her arms, murmuring soft reassurances.

"Oh, honey, do you want to talk about it?" she asked gently.

"I'm just really tired, Mom. I think I'll head to bed," I replied, my voice muffled against her shoulder.

She nodded in understanding, her touch tender as she let me go.

As I retreated to my room, the weight of the day pressed heavily upon me. I readied myself for bed, clinging to a fragile whisper of hope.

Tomorrow will be better. It has to be.

Chapter 3

Cain

I stood in my dimly lit office, fists clenched at my sides. The faint scent of Everly still lingered subtly, yet inescapably. My muscles tensed as I exhaled slowly through my nose, forcing myself to remain still when every part of me demanded movement, demanded release, demanded I fight to burn off this gnawing irritation.

A hybrid. Inexperienced. Untrained. The queen had saddled me with a damn trainee who was more liability than asset. I had dedicated my life to ensuring the Royal Guard produced warriors, not softhearted recruits with no discipline, no skill, no comprehension of what it truly meant to stand in the palace's shadow and protect it. And yet, she expected me to turn Everly into a soldier.

I scoffed and raked a hand through my hair. This wasn't just frustrating; it was insulting.

I had fought for everything, clawed my way up from nothing, proving again and again that I was capable. That I was worth something. My father never made it easy to forget that perfection was the only acceptable standard. If I failed, if I let anyone slip through the cracks, it would only confirm what he had always believed: that I was weak. Useless.

I would not let that happen. And yet…

My jaw tightened as Everly's wide, determined eyes surfaced in my mind. The way she had faced me without flinching, despite the obvious gap in skill between us. There was something in her something that irritated me almost as much as it intrigued me.

She wasn't weak. No, there was fire in her, even if it was buried beneath layers of doubt and inexperience. She wasn't the polished recruit I wanted, but I couldn't deny that she had… potential. And that wasn't the only thing I couldn't deny.

I cursed under my breath. I wasn't blind. I'd noticed the way her hair caught the light, the subtle part of her lips when she focused. How her scent was different, unfamiliar stirred something in me I didn't want to name. I didn't want to acknowledge it, didn't want to feel whatever this was. Attraction? No. Impossible. I had spent years forging myself into something untouchable, something immune to weakness, distraction, temptation.

But she made me feel. And that was dangerous.

Unable to endure the suffocating air of my office any longer, I left, abandoning the remnants of her presence. The palace corridors were silent, save for the heavy rhythm of my boots against stone. Shadows stretched long across the walls, the torchlight flickering, barely pushing back the darkness. My destination was clear: the courtyard beyond the palace, where I could finally breathe without the weight of expectation pressing down on me.

The night air was cool, carrying with it the faint perfume of flowers drifting from the queen's private garden. I wandered through the courtyard without purpose, my thoughts knotted with frustration. The training, the expectations, the damn hybrid, it all gnawed at me. I couldn't decide what unsettled me more: Everly's lack of experience, or the fact that I couldn't seem to push her from my mind.

I found a stone bench near the center of the courtyard and sat heavily, dragging a hand down my face. Silence cloaked me like an old companion, granting a moment's reprieve.

Until she arrived.

The queen approached with the quiet grace only she possessed, her silver hair catching in the moonlight. I stiffened, instinctively straightening as she seated herself beside me without a word. For a long moment, she merely gazed at the night sky, letting the silence stretch before she finally spoke.

"You are troubled, Cain." Her voice was soft but unwavering.

It was not a question.

I exhaled slowly, leaning forward, elbows braced on my knees.

"I don't understand why you assigned her to me."

The queen's lips curved, though her eyes carried a knowing weight. "Because you are the best."

My jaw tightened.

"You expect me to mold an inexperienced hybrid into a warrior worthy of the Royal Guard. That isn't realistic."

"Do you believe a hybrid is incapable of greatness?" she asked, tilting her head slightly. Her tone held no accusation, only curiosity.

I hesitated.

"No. But she's untrained, undisciplined. The Guard demands the best."

"And she will be," the queen replied with quiet conviction. "Just as you were not always as skilled as you are now, she, too, will grow if given the chance."

Frustration burned beneath my skin.

"You're asking too much."

"I am asking you to trust," she corrected gently. "Everly is not like other recruits. She carries a fire within her, a strength she has yet to claim. And you"

She paused, her eyes searching mine.

"You are the one who can draw it out."

Her words carried something deeper, unspoken yet heavy. A weight pressed against my chest, unfamiliar and unsettling.

"Why are you so certain about her?"

A small smile softened her features.

"Because I knew her mother well. And I have seen the kind of person Everly is destined to become."

I exhaled sharply, dragging a hand through my hair.

"You truly believe she belongs in the Guard?"

"I believe she belongs where she is meant to be." The queen's gaze was unwavering. "And perhaps, Cain, she is exactly where you are meant to be as well."

Her words twisted in my stomach, but I forced the thought aside. This wasn't about me. It was about the Guard. About proving my worth. About ensuring I didn't fail.

I turned back to the queen and gave a firm nod.

"I'll keep trying."

Her smile held approval, though it carried the shadow of something deeper, something I wasn't ready to face.

"That is all I ask."

She rose with effortless grace, leaving me alone beneath the vast, endless night.

Chapter 4

Everly

The early morning light crept through my window, chasing away the remnants of a restless night. Despite the emotional turmoil and little sleep, my resolve had hardened into determination. Pages from the textbook I had studied the day before lay scattered around me.

Unable to rest, I had stayed up late preparing for whatever Cain might throw at me. From his vast collection, I had borrowed a tome titled Arcana of the Ancients. I skimmed through it until a chapter immediately captured my attention: "The Ethereal Brethren: An Account of the Fae's Diverse Kin."

Under the soft glow of my desk lamp, I pored over the detailed descriptions and illustrations of various fae species, each more captivating than the last. The chapter began with the Sirens creatures renowned for their otherworldly beauty and deadly allure. Their songs, it was said, could bewitch the hearts of sailors and stir the oceans into fury. The illustration depicted a siren with cascading hair that flowed like water, her piercing eyes hinting at the depths of her power.

Next were the Shapeshifters, or Changelings as they were sometimes called, beings gifted with the ability to alter their forms at will. The text described their remarkable adaptability a survival trait that allowed them to mimic anything from woodland creatures to other humans entirely. The illustration showed a shapeshifter mid-transformation, its features a mesmerizing blend of human and beast.

Then came the Oracles, revered across realms for their foresight. These mystical beings could glimpse the threads of destiny, a gift that was both blessing and curse. The accompanying artwork showed an oracle with luminous eyes fixed on a glowing orb, wisps of fate curling around her fingertips.

Finally, the Nymphs, guardians of the natural world, are each bound to an element of nature. The text described how they protected sacred realms, from lush forests to bubbling streams. The illustration portrayed a forest nymph seamlessly merging with her wooded surroundings, her skin patterned with leaves that rendered her nearly invisible to the untrained eye.

At the back of the tome, I discovered a section on the Mystics fae of profound psychic and mental abilities. These rare beings were both revered and feared for their power to delve into the minds and emotions of others. Mystics could extract thoughts as easily as one might pluck a leaf from a tree, and their ability to manipulate emotions made them powerful allies and dangerous foes.

Their talents also included telekinetic travel, allowing them to move objects or themselves by sheer will, and the creation of vivid illusions capable of deceiving even the most discerning observer. The accompanying illustration showed a Mystic with eyes closed and hands outstretched, waves of shimmering energy radiating from their fingertips, bending the very fabric of reality.

The final section described the Elementals, fae who commanded the raw forces of nature itself. Each was tied to one of the four elements, earth, air, fire, or water, and their powers embodied the essence of those forces.

Earth Elementals could shift the ground, raise barriers, or tear fissures at will, while Air Elementals

They could summon gusts strong enough to lift massive objects or even shift the weather itself. Fire

Elementals wielded flames that could either warm the chill of night or consume an entire forest in their fury, while Water Elementals bent liquid to their will with such precision that they could draw moisture from the air or sculpt it into intricate forms. Their powers were bound only by their connection to their element and the breadth of their imagination.

The text emphasized that these fae were among the most respected in the realms, their gifts both breathtakingly creative and devastatingly destructive. The illustration depicted a circle of Elementals, each encircled by their respective forces, in a display both harmonious and formidable.

As I studied the pages, I felt a profound connection to the vast tapestry of fae lineage. With every paragraph, I wasn't just preparing for my upcoming test I was deepening my understanding of the mystical world to which I belonged. This knowledge was no longer simply academic; it was a lifeline, a claim to a world that was part of me. And I was more eager than ever to protect and serve it.

That morning, I stepped into the testing room with a quiet confidence. The test a blend of historical facts and tactical scenarios felt almost trivial compared to the challenge I had faced with Cain the day before. My pen moved swiftly across the paper, each answer a strike of defiance against any lingering doubts about my worth.

When the results came back, the instructor's approving nod felt like my first victory in a much larger battle. I had not only met expectations I had surpassed them. This triumph in the academic realm was a stepping stone, the first foundation of a reputation I intended to build: one as formidable as any guard in the history of the Imperial Counsel, or under the queen's command.

For combat class, I gratefully shed the gaudy yellow of my usual uniform for something far more practical: tight black pants, a fitted tank top, and sturdy calf-high boots. My fiery, untamable hair was neatly woven into a braid trailing between my shoulder blades. It was also a relief to anticipate interaction with someone other than Cain, whose dour presence had begun to weigh heavily on me.

Yet, stepping into the gym, my relief quickly curdled into apprehension. The room brimmed with my peers every one of them a Mystic and their stares burned into me as I entered. Some sneered, others simply watched with wary eyes. Only one girl broke through the collective chill, lifting her hand in a friendly wave. I returned it with a hesitant smile and made my way toward her. Unfortunately, nerves got the better of me, and I nearly collided with a boy built like a tree trunk. His scowl as I sidestepped him sent me scurrying faster toward the girl.

"Hello. I'm Lyla. Don't mind them. They hate change. They all threw a fit when someone added another couch to the lobby last spring." Her voice was enchantingly melodic, like a harp playing a lullaby.

Lyla was striking, her heterochromatic eyes one silver, the other blue shifting colors as I glanced away and back again. Her hair cascaded in soft shades of pink, reminiscent of a rose petal or a kitten's nose. Her manner reminded me of Ferra: quick-tongued, unfiltered, petite, yet radiating warmth. Almost too saccharine for my taste but a welcome break from the hostility.

"I'm Everly. You're literally the first person here who hasn't treated me like shit," I said, throwing a challenging look at the others who had given me the cold shoulder. Watching them squirm under my gaze? Yeah, that felt good.

"Oh, I know who you are," Lyla chirped, brushing past the weight of my name as if it were nothing at all.

Another gossip tidbit: "You're the first-ever halfling to join the Guard." Her casual use of the word halfling, usually a loaded term around here, was oddly jarring.

The gym was fully equipped, with state-of-the-art machines lining one wall, blending features of ellipticals and treadmills. Thick mats covered the entire floor, while weight benches stacked with hundreds of pounds of iron occupied the opposite side. Medicine balls and tension ropes lay scattered about. As Lyla chatted, my pulse quickened not just from the nerves of socializing but also from the looming dread of physical exertion in front of this critical audience. My physique, curvier and less athletic than most, was rarely seen in this warrior caste. The thought of exposing my lack of fitness in such a setting was daunting.

Attention shifted when the instructor lumbered forward, his presence surprisingly commanding despite his unassuming appearance. He was short and stout, his round belly hinting at a fondness for good meals rather than rigorous training. His hair, a pale blue streaked with silver, matched his wings—dull blue-grey and sagging toward the floor as if tired of holding themselves up. With a grunt, he settled onto a stool placed centrally for all to see.

"Welcome to combat class. Yous won't leave here a badass, but yous will learn to defend yourself. Never know when a call to action will happen," he barked, his accent rough and difficult to place. His lack of the polished eloquence typical of the fae folk piqued my curiosity. How had someone like him secured such a prestigious palace posting despite his less-than-ideal physique?

He continued with gravelly seriousness: "Yous were chosen based on your physical academic scores. That, compared to your mental scores, shows great promise in aiding' the war against magic-stealing' crotch goblins. First and foremost is keeping' the Counsel and the queen safe. Then yourself. Today, we start with blocking'. Pair up!" With a sharp clap of his hands, the room exploded into motion as everyone scrambled to choose partners.

I turned to Lyla, hoping she'd choose me. To my relief, she grabbed my hand. "I will be with Everly, and it will be magical. We are going to be the best of friends and the best of fighters," she declared, her face shining with enthusiasm. Her optimism was infectious, and I laughed softly a genuine sound that surprised me after the tensions of the previous day.

Together, we found a space on the mats and began practicing defensive stances, mirroring the instructor's demonstrations. About an hour in, I noticed Mr. Franklin speaking with someone familiar. My focus slipped from the drills to the curious sight of our instructor engaged in serious conversation with a figure whose presence in the gym felt out of place. The encounter sparked a flicker of unease and curiosity about what might be unfolding beyond our exercises.

I must have stared too long, because a fist caught me hard at the temple. Lyla squealed, drawing the attention of the pairs around us. Unfortunately, it also caught Mr. Franklin's notice.

"Shake it off, halfling," he called out before turning back to his conversation.

That was when the other man shifted, and I froze. Cain. His eyes locked on mine, and my stomach knotted. So, I guess everyone here is just going to throw that word around. Perfect. And… is that pity I see in his eyes?

I shoved the thought of Cain aside for the rest of class. As we packed up, Lyla nudged me with her shoulder.

"A few of us are going to the Raindrop Café after class. You should come!" she exclaimed, her ever

Her eyes twinkled as I caught sight of three guys nearby, whispering just within earshot. There was no doubt in my mind that they had overheard the invitation.

"Thanks, Ly, but I think I'll just head home and study. Cain is on my case about starting volume two or something. His workload is intense." I smiled at her, hoping my rejection hadn't hurt her feelings.

"Oh, of course. How lucky are you to have Cain Campbell as a mentor? He's so dreamy. And those pants, his butt looks good enough to bite." She snapped her teeth playfully. I hadn't even known his last name. No one ever addressed him by it or his father's, for that matter. It was wild how a single scandal could wield such power that people avoided a name entirely.

Lyla's graceful flip of her vibrant hair, followed by a tender kiss on my cheek, left a lingering trace of warmth as she disappeared through the doorway, her laughter trailing behind like a whispered promise of friendship. I exhaled deeply, a blend of confusion and amusement filling me as I hoisted my bag over my shoulder. The day's toll pressed into my muscles, made heavier by the restless nights that had become all too familiar.

Navigating the dimly lit halls of the sprawling palace, the echo of my footsteps a somber soundtrack, I halted suddenly. I had left my textbook in Cain's office that morning. Twilight deepened outside, and I assumed he had already gone, perhaps retreating to his quarters or tending to more pressing matters.

Yet, as I neared his door, a soft glow seeped from beneath it, betraying my assumptions. Steeling myself for an encounter I hadn't expected, I pushed the door open with more force than intended.

"Sorry. Left my book. Just grabbing it and leaving," I announced, my voice sharper than I meant it to be, as I strode to the table where I had worked earlier. The familiar weight of the book in my hands brought a small comfort, and I was about to retreat when the screech of a chair broke the silence.

Cain rose; his movements deliberate.

"Miss Walker, I owe you an apology," he said, his voice soft yet strained, as if weighed down by discomfort. "I was too harsh yesterday. For us to work effectively, we need a functional student-mentor relationship. I overstepped, and I'm sorry." His gaze avoided mine, settling somewhere beyond my shoulder. "And you aced your test today. Impressive work." The words tumbled out almost as an afterthought.

The air grew heavy with his sincerity, awkward yet undeniable, thick as the humid night outside. His rare apology mingled with the praise, stirring a storm inside me, shock, a sliver of vindication, and still the faint sting of yesterday's barbs.

"Thanks. See you tomorrow," I replied evenly, masking the chaos within. Was this apology genuine, or simply a strategy? Either way, I claimed it as a win. A small smile tugged at my lips as I left his office, carrying a trace of newfound confidence in my step.

The train ride home was reflective, a quiet lull after the storm of the day. Dinner with my mother brought cheerful reprieve; her stories dominated by Anezka's latest misfortune, floor scrubbing. Not as grim as toilet duty, but still fitting. Retelling it made me smirk, the satisfaction easing the day's weight.

That night, Cain invaded my dreams. We were secluded in a forest beneath a sky so clear the stars seemed touchable. A crackling fire flickered before us, its warmth barely rivaling the closeness of our makeshift shelter. Pressed together under a blanket, we shared heat. Firelight softened his sharp features into something gentler.

He turned toward me, his eyes glowing with reflected flames. His lips moved, though the words were lost to the wind. They made me smile anyway, filling me with contentment. Then his hand cupped my cheek, and his lips brushed mine, tentative, then deepening into urgency. The second kiss was fervent, hungry, as though he had starved for this moment, and I was the feast. Heat spiraled through me, not from the fire but from his touch. My breath hitched, breaking free in a soft growl that carried his name into the night air.

His lips trailed fire down my neck, each touch like kindling until every nerve felt ready to combust.

Suddenly, I awoke. The dream shattered into the cold reality of my bedroom. I sat up, drenched in sweat, heart pounding as the clock read two a.m. Moonlight streamed through my window, silver and mocking. With a frustrated sigh, I lay back down. The dream faded into shadows, leaving me to a deep, dreamless sleep for what remained of the night.

Chapter 5

Cain

The evening air hung heavy with the remnants of a long day, exhaustion weighing down my muscles. Hours had been spent drilling Everly, testing her limits, yet frustration and something else I refused to name churned within me. The Queen's words lingered, unsettling me in ways I couldn't understand. I shook my head, shoving the unease aside. Everly was my trainee. Nothing more.

Craving escape, I left the palace and slipped into the city, heading toward the only place where I could unload my frustrations freely. The tavern was already alive with the murmur of early patrons, and in the far corner, right where I knew he'd be sat my oldest friend, Jasper.

Dim lanternlight flickered across the worn wooden walls, casting long shadows. The air smelled of ale, roasted meat, and the faint tang of smoke from the hearth in the corner. A low hum of conversation filled the space, broken by bursts of laughter or the clatter of dice on nearby tables. It was a familiar place, a kind of refuge, though I wasn't sure if it was the company or the whiskey that kept me coming back.

Jasper raised a brow as I slid into the seat across from him, his lips curving in amusement.

"You look like hell."

"Feel like it too," I muttered, signaling for a drink. The bartender, an older man with a knowing look, nodded and poured my usual without asking.

Jasper, ever the observer, studied me with sharp eyes. He'd always been that way, perceptive, attuned to every detail.

It was part of why we'd become friends so long ago: he never pried, but he always knew when to push.

"I got assigned a trainee," I said after a pause.

"About time," Jasper replied, leaning back in his chair as his dark wings shifted against the wood. "I thought they'd let you run the place before they trusted you to train someone."

I scoffed and took a drink. "She's a hybrid."

His face twisted, tightening with disgust in a way I'd seen too many times before. "You're joking."

My jaw clenched. I forced myself to stay calm, though irritation prickled beneath my skin. The reaction wasn't surprising, but it still grated on me.

"No. And she's completely untrained. The Queen expects me to make her into a Royal Guard."

Jasper exhaled sharply and shook his head, lifting his glass.

"That's madness. The Guard isn't a place for a half-blood."

There it was — the same prejudice I'd heard a thousand times before. The same belief I'd once shared. The belief I should still hold. And yet, after only a short time with Everly, it felt… different. Off. Wrong.

Jasper and I had known each other since boyhood, both raised beneath the crushing weight of expectations drilled into us from the moment we could walk. We had trained together, fought together, bled together. He was one of the few who truly understood what it meant to be forged in the relentless fire of the Guard. We had always seen the world the same way or so I had thought.

"She's not as weak as you think," I said carefully, though even I wasn't sure why I was defending her.

Jasper scoffed, swirling the whiskey in his glass.

"Come on, Cain. You of all people should know better. They don't belong in our ranks."

I wanted to agree. I should have agreed. But the words caught in my throat.

Instead, I drained my glass, the burn of alcohol doing little to quiet my irritation. The Queen had made her decision, and like it or not, Everly was my responsibility. No matter how much Jasper and a part of it represented- I wasn't about to let her fail.

"The Queen insists she's just as capable as the Mystic-born," I said, keeping my voice measured.

Jasper let out a sharp laugh, tipping his glass back before setting it down with a decisive clink. "Of course she does. She's always had a soft spot for strays. What's her connection to this one?"

I hesitated before answering, my fingers tightening around my drink. "She's the daughter of the royal seamstress."

Jasper rolled his eyes, a smirk tugging at his lips. "Figures. The Queen's been keeping her pets close lately."

I drained the rest of my drink, the burn doing little to ease my frustration. "I don't have a choice in this, Jasper. The Queen is forcing my hand."

"Then go through the motions. Train her just enough to pass her off to someone else."

That had been my plan. A simple, efficient solution. But I knew now it wouldn't be so simple. Everly had a way of making me feel things I didn't want to feel: irritation, protectiveness, something dangerously close to admiration. And that was dangerous.

I pushed back from the table, the chair scraping against the worn wooden floor. "I need air."

Jasper smirked, tilting his head slightly as he studied me. "Or maybe you need to get your head on straight. Don't let this half-blood cloud your judgment."

I didn't respond. I wasn't sure I could. His words felt hollow now, as if I were the one clinging to an old belief that no longer fit.

When I returned to the palace, I went straight to the small apartment tucked behind my office. The Queen had granted me permission to stay here, knowing I spent more time buried in my books than anywhere else. I had enough money to live in the city, but what was the point? My work was here. My solitude was here.

I preferred it that way. The quiet, the isolation, it was a sanctuary of sorts. No prying eyes, no judgments, no expectations beyond the ones I placed on myself. Beyond these walls, the world carried its noise, its whispers, its endless demands. Here, I could breathe, even if each breath was sometimes edged with loneliness.

Stepping inside, I flexed my wings, stretching the tension from them. The deep gray feathers shimmered faintly in the candlelight, their edges darker than the rest. My father always said they were the mark of my lineage, a sign of strength. But to me, they were just another weight I carried.

Strength. That was his creed. Strength of body, strength of will, strength of mind. I had spent my entire life trying to prove to him that I possessed all three. Yet no matter how many battles I won, how many promotions I earned, his approval remained just out of reach. Maybe it always would.

I sighed, dragging a hand down my face before moving to the small desk against the wall. Books were stacked haphazardly, tomes on battle strategies, histories, and the occasional personal indulgence: stories of legendary warriors, men and women who carved their names into history with their own hands. Sometimes I wondered if they, too, had spent sleepless nights questioning whether they would ever be enough.

The flickering candle cast uneven shadows across the walls, and for a moment, I let myself sink into the silence. My fingers traced absent patterns along the spine of a leather-bound book, but my mind was elsewhere, suspended between the weight of the past and the uncertainty of what lay ahead.

I sat on the edge of my bed and reached into the drawer of my bedside table. My fingers brushed against the worn edges of an old photograph, and I pulled it free. The image was faded, creased from years of handling, a snapshot of my family, frozen in time. My father stood tall and rigid, his stern gaze an unspoken command. My mother's smile was soft yet distant, as though she already sensed the grief that would come. My older brother had his arm slung around my shoulders, his grin easy and full of life, a sharp contrast to the heaviness that often haunted our home.

He had been everything my father wanted: strong, capable, the perfect son.

And then he was gone.

The accident had taken more than just his life. It had shattered my mother, leaving her a shadow of who she once was. The warmth in her eyes had dimmed, her voice reduced to a murmur, as if she were always waiting for something that would never return. I still visited her, but she wasn't truly there anymore, not in the way that mattered. She would hold my hands and smile, but the light in her eyes never came back.

I traced the edges of the photo, my thumb running along the crease that split through my brother's face. The ache in my chest was familiar, a wound that had never fully healed. Swallowing against the tightness in my throat, I placed the picture back in the drawer, shutting it away like the emotions I didn't have the strength to face.

Lying back, I stared at the ceiling, but sleep wouldn't come. My thoughts drifted, unwillingly, to Everly.

I remembered the first time I saw her, before I even knew her name. She had bumped into me on the street so unexpectedly that I barely registered the impact before she muttered an apology and hurried off. I should have been irritated, but instead, I found myself staring after her, momentarily caught off guard by the striking contrast of her fiery red hair and vivid green eyes. Something about her had drawn me in, holding me just a moment longer than it should have.

And then, days later, when I walked into the lobby and saw her standing there asking for me, it felt like some kind of cruel joke. She was my trainee? I had scoffed at the idea, frustrated that the Queen would assign me an inexperienced hybrid when I had a reputation to uphold. But even then, despite my irritation, I couldn't deny that same captivation. It unsettled me. I had trained countless recruits before, yet I had never felt… this. A pull I couldn't name, something beyond logic or reason.

How was I supposed to focus on duty when my thoughts kept drifting to her? When the weight of my responsibility was challenged by something I couldn't understand? My mind refused to quiet, churning endlessly over the day, over Everly, over my own damn confusion. I had spent years molding recruits into warriors, but she was different. She wasn't just another soldier. She was a puzzle, and I wasn't sure I wanted to solve her.

With a frustrated sigh, I pushed off the bed and grabbed my boots. If I couldn't sleep, I could at least run until I was too exhausted to think.

The combat wing was silent at this hour, the halls empty. Stepping outside, I stretched my wings before setting off at a steady pace along the perimeter. The night air was cool against my skin, the rhythmic pounding of my feet the only sound in the darkness. The moon hung low in the sky, casting long shadows across the palace grounds. My breath came in sharp exhales, my muscles burning with every stride, but I didn't stop. I welcomed the ache, the push past exhaustion.

I ran until my breath came in ragged gasps, until my mind was finally, blissfully blank.

Only then did I return to my quarters and collapse onto the bed. The weight of the day, of memories and unspoken thoughts, finally faded as sleep claimed me before I had the chance to think again.

Chapter 6

Everly

The days slipped by in an uneventful cadence. The vivid dream I had of Cain did not return, leaving me oscillating between relief and a quiet sense of loss. In reality, Cain kept a professional distance, offering little more than necessary comments on my academic progress. His praise for my flawless test scores was sparse, though it carried a genuine weight. By the fourth day under his mentorship, I had devoured all the volumes of Origins of Fae and progressed to Magical Properties of Erynvale Waters. The bias in my curriculum became clear—there was a strong emphasis on mystic magic, with little exploration of Elemental magic, except when it was framed in terms of its benefits to Erynvale.

Growing up in Verdanis, I had been taught the sanitized version of Laseel, the land of the Elemental fae. Still, even the limited images I had seen suggested a hauntingly beautiful landscape: trees as dark as the deepest night with shimmering silver leaves, and a perpetual veil of clouds maintained by weather faeries to shield the land from daylight. By night, the clouds would part, revealing a starlit sky that lent a fragile brightness to the gloom. Pure-blooded Elementals were more sensitive to sunlight, with paler skin and delicate eyes, traits my kind rarely inherited.

Verdanis, by contrast, was a realm of whites, golds, and yellows. Trees bore stark white bark and golden leaves, and even the waters ran brighter than those of Laseel. Everything shimmered in vibrant light and color, a world shaped to reflect its people's preference for brilliance.

On the fifth day, as I unwrapped the burrito my mother had packed, Cain finally broke his reserve.

"Your mother must not have much faith in your ability to feed yourself," he remarked casually, eyeing the meal.

"Why would you say that?" I asked, puzzled by his sudden interest in my lunch.

He shrugged, glancing toward the palace cafeteria. "Well, considering she knows the palace has a cafeteria for each department but still packs your lunch… she must think you'd never make it there yourself." His hand drifted closer as he picked up the note my mother had left beside the food. It read: You are destined for greatness!

He lifted a brow and handed me the note. Our fingers brushed lightly, and a spark of warmth shot through me, reminiscent of the dream that had lingered in my subconscious. Heat flushed my cheeks as memory and reality collided, my pulse quickening. His touch lingered just a heartbeat too long before he pulled away, leaving a tingling trail across my skin.

I steadied myself, swallowing my bite before meeting his gaze, now weighted with an unspoken question. My voice came out firm, though my chest thrummed with nervous energy.

"I'm her only child. She just wants to make sure I know I'm loved," I said evenly, though my heart pounded in defiance. His gaze unsettled me with a disorienting mix of fear, thrill, and something dangerously close to longing. How could a man who clearly disdained my heritage unravel me so easily?

For the briefest moment, his expression faltered, revealing something unguarded before his mask slipped back into place. I refused to look away, though my nerves burned under his scrutiny. His aversion to what I was contrasted too sharply with the inexplicable pull that seemed to tether him to me. Finally, Cain looked away, his posture tightening.

"You've shown great discipline this week," he conceded, his voice cool again. "You continue to impress me. I think you deserve a little break. Take the rest of the day off. Surely you have some girlfriends to gossip with or shop with."

His attempt at lightness landed awkwardly, as if he wasn't sure how such interactions worked, or perhaps doubted I had those connections at all.

I packed my notes briskly, seizing the excuse to retreat from his confusing presence.

"Yeah, sure. I can find something to do. Weighing my options, I guess," I replied with forced nonchalance, though my mind reeled at the freedom of the chance to see Ferra or Paris, whom I hadn't spoken to since our first day.

As I rose, I expected Cain to step aside, but instead, I found myself standing startlingly close. His scent of cedar and leather surrounded me, intoxicating and impossible to ignore. For the first time, I realized how neatly his height aligned with mine, my nose just brushing his chin. The fit felt unsettlingly right.

No, I reminded myself sharply. He's not for you. Remember who he is, the man who judged you the very first day.

Before I could step past him, Cain lifted his hand, brushing back my bangs with a touch so light it sent a trail of heat across my forehead. The warmth burned slowly, radiating down to the pit of my stomach. My skin tingled where his fingers had lingered, and for a moment, his features softened, his eyes sweeping over my face with an intensity that stole my breath.

Then, as if catching himself, he stepped back abruptly, and the moment shattered.

"Hmm… yes, uhm… I also need to inform you that a new trainee is starting on Monday," he said, his voice a velvet rumble that didn't match his usual gruffness. But almost instantly, his professional mask slipped back into place. "I expect you to stay on the path you're on, despite my divided attention."

My head snapped up, and the words tumbled out before I could stop them.

"Oh, right, because I get so much attention now, besides, 'Read this, Miss Walker. Take this test, Miss Walker,'" I shot back, my voice dripping with sarcasm, pitched higher as I mocked his stern demeanor. I may have let my eyes roll, a small gesture of exasperation I hoped he hadn't noticed.

"See you on Monday, Miss Walker," he replied, deliberately slowing down the pronunciation of my name as though stamping the distance he wanted to keep. With a curt nod, he turned and left the room.

As I followed after him, the confusing mix of his disdain and the undeniable pull I felt left me tangled in emotions. The door closed behind me with a soft click, sealing away the charged air as I stepped into the cooler, calmer corridor. Still, his scent lingered, a ghostly imprint that kept the memory of our closeness alive.

Later, when I settled into the quiet comfort of the Mystwood Bistro with Peris, I couldn't help appreciating the little café's softer atmosphere, a welcome contrast to the noisy Raindrop Café where most of the trainees gathered. Peris, brimming with energy and gossip, seemed mildly annoyed at my choice but soon launched into his usual palace tales.

"Sheila dyes her hair blue because her husband once looked at another woman with blue hair. Are you even listening, girl? Ohhh, you've got that mentor boy-toy on your mind, don't you? Better spill," Peris teased, snapping his fingers in front of my eyes.

I blinked, dragged from the fog of my thoughts, not of Cain, but of the heavy week finally easing from my shoulders.

"No. I was just… finally letting my body unclench from the weight of this week. I don't get to sit around and have gossip sessions all day. My so-called mentor just keeps slapping book after book at me. It's real work," I blurted, harsher than I meant.

"Okay, Miss Attitude. Tell me how you really feel," Peris replied with a playful roll of his eyes, softening the tension.

I sighed, guilt pricking.

"I'm sorry, Peris. It's not you. Like I said, Captain Cranky Pants dumped a workload on me that's impossible to finish. I've been burning the candle at both ends just to prove a hybrid can be just as good as a Mystic."

I reached across the table, taking his hand in gratitude. He squeezed gently and gave me a sympathetic smile.

"Girl, I get it. We don't just sit around gossiping, you know. I tried to share some of my design ideas, and they practically laughed me out of the room. I thought I could make real changes," Peris admitted.

My heart softened. I'd assumed Peris was managing better than Ferra and me, but clearly none of us had found the transition easy. We lingered at the bistro, sipping lattes and catching up, steering carefully away from any mention of my mentor.

Later, even on the train ride home, my mind betrayed me when I caught sight of someone who resembled Cain from behind. A surge of excitement rushed through me, chased swiftly by confusion.

That night, I dreamt of him again. The dream replayed the same scene as us under a blanket beside a fire beneath the stars. He whispered something I couldn't make out, and as before, his hand brushed the hair from my face before he kissed me. The warmth ignited within me, but this time, dream-me pulled away. I rose from our cozy place by the fire and walked toward the shelter. Cain remained behind, sitting alone before finally rising and vanishing into the dark woods.

The dream left me restless, emotions churning, the line between waking thoughts and subconscious long since blurred.

Chapter 7

Cain

The morning sun had only begun to creep over the horizon when I stepped into the training yard, my muscles still stiff from last night's run. I'd barely managed a few hours of sleep, but that wasn't unusual. What was unusual was the irritation gnawing at my insides. Dante. His name had reached me the night before, carried through the ranks like the warning of an approaching storm. A new trainee, supposedly skilled, and someone I was told to keep my eye on. I wasn't exactly thrilled.

Dante, of course, looked entirely at ease when I found him outside the meeting hall, arms folded across his chest, that infuriating smirk plastered on his face. He straightened slightly as I approached, though his expression didn't change. He retracted his wings. Tall and broad-shouldered, with a bronze complexion that made him look like he belonged under the sun rather than in the palace's shadow, he already radiated defiance. The spiked mohawk screamed rebellion, arrogance wrapped in style, and the piercings at his lip and pointed ear only reinforced the image.

His eyes found mine, dark and steady, the smirk tugging at his mouth as if he already knew the outcome. Cocky. Confident. The kind of recruit who believed he had nothing to prove because he was already convinced, he was the best. I'd met his type before, and I wasn't in the mood.

"So, you're Cain," Dante drawled, shifting his weight onto one foot as though this were a casual chat rather than the start of his training. "I was expecting someone… taller."

I clenched my jaw, exhaling through my nose as I stepped closer. "And I was expecting someone with a little more humility."

He grinned, unfazed. "Confidence and humility aren't the same thing, boss."

I already hated him. Standing beside him, I felt annoyingly self-aware. He had that effortless kind of presence that made everyone else seem a little dimmer. The sharp angles of his face, the way he carried himself, it was like he knew exactly how he looked and wielded it like a weapon. I wasn't used to being the one overshadowed, but in his presence, that's exactly what I was. I shoved that thought aside, focusing on what mattered.

"You're here to train, not talk," I said evenly, leaving no room for argument. "Let's see if you can back up that attitude with skill."

"You look thrilled," he said.

"I don't like surprises," I muttered, pushing open the heavy doors and stepping inside.

Saturday mornings were supposed to be mine. Not that I had plans, I never did, but it was the principle of the thing. If I wasn't scheduled for training, I expected at least a few hours of solitude. So when I was summoned to meet with a member of the Imperial Council alongside Dante, irritation was already brewing. This was going to be a long day.

Councilor Hadrian sat at the long wooden table, a sharp-featured man with graying hair and a calculating gaze. He wasted no time.

"Dante's placement here was arranged as a favor to the Queen," Hadrian explained, folding his hands before him. "He's already undergone preliminary training over the summer with his uncle, who serves in the palace guard. This is simply a continuation of that preparation."

I kept my expression neutral, though my mind spun. A favor. That meant someone in power had taken an interest in Dante, and I didn't like unknown variables. I had spent my career earning my place. I didn't trust anyone who had theirs handed to them.

"So what exactly am I supposed to do with him?" I asked, my voice measured.

Hadrian's small smile told me he knew what I was thinking. "Train him as you would any other recruit. Ensure he meets our standards."

I nodded stiffly and turned toward Dante. "Come on. I'll show you around."

The tour was mostly for formality. I knew Dante had likely been in and out of the palace before, thanks to his uncle's position, but I wasn't about to cut corners. If I had to do this, I'd do it properly.

We walked through the grand halls, the air heavy with centuries of history. Sunlight streamed through massive windows, spilling across the polished stone floors. Every so often, a servant or guard nodded in acknowledgment as we passed.

"So," Dante said, hands tucked in his pockets as he strolled beside me. "You're always this grumpy, or is it just me?"

I didn't glance at him. "I don't waste time on unnecessary conversation."

"That's a yes," he chuckled. "Good to know."

We crossed into the training yard, where a few early risers were already practicing their forms. I gestured toward the sparring rings.

"You'll spend most of your time here. Expect drills every morning."

Dante tilted his head. "You're a morning person, huh?"

"I'm a disciplined person," I corrected.

Right, right." He let the silence stretch for a moment before casually adding, "What about when you're not playing drill sergeant? You got a life outside this place?"

I shot him a look, and he raised his hands in mock surrender. "Just making conversation."

"Don't."

"Ouch," he said, grinning. "Must be lonely, though. Living in that little apartment behind your office. No girlfriend? No late-night tavern escapades?"

I clenched my jaw. "Focus on the tour."

"You're really bad at this whole casual conversation thing, you know that?"

I ignored him and kept walking. Suspicious favor or not, Dante had a long way to go before I'd let my guard down. And something told me he would enjoy every second of trying to break through.

The rest of the weekend passed in quiet solitude, just the way I preferred it. I spent most of my time buried in books, flipping through old battle strategies, tactical reports, and history tomes I had read a dozen times before. The familiar words kept my mind occupied, offering a safe escape from the tangled mess of thoughts I refused to acknowledge.

But despite my best efforts, my focus wavered. Every so often, my mind drifted, unbidden, unwanted, to the thought of Monday. To training. To Everly.

It didn't make sense. I had trained dozens of recruits before, had seen all kinds come and go. There was nothing special about her. And yet, the thought of seeing her again, watching her push herself, challenging her sent an odd thrill through me. It was irritating.

I shoved the thought aside, reminding myself it was nothing. I was her instructor. That was all.

Still, for the first time in a long while, I found myself counting down the hours until Monday.

Chapter 8

Everly

The weekend brought a welcome pause from the palace's relentless energy, and I spent it luxuriating in rest, wrapped in the fluffiest pajamas I owned and indulging in far too much TV. By Sunday, Peris and Ferra had joined me for a lounge fest in my living room, which soon transformed into a sanctuary of peace as we sprawled across the couch, letting conversations flow as effortlessly as the sunlight streaming through the windows.

"So, how's the seamster life treating you?" I asked Peris, passing him a bowl of popcorn. His eyes lit up, the passion for his craft unmistakable as he launched into an enthusiastic reply.

"It's amazing! The threads, the fabrics, I feel like a kid in a candy store. And to think I get to design uniforms people might actually want to wear," he said, his excitement infectious.

"And Ferra, what about the kids? How's teaching going?" I asked, genuinely curious about her new role.

Ferra's smile was soft, her sincerity radiating through every word. "It's more rewarding than I ever imagined, Everly. The kids are so open and eager to learn. And Ms. Hendricks, my mentor, is incredible, such a powerhouse of knowledge, but also so nurturing. I really feel like I've found where I belong."

Her words warmed me, though they also stirred a pang of envy for her clearly defined path. As the conversation shifted toward our lives at the palace, Ferra leaned forward, her eyes bright with curiosity.

"So, Everly, you've been awfully quiet about your mysterious mentor, Cain. What's he like?"

Before I could answer, Peris smirked. "Oh, Cain? I saw him the other day. That man is as handsome as they come, like he stepped out of some hero's tale, all brooding and mysterious."

I sighed and rolled my eyes, though an involuntary smile tugged at my lips. "Handsome? Maybe—if you like them frosty. He's… complicated. One minute he's all business, the next he's apologizing for being harsh. I can't figure him out. It's like he's balancing between mentor and drill sergeant."

Peris leaned in, intrigued. "Sounds like you're not entirely immune to his charms. Is there a soft side to the infamous Cain?"

"It's more confusing than anything," I admitted, tucking a strand of hair behind my ear. "He's got this intensity that could make him either an incredible mentor or just an intimidating enigma. And after stumbling on some secretive things in his paperwork, I'm not just curious, I'm caught up in trying to understand what he's really hiding."

Ferra, ever the peacemaker, placed a reassuring hand over mine. "Well, whatever happens, remember you're not in this alone. We're all finding our way through this crazy new world together."

"Yeah," I chuckled, shaking my head. "Between your teaching adventures, Peris's fashion revolution, and my mentor mysteries, we're basically living a novel."

"Speaking of writing," Peris teased with a mischievous twinkle in his eye, "if you do figure Cain out, jot down some notes for me. Strictly for… research purposes."

We burst into laughter, the tension melting away as the moment wrapped us in easy camaraderie. The conversation lifted my spirits, reminding me that no matter how daunting the figures in our lives seemed, we always had each other's backs.

The lingering confusion about Cain's behaviour was like a persistent itch. Why had his stern voice softened? Why had his brisk demeanour relaxed, even if only for a moment? I mulled over our last interaction, sifting through my jumbled feelings. Was there more to him beneath that icy exterior? Despite myself, I found my thoughts drifting back to him throughout the train ride and even during dinner. The complexity of my feelings unsettled me; it was easier to stay angry than to admit any flicker of admiration or curiosity about him.

When the laughter subsided, I seized the moment to steer the conversation towards something brighter. Leaning forward, energised by the thought of introducing my new friend, I said, "Speaking of new faces, I met someone at combat training her name's Lyla. You'd love her," I added, my tone bubbling with genuine excitement.

Ferra perked up, her interest clearly caught. "Lyla? What's she like?"

"She's incredible, like a burst of sunshine. Friendly, chatty, and the kind of person who makes you feel at ease, even in the middle of a grueling workout," I explained, my eyes lighting up at the memory of our training session. "She made the whole class feel far less daunting."

Peris raised an eyebrow, a smile tugging at his lips. "Sounds like you've found your combat guardian angel. Anyone who can keep you from kicking your own butt in training must be special. We definitely need to meet her."

"Yeah, she's got this positive energy that's really infectious," I continued. "And she seems to understand the whole palace dynamic; she made me feel a lot less like an outsider. I was thinking, maybe we could all hang out sometime? Grab lunch together at the cafeteria?"

Ferra nodded eagerly. "I'm in. It's been a while since we added anyone new to our little crew, and it sounds like she could bring a fun new spark."

Peris grinned. "Absolutely. Let's invite her to join us. It'd be great to have another friend in the palace, especially one so spirited."

"I'll ask her tomorrow," I said, a warm surge spreading through me at the thought of bringing Lyla into our circle. "I think she'll fit right in."

The idea of expanding our small group and leaning on each other's support was comforting. Despite the uncertainties and challenges of palace life, forging connections like the one with Lyla made the daunting new world feel a little more like home. It had been just the three of us for so long. I hoped that introducing Lyla, a Mystic, would help dispel some of the stereotypes about hybrids in the palace. Her warmth and openness could be exactly the example needed to challenge the all-too-common prejudices

Dinner with my mom was usually our time to reconnect, and that night was no exception, even as my thoughts kept drifting.

"Mom, I think I might try eating in the cafeteria this week," I said, poking at my food

"Oh? Planning to mingle with the crowd?" she teased, a glimmer of amusement in her eyes.

"Yeah, I figure it's time I see more of palace life beyond Cain's chilly training room," I replied with a wry smile. She nodded, understanding my need to stretch my wings, even if I wasn't quite sure what I was looking for.

Monday morning brought an unexpected sight in the office: a guy was sitting in my usual seat. And he wasn't just any guy; there was something about his presence that caught me off guard. He looked about my age, but it was his violet eyes and blue-black hair, styled with spiky edges and shaved sides, that grabbed my attention. The lip piercing only added to his rebellious charm.

The pointedness of his ears marked him as a hybrid, like me, instantly softening a part of myself I hadn't realized.

I was on edge. Here was someone who might understand the nuances of not fully belonging to one world or another, a potential ally amid a sea of full-blooded peers.

"Hello," he said, his voice smooth and deep, resonating directly into my core and unsettling the calm I usually maintained. His casual confidence was disarming, and when he flashed a quick, crooked smile, I felt my composure waver under his gaze. "My name is Dante. Who might you be?"

His question hung in the air with an ease that drew people in. Before I could gather my thoughts into a coherent response, Cain's voice cut through the tension from behind me.

"Miss Walker, I see you've met our new trainee." Cain strolled in, nonchalant as ever, and took his seat. "Mr. Phillips, you have a long way to catch up with my star pupil here. I suggest you get started with Origins of Fae, Volume One."

Star pupil? His words caught me off guard. I had been the only pupil until Dante showed up. I took a seat across from Dante, trying to focus on organizing my work without being distracted by his intriguing presence. Cain's stern voice broke the silence again.

"Mr. Philips, is there an issue?"

"It's Dante, sir," he corrected Cain smoothly, unfazed

I couldn't help but scoff under my breath. "Good luck with that."

Dante continued unabated. "I do not have an issue, sir. I've already read Origins of Fae, volumes one through five. Twice. I'm ready for any test you have on the subject."

I turned to Cain, my expression mirroring the shock his unchanging demeanor tried to mask. This was not the response I or seemingly Cain had expected. Composed as ever, Cain handed Dante a large stack of prepared tests. I refocused on my book, though my attention was now split between reading and watching Dante handle the tests with surprising ease.

Chapter 9

Cain

Walking into the office on Monday morning, I expected the usual routine: Everly at her desk, ready to be drilled on the day's training. Instead, I walked into a scene that sent a sharp irritation straight through me.

Dante was there, leaning too close to Everly, his cocky smirk firmly in place. His dark, bronze-toned hands rested on the desk beside her, his posture casual enough to seem effortless but deliberate enough to make my teeth clench. And then there was the way he looked at her like he was genuinely interested.

I noticed it the second his eyes landed on her: that gleam of attraction, the way he studied her, the brief brush of his fingers against hers when she passed him a book. It was subtle, but it was there, and it was enough to make something ugly coil in my chest.

I had no right to feel this way. I knew that. But that didn't stop my pulse from spiking or my jaw from tightening as I stepped further into the room. Everly barely registered my presence, too absorbed in whatever Dante was saying. And he was enjoying this. His lingering touch, his too-smooth tone. He was testing me.

Sitting at my desk, I began grading Dante's tests, my eyes flicking up occasionally to watch him and Everly when they thought I wasn't looking. The kid was smart; I had to give him that. His answers were well thought out, and his grasp of strategy was impressive. I couldn't fault his intelligence, but that didn't mean I had to like him. When I finished, I stood and walked over, placing the marked tests on Dante's desk. "Good marks," I said, keeping my voice neutral.

Dante barely glanced at the papers before his gaze returned to Everly. He wasn't even trying to hide it, just staring at her like she was something to be studied, something to be admired. My hands clenched into fists at my sides before I forced them to relax. The word echoed in my head before I could stop it.

Mine.

I exhaled sharply through my nose and turned away before I could do something foolish. Instead, I let my eyes linger on Everly. She was deep in concentration, brow slightly furrowed, lips pressed together as she worked through a problem on the parchment in front of her. Something about the way she focused was captivating; her entire body seemed to lean into her thoughts. I'd watched her improve so much in such a short time, and damn if I wasn't impressed.

Then there was Dante. The punk had a leg up, with an uncle in the Royal Guard who had likely been grooming him for this since childhood. It wasn't fair not to Everly, who had to fight for every bit of ground she gained. It irritated me. She deserved the same head start, the same advantages, but instead, she had to claw her way up on her own. And she would. She was proving that every single day. At the very least, their progress would make me look good. Producing two competent recruits would solidify my reputation as an elite trainer, someone who could mold even the roughest fighters into warriors. That was the excuse I clung to as my eyes drifted back to Everly.

Combat class was when I watched her most, the way she moved, the determination in every strike, the controlled power behind each step. It was exhilarating to witness. The first time I saw her dodge and counter without hesitation, something inside me tightened. The fluidity of her body, the way she handled herself it stirred something I wasn't ready to name. It was more than admiration. It was something deeper. Something dangerous.

I pushed the thought away and forced myself back to grading, but my mind remained filled with the image of Everly, her body moving like a blade, sharp and precise, and the undeniable heat that spread through me whenever I watched her fight.

Chapter 10

Everly

As lunchtime rolled around, I navigated my way to the cafeteria, a decision that felt liberating, breaking the monotony of my routine. Rounding the corner, lost in thought about my new lunch plan, I collided with a solid figure. My heart raced, fearing I had once again bumped into Cain.

Looking up, relief washed over me. It wasn't Cain, but Dante. My pulse didn't slow, though; his presence seemed to electrify the air around us.

"Hello, Miss Walker," he said, his hands lightly grasping my elbows to steady me as I nearly stumbled into him. The warmth of his touch sent a surprising rush of heat under my skin.

"It's Everly," I managed to whisper, feeling an unexpected flutter in my stomach.

"Hello… Everly," he repeated, his voice dipping into a soft, melodious cadence that made my name sound like a secret he cherished. The pause, heavy with unspoken curiosity, sent shivers down my spine. My thoughts clouded as a dizzying mix of his proximity and the faint minty freshness that seemed to emanate from him took over. I was hyper-aware of every detail, the way his pupils dilated as he looked at me, drawing me deeper into the moment.

"Sorry. Hungry," I blurted, wincing at how mundane my words sounded against the backdrop of our charged encounter. How could I reduce this electric moment to something so trivial?

His grin widened, acknowledging the awkwardness yet somehow appreciating it. As he gently released me, the cool air clashed sharply with the residual warmth of his touch, leaving a tingling sensation on my skin. I cast my eyes downward, letting my bangs shield my flushed cheeks, and hurried into the cafeteria, hoping the bustle would help me regain composure.

Reaching for a tray and beginning to pile it with fruit, another hand darted out for the same apple I had in my sights. I looked up to apologize, but my breath hitched when I saw who it was. I groaned inwardly, realizing the universe might have a peculiar sense of humor.

Of course, it had to be Cain. If I didn't get away from all this masculine energy, I was going to lose it. A small,

He released me, and the cool air clashed sharply with the lingering warmth of his touch, leaving a tingling sensation on my skin. I cast my eyes downward, letting my bangs shield my flushed cheeks, and hurried into the cafeteria, hoping the bustle would help me regain my composure.

Reaching for a tray and piling it with fruit, I was stopped by another hand darting for the same apple. I looked up to apologize, but my breath caught when I saw who it was. I groaned inwardly. Apparently, the universe had a peculiar sense of humor.

Of course, it was Cain. If I didn't get away from all this masculine energy, I was going to lose it. A small, almost mocking smile played on his lips as he noticed my surprise. Exasperated and unwilling to engage, I let him take the apple and retreated quickly.

Grabbing an orange juice from the counter, I paid without another word and scanned the cafeteria for a quieter spot. Lyla was alone in a corner that seemed to shield her from the rest of the world. I headed over, the cool juice bottle a small comfort against my rising irritation.

"Anyone sitting with you?" I asked as I settled beside her.

"Nope, they prefer the staff cafeteria's better food, they say," Lyla replied with a shrug, her voice low. "I stay here. It's quieter. How was your weekend?"

"Gloriously boring," I said, studying my meager meal: a banana and a handful of grapes. In my mission to avoid Cain, I'd forgotten to grab anything else. Contemplating a return to the line, I sighed.

Just as I was about to tell Lyla I'd be right back, her eyes widened, fixating on something or someone across the room.

"Who is that?" she asked, her finger subtly pointing. I followed her gaze and spotted Dante.

Oh, that's Dante. He's the new trainee under Cain," I explained, feeling a surge of annoyance even mentioning it.

Her eyebrows shot up. "Under Cain? But mentors usually don't take more than one trainee at a time."

"Yeah, I know," I muttered, stirring my juice with the straw. "And it gets weirder. It's his first day, but he claims he's already up to speed with everything I've learned. Took the tests today without a hitch." I chuckled dryly, realizing I had become the very gossip I often mocked. Peris would get a kick out of this later.

"That is odd," Lyla mused, her gaze thoughtful as she glanced back at Dante.

"Looks like he might be a hybrid, too. That's great news for you, Everly. Finally, someone you can relate to here."

Her use of the term hybrid, which I had explained as the respectful term for people like me, struck a chord. Despite her sometimes overly sunny disposition, which could be cloying, I couldn't deny the comfort her friendship brought. She was right; perhaps Dante could be more than just another complication at the palace. Maybe he could even be a new ally or a friend.

"That is true," I admitted, allowing myself a small smile. Her optimism, infectious as it was, sometimes made the unbearable a little more tolerable.

"He's just distracting! I mean, even you have to admit he's pretty attractive. Add Cain, the Heartthrob of Erynvale, and it all has me acting like a schoolgirl. I've always been able to keep my wits about me, especially around guys. I'm getting on my own nerves over it," I continued.

She snorted, trying to hold back a smile. I smiled too, realizing how ridiculous I sounded. My face reddened, and I softly apologized for my outburst.

"Oh, don't act like you never swooned over a guy at your old school. Didn't you tell me your friend Peris is a flirt? You don't have to put on this tough-girl façade here just because others are scrutinizing you. We survived a whole week of combat training, we're practically besties now." Her words felt like a warm embrace. I actually made a new friend? A Mystic?

"What is his last name anyway?" she asked.

"Oh, uhm… Philips," I replied.

Lyla's face scrunched up. Even with her eyebrows furrowed and nose scrunched, she looked angelic. Then her expression softened, and she sighed.

"I've heard that name before, but I can't place where."

We finished our lunches with no more talk of Dante or Cain.

In the sweltering heat of the gym, combat class had morphed into a brutal agility session. As someone who had never excelled at running, I struggled to keep pace, each lap leaving my lungs burning and muscles screaming for relief. Sweat dripped into my eyes, stinging sharply, while my fire-engine red hair, pulled into a high ponytail, offered little respite as damp bangs clung to my forehead.

"Guards need more than strong fighting skills. They need strong calves!" Mr. Franklin's voice boomed through the gym, punctuated by the rhythmic thud of our feet on the mats.

A blur of white zipped past me, Amaya, her bleach-blonde hair streaming behind her like a comet's tail. She glanced back with a smug smirk before accelerating. Her focus wasn't just on overtaking me; it was clear she aimed to catch Dante, the unofficial leader of our pack.

Rolling my eyes at her obvious display, I immediately regretted the gesture as sweat ran into my eyes. Grimacing, I wiped my forehead with my collar, silently cursing the burning sensation.

The shrill blast of Mr. Franklin's whistle cut through the air, mercifully ending our ordeal.

Chapter 11

Cain

The summons came just after sunrise, a sealed letter handed to me by one of the Queen's attendants. My stomach twisted as I made my way up the grand staircase to her chambers, my boots echoing against the polished marble. The Queen didn't call me often, and when she did, it was never for good news.

The heavy doors groaned open, revealing Queen Anastasia seated on her throne. Her violet eyes pinned me in place, sharp and unreadable. There was no one else present—just me, her, and whatever grave news she had summoned me for. Whatever this was, it wasn't just about me.

"Cain," the Queen said, her voice even, controlled. "I will not waste time with pleasantries. Your father's unit has been found abandoned."

My heart stopped. "What?"

Her words were deliberate, each one hitting like a blow. "Every soldier in his command was discovered slain. The camp left in disarray. But your father was not among them."

A cold rush of disbelief washed over me. My father was not an easy man to kill. If he had been there, he would have fought, left a trail of bodies in his wake. The fact that they found no trace of him made my chest tighten.

"I am sending a search party," the Queen continued, her fingers drumming lightly on the gilded armrest. "A small, capable group. A battalion would draw too much attention. This mission requires subtlety. You and your trainees will go."

I barely heard her. My father—missing. His men were slaughtered. None of this made sense. My mind raced, running through the possibilities, none of them leading anywhere good.

"Just us?" I asked, my voice hoarse.

Her gaze didn't waver. "You will be my blade in the dark. You will move unseen and uncover the truth before whoever did this realizes we are watching."

I exhaled sharply, my fists tightening at my sides. This wasn't a request; it was an order. One, I had no intention of refusing. I wasn't going to sit back and wait for answers. If my father were out there, I would find him. But I couldn't take Everly and Dante along. How would that even work?

I frowned, crossing my arms over my chest. "This is a mistake."

The Queen's expression remained cold and decisive. "Explain."

"Everly is untrained," I said flatly. "Dante is too new. I don't trust him yet. And I am not enough on my own." I took a step forward, my voice lower but firm. "If my father's entire unit was wiped out, we need more than just three of us."

The Queen's gaze didn't waver. "And yet, you will go. This is not a battle won by numbers, Cain. It is a mission of precision. And I have a feeling about Everly."

I frowned. "A feeling?"

Her expression remained unreadable, but there was something in her tone—something sure. "There is strength in her that has yet to fully awaken. You've seen it yourself. She is not like the others."

I wanted to refute her, to tell her Everly wasn't ready, but the words caught in my throat. Because the truth was, Everly had already surprised me. Again and again.

She had gone from stumbling through her first drills to holding her own in combat class. Her mind was sharp, and her body was growing stronger and more disciplined. I had seen the fire in her eyes when she fought, the way she refused to yield even when she should have. It was reckless, but it was also… thrilling to watch.

My thoughts strayed further than I wanted them to, lingering on the way she moved, the quiet determination in every motion, the way she looked when she concentrated—lips slightly parted, brows furrowed, utterly focused. And then there were the moments between training, the rare glimpses of her unguarded. The way she laughed when she thought no one was listening. The way my chest tightened when she did.

I clenched my jaw, my fists tightening. I wanted to argue, but what good would it do? The decision had already been made.

I exhaled sharply. "When do we leave?"

Her expression remained cold and decisive. "At dawn."

I nodded once. No hesitation. No second thoughts. I had a mission. And I would not return empty-handed.

Chapter 12

Everly

Nestled amidst a sea of ancient texts and maps in Cain’s dusty office, I pored over every tome that detailed the arcane lore of the fae, from the solemn histories of Erynvale to treatises on magical disciplines. Despite the silence, a restive atmosphere filled the room, amplified by Cain's unexplained absence throughout the week. It allowed me to dive into the complexities of the Mystic arts. However, my heart yearned to uncover the secrets of Elemental magic that eluded my grasp. My table, a meticulous array of notes and faded maps, was a testament to my relentless quest for knowledge.

As I annotated a particularly elusive passage, the feeling of being watched crept over me. Lifting my gaze, I caught Dante lounging in his chair, his eyes fixated on me with an unsettling intensity.

“Can I help you?” I snapped, my voice laced with irritation.

“You haven’t talked to me all week, and that’s the first thing you say?” Dante's smile was lopsided, disarmingly charming. “I thought we were going to be good friends.”

His words sparked a flare of annoyance within me. “I don’t know what gave you that impression, but I’m not interested. I just want to do my work and finish my training. Unlike some people who clearly had a heads-up not only on their assignment but the curriculum, I actually have to study.”

Keeping my eyes resolutely on my papers, I avoided his gaze. If I looked into those deep blue eyes, I feared my resolve might crumble. After all, discussions with Ferra, Peris, and Lyla had confirmed my unfortunate tendency towards becoming distracted by attractive distractions.

As I began to pack up for the day, Dante rose and approached with a casual swagger that made my heart skip despite my intentions. He halted just short of my table, and after a tense pause, I finally met his gaze.

"Would you like to grab dinner with me?" he asked, his voice smooth and inviting.

The question caught me off guard, and I stared back in disbelief. "Like a date?!" I blurted out.

"Well, I did say I wanted to be friends. So like a friend date, if you prefer," he clarified, a hint of playfulness in his tone.

"Yeah, I don't think so," I muttered, scanning the room, relieved Cain wasn't there to witness this exchange. "I really don't know you."

His eyes, a stormy blend of blue and violet, seemed to pierce through to my very soul. "That is kind of the point of dinner, to get to know me."

As he stood there, waiting for an answer, the spicy scent of musk and mint that clung to him filled the space between us, making it harder to think. *Was I really about to decline an opportunity to peel back the layers of the enigmatic Dante, or was I afraid of what I might discover—not just about him, but about myself?*

I made a brief stop at home, informing my mother of my dinner plans in a tone that was casual yet deliberately vague. I skirted around the particulars—after all, discussing Dante felt like stirring a pot of chaos I wasn't ready to address with her just yet. Without changing from my day's attire, as this was merely a friend date (or so I reminded myself sternly), I left for Raindrop Café. There was no need to embellish my appearance; this wasn't a date, despite the fluttering in my stomach that suggested otherwise.

The walk was a short one, just a few blocks that I traversed under the waning light of the day. The evening sky was a canvas of fiery reds and deep purples, the fading sun casting a dramatic backdrop as the city began to shimmer with the first signs of night. As I approached the café, a silhouette detached itself from the shadows—the unmistakable posture of someone waiting with a patience that seemed both casual and charged.

It was him, Dante, leaning against the exterior wall with a nonchalance that belied the tightness in his shoulders. He straightened as I drew closer, pushing off from the wall with a grace that caught the dimming light. His usual smirk was replaced with something softer, more tentative, as if he too sensed the undefined boundaries of this meeting. As our eyes met, the ambient glow from the café's windows illuminated his features, highlighting the striking contrast of his violet eyes and the dark spikes of his hair.

"Everly," he greeted, his voice smooth as velvet yet laced with an undercurrent of something akin to nervous anticipation. This wasn't the confident, almost cocky persona he paraded around during training. Tonight, he seemed genuinely eager, nearly vulnerable, and it piqued my curiosity even further.

Stepping closer, I could see his usual smirk had morphed into a genuine smile, one that reached his eyes and softened his typically sharp features. This Dante was someone I hadn't yet encountered—one who might just be as complex and layered as the skies above us.

“Glad you could make it,” his voice a low, inviting timbre that somehow matched the twilight hues. I noticed the day’s casual attire was gone; in its place, he wore a form-fitting dark blue t-shirt that emphasized the broad expanse of his chest and the sculpted cut of his biceps, a stark contrast to the subtlety of his presence.

"Yeah, well, it sounded like you were going to whine about it next week if I didn't show," I quipped, stepping closer, my gaze unintentionally catching on the stubble shadowing his jaw—a hint of ruggedness that suggested a history as complex as the scar barely visible on his nose.

He chuckled—a deep, resonant sound—and held the door open for me, his manners flawlessly in place despite my barbed greeting. As we entered, the ambiance of the café enveloped us like a serene sanctuary. The interior was an escape into a lush oasis, with walls adorned in murals depicting tranquil waterfalls and verdant hot springs. The furniture, made of bamboo, complemented the theme, adding to the sense of being in a secluded retreat.

We chose a cozy corner booth, the murmur of water from the themed decor blending seamlessly with the low hum of conversation around us. A waitress approached swiftly, her smile warm and welcoming as we settled in. The menu was a blend of exotic flavors, carefully curated to complement the decor, offering an array of dishes as vibrant as the murals on the walls.

As I glanced through the menu, the reality of sitting across from Dante began to sink in. This wasn't just any dinner; it was a test of sorts—a dance around each other's personalities and a probing of boundaries. I was here under the pretense of friendship. Yet, the electric charge of his nearness spoke of potential complexities I hadn't fully anticipated.

Settling back into the booth, I decided on my usual comfort fare—a burger and fries. After placing the menu aside, I glanced across the table. Dante mirrored my actions, and an uneasy silence stretched between us, thick with unspoken thoughts. Resolved to break the tension, I leaned forward, my curiosity piqued and ready to dive into the depths of this enigmatic newcomer.

"So, you obviously didn't grow up here in the capital," I started, my tone casual but edged with a hint of suspicion. "I've been here since birth and know all the hybrid families around. Where are you from?" I asked, taking a sip of water to steady my nerves.

Dante's gaze flickered with a mixture of nostalgia and something darker as he replied, "You're right, I didn't. I'm originally from Laseel. My father was an Elemental. My mother's family has deep roots here, all Mystics. We moved here only recently, after... after my father passed away." His voice was a soft murmur, laced with a pain that briefly shadowed his striking features.

My curiosity deepened, stirring the waters of our budding acquaintance. "You received a blue box then?" I asked, referring to the somber packages sent to families of fallen soldiers, often shrouded in secrecy and sorrow. The idea nagged at me—would my new role in the royal guard unveil the truths hidden behind these veiled sacrifices? The rumors of monstrous creatures born from desolate lands often circulated, whispered among the ranks, but solid details were elusive, bound by magical oaths of silence.

Dante shook his head, his voice barely above a whisper. "No, my father wasn't a soldier at his end. He... he died a hero in his own right, defending a woman from harm in our neighborhood. It was rough, and he got involved in a bad situation."

I nodded, absorbing his words. The story tugged at me—a mix of raw honesty and something he might be withholding. "I'm sorry to hear that. It's a harsh reminder that despite our extended lifespans and quick healing, we aren't truly immortal," I said softly,

"Indeed. We moved here to be closer to my mother's family, but to their dismay, she was ostracized when I was born. Only my uncle, her brother, would take us in," Dante confided, his voice tinged with a mix of resignation and defiance. He shrugged slightly, as if the weight of his family's judgment was a familiar burden he had long learned to bear.

As he spoke, the waitress arrived, placing our orders in front of us. The aroma of the burger immediately captivated my senses, tightening my stomach with hunger. We fell into a comfortable silence, focusing on the food in front of us, until Dante decided to slice through the quiet.

"I love a girl who isn't afraid to eat something that once had a face," he remarked, his lopsided smile revealing a charming dimple on his right cheek.

"I can't stand girls who pretend they don't. Who am I trying to impress anyway? Bring on all the faces!" I blurted out, more boldly than intended. My face flushed a bright red—a stark contrast to my usual calm demeanor.

His soft chuckle helped cool the heat that had crept up to my pointed-tipped ears, and encouraged by the lighter mood, I probed further into his life.

"So, how did you land an assignment with the royal guard?" I asked, my curiosity piqued.

He hesitated, his fingers idly pushing around the pasta on his plate. "My uncle is a palace guard. He discussed my unique situation with the Queen and managed to arrange something special for me. The selection committee and imperial counsel reviewed my transcripts from Laseel," he explained, his voice casual but measured.

"And does Laseel have the same resources we've been using in Cain's library? Most of those books are centered around Mystic lore," I inquired, leaning in slightly, intrigued by his ease with the curriculum.

"I'm a quick learner," he said with a shrug. "Once my uncle secured the Queen's approval for my residency and my assignment, I studied independently. It helps to have connections in high places, as I'm sure you understand, being the daughter of the Queen's seamstress," he added, giving me a knowing look over his drink.

I paused, slightly taken aback by his awareness of my mother's role. While I had never mentioned it, it wasn't surprising that he had gleaned that information, given his uncle's position at the palace. His mention of connections resonated with me, weaving a thread of commonality between us that was both unexpected and intriguing.

Dante swirled the straw in his drink lazily, the ice cubes clinking against the glass. I leaned back in my seat, deciding to steer the conversation toward something that had been on my mind for weeks.

"So," I began, trying to sound casual as I stabbed a fry into the small pool of ketchup on my plate. "Do you have any powers yet? You know, Elemental or Mystic?"

Dante's lips quirked into a knowing smile, and he set his glass down with a soft clink. "Yeah, mine showed up not long before I moved to Vedanis," he admitted, his voice smooth and even, like he wasn't about to casually reveal a piece of himself. "Elemental—water."

I froze mid-bite, my fry hovering in the air as I processed his words. "Water?" I repeated, a mix of surprise and fascination in my tone. I hadn't even thought about Elemental powers being an option for me. I'd always assumed, no, *expected*, I'd end up with something Mystic, like my mother's aura-reading or my aunt's illusion casting.

"I never even considered Elemental powers," I admitted, setting the fry down. "I mean, I've always imagined I'd get something Mystic, but so far…" I gestured vaguely, trailing off as frustration bubbled up. "Nothing. Not even a spark."

"They'll show up," Dante said confidently, leaning forward as his violet eyes met mine, a hint of amusement sparkling in their depths. "Probably when you're not expecting it. That's usually how these things go." His calm certainty made me want to believe him, although it didn't make the waiting any more straightforward.

I tilted my head, narrowing my eyes at him. "How do you even know that? Did some grand mystical power bestow you with the patience of a saint?"

He chuckled softly, shaking his head. "Hardly. It just makes sense. Besides, you're still figuring out who you are. Maybe your powers are waiting for you to catch up." His words felt like they held more weight than he let on, but I wasn't sure if I wanted to peel back those layers just yet.

I took a sip of my drink, mulling over his response. "I guess it's possible. I mean, Cain's powers are tied to who he is. That mental shield of his? Pretty sure it's inherited from his father. It makes sense, considering they're both guarded as hell and impossible to read."

Dante nodded, watching me closely. "Exactly. Your powers—whatever they are—they'll reflect something deep about you. Something you might not even realize about yourself yet."

I sat back, digesting his words, the noise of the café fading into the background. It was such a simple thought, but it left me feeling both comforted and unsettled. What if I wasn't ready to discover what was hidden inside me?

As we continued our meal, the air between us shifted. Dante seemed to grow more pensive with every passing moment, his usual easy confidence replaced with something quieter, heavier. He swirled his pasta absentmindedly, his gaze flicking toward the window as though he were expecting someone to walk in and interrupt us.

"You're quieter than usual," I remarked, raising an eyebrow. "Let me guess—you've run out of clever one-liners?"

He smirked faintly, but it didn't reach his eyes. "Not quite, Angel Eyes. Just...thinking."

"About?" I pressed, leaning forward. His hesitance was unusual, and for some reason, it put me on edge.

Dante exhaled and rubbed the back of his neck, his gaze darting to the door again. "Look, I probably shouldn't be saying this, but since you're training under Cain, I feel like you should know... there's more to him than meets the eye."

I scoffed, spearing a fry with unnecessary force. "Yeah, no kidding. The man's a walking enigma with a superiority complex. What else is new?"

Dante shook his head, his expression darkening. "I'm not talking about his attitude. I'm talking about his past—and his father."

That made me pause. My grip on the fork tightened as I narrowed my eyes at him. "Cain's father? What does he have to do with anything?"

Dante hesitated, clearly debating whether to continue. Finally, he leaned forward, his voice dropping to a near-whisper. "Cain's father was involved in something—something big. Something the palace has worked hard to keep under wraps. From what I've pieced together, he was one of the few people standing between us and... whatever's out there."

My heart skipped a beat. The vague references to "threats" and "dark forces" from my studies at the palace flashed through my mind, but no one had ever been specific. No one had dared.

"Are you saying Cain's father was dealing with whatever it is the army's been fighting beyond the borders?" I asked, my voice sharper than I intended.

Dante's jaw tightened, and he glanced around the room as though the very walls might be listening. "Yes. But it wasn't just the army. Cain's father was part of a... select group. People who knew what we're really up against. People who understood that the threats out there aren't just monsters or rogue Elementals. They're older, darker, and far more dangerous."

My stomach churned. The idea of such threats existing in the first place was unsettling enough. Still, the thought that Cain—stoic, unyielding, frustrating Cain—might be tangled up in this legacy made my pulse quicken.

"And how do you know all this?" I demanded, my voice low but insistent.

Dante's lips pressed into a thin line. "Let's just say my family's path crossed with Cain's father's more than once. My mother told me enough to piece some things together after my father...died."

Something about the way he said it—how his words lingered on the edge of something unsaid—sent a chill down my spine. "And Cain? Does he know?"

Dante leaned back in his chair, his eyes meeting mine with a strange mix of seriousness and regret. "Oh, he knows. He knows more than anyone else. And that's why you should be careful, Everly. Cain's carrying secrets—secrets that could get people killed."

The weight of his words settled heavily between us, and for a moment, I couldn't respond. My mind raced, trying to reconcile the stoic, infuriating man I'd been training under with the image Dante was painting—a man steeped in shadows and burdened by a dangerous legacy.

"I don't need to be careful," I finally said, my voice steadier than I felt. "But maybe Cain does, if he thinks he can keep me in the dark."

Dante chuckled softly, though there was no humor in it. "Good luck with that, Angel Eyes. Cain's walls aren't easy to break through. But if anyone can do it...I'd bet on you."

His words hung in the air as the waitress returned with the check, her cheerful demeanor at odds with the tension now thrumming between us. Whatever Dante had just shared was only the tip of the iceberg. And something told me that uncovering the rest wouldn't just be difficult—it would be dangerous.

Chapter 13

Cain

The streets of downtown were alive with energy as I walked, the hum of conversation blending with the distant sound of music spilling from the taverns. The scent of fresh bread and roasting meat carried on the cool evening air, but I barely noticed it. My thoughts were tangled, my mood sour.

I hadn't meant to come this way. Maybe I was looking for a distraction. I needed to clear my head before we left at dawn. Either way, the last thing I expected was to see her.

Everly.

Through the large window of a restaurant, candlelight flickered against the glass, illuminating the inside in a golden glow. And there she was, sitting across from Dante, her red hair catching the soft light like fire. She was smiling—laughing even.

My stomach twisted, a sharp and immediate reaction that I didn't like.

Dante leaned in, elbows on the table, his posture relaxed, his eyes locked on hers. He said something, and she laughed again, the sound muffled through the glass but no less impactful. The sight of it set something hot in my chest. It wasn't anger exactly, but it was close to it.

Jealousy.

The realization hit me hard, settling in my gut like a stone. I had no right to feel this way. Everly wasn't mine. She was my trainee, nothing more. And yet, seeing Dante look at her like that, so easy, so sure of himself—it made my hands clench at my sides.

Dante had always carried himself like he had the world figured out. Like nothing could shake him. And now, here he was, encroaching on something—someone—that wasn't his to claim. I didn't trust him, not in battle, and certainly not with Everly.

I knew I was being irrational. I knew Everly deserved to have a moment of peace, of normalcy, before we set out on a mission that could very well get us all killed. But knowing it didn't make the jealousy go away.

I watched her a moment longer, letting my eyes linger on the way her lips curled when she smiled, the way her green eyes sparkled under the dim light. She had come so far in such a short time. She was strong. Resilient. And something deep inside me whispered that she deserved better than a cocky recruit who had barely proven himself.

I turned away, my chest tight. I had no claim to her. No right to interfere. But that didn't mean I had to like what I saw.

With a scowl, I kept walking, hands shoved into my pockets, jaw set. Tomorrow, we would leave for the mission, and I would make sure she stayed focused. I would make sure Dante knew his place. And maybe, just maybe, I'd figure out why the hell I couldn't stop thinking about her.

I found myself at The Rusted Fang, a dive bar that catered to the roughest kind of crowd. A place where fights were encouraged, bets were made, and pain was both the prize and the punishment. It was exactly what I needed.

The underground ring was loud with cheers and jeers as two fae clashed in the center, their blows brutal, their movements a blur. I let my anger toward Dante fuel my steps as I walked up to the pit master.

"Put me in."

The fae eyed me, sizing me up, before nodding. "Next round."

I stripped off my jacket and stepped into the ring. My opponent was a broad-shouldered fae with dark horns curling from his forehead, his knuckles wrapped tight, his smirk confident. He thought he could beat me.

He was wrong.

The bell rang, and he lunged first. I dodged, letting him overextend before driving my fist into his ribs. He grunted but recovered quickly, throwing a sharp right hook that caught my cheekbone. Pain flared, but I welcomed it.

We circled, trading blows, my body absorbing the punishment, my fists returning it tenfold. Blood dripped from a cut above my brow, blurring my vision. My ribs ached, my jaw throbbed, but I pushed through, my mind singularly focused on one thing—winning.

Then I saw my opening. He hesitated, just for a fraction of a second, and I took it. My fist slammed into his gut, knocking the wind out of him. As he doubled over, I brought my elbow down onto the back of his head, sending him sprawling onto the floor. The fight was over.

I stood over him, breathing hard, blood dripping from my face, adrenaline still surging through my veins. The crowd roared, but I barely heard it.

One of the pit medics approached me, hands glowing with healing magic. I shook my head. "No."

"You need—"

"I said no."

I wanted the pain. Needed it. It grounded me, reminded me that I was still in control. That no matter what I felt when I saw Everly and Dante together, I could still dominate something.

I left The Rusted Fang, my knuckles throbbing, my body sore but satisfied. Blood still dripped from the cut above my brow, my lip split from a particularly nasty right hook, but

I didn't care. The pain is a distraction from the rage still simmering beneath my skin.

As I walked past the restaurant, I saw them leaving. Everly's expression was soft, amused, her lips curved in a small smile as Dante leaned in close, whispering something into her ear. The easy way they moved together, the familiarity—it made my jaw tighten, my breath come just a little sharper.

Without thinking, I followed.

They walked together for a few blocks, their conversation easy, casual. Everly brushed her hair behind her ear, laughing softly at something Dante said. It was the kind of laugh she rarely gave, one without restraint. A private moment, meant for them.

I shouldn't have been watching. Shouldn't have cared. But I did.

When they reached the crossroads, Everly turned down the road leading to the palace. Dante stood there, watching her go, his eyes lingering on her retreating form for too long, too long for my liking.

That's when I struck.

I stepped into his path, backing him into the mouth of a dark alley. The shadows swallowed us, the only light spilling in from the streetlamps behind me.

"What are you doing with Everly?" My voice was low, steady, but my hands clenched at my sides, aching to take action.

Dante blinked at me, then smirked, his violet eyes gleaming with something close to amusement. He reached up, rubbing his jaw where I'd slammed him against the wall. "That's quite the bruise, Cain. Someone finally knock you down a peg?"

I grabbed his collar and shoved him back, his head knocking against the brick. My breath was uneven, my pulse hammering in my ears. "Answer me."

His smirk didn’t falter, though his fingers curled into fists at his sides. "Relax. We had dinner. That’s all."

I didn’t move, my grip still tight on his collar. "Stay away from her."

Dante exhaled a soft chuckle, his head tilting as if he were studying me, peeling back my anger layer by layer. "That’s what this is about, huh?" He licked his split lip, amusement flickering in his eyes. "You don’t like seeing someone else get close to her."

I shoved him harder, my nails digging into the fabric of his shirt. "You don’t know what you’re talking about."

"I think I do." His voice dropped, no longer teasing but sharp, edged with something unreadable. "And I think you do, too."

The weight of his words settled between us, thick and heavy. I wanted to hit him. Wanted to rip that smug look off his face. But that would mean giving him precisely what he wanted—proof.

Instead, I let go, stepping back. "Whatever game you're playing, end it."

Dante adjusted his collar, rolling his shoulders as if shaking off the moment. "Wouldn’t dream of it."

I turned on my heel and stalked off, but the fire in my chest didn’t burn out. If anything, it burned hotter.

Chapter 14

Everly

The next day, Dante and I were back in Cain's office. I had claimed my usual spot at one of the scarred wooden tables, my notes spread out like the chaotic mind map of someone teetering on the edge of unraveling. Dante sat at the other table, his long legs sprawled as he lazily flipped through one of the thicker books Cain had assigned.

"What are you even reading?" I asked, unable to mask the irritation in my voice. While I was drowning in the history of magical treaties, he looked as though he were skimming a novel for leisure.

He glanced up, his violet eyes gleaming with mischief. "Something light. You know, the Origins of Fae Wars is a real page-turner. You'd love it, Angel Eyes."

I rolled my eyes so hard I half expected to see the back of my skull. "Must be nice to sit there looking pretty while some of us actually have to work."

"Jealousy doesn't suit you," he quipped, flashing a grin equal parts charming and infuriating.

Before I could retort, the heavy creak of the office door cut through the room. Cain stepped inside, his presence immediately commanding. He looked more tense than usual, sharp features carved into a grim expression. His uniform was immaculate, but the faint shadows beneath his piercing gray eyes betrayed a lack of sleep. Whatever had kept him away last week, it hadn't been rest.

"Good. You're both here," Cain said

Cain entered without preamble, his voice cool and clipped as always. He strode to the front of the room, folding his arms across his broad chest as his gaze swept over us.

"Well, nice to see you too, boss," I muttered under my breath, earning a soft chuckle from Dante. Cain's eyes flicked to me, sharp and unamused, and I immediately straightened in my seat.

"I've been meeting with the Defense Counsel," Cain began, his tone leaving no room for interruption. "Something has happened beyond the wall."

The air in the room shifted, a palpable tension pressing down on us. Dante straightened, his casual demeanor vanishing as his gaze locked onto Cain.

"Something big," Cain continued, his jaw tightening. "An entire patrol unit is gone. No survivors, no signs of what attacked them. The scouts sent to investigate found… nothing. Just empty terrain where they should have been."

A shiver ran down my spine, my stomach twisting. The wall had always been a mystery, a looming barrier separating our kingdom from whatever horrors lay beyond. The soldiers who patrolled it were rarely spoken of, their work shrouded in secrecy. For an entire unit to vanish was unheard of and terrifying.

Cain's gaze shifted between the two of us, his expression unreadable.

"The queen has tasked me with leading a reconnaissance mission beyond the wall to gather intel. Since you're both my trainees, you'll be coming with me."

My mouth fell open. "What? Us? On a mission? Beyond the wall?"

"You've got to be joking," Dante said, though his tone carried more intrigue than fear. "I thought trainees were supposed to stay behind and fetch coffee, not risk life and limb."

Cain's eyes narrowed. "This isn't a democracy. You're both coming, and you'll follow my orders without question. The Defense Counsel agrees that hands-on experience is crucial, and you've proven capable enough to handle yourselves."

I snorted. "Capable? I nearly passed out running laps last week."

Cain arched an eyebrow. "Which is why we'll be focusing on stamina and combat drills for the next two days. You'll need every ounce of strength and focus you can muster. Beyond the wall, there's no room for mistakes."

His words landed like stone, heavy and undeniable. I exchanged a glance with Dante, whose usual smirk had faded into something more somber. Excited, maybe. A little apprehensive, definitely. Either way, he didn't look nearly as horrified as I felt.

"When do we leave?" Dante asked, his voice steady.

"Three days from now," Cain replied. "That should give you enough time to prepare. Gear up, train hard, and study everything you can on past expeditions. Dismissed."

He turned on his heel and left, a suffocating silence filling the space he vacated. I stared after him, my mind racing beyond the wall. The thought alone made my pulse thunder.

"Well," Dante said after a beat, his voice lighter than the situation deserved, "this should be… interesting."

I shot him a glare. "Interesting? We're about to march straight into the unknown, probably to die horribly, and you think it's interesting?"

His lips twitched into that infuriating smirk. "What can I say? I like a little excitement. Besides, if we're going to die horribly, at least we'll do it together, Angel Eyes."

I groaned and buried my face in my hands. This mission was going to be the death of me, and not just because of whatever waited beyond the wall. It was insanity. Two trainees, barely weeks into their training, are being sent on a mission like this? My thoughts spun with the sheer absurdity. What was Cain thinking? Did the Defense Counsel honestly believe two green recruits could survive whatever they feared out there? Or was this just some cruel trial by fire?

The weight of it hit me like a punch to the gut. I wasn't ready not for something like this. I had only just begun to grasp combat training and palace protocols. And Dante, for all his cocky confidence and mysterious past, couldn't have been much more prepared than I was. Sure, he had bravado, but could it hold up against whatever was waiting for us out there?

How insane was this? It wasn't just reckless, it was downright irresponsible. We weren't seasoned guards; we were barely rookies. And yet here we were, being dragged into the unknown on the whims of people who clearly valued secrecy over sanity. Later that evening, I sat at the kitchen island, watching my mother chop herbs from her garden with meticulous care. The soft scent of basil and rosemary filled the air, but even that couldn't soothe the knot of anxiety in my stomach. I had been dreading this conversation, knowing her protective streak ran as deep as her healing abilities.

"So," I began, picking at a loose thread on my sleeve. "I'm going on a mission. Beyond the wall."

Her hands froze mid-chop, the steady rhythm of the knife against the cutting board falling silent. Slowly, she turned to face me, her silvery eyes narrowing with concern.

"Beyond the wall? With Cain?"

I nodded, swallowing hard. "Yeah. He says it's... important. Something happened to a patrol unit, and the Defense Counsel wants answers."

She set the knife down and crossed her arms, leaning against the counter as she studied me. "Everly, that's dangerous. You know that, right? No one knows what's out there."

"I know," I admitted quietly. "But I can't exactly say no, can I? Cain seems to think I can handle it, and maybe he's right. Maybe I can."

Her expression softened as she stepped closer, placing a gentle hand on my cheek. "You're strong, my love. Stronger than you realize. Your father's bravery and determination run in your veins I've seen it in the way you face challenges, even when you don't want to." Her lips curved into a faint smile. "And if it eases your mind, I'm close to the queen. I'll know everything about the mission as it happens. If anything goes wrong... I'll know."

A lump rose in my throat, fear and gratitude threatening to overwhelm me. "I don't want you to worry."

Her laugh was soft but warm. "Oh, sweetheart, worrying about you is what I do best. But I also trust you. And Cain, for all his gruffness, wouldn't take you on this mission if he didn't believe you were ready. Just promise me you'll be careful."

I nodded, leaning into her touch for a moment before pulling back. "I will. And... thanks for believing in me."

She returned to her chopping, though slower now, more deliberate. "Just remember you're not alone. And when this is all over, you'll have one heck of a story to tell."

I smiled faintly, her words wrapping around me like a protective shield. The mission still loomed large in my mind, but at least I knew someone was waiting for me on the other side. Someone who believed I could do this even if I wasn't entirely sure myself.

Chapter 15

Cain

I had them gathered at the edge of a clearing, the morning sunlight filtering through the dense canopy above. The chill of the night still clung to the air as I leaned against a tree, Starfire sword glinting faintly at my side.

I eyed them both carefully. "Alright," I began, keeping my voice even. "Let's talk about your magic. Or, in your case," I glanced at Everly, "the lack of it so far."

Dante stepped forward before she could answer, his smirk as cocky as ever. "Well, I don't mind going first." He lifted his hands, palms facing outward, and a bead of water formed in the air, hovering effortlessly. With a flick of his wrist, it split into two, swirling in a mesmerizing dance. I had to admit, his control was decent.

"That's enough, Dante. It's not a circus act," I muttered, though I caught myself smirking slightly. Dante bowed dramatically before stepping back beside Everly, clearly pleased with himself.

Turning my attention to Everly, I studied her carefully. "And you? Nothing yet?"

She sighed, shifting uncomfortably. "I haven't noticed anything. No glowing hands, no mysterious energy bursts. Just... nothing."

I stepped closer, watching her reaction. "What about your wings? Usually, when magic starts to emerge, the instinct for your wings to grow and spread kicks in. Have you felt anything there? A tension, maybe?"

She shook her head. "Not that I've noticed."

“Turn around,” I instructed, keeping my voice firm but steady. Hesitant, she obeyed, her shoulders stiff. As she turned, my eyes traced the curve of her spine, the way her breath hitched slightly in anticipation. I reached out, my fingers brushing lightly against her back, stopping at the space between her shoulder blades. Her skin was warm beneath my touch, softer than I expected. I felt her shiver, and for a moment, I wasn’t sure if it was from the cool air or something else entirely.

My fingers lingered just a fraction longer than necessary, pressing gently against the spot where energy should have been building. The silence stretched between us, thick, charged. I could feel the way her body tensed, like she was holding herself still, waiting. I swallowed hard, forcing my voice to remain even. But something about the way she reacted to me—how her body responded, the way I could feel the slight rise and fall of her breath beneath my fingertips—was dangerously distracting.

“Feel that?” I asked softly, pressing slightly against a point where energy should have been gathering.

She nodded, barely above a whisper. "Yeah... it’s... warm."

“That’s a good sign,” I said, keeping my hands steady even though something about this moment felt... intimate. “Your wings might be ready to emerge soon. You’ll know when it happens—it’s not exactly subtle.” I stepped back, clearing my throat.

Everly turned to face me, curiosity flickering in her green eyes. "Why don’t we see more fae flying around? My mother always said it wasn’t practical, but she never really explained."

I crossed my arms. "She’s right. Flying burns through energy fast. Your metabolism speeds up, meaning you’ll need to eat more frequently, and it can leave you exhausted. Most fae save their wings for short distances or emergencies.

Around the city, public transport is just easier, especially when you're coming home after a long day of work."

Everly seemed to consider this, her gaze drifting slightly. I could tell she was imagining what it would be like to fly.

I snapped my fingers, bringing her back to the moment. "Alright. Let's see if we can coax out any magic. Common magic is a good place to start. Simple things, like healing. Focus on your palms and try to feel for any tingling or heat."

She held out her hands, palms up, eyes narrowed in concentration. I oversaw her, looking for any sign of magic stirring. But after a few minutes, she sighed, shaking her head. "Nothing."

I frowned. "Maybe you need some motivation."

Everly shot me a suspicious look. "What?"

I pulled a dagger from my boot, flipping it in my hand before extending it toward her. "Hold out your hand."

She hesitated, looking between me and the blade, but I didn't waver. Finally, she relented, extending her hand. As I took it in mine, a spark of something unfamiliar settled in my chest. Her skin was warm against mine, and for a brief moment, I hesitated.

"This will only sting," I murmured, not sure if I was reassuring her or myself. With a quick, precise motion, I made a small cut across her palm. A sharp hiss escaped her lips.

"Now," I said, releasing her hand. "Put your palms together and focus on your core. Feel for that warmth or tingling and imagine it traveling down your arms and into your hands."

She did as I instructed, her face tightening in concentration. But after several moments, nothing happened. Just the dull throb of her wound and the frustration in her eyes.

After a few more failed attempts, I sighed, slipping the dagger back into my boot. "Not everyone's magic emerges the same way," I admitted, though part of me hated saying it. "We'll keep trying, but in the meantime, we'll stock up on potions for anything we might face. They'll handle most ailments."

Everly nodded, but I could see the disappointment in the way she held herself. Dante clapped her on the shoulder, his hand lingering a second too long. "Don't worry, Angel Eyes. Your magic will show up when you least expect it. Just try not to burn anything down when it does."

My teeth clenched at the casual way he touched her, the way his fingers curled slightly against her shoulder before he finally pulled back. It wasn't just encouragement—it was deliberate. He knew exactly what he was doing. Testing me.

Dante met my gaze, his smirk infuriatingly smug. The flicker of amusement in his eyes confirmed my suspicion—he knew. He knew how I felt, even when I barely understood it myself.

Everly, oblivious to the tension crackling between us, laughed at his remark, but my fists curled at my sides. She had no idea how much of a game Dante was playing. And I hated that he was winning.

I forced myself to look away, masking my irritation. Whatever this was—whatever strange pull I felt toward Everly—I needed to bury it. Fast.

She laughed, the sound lighter than before. But as I watched them interact, I found my jaw tightening. Dante was getting too comfortable around her.

I forced myself to look away, masking my irritation. Whatever this was—whatever strange pull I felt toward Everly—I needed to bury it. Fast.

Chapter 16

Everly

The morning of our departure dawned cold and quiet, the sky painted in muted shades of gray as if the heavens themselves held their breath. Cain had instructed us to meet him in the armory. When Dante and I arrived, our new uniforms were waiting—sleek black tunics with high collars, tailored to perfection. The fabric was surprisingly lightweight but reinforced in all the right places, a blend of utility and subtle elegance. The black combat pants, lined with pockets for every imaginable purpose, and sturdy boots completed the ensemble. It wasn't ceremonial; it was designed for survival. Yet, there was something about slipping into that uniform that made my pulse quicken.

Dante tugged at the cuff of his sleeve, his lip curling in a half-smile. "Not bad," he said, turning to me with a wink. "Black suits you."

I rolled my eyes, smoothing the front of my tunic. "Let's hope I don't ruin it with whatever's waiting for us out there."

We were issued matching black backpacks, stocked with essentials: rations, first aid kits, maps, and a small vial of something Cain cryptically referred to as "emergency reserves." The weight of the pack on my shoulders felt heavy, but not as heavy as the tension simmering in the air.

The real surprise came later when Cain escorted us to a private chamber deep within the palace. The room was dimly lit by golden sconces, their glow dancing off the polished marble walls. At its center stood Queen Anastasia herself, flanked by the Imperial Council. The queen's presence was commanding yet unnervingly familiar—her golden hair cascaded in waves, and her silver eyes seemed to pierce straight into my soul. Yet, it was the way she looked at Cain that made me pause. There was something there—a warmth, a shared history that felt too personal for the occasion.

"You're early," she said softly, her voice carrying a note of something unspoken as her gaze lingered on Cain. He inclined his head but said nothing, his expression unreadable.

The ceremony was brief but unforgettable. A velvet-covered table held two sheathed swords—Starfire swords, forged with ancient rituals and power. Their hilts gleamed with intricate patterns that pulsed faintly, as though alive.

The queen stepped forward, a ceremonial dagger in her hand. "These swords are bound to their wielders," she began, her voice steady. "A drop of my blood, a drop from the Imperial Counsel, and a drop from each of you will tie their magic to your very essence. Wield them wisely."

One by one, the ritual began. The queen pricked her finger, a single drop of shimmering silver blood falling onto the blade of my sword. One of the council members followed, their deep crimson adding to the ethereal glow. Then it was my turn. Cain handed me the dagger, his fingers brushing mine for the briefest moment—a touch that sent an unexpected jolt through me.

I pressed the blade to my fingertip, watching as a bead of my own blood joined the others. The sword hummed in response, as though recognizing me. I wrapped my hand around the hilt, and a surge of warmth shot up my arm, filling me with a strange, electric energy. This was no ordinary weapon—it was alive.

Dante's turn followed, and he took to the ritual with a surprising seriousness, his usual smirk replaced by a look of quiet reverence. His sword reacted just as mine had, the hum resonating in the silent room.

When it was over, the queen stepped back, her eyes scanning the three of us. "You are venturing into the unknown," she said, her tone carrying the weight of centuries. "Trust your instincts. Trust each other."

As we turned to leave, I couldn't help but glance back. Cain lingered for a moment longer, his posture rigid as the queen's gaze softened. "Be careful, Cain," she said quietly, almost too quietly for me to hear.

His jaw tightened, but he nodded once before following us out. My mind raced with questions as we made our way to the waiting transport. The weight of the sword on my hip was nothing compared to the new questions swirling in my head—questions about the queen, about Cain, and about what lay ahead.

"We will take the train to the end of the line, near the border between Verdanis and Laseel. From there, we'll ride horseback to Laseel and beyond, toward the wall at the kingdom's edge where the unit was last seen. It's roughly a week-long ride." The rhythmic clatter of the train against the tracks filled the silence as Cain laid out the plan in his low, commanding voice. His gaze flickered to me, sharp and assessing, as if he were gauging whether I'd survive the journey.

To say I was nervous was an understatement. The last two days had passed in a blur of grueling training and restless nights. My muscles were on fire from combat drills, and I hadn't decided if the ache was from genuine effort or if my body was trying to distract me from the storm of anxiety swirling in my chest. Either way, I was too drained to overthink—for once.

The train was quiet and mostly empty, save for a few older fae and midday commuters in the distance. The last car, reserved for guardsmen, was eerily still, and I relished the reprieve from constant movement. Trying to calm my nerves, I closed my eyes, letting the steady sway of the train lull me into a meditative state. My mother's old breathing techniques echoed in my mind, and I counted slowly, attempting to push the chaotic thoughts aside.

But instead of calm, images began to flicker behind my eyelids. A dark forest stretched out before me, shadows twisting and stretching like living things. The acrid scent of burning wood filled my senses, thick and cloying. A fire blazed in the distance, casting dancing orange light against the trees. A figure stood at its edge, back turned to me. I stepped closer, my breath catching as I recognized Dante. But something was wrong—his eyes. They were completely black, voids that swallowed all light and warmth. A chill raced through me as I noticed another figure kneeling before him. Cain. His head bowed, his eyes black as midnight.

My eyes flew open, heart pounding. My fingers were tangled together in a tight grip, and sweat dampened my palms and forehead. The train screeched to a halt, jarring me back to the present.

"Hey, are you okay?" Dante's voice came from beside me, soft but edged with concern. His violet eyes, so vivid and alive, were a stark contrast to the version I had seen moments ago. I shifted slightly away from him, unable to shake the memory of that vision.

"Yeah," I said, my voice a little shaky. "I was just meditating… I must've dozed off and had a bad dream."

Dante tilted his head, studying me with an intensity that made me feel like he could see right through me. Before he could say anything more, I looked to the other end of the car. Cain stood there, deep in conversation with another royal guard escorting us to the stables. Relief washed over me as his steel-gray eyes, flecked with blue, locked onto mine. A crease formed between his brows as he crossed the car toward us with that effortless, predatory grace of his.

"You alright, Miss Walker?" His voice was firm, but a hint of warmth lay beneath the authority. It was disarming, and for a moment, I just stared.

“She fell asleep and had a bad dream, apparently,” Dante interjected with a low chuckle, the sound rolling out like a lazy taunt.

Cain’s eyes narrowed, his gaze shifting between the two of us. Concern gave way to suspicion, his expression hardening as if he could sense the tension clinging to the edges of my nerves. “Keep your focus. We’ll need it where we’re going,” he said curtly, but his gaze lingered on me for a moment longer before turning to leave.

The stables at the edge of the capital were sprawling and smelled heavily of hay and leather. Rows of stalls stretched down the wide barn, each housing sleek, strong horses that eyed us curiously as we entered. My gaze immediately landed on a brown and white spotted horse in one of the larger stalls, its coat patterned like a patchwork quilt. It leaned over the stall door, ears twitching in my direction, as if assessing me.

Cain was already talking to the stable master, a no-nonsense fae with deep lines etched into his sunbaked skin. "We’ll need three fit for long travel. Strong, obedient, and sure-footed," Cain said, his authoritative tone leaving no room for debate.

"Got just the ones," the stable master replied, gesturing for his staff to start prepping. Moments later, a massive black horse was led out, its sheer size and presence mirroring Cain’s intimidating demeanor. Cain gave a rare approving nod, running his hand along the horse’s neck as if they were already in silent agreement. The beast’s dark eyes seemed to gleam with intelligence.

Dante's horse came next, a sleek, dark brown creature with a single striking white blaze down its face. Dante approached with surprising ease, his usual cocky demeanor tempered by an unfamiliar gentleness. The horse snorted, bumping its nose against him in what looked like instant camaraderie. Of course, Dante even charmed animals.

And then there was mine. The stable hands brought out the spotted beauty I'd noticed earlier, her coat glossy in the late afternoon light. She looked a little smaller compared to Cain's monster of a horse, but still strong and solid. I reached out hesitantly, and her soft nose pressed into my palm as if to say, *I suppose you'll do.*

"That one's Spirra," the stable master said. "Gentle, but don't let her get lazy on you. She's clever enough to take advantage of a first-time rider."

"Fantastic," I muttered under my breath, trying not to let my nerves show.

As we began loading the saddlebags with supplies, Cain laid out the plan. "We'll stay with locals as much as we can along the route," he said, his deep voice cutting through the bustle of the stables. "But there will be nights when we'll have to sleep outside. Be prepared for that."

I grimaced at the thought, my arms sagging slightly under the weight of the rolled-up bedroll I'd just slung over Spirra's saddle. The idea of sleeping on the ground, with bugs and damp air, made my stomach turn. Cain noticed my expression, but only gave me a look that said, *You'll survive.*

"I've never ridden a horse before," I admitted, hoping this revelation wouldn't somehow make me seem even more unprepared than I already felt.

One of the stable hands overheard me and stepped forward. He was taller than me by at least a head, his long blond hair tied back in a messy top knot. His face was unremarkable—plain and unassuming—but his golden eyes glowed faintly, giving him an ethereal quality that marked him as Mystic. His wings, a pale gold so light they were almost off-white, stretched slightly as he adjusted his stance. When the sunlight hit them, they shimmered like spun glass.

"Duncan," he introduced himself, his voice smooth and easy. "I can give you a quick rundown. It's not as complicated as it seems, but it does take practice." He flashed a smile that didn't quite reach his eyes, though it wasn't unfriendly.

I nodded, feeling a mix of relief and nervousness. Duncan guided me to Spirra, explaining the basics of saddling up, holding the reins, and keeping my balance. His hands were rough as he adjusted the stirrups to my height, his touch professional yet firm.

"Hold here," he instructed, placing my hands on the saddle horn and the edge of the seat. "And use the stirrup to push yourself up. Don't just try to pull yourself on—it won't end well."

I followed his instructions; my first attempt was clumsy but successful. Sitting atop Spirra felt strange; the ground suddenly felt farther away than I liked, but there was also an odd sense of exhilaration. Duncan walked me through a few more basics, like steering and stopping, his tone patient but firm, as if he'd done this a hundred times before.

"You're doing better than most first-timers," he said, stepping back and folding his arms. "Spirra seems to like you, which helps."

"Thanks," I muttered, still feeling awkward but grateful for his guidance. His glowing eyes caught mine briefly, and there was something in his expression—curiosity, maybe—but he said nothing further.

As the others finished loading up their horses, I couldn't help but glance at Cain and Dante. Cain, of course, looked entirely at ease, towering atop his enormous black horse like some ancient warlord. Dante, meanwhile, looked infuriatingly good, his relaxed posture and easy smile making it seem like he'd been born in the saddle.

"Alright, mount up," Cain barked, his voice breaking through my thoughts. "We've got a long ride ahead, and I'm not waiting for anyone."

With a deep breath, I gripped Spirra's reins and urged her forward, the unease in my chest mixing with a spark of anticipation for the journey ahead.

Chapter 17

Everly

The ride out of the capital was both awe-inspiring and grueling. The cobblestone streets slowly gave way to the dirt paths that twisted and turned through the outskirts, leading us into the hilly countryside. The horses moved steadily beneath us, their hooves crunching against gravel and packed earth. Spirra, my brown-and-white spotted horse, had a surprisingly smooth gait. However, I was quickly learning that even a "smooth" ride could wreak havoc on muscles I hadn't known existed. My backside had gone numb within the first hour, and I found myself shifting in the saddle constantly to keep the tingling sensation at bay.

Exiting the capital of Verdanis meant passing through the Luminite Crystal wards that protected the city. As our group moved through the shimmering barrier, a brief prickling sensation danced along my skin, like walking through a field of static. It was a sensation many had grown accustomed to. Still, for me, it served as a tangible reminder of the magical protection we were leaving behind.

The landscape was breathtaking, with rolling green hills bordered by thick woodlands that stretched out as far as the eye could see. Birds flitted between trees, their songs mixing with the occasional rustling of underbrush as small animals—rabbits, deer, and once, something resembling a fox but with shimmering silver fur and antlers—darted away at our approach. The occasional winged creature soared overhead, some real and recognizable, like hawks and eagles.

In contrast, others were distinctly mythical, their shimmering scales or elongated, serpentine tails setting them apart from anything mundane.

From the tops of the hills, I caught glimpses of the Saffron Sea, its golden waters glistening under the midday sun. Ships dotted the horizon, their sails bright against the azure sky as they moved toward the capital's bustling ports. The view was enough to momentarily distract me from my discomfort, though it also stirred an unexpected pang of homesickness. Looking back, the capital sprawled like a jewel across the land, its towering spires catching the light. It was both a comfort and a reminder of what I was leaving behind.

I felt a sharp twist of guilt in my chest. I hadn't told Peris or Ferra about my departure; the secrecy of our mission had made it impossible for me to do so. I knew they would notice my absence soon enough, just as Lyla would undoubtedly question where Cain and Dante had gone. The thought of Lyla made the guilt worse, even though our friendship was still new. She deserved better, and I hated that I'd left without a word. I silently promised myself that if—*when*—I returned, I'd make it up to all of them.

We reached the edge of Verdanis by late afternoon, the place where an old, crumbling wall once stood to close off the kingdom's borders from Laseel. Only fragments of the wall remained now, moss-covered and weathered with age. It was strange to think that this barrier had once been so fiercely guarded, now reduced to a ruin overtaken by nature. The sight marked a change in the air, a subtle shift as the forest deepened and the hills grew steeper.

The journey was far from glamorous. We ate rations on horseback—dried meats, cheeses, and hard bread—which was awkward enough while bouncing along the trail. Short breaks allowed us to stretch our legs, but stopping too often wasn't an option. Even more embarrassing was dealing with the necessary bathroom breaks. As the only female, I had to wait for Cain and Dante to move far enough away to give me some semblance of privacy. Still, it wasn't lost on me how exposed and vulnerable I felt squatting behind a tree in the middle of the wilderness.

The sun rose higher, warming the air and making the long sleeves and heavy black fabric of our uniforms unbearable. I tried to keep my hair down at first, but it wasn't long before sweat made it stick to the back of my neck, forcing me to twist it up into a messy bun. Cain rolled up his sleeves without a word, his forearms catching the light and revealing intricate tattoos. The ink swirled in shadowy patterns, almost alive, coiling into shapes that seemed to shift with every movement of his arms.

A Starfire sword stretched along the length of his right forearm, its blade shimmering faintly as the sun hit it, as though the tattoo itself held a fragment of light. On his left arm, the crest of Erynvale stood out boldly—a crown encircling a shield flanked by two crossing swords, the symbol of the kingdom's strength and unity. Scattered among these larger designs were smaller symbols that I couldn't quite place; the lines and curves spoke of secrets and stories left untold. One particular phrase ran just below his elbow, the letters etched in sharp, elegant script: *"Mask the truth to protect what matters most."*

The sight of his tattoos made my breath catch. They seemed so out of place on someone like Cain, whose demeanor was as sharp and unyielding as steel. These marks, intimate and deliberate, hinted at a deeper layer to him—a part of his story he kept carefully hidden beneath that controlled exterior. It made me wonder just how much he had masked, how much of the man beneath the guard I had yet to see.

Dante rolled up his sleeves next, and while his forearms were bare compared to Cain's, the play of muscles under his skin was enough to draw attention. His smirk suggested he noticed my wandering eyes. However, I quickly looked away and focused back on the trail ahead, gripping Spirra's reins tighter. My horse snorted in response, as if to remind me that I wasn't exactly riding gracefully.

"Why are we wearing black and long sleeves for this journey, anyway?" I finally asked, tugging at the fabric clinging to my skin. "Seems a bit impractical for riding through the countryside in the sun."

Cain didn't look back, his voice calm but firm, as though he'd anticipated the question. "Laseel is much cooler than the capital. You'll be glad for the layers soon enough."

Dante chimed in, his tone lighter, though tinged with his usual teasing edge. "The Elemental fae in Laseel keep their territory darker. Something about their sensitivity to light. Sunlight's not really needed for vegetation there—earth elementals use their magic to keep plants healthy. And fire elementals keep the cities warm, but the woodlands and uninhabited areas? They can get *really* cold."

I glanced back at Cain, my eyes retracing the tattoos. I couldn't stop wondering what stories those swirling shadows told—and what kind of man had decided to mark his skin with them, as though the memories they carried were too important to ever forget.

I absorbed the information, trying to imagine a land so different from Verdanis, where magic dictated the climate and the environment bent to its will. It was both fascinating and unsettling. The closer we got to Laseel, the more I realized how little I truly knew about the world outside my home. Spirra snorted beneath me, as if sensing my unease, and I reached down to pat her neck.

"You and me both, girl," I muttered under my breath. "We're in for an adventure."

As the sun dipped below the horizon, we arrived at the settlement of Ashmoor—a small town nestled between the borders of Verdanis and Laseel. It had clearly sprung up after the boundaries came down, a testament to the alliance between the two territories. The air was cooler here, carrying the faint scent of pine and the tang of the nearby sea, and the flickering lanterns that lined the cobblestone streets gave the settlement a rustic charm.

The stables were our first stop, where a pair of young stable hands hurried to take our horses. Spirra whinnied as I slid off her back, my legs trembling slightly after the long day's ride. Cain wasted no time, immediately striding toward a man waiting near the entrance to the Inn. He was broad-shouldered, clad in a dark uniform adorned with insignias that marked him as a guard—Petty Officer Joseph Grant, Cain's contact. Their exchange was brief, words murmured low enough to be drowned out by the buzz of the settlement, but I caught the occasional glance in our direction. Whatever they were discussing, it was a serious matter.

The Inn, like the rest of Ashmoor, had a rugged simplicity to it. The great hall served as both a dining area and a gathering place, with long wooden tables arranged beneath low-hanging lanterns. The walls were decorated with mismatched banners and shields—tokens of pride, no doubt—but it was clear this was a place run by men. The few women and children present appeared to be the family of the guards stationed here, and they moved comfortably among the Elementals and Mystics alike. What struck me most was the camaraderie between them, the way they laughed, worked, and dined together as though their differences in magic were inconsequential.

The children ran in and out of the hall, their laughter ringing out like music. My gaze caught on a small group playing near the hearth, their pointed ears marking them unmistakably as hybrids. A warmth spread through my chest at the sight, but it was bittersweet, mingled with a longing I couldn't quite put into words. They looked happy here, accepted. Was it possible to build a life like that, even as a *halfling*?

We were offered a hot meal, and I didn't hesitate to accept. The savory aroma of roasted meat and hearty stew made my mouth water as I sat down beside Dante. Across the hall, a group of older fae played cards near the hearth, their laughter echoing warmly through the room. Two of them, identical down to the tilt of their grins, caught my attention. Twins. The sight made my chest tighten with a pang of longing. What would it be like to have a sibling? Someone who understood you so profoundly that they were practically another version of yourself?

"You've been quiet," Dante murmured beside me, his violet eyes catching the light in a way that made them almost glow. His tone was casual, but there was curiosity behind it.

"Just... thinking," I replied, my gaze lingering on the twins. "It must be amazing to have a sibling, let alone a twin."

Dante's lips quirked into a soft smile. "I actually have a younger sister," he admitted, his voice lowering as though he hadn't meant to share. "She's back in Laseel with my mother."

His words stopped me cold. My mind flashed back to our earlier conversations, to the story he had told me about moving to the capital after his father's death, because his father had no family left. My brow furrowed, but I forced a smile and didn't press him—not in front of the older fae, who were now inviting us to join their game.

The cards provided a welcome distraction, the simple game giving me a chance to laugh and relax for the first time in days. I savored the hot dinner, the warmth of the hall, and even Dante's sly comments whenever I fumbled a play. For a moment, I let myself forget the mission ahead and the mounting mysteries swirling around us.

Cain returned just as the game was winding down, his expression as unreadable as ever. "Your room is ready," he announced, his deep voice cutting through the chatter. My relief was short-lived, however, as he added, "The three of us will be sharing."

"Wait, all three of us?" I blurted, staring at him in horror.

He raised an eyebrow, clearly unimpressed by my outburst. "This is a small settlement, Miss Walker, not the royal palace. Accommodations are limited."

Dante, of course, found the situation highly amusing, his grin widening as he leaned back in his chair. "Don't worry, Angel Eyes. I promise not to snore."

I shot him a glare, my cheeks heating as I stood to leave. *This was going to be a long night.*

Dante stayed behind, absorbed in another round of cards, his laughter mingling with the deeper voices of the other players. Cain, however, stood by the door, waiting for me with an air of impatience. With a reluctant sigh, I followed him up the creaky wooden stairs, my boots echoing softly on the worn steps.

The air between us was thick with unspoken tension as he led the way to our shared room. I hated silence, and Cain seemed to revel in it, so naturally, I couldn't resist trying to fill the void.

"So... does brooding come naturally, or is it a skill you've perfected over the years?" I quipped, hoping to needle him out of his icy demeanor.

His jaw tightened, and for a moment, I thought he might ignore me entirely. "I'm not here to entertain you," he replied curtly, his voice clipped and cold.

I stopped dead in my tracks, my patience snapping. "Alright, enough. What is your problem?" I demanded, planting my hands on my hips. "You've been like this since day one, and it's getting old. If you have an issue with me, just say it, but don't treat me like dirt when I have no idea what's going on!"

He stopped a few steps ahead, exhaling sharply as if I'd struck a nerve. Slowly, he turned, the hard lines of his face softening ever so slightly. "You want to know my problem?" he asked, his voice quieter now but no less firm. "I'm not happy about this mission, about dragging two unskilled, unmanifested magic trainees—trainees who can barely keep up in combat class—into a situation that could get us all killed."

His words stung, even though they weren't entirely untrue. My lips parted to protest, but he cut me off, his tone shifting. "But it's not my choice. The queen specifically requested I take you both. She didn't want me going alone, and apparently, she has a gift for these things."

I tilted my head, my frustration giving way to curiosity.

"Her intuition? You mean the queen's famous ability to sense people's intentions?" Cain nodded, his arms crossing over his chest.

"She's convinced you and I are meant to work well together," Cain continued, his gaze locking onto mine. "Although she couldn't get a proper read on Dante. She only saw him briefly during the Starfire ceremony and told me to keep my guard up around him. That's why I'm cautious."

I nodded, feeling a pang of guilt for the times I'd brushed off his intensity as paranoia. "I get it," I admitted softly. "Honestly, I'm suspicious too."

That caught his attention, his eyes narrowing slightly. "What do you mean?"

I hesitated, then decided to be honest. "On the train, when I was meditating, I had this... vision. It felt so real. There was a fire, and Dante was standing there, but something was wrong. His eyes were completely black, like voids. And you... you were there too, kneeling in front of him, and your eyes were the same."

Cain's expression darkened, his brow furrowing as he processed my words. "A vision?" he repeated, his voice weighted with something I couldn't quite place. "That could be your magic starting to manifest."

The possibility sent a shiver down my spine. Was that truly what it was? A manifestation of my latent abilities? Or was it just my nerves playing tricks on me? Either way, the look in Cain's eyes—half concerned, half calculating—told me that whatever was happening, this mission was only the beginning.

Once the door clicked shut behind us, I took in the room. It was small but charming, bathed in the warm glow of lantern light. A large bed dominated the space, its carved wooden frame ornate but well-worn, flanked by two modest end tables. A crackling fire danced in the hearth, its soft glow reflecting off a polished oak table and two mismatched chairs. Off to the side, a door led to a tiny bathroom with a clawfoot tub and a porcelain sink—luxuries but understated. The running water felt like a small blessing, though the lack of modern lighting gave the space an old-world charm.

Cain shrugged off his cloak, draping it over the back of one chair. "The elementals here prefer it this way," he explained, motioning to the lanterns. "They don't care much for the harsher lighting mystics use, and the mystics here are... accommodating."

I nodded, tracing the rim of the table with my finger, feeling the grooves etched into the wood by time. "It's interesting," I murmured, my thoughts drifting. "Seeing how they've built this life together. The elementals and mystics, I mean. Even the children here—so many with pointed ears marking them as hybrids. It's strange for me to see. I thought I was part of the first generation."

Cain leaned back against the fireplace, his arms crossing over his chest as the lanterns cast shadows that danced across the tattoos on his forearms—the swirling symbols and crests coming alive in the flickering light. "You were," he said after a pause, his voice low. "But time doesn't stop just because your life feels singular. The moment the walls came down, everything began to change. There's more mixing now than there ever has been, especially in places like this—outposts where people rely on each other to survive. It doesn't matter what kind of magic you have when you're facing the same dangers."

His words settled over me like a heavy blanket, warm yet suffocating. I turned toward the fire, watching the flames lick at the logs as my thoughts swirled. "I used to wonder," I said quietly, "if I was some kind of mistake. A test run for what happens when two worlds collide." I glanced at him over my shoulder. "But seeing the kids here, maybe I wasn't such an anomaly after all."

Cain's gaze was unreadable, but the weight of it was unmistakable. "You're not a mistake," he said, his voice firm, his grey-blue eyes catching the firelight like molten steel. "Don't ever think that."

For a moment, the room felt too small, the air too thick. His words lingered, a declaration that felt too intimate for the space between us. I turned back to the fire, trying to steady the sudden flutter in my chest. "I just hope this mission doesn't make us a cautionary tale for the next generation," I said lightly, though the edge of truth in my voice betrayed me.

Cain's lips quirked into a faint smile, but there was no humor in it. "Let's make sure it doesn't," he said simply, his words holding more weight than I was prepared to carry.

The silence stretched between us as the fire crackled, the shadows flickering like secrets waiting to be unearthed. The firelight flickered against the walls, casting long, shifting shadows that seemed to echo the weight of the conversation we were about to have. Cain leaned back against the table, his sharp features softened but not diminished by the warm glow of the lamp. The silence between us was heavy, almost expectant. Gathering my courage, I finally spoke, the question tumbling out before I could overthink it.

"Cain," I began hesitantly, "is there... a personal connection between you and Queen Anastasia?"

His blue-flecked, gray eyes narrowed slightly, a flicker of something unreadable crossing his face. For a moment, I thought he might brush me off. But then he sighed, running a hand through his tousled blond hair, the firelight catching it and making it glow like molten gold.

"Yes," he admitted quietly, his voice low and deliberate. "There is a connection." He hesitated, as though weighing his words. "She's my grandmother. My father is her son."

The air seemed to rush out of the room. My heart stuttered as the weight of his revelation sank in. I stared at him, wide-eyed, as memories of the mourning period the entire kingdom had taken flashed through my mind. When his grandfather, King Aldren, passed away, it was a nationwide tragedy. The bells had tolled for days, and Queen Anastasia wore black for an entire year to honor him. Her grief had been palpable, almost tangible, even to someone like me who had only seen her from a distance. It was a sorrow the kingdom shared, though no one dared to speculate too loudly about the mysterious circumstances surrounding the king's death.

"But..." I started, my voice trembling slightly, "that's not in the histories. The books mention the queen's sons, but they don't..." I trailed off, realizing the significance of what he was telling me.

Cain's jaw tightened, the flickering firelight emphasizing the hard lines of his face. "It's not something we let the world know," he said, his tone laced with a quiet intensity. "For the safety of my family. My grandfather's death—" He stopped himself, exhaling sharply. "There are... things about it that aren't as they seem. Things that fuel this mission."

His words hung in the air like a storm cloud, heavy and foreboding. I wanted to press him, to demand he tell me more, but something in his demeanor—his tightly coiled restraint—held me back. There were secrets here, dangerous ones, and it felt like he was only letting me glimpse the edge of them.

"That's..." I swallowed, unsure what to say. "A lot."

Cain gave a small, humorless smile. "You have no idea."

Before I could respond, he straightened, brushing the tension away as if it hadn't existed. "You should wash up," he said, gesturing toward the small bathroom. "The tub should still have hot water."

Taking the hint, I nodded and slipped into the bathroom. The hot bath was a welcome distraction, the steam wrapping around me like a cocoon as I tried to process everything he'd told me. But when I stepped out, wrapped in a robe, I realized something that made my stomach sink—I hadn't packed anything to sleep in. The robe was all I had.

"Great," I muttered to myself, wringing out my damp red hair. I cracked the door open and peered into the room, spotting my bag near the bed. Quietly, I padded out, the soft rug brushing against my bare feet.

Cain was sitting on the edge of the bed, his shirt discarded, leaving his broad chest and arms exposed. His pants rode low, revealing the deep V just below his navel. My gaze lingered on the starlight sword inked down his forearm, its blade gleaming like it held absolute power.

I froze, my heart hammering in my chest. The sight of him, all hard edges and quiet strength, stirred something deep and dangerous inside me. My pulse quickened as I tried to focus on the bag, but my clumsy feet had other plans. I tripped on the edge of the rug, stumbling forward with a startled yelp.

Cain was on his feet in an instant, his hands steadying me before I could hit the floor. The sudden motion loosened the tie on my robe, and the fabric parted just enough to expose the curve of one breast. His sharp intake of breath was audible, and when I looked up, I found myself caught in the smoldering steel of his hooded gaze.

Time seemed to stretch, the space between us charged with something electric. Molten lava pooled deep inside me. Our faces so close, I could feel his breath on my lips. His eyes flickered downward, lingering for a moment that felt far too long. My skin prickled as I realized my nipples had hardened under his gaze, and heat bloomed in my cheeks as I fumbled to pull the robe closed.

"Thanks," I managed to stammer, my voice barely above a whisper. I quickly stepped back, my heart racing as I tried to gather myself.

Cain's expression was unreadable as he turned and grabbed something from the foot of the bed. "Here," he said, holding out a neatly folded set of pajamas. "One of the wives in the settlement thought you might need these."

I took them from him, our fingers brushing for a fleeting moment. "Thanks," I said again, avoiding his eyes as I turned back toward the bathroom, the fabric clutched tightly in my hands.

As the door clicked shut behind me, I leaned against it, my chest heaving with the weight of emotions I couldn't quite name. Whatever this was between us, it was a dangerous situation. And I wasn't sure I wanted to resist stepping into the fire.

I heard Dante enter the room while I was still in the bathroom, the faint creak of the door followed by his familiar footsteps. Their voices carried through the wooden walls, low and gravelly as they discussed the sleeping arrangements. I paused, towel in hand, as Cain's voice cut through the murmur.

“We've agreed you get the bed,” he said flatly when I stepped out. His eyes lingered for a moment, taking in my damp hair and borrowed pajamas. “Unless, of course, you'd rather pick one of us to cuddle up with—or better yet, have both of us in your bed."

I blinked, his words settling like hot embers on my skin. The corner of his mouth twitched upward, a ghost of a smirk daring me to react.

"Very funny," I said, crossing my arms to deflect the heat creeping up my neck. "I'll take the bed."

That night, my dreams came alive again, vivid and haunting like the ones before. I was in the forest, the air thick and suffocating, the shadows impossibly dark. The towering trees around me, once so vibrant and shimmering with silver leaves, now wilted and crumbled as a giant shadow loomed above them. It cloaked the entire forest in darkness, devouring everything in its path.

My heart raced as I turned, the forest shifting around me like it was alive. Then I saw him—Cain. He was on the ground, his silver hair darkened with blood, the glint of a Starfire sword protruding from his chest. His face was twisted in pain, his piercing grey eyes dulled, staring blankly at the sky.

"No!" I screamed, but the sound felt swallowed by the darkness.

A chill ran down my spine as I shifted my gaze upward. Standing over Cain was Dante, his broad shoulders rigid, his presence cold and unfamiliar. His eyes—once such a striking violet—were now completely black, as though they'd been swallowed by the void itself.

"It had to be done," he said, his voice deep and resonating, echoing all around me as if the forest itself spoke through him. The timber of his tone sent shivers racing through my veins, a mixture of fear and something unexplainably magnetic. His expression was calm, almost serene, as though betraying Cain was inevitably destined.

I couldn't breathe. My legs felt rooted to the ground, no matter how desperately I tried to move. The Starfire sword in Cain's chest pulsed with a faint light before it flickered and died, and I was consumed by the realization that Cain wasn't moving. He was gone.

I woke with a start, my chest heaving as though I'd been holding my breath for hours. My skin was damp with sweat, and my hands trembled as I raked them through my hair. The dream clung to me like a second skin, the image of Dante's blackened eyes and Cain's lifeless body seared into my mind.

I turned, bleary-eyed, to find Dante sprawled beside me, his head resting on one arm like he owned the damn place. Cain was nowhere to be seen. My temper flared as I shoved him hard, sending him tumbling to the floor with a loud thud.

"What the hell, Dante?" I snapped, sitting up and glaring down at him.

He rubbed the back of his head, looking up at me with a boyish grin that only fueled my irritation. "I got cold," he said as if that explained everything. "You were sleeping so soundly, I figured you wouldn't mind."

"Mind?!" I threw the blanket off and stood, jabbing a finger in his direction. "You don't get to just climb into bed with me because you're chilly!"

"Well," he said with an infuriating shrug, "at least I didn't snore. You should be thanking me."

I stormed off to the bathroom, slamming the door behind me as I tried to shake off the lingering embarrassment and the way my heart had inexplicably raced when I woke up to find him there. By the time I emerged, dressed and brushing my damp hair, Dante had stripped off his shirt, standing with his back to me as he rummaged through his bag.

"Do neither of you know how to wear a shirt?" I muttered, keeping my eyes stubbornly fixed on the wall.

Dante turned, his lips curving into a devilish smile as he caught my flustered expression. "Oh, so you've seen Cain shirtless?" he asked, his tone teasing. "And here I thought I'd be the one inspiring you're what do they call them? Wet dreams?"

"Excuse me?" I sputtered, my face burning as he laughed, the sound low and warm like a crackling fire. He leaned back against the wall, arms crossed over his chest, utterly unapologetic.

"If you wanted to see more of me, Angel Eyes, you could've just asked."

I didn't dignify that with a response. Instead, I grabbed my bag and stormed out, cursing the fact that I had to spend another day with these infuriating men and cursing even more the flicker of something thrilling that Dante always managed to ignite.

When I saw Cain in the great hall, there was a noticeable shift in his demeanor. He seemed friendlier, less guarded than before. Our late-night conversation had melted a fraction of the ice between us. As we sat together, a kitchen attendant approached, balancing plates of breakfast foods that she placed in front of each of us with practiced ease. The savory aroma of fresh bread, spiced sausages, and roasted root vegetables filled the air, and my stomach grumbled in anticipation.

The woman's gaze lingered on me, and with a kind smile, she asked, "Did the clothes fit you well, dear?"

I realized with a start that she was the one who had lent me the pajamas. "Yes, thank you. They were perfect," I said, my tone soft with gratitude. I ventured further, asking her name.

"Matilda," she replied warmly, her pale gold eyes twinkling. She didn't flinch or shy away from me as so many others had upon realizing I was a hybrid. Before I could respond, a small child ran into the hall, his tiny legs moving as fast as they could. He latched onto Matilda's leg with a giggle, and I noticed the faintly pointed tips of his ears. A hybrid child.

Matilda lifted the boy into her arms effortlessly, whispering something to him that made his face light up. "This is Miss Walker," she said to the boy. "She's a hybrid like you. And one day, if you're brave and strong, you could be a royal guard just like her."

My chest swelled with an unexpected warmth. A slow smile spread across my face, and for the first time, I felt pride in the part of me I'd always been told was a weakness. Across the table, Cain watched the exchange with a rare, genuine smile. But when I glanced at Dante, his expression was more complex to read, somewhere between thoughtful and wary.

"Finish up," Cain said, his tone commanding but not unkind. "We have to discuss our journey."

We followed him out of the hall and across the settlement to a sturdy building that housed the local guards. Inside, he led us to a private room that bore an uncanny resemblance to his office back home, maps pinned to the walls, papers strewn across the wooden table, and a palpable air of strategy and secrecy. Petty Officer Grant joined us, his expression grave.

"This information stays between us," Cain began, his voice dropping into a low, authoritative tone. "It's sensitive."

The atmosphere shifted, the weight of his words sinking into the small room. He took a deep breath before continuing. "The unit that disappeared beyond the wall it was my father's. The Supreme Commander of Erynvale has been missing for two weeks. None of the outposts within our borders has heard from him, and the battalion outside the wall is unaccounted for."

My breath caught, and I fought to keep my expression neutral, my mind flashing back to the royal bloodline I now knew Cain was tied to. His father, the queen's son, is missing in enemy territory. I glanced at Dante, who looked contemplative but unaware of the more profound implications. I resolved to keep Cain's royal connection to myself. It wasn't my secret to share, especially not with someone I was still figuring out if I could trust.

"Another unit was sent to investigate," Cain continued. "They found the outpost in ruins. Most of the soldiers were accounted for…dead. My father is the only one unaccounted for."

Dante broke the heavy silence. "Were any maps, documents, or other sensitive materials missing?"

"No," Cain replied sharply, his tone like steel. "But that doesn't mean they weren't compromised. We have to assume the worst."

The conversation shifted as Cain moved to logistics. "Our next destination is Laseel. It's about a day's ride from here. From there, we'll head to an outpost between Laseel and the wall, which will take another two days. The final stretch to the wall itself will be a day and a half."

The enormity of the mission sank in as Cain spoke. I glanced between the maps and the resolute look in his eyes. This wasn't just a routine mission—it was deeply personal for him. And for some reason, knowing that made my resolve stronger. Whatever awaited us beyond the wall, I was determined to prove I belonged on this mission, even if every mile we rode brought us closer to a danger none of us were fully prepared for.

"What exactly is out there that we're expecting to find?" I asked, my tone sharper than I intended as I turned to Cain. "Sorry, but I've spent my entire life hearing about this 'grave threat,' and no one even seems to know what it is."

Cain's expression hardened, his jaw tightening as his eyes narrowed. "That's above your pay grade, Miss Walker," he said curtly. His voice was as cold as winter frost. "The information is need-to-know, and you'll know it when it's needed."

Of course. Back to stone-cold Cain. But the flicker in his eyes, a glint of hesitation, made me think he wanted to tell me. That whatever it was gnawed at him in ways he couldn't show. My eyes flicked to Petty Officer Grant, who stood stoically nearby, and it hit me—Cain wasn't withholding because of me. He didn't trust Dante. The thought made my stomach churn. Why bring him along at all, then? Cain's gaze lingered on me for a moment longer before he barked another order.

"We leave within the hour. Pack up and meet me by the stables. Don't waste time."

As we walked back to our room, Dante sidled closer, his voice dropping to a conspiratorial whisper. "Do you have any idea what they're hiding?" His violet eyes gleamed, a spark of something dangerous lurking beneath their surface.

"No," I replied, my own voice low. "But I'm starting to think it's worse than we've been told."

He smirked, that mischievous twist of his lips making him look both charming and infuriating. "I know things," he said, his tone teasing at first, then darkening. "Things about what's beyond the wall."

I stopped walking and turned to face him fully, my heart beating faster. "Like what?"

"The Blight that desolated the land, it's not just some natural disaster or a consequence of war," Dante began, his voice soft but weighted. "It's the result of very dark magic. The kind that takes the life from everything and then twists it, creates something entirely new and utterly horrifying. The dead trees? Their wood transforms into Timber Wolves—massive, savage creatures. Rocks? They reshape into fearsome, steed-like beasts. The animals that once lived there? Turned into weapons of death. Even the skeletons of those who died in those cursed lands rise as warriors."

I shivered, the vividness of his words painting pictures in my mind that I wished I could erase. "And it's all just...happening on its own?" I asked, though a sinking feeling told me I wouldn't like his answer.

"No," Dante said grimly. "It's all controlled by one person. Someone with magic as powerful as the royals. He calls himself Nightshade."

"Nightshade? Like the herb?" I asked, the laugh that escaped my lips more nervous than amused. "That doesn't sound terrifying at all."

Dante's smirk returned, though it lacked its usual playfulness. "You won't be laughing if you ever see him," he said, his tone a warning. "The name might sound harmless, but what he's capable of? It's anything but."

I swallowed hard, suddenly feeling the weight of the mission pressing on my shoulders. Whatever lay ahead of us, I knew one thing for sure, I wasn't ready for it.

Chapter 18

Everly

We mounted our horses once again and headed north. As we left the coastline behind, the crisp scent of saltwater dissipated, replaced by the rich, earthy aroma of the forest. The trees here were nothing like the meticulously groomed ones in the capital. They were wild and ancient, towering above us with thick canopies that dappled the sunlight on the ground. Birds chirped from unseen perches, their melodies weaving through the quiet rhythm of hooves on the dirt path. My heart swelled with wonder. I'd never felt so free, so untethered, riding through untouched nature. It was a far cry from the structured life I'd grown up in, and I found myself eagerly anticipating what other marvels lay ahead.

We traveled in a line, Cain leading with that confident ease of his, me following a few paces behind, and Dante bringing up the rear. Hours passed in near silence until, finally, Dante nudged his horse forward to ride alongside me. His violet eyes sparkled mischievously as he slowed his pace to match mine, just out of earshot of Cain.

"How do you know all that stuff you told me back in Ashmoor?" I asked, breaking the silence. My voice was hushed, though I wasn't sure why.

He hesitated, his hand brushing absently along the reins. "My father used to be somebody when he served the Elysian Army," he said carefully.

I raised an eyebrow. "How is that possible? Weren't all soldiers magic-bound from revealing anything about what's beyond the wall?"

A shadow crossed his face. "Not everyone was," he admitted, his voice barely audible. "In the early days of the conscription, before the Blight, the elementals of Laseel didn't trust the mystics enough to make such promises. There was too much tension, too much history of betrayal between the two sides. My father… he told me things, things I don't think even he fully understood. He didn't survive long enough to see what it became."

I let that sink in, the weight of his words settling heavily on my chest. "So this… Blight. It started before Queen Anastasia broke down the barriers between mystics and elementals?" I asked.

He nodded. "Long before. Back when the old king and Queen still ruled, they were the ones who built the walls, who made the divide. It wasn't until Anastasia married their son, King Aldren, that things began to change. She was the one who tore those barriers down, but by then, the Blight was already here, spreading beyond the kingdom's walls."

Before I could ask more, Cain's voice carried back to us, sharp and unexpected. "You two trading secrets?"

His tone was light, but his posture on his horse was as rigid as ever. He didn't turn around, but I caught the flicker of amusement in his voice. I rolled my eyes and urged Spirra forward, leaving Dante behind. I wasn't about to give Cain the satisfaction of thinking we were scheming.

By the time the sun climbed high into the sky, we stopped near a bubbling spring. The horses drank greedily as we refilled our canteens, and I let my gaze drift to the clear stream, where fish darted between the rocks. The simplicity of the moment was grounding, even as my mind buzzed with thoughts of everything Dante had said.

I glanced toward Cain, who was tending to his massive black horse with surprising tenderness. The sight of him, his strong hands brushing along the horse's mane with careful precision, stirred something unexpected in me. Gathering my courage, I walked over.

“What’s his name?” I asked softly, gesturing to the horse.

Cain’s lips quirked into a faint smile, his face softening. “Shadow.”

“Fitting,” I said with a small laugh, brushing my fingers along Shadow’s velvety nose. “You seem… comfortable with horses.”

"I was," he admitted, his voice carrying a hint of something more profound. "Before the accident."

He didn’t elaborate, but he didn’t need to. I’d noticed the stiffness in his movements, the limp he tried to mask. His leg was the reason he’d never rise higher than a corporal, relegated to training rather than leading. Yet here he was, on this mission with us, defying the limitations that had been placed on him.

I studied him, my chest tightening. “You know, I think your father would be proud,” I said quietly.

His hand stilled on the horse, and for a moment, I thought I’d said too much. But when he turned to look at me, there was something unspoken in his eyes—a mix of gratitude and vulnerability he rarely allowed himself to show.

“Let’s hope this mission gives me the chance to prove that,” he said, his voice steady but tinged with determination.

I nodded, feeling a newfound respect for him settle in my chest. Cain was far more than the stoic, unyielding trainer I’d pegged him as. There was depth there, layers I wasn’t sure I’d ever be able to unravel. But, gods, I wanted to try.

We continued riding in silence, the rhythmic sound of hooves on the forest floor filling the air. The trees around us began to change, their transformation subtle at first. Here and there, a few massive trunks loomed, black as midnight, with leaves that shimmered silver like moonlight. They stood in stark contrast to the vibrant green trees of the capital, where I had grown up. The further we rode, the more these dark, ethereal trees took over, the lush greenery fading into memory. The temperature dropped sharply, biting through the air and chilling my skin despite the long sleeves and pants Cain had insisted on. For once, I had to admit he was right.

Looking up, I noticed the sun, usually hidden by the canopy above, had vanished entirely. Heavy clouds cloaked the sky, sealing us in a dim, shadowed world. It was disorienting, the perpetual twilight making it impossible to guess how much daylight we had left. I gripped Spirra's reins tighter, my eyes scanning the eerie landscape. The silence felt too deep here, too unnatural, broken only by the occasional rustle of the wind through the silver leaves. My stomach tightened with unease, though I fought to suppress it.

Just as I began to wonder how much longer this unsettling journey would last, the trees thinned, giving way to a broad river. Beyond it, nestled on the other side, was the city of Laseel. The sight of it took my breath away. Laseel rose from the ground like something out of a storybook—its dark stone buildings almost glowing under the silver sky. A long wooden bridge stretched across the river, welcoming us to the city like a threshold to another realm.

We crossed the bridge, the wooden planks creaking beneath the weight of our horses. At the other side, city sentinels waited, their sharp eyes assessing us as we approached. Cain dismounted with practiced ease, pulling a sealed document from his saddlebag. He handed it over to one of the guards, who scanned it with a solemn expression before giving a curt nod. With that, we were waved through, no questions asked. I watched them as we passed. One of the sentinels, a striking fae with eyes like dark maple syrup, met my gaze. His hair, dark as midnight, fell in soft waves, and his wings, tucked neatly against his back, were unlike any I'd seen before. The feathers were a gradient of shadowy grey, deepening to black at their base and fading to white at their tips. He stared at me a moment too long, his expression unreadable.

The city of Laseel was unlike anything I'd ever experienced. As we moved down the packed dirt roads, fae emerged from their homes and shops to watch us. Their faces peered out from windows and doorways, curious and cautious. Whispers carried through the air, and I couldn't shake the feeling of being on display, a strange animal paraded through their streets. I sat straighter in my saddle, trying to project confidence, though inside I felt unmoored.

"They're staring," I murmured to Dante, who had ridden up beside me.

"They're still cautious about Mystics here," he whispered, his violet eyes scanning the streets. "Hybrids like us get a little more acceptance—out of respect for the Elemental side—but don't get too comfortable."

I followed his gaze, noting the curious stares from the townsfolk. It wasn't me this time causing a stir, thankfully. Cain, riding confidently ahead, was the spectacle. His commanding presence drew attention wherever we went. For once, I was glad to blend into the background.

We rode up to a cozy inn, its exterior aged but charming, with guardsmen waiting out front. Spirra perked up as I caught sight of the fenced pasture beyond the stables, imagining her enjoying the space after a long day. As we dismounted, Cain handed the reins to one of the stable hands and turned to me, his tone casual but his words anything but. "I'll let you check us in. They'll feel more comfortable with someone of your... background."

I froze, raising a brow at him. "Well, damn. That's only one step away from calling us '*halflings*,' isn't it?" My voice dripped with sarcasm, but the weight behind my words was unmistakable.

His expression faltered, his eyes widening in realization. “I didn’t mean it like that,” he said quickly, almost apologetically.

I crossed my arms and let the silence stretch long enough to make him squirm before finally rolling my eyes. “Fine. Whatever.” He seemed to take the hint and turned toward the lobby himself, probably to avoid my icy stare. A few moments later, he returned, his usual confident demeanor intact.

“So,” I asked, unable to resist, “are we all sharing again? Or did you finally decide we deserve some personal space?”

Cain’s lips curled into a mischievous smile, one that made the crinkles at the edges of his eyes deepen. It sent an unwelcome flutter through my chest. “Nope. We’ve got two rooms, but you’ll have to pick which of us to share it with.”

I groaned. “Or, hear me out—how about you two cuddle up together while I take one to myself?” My sass earned a deep laugh from him, one that warmed the chilly evening air more than I cared to admit.

Cain shook his head, the amusement lingering in his expression. "The smaller room has a single bed. I'll take that one. You two can sort out the bigger room." The finality in his voice made it clear the discussion was over. However, the lighthearted tone kept me from arguing further.

Inside, Dante and I began unpacking in companionable silence. I slipped into the bathroom to wash up, taking a moment to let the warm water ease the tension from my face. When I emerged, Cain was standing in the doorway, casually leaning against the frame as he addressed Dante.

“This inn doesn’t have a hall or kitchen, but the stablemen mentioned a tavern down the road. Apparently, their chicken pot pie is exceptional.” He turned his gaze to me, and for a brief moment, the firelight caught the flecks of silver in his stormy eyes. "Probably not as good as your mother's, though."

I felt a blush creep up my cheeks, the memory of that lunchtime in his office suddenly vivid. Before I could respond, Dante chimed in. "They must be talking about Sal's. Good food, great people."

With that settled, we walked to the tavern. Sal's was lively but not overwhelming, and the warm scent of spices filled the air. The pot pie was decent, though it didn't hold a candle to my mother's cooking, and I didn't bother pretending otherwise. The drinks, however, were another story. The ale here was dark and bitter, a stark contrast to the effervescent cocktails of the capital. It was heavy, both in flavor and potency.

The first sip burned its way down my throat, lighting a fire in my stomach that dulled the ever-present chatter in my mind. By the second sip, the world seemed softer, the edges blurred. I caught Dante watching me, his gaze curious. "Do you like the ale?" he asked, his voice warm with amusement.

I tipped the mug back again, wincing slightly. "Tastes like shit, but it's strong. Stronger than the drinks back home." My words slurred just enough to betray how quickly it had hit me.

Cain reached over and plucked the mug from my hands, a laugh rumbling deep in his chest. "That's enough for you, then. We don't need you falling over on the way back."

I didn't argue, especially as the room began to tilt. Dante was at my side in an instant, his arm steady around my back as he helped me to my feet. His touch was solid and warm, his strength evident as he supported me effortlessly. "Your arms," I murmured, my voice hazy, "they're like... really big tree branches."

His laugh was low and rich, vibrating through me as he guided me out of the tavern. "Come on, lightweight. Let's get you back to the inn."

Through the fog of my thoughts, I caught a glimpse of Cain's face. For the briefest moment, something unreadable flickered in his expression—reluctance, maybe regret? But he nodded curtly, muttering something about checking on the horses before heading to bed. By the time we reached the inn, the world around me felt submerged, everything muffled and slow.

Once inside the room, Dante unceremoniously dropped me onto the bed. My body hit the mattress with a soft bounce, and I let out a breathy laugh, trying to mask how the world was still spinning around me. The dizziness was relentless, and I pressed the heels of my hands to my temples in a futile attempt to ground myself.

Dante disappeared into the bathroom and returned moments later, holding a cool, damp cloth. Without a word, he handed it to me, his expression unreadable but not unkind. I placed the cloth on my forehead, the chill soothing against my flushed skin. The weight shifted on the bed as he sat beside me, so close that the heat radiating from his body seemed to seep into mine. He passed me a glass of water and a stale piece of bread from his rations, his fingers brushing mine for a fleeting second.

"Eat this, drink this. It'll help," he said, his voice low but firm, leaving no room for argument.

I did as I was told, nibbling on the bread and sipping the water. Slowly, the spinning began to ease, and the edges of my vision cleared. The warmth from the ale still coursed through me, leaving a pleasant hum in my veins, though my thoughts were still tangled and loose.

I sat up, the damp cloth slipping from my forehead onto my lap, and turned to look at him. His profile was sharp in the dim light, the soft glow from the lanterns catching the chiseled line of his jaw and the faint Shadow of stubble there. The scent of mint and musk surrounded him, stronger now, and I couldn't help the way my gaze lingered on him.

"Why are you so nice to me?" I asked softly, my voice unsteady from more than just the ale. "You don't even know me."

He turned his head to meet my gaze, his eyes—violet and endless—piercing straight through me. "I know enough, Angel Eyes," he said, the nickname falling from his lips like silk. "I've seen how you interact with people—all kinds of people. That's all I need to know about you to decide I like you."

His honesty was disarming, and for a moment, I was at a loss for words. *He likes me?* The words echoed in my mind, and I felt the heat in my cheeks intensify, though whether from the ale or his proximity, I couldn't tell.

Sitting this close, his scent was intoxicating, more potent than the ale that had muddled my thoughts. My gaze dropped to his lips, and before I knew it, I was leaning closer, drawn in by the magnetic pull between us. My breath hitched as the space between us dwindled, my heart pounding against my ribs.

For a second, the world faded—the inn, the mission, even my own inhibitions. There was only him, the warmth of his presence, and the electric tension that crackled in the air between us. I felt my lips part slightly, my chest rising and falling with shallow breaths as I hovered, waiting, wondering if he would close the gap or leave me hanging in this unbearable moment of anticipation.

Dante closed the space between us, his hand sliding to cradle my face before tangling in my hair. His kiss started slowly, teasing, as if he were savoring the moment, but it quickly deepened, turning urgent and consuming. His lips moved against mine with a heat that left me breathless, and the gentle stroke of his tongue sent a spark racing down my spine.

I found myself leaning into him, the pull between us undeniable. Without thinking, I pressed forward, pushing him back onto the bed. His body beneath mine was firm, warm, and perfectly aligned with every curve of my own. My chest brushed against his, and the sensation sent a shiver through me, every nerve coming alive. My nipples peaked in response. The warmth of the ale was nothing compared to the fire igniting in the pit of my stomach, a tension coiling tighter with every touch, every movement.

As I straddled him, his hands moved to my waist, gripping me with a mix of tenderness and need. I felt the heat radiating between us, the thin barrier of our clothing doing little to dull the connection. My legs tightened around him instinctively, and his breath hitched, the sound sending a rush of exhilaration through me.

I felt the evidence of his desire grind against the very core of me. Grinding on him, electric pulses ignited from between my thighs. My actions fueled by need and the ale, I kissed him harder. I ran my fingers through his dark, close-cropped hair and down the front of his chest. Our mixed breathing picked up in pace until I looked down at him. His gaze met mine, dark and hungry.

"We have to stop, Everly." His use of my actual name, not the teasing pet name he'd given me, cut through the haze clouding my mind. Oh gods, what was I doing? For a moment, I just lay there, sprawled across his chest, staring blankly at the floor as reality came rushing back in. His chest rose and fell beneath me, steady yet charged with tension. Finally, I scrambled up, sitting on the edge of the bed, my back to him.

"Yeah, I'm sorry," I muttered, my voice tight with embarrassment. "I definitely didn't mean for that to happen. I think that ale was just… too strong."

"Don't get me wrong," he said, his voice low and rough, tinged with barely restrained desire. "I want to. Gods, do I want to." There was no mistaking the hunger in his eyes when I glanced back at him. "But that's just it. The ale. I'm not willing to put us in a situation where I'm taking advantage of you under the influence of magical drinks."

I scoffed softly, trying to mask the sting of rejection with sarcasm. "Well, thanks. I'd rather not be someone's mistake."

"You wouldn't be a mistake," he said firmly, sitting up. His tone softened as his gaze pinned me in place. "I just don't want anything clouding the moment if we ever… If we were to ever be together. I don't take sleeping with someone lightly, Everly. Especially when I've already told you—I like you. Feelings get messy. And we're stuck working together for the foreseeable future."

I rolled my eyes at the "feelings get messy" excuse, but his words still sent a flutter of something traitorous through my chest. He paused for a moment, like he was carefully choosing his following words. "And, like you just pointed out, we don't know each other all that well. I don't need to know everything about you to feel this way, but I'd like to know more. Like… what's your favorite fruit? What makes you happy? What about your friends, your family, your first kiss—" He suddenly stopped, his expression shifting into mock horror as he ran a hand over his face. "Wait… you have had a first kiss, right? Oh gods, please don't tell me you're a virgin."

"What? No!" I blurted out, turning to face him so fast I nearly lost my balance. The words spilled out louder than I intended, and his lips twitched, fighting a grin.

"Well, you hesitated," he teased, leaning back on his hands, his muscles flexing in a way that made it hard to focus on being annoyed. "For a second, I thought I was going to have to walk you through all of this."

I groaned, covering my face with my hands to hide the heat rising in my cheeks. "Dante, I swear to gods—"

His laughter broke the tension, warm and easy, and I couldn't help but peek through my fingers, catching the mischievous glint in his violet eyes. "Relax, angel eyes. I'm just giving you a hard time. But seriously… next time, no ale. Just you and me."

The intensity in his voice made my breath hitch, and for a moment, I couldn't tell if it was a promise, a warning, or both.

I stood abruptly, the suffocating tension between Dante and me too much to bear. "I need some air," I said, grabbing my cloak. Dante's brows furrowed with concern as he stood halfway from his seat.

"You sure? It's late," he said, his voice low and edged with worry.

"I'm fine," I reassured him, forcing a faint smile. "I just need to clear my head. I'll stay close."

Without waiting for more questions, I slipped out the door and found myself wandering down the hallway. Before I knew it, I was tapping softly on Cain's door. His curt voice from within called, "Come in."

Pushing the door open, I stepped inside. Cain had somehow turned the plain inn room into a scene from his chaotic office back home. Maps and papers covered the bed and table, spilling onto the floor in an organized mess only he could understand. He sat at a small desk, leaning over a document, his fingers trailing absentmindedly across the lines of text. When he looked up and his grey eyes locked on mine, the fire I'd been trying to extinguish flared back to life.

Why did his lashes have to frame those eyes so perfectly? And gods, the way his shirt strained against his shoulders as he leaned back in his chair—stop. I cursed myself silently. This was ridiculous. I was still buzzed, and Cain was the last person I should be looking at like that. I blinked and forced the words out before my traitorous thoughts took me further down that dangerous path.

"I'm going for a walk," I said, my voice steady despite the tension simmering in my chest. "I'll stay close."

He studied me for a beat, his expression unreadable, then gave a brief nod. “Good.”

I closed the door quickly, as if that would keep the heat of his gaze from following me. Wrapping my cloak tighter around me, I headed to the stables. Spirra stood in the pasture, her sleek brown-and-white coat glowing faintly under the moonlight. She stayed near Shadow, Cain’s massive black horse, their quiet companionship grounding me. I leaned against the fence, sighing deeply as a wave of homesickness hit me. I missed Peris and Ferra so much. If they were here, I could pour out all my boy drama to them and let their advice—or their laughter—sort it out.

As if answering my silent plea to the gods, a woman about my age emerged from the stable, her boots crunching softly in the grass. She had dark brown hair cut just below her chin and piercingly familiar eyes that tugged at a memory I couldn't quite put my finger on. She wore a deep purple tunic and black leggings, her riding boots scuffed but sturdy.

“Which one is yours?” she asked, her voice like a soft melody carried on the night breeze.

I pointed to Spirra, who, I realized with a pang of amusement, was sticking close to Shadow. “Her name is Spirra.”

The woman’s lips curved into a knowing smile. “Ah, Spirra. An ancient word—it means Spirit.”

I tilted my head, intrigued. “You know your languages.”

“I dabble,” she said with a teasing lilt. Her gaze flicked back to me, sharp but not unkind. “I saw you come in with the Mystic. Are you some kind of prisoner?” Her tone was playful, and I couldn’t help but laugh.

“Not a prisoner,” I replied, smirking. “Although, with the way he acts sometimes, it feels like it.”

“I’ve heard he can be a hard one to get along with,” she said, nodding toward the inn. “But I already felt bad enough for you having to deal with Dante.”

The mention of Dante snapped my attention to her, and I narrowed my eyes. “How do you know Dante?”

Her smile turned sly. “He’s my brother.”

My breath caught. Of course. The eyes—the same haunting, deep blue that seemed to see straight through me. That’s where I’d seen them before.

Just when I thought the gods were blessing me, it turned out to be a curse. I let out a short laugh, trying to mask my growing unease. She tilted her head, studying me with an intensity that made my skin prickle.

“Why is that funny?” she asked, her tone playful but her eyes sharp, like she was trying to read between the lines.

“Oh, no reason,” I said, waving her off with a forced smile. “Just... the irony of asking the gods for help and getting Dante’s sister instead.”

Her lips curved into a smirk that felt just as dangerous as Dante’s lopsided grin. “He does have that effect on people, doesn’t he? Always making things... complicated.” Her words hung in the air, heavy with unspoken meaning.

I arched a brow. “You don’t seem too thrilled about him either.”

Her smirk softened into something more thoughtful. “Dante is... Dante. You’ve probably figured out by now that he has a knack for charming his way into hearts and trouble in equal measure.” She paused, her gaze flicking to Spirra in the pasture. “But he’s not all bad. There’s more to him than what you see.”

“Yeah, I’m starting to figure that out,” I muttered, the memory of his confession back at the inn still fresh in my mind. “He’s full of surprises, that’s for sure.”

She gave me a look that felt oddly like a warning, though I couldn't be sure. "Just be careful. My brother doesn't let people in easily, but when he does... he's relentless."

Her words sent a shiver down my spine, though whether it was fear or anticipation, I couldn't say. Before I could respond, she turned back toward the stable, her voice floating over her shoulder as she walked away.

"It was nice meeting you, Spirra's rider. Try not to let Dante drive you too crazy."

I stared after her, my mind swirling with questions. Who was this woman really? And what exactly did she mean by "relentless"?

The night suddenly felt colder, and I hugged my cloak tighter around me as I turned back to Spirra. The gods weren't just testing me—they were throwing me into the fire, and I wasn't sure if I wanted to run or burn.

Chapter 19

Cain

The room was quiet, save for the occasional creak of the old wooden chair beneath me. My desk was littered with maps, reports, and scattered notes, but I couldn't bring myself to focus on any of them. The ink on the page blurred together, my mind refusing to settle. Everly had just left, saying she was going for a walk, and I told myself it didn't matter. I told myself I didn't care.

But I did.

I leaned back, rubbing a hand over my face, exhaling sharply. I had been pushing her away on purpose. Telling myself it was for her own good, that she needed to focus. That I needed to focus. But the truth of it sat heavy in my chest—I was the one who wasn't ready. Everly deserved better than me, better than the weight I carried, better than the walls I built around myself. And yet, the thought of her finding comfort in someone else, in Dante, twisted something sharp and ugly inside me.

I reached for the glass of water on my desk, taking a sip, only to realize my hands were clenched so tight around it that my knuckles had turned white. I set it down with more force than necessary, cursing under my breath. I needed to get a grip. I needed to let this go.

The mission should have been my only concern. My father was missing, his unit slaughtered, and yet here I was, letting my thoughts spiral around a woman I had no right to claim. But every time I saw Dante standing too close to her, every time I caught the way her green eyes softened when she looked at him, something inside me snapped.

Damn him.

I tried to refocus, pulling a report closer, scanning the words without truly processing them. But my mind kept drifting to Everly, to the way she had lingered at my door, hesitation flickering across her face before she left. To the way I had wanted to call her back, to tell her—what? That I didn't want her to go? That I wanted her here, with me?

I couldn't. I wouldn't.

Because the alternative—watching her slip closer to Dante—wasn't an option I was willing to accept.

With a frustrated growl, I pushed away from the desk, standing abruptly. My wings flexed instinctively at my back, the tension settling deep into my muscles. The room suddenly felt too small, the air too thick. I needed an outlet, something to burn off the restless energy clawing at my chest.

I paced, running a hand through my hair, breathing hard. It wasn't just jealousy—it was something deeper, something far more dangerous. I had spent years keeping people at arm's length, ensuring no one got close enough to be a weakness. But Everly had slipped past my defenses so effortlessly, without even realizing it. And now, the idea of her being close to Dante made my blood boil.

I knew what Dante was doing. He wasn't just interested in her—he was testing me, pushing to see just how far I'd let this go before I snapped. And gods help me, I was close.

I sat back down, forcing my hands flat against the desk, grounding myself in the cool, solid wood beneath my palms. I had to control this. I had to control myself. Because if I didn't, I wasn't sure what I'd do next.

Everly deserved better than this. Better than me. But that didn't mean I'd stand by and let Dante have her, either.

My gaze flicked to the bottle of whiskey sitting on the shelf across the room, half-empty from previous restless nights.

Screw it.

I poured myself a glass, the amber liquid burning its way down my throat. One sip turned into two, then three, until the fire in my chest dulled just enough to settle the storm raging in my head. But the more I drank, the more the irritation festered. Dante. His smugness. His too-easy way of making Everly laugh, of making her comfortable. I could still see the way she looked at him, her guard slipping in a way it never did around me.

Before I realized it, I was out the door, my steps heavier than they should have been as I made my way down the dimly lit hall. My knuckles rapped against Dante's door, more complicated than necessary.

It took a few moments before the door swung open, revealing Dante—shirtless, his hair tousled like he had just been about to sleep. His violet eyes flicked over me, amusement curling at the corner of his mouth.

"Well, well," he drawled, leaning against the doorframe. "Didn't expect a visit from you tonight, Cain. To what do I owe the pleasure?"

I ignored his tone, shoving past him into the room. He sighed dramatically, but didn't stop me. "Getting comfortable, are we?"

"Shut up. I want answers."

Dante sighed, rubbing a hand over his face before closing the door behind me. "Answers? About what?"

I turned, my glare sharp despite the haze in my head. "Who are you, really?"

Dante's amusement faded just slightly, his smirk thinning at the edges. "I think we covered this already. I'm Dante. Your charming, infuriating trainee."

I took a step closer. "You're hiding something. I see the way you move, the way you fight. You knew things back in Ashmoor that you shouldn't have. And now, the Queen is putting you on this mission? Why?"

Dante's violet eyes flickered, his expression unreadable. "Maybe I'm just special."

I scoffed, shaking my head. "You've been keeping secrets since the moment you got here. And I don't trust you."

Dante sighed, crossing his arms over his chest. "Cain, you don't trust anyone."

He wasn't wrong. But this was different. There was something about him that didn't sit right. "What are you really after?"

For a moment, Dante was silent. Then, slowly, he smirked. "Wouldn't you like to know?"

My fists clenched at my sides. I was too drunk for this. Too angry. Too frustrated. "Stay out of my way, Dante. I don't have time for your games."

He tilted his head, studying me in that infuriating way he did. "You sure about that? Because it seems like I'm the only thing keeping your mind off her."

I turned to face him, arms crossed, the alcohol making my blood burn hotter. "What are you doing with Everly?"

His smirk deepened. "Ah, there it is." He took a step closer, his gaze sharp. "You know, I was wondering how long it would take before you came storming in here like a jealous husband."

I stepped forward, my jaw tightening. "Answer me."

Dante exhaled, shaking his head. "We're friends, Cain. Not that it's any of your business, but she actually enjoys my company." His tone was light, but I saw the challenge in his eyes. "You don't get to dictate who she spends time with."

Something about the way he said it made my pulse spike. I clenched my fists, resisting the urge to hit him. "I don't trust you."

He laughed, slow and knowing. "No, you just don't trust yourself."

I stiffened.

Dante stepped around me, deliberately brushing past my shoulder as he crossed the room. "You know, for someone so possessive, you sure have a funny way of showing it. Assigning her to share a room with me? That's practically pushing her into my arms."

My jaw tightened. "That's not—"

"Isn't it?" He cut me off smoothly. "You keep telling yourself you're keeping her at a distance for her own good, but maybe you just don't want to admit the truth—that you're the one running away."

I inhaled sharply, my nails biting into my palms. The whiskey in my veins fueled the fire inside me, but Dante's words hit their mark.

I turned sharply, fixing him with a glare and repeated, "Don't get in my way."

Dante held my gaze, unfazed. "Make me."

For a moment, I considered it—considered swinging, letting the jealousy boil over into something real, something tangible. But I didn't. Instead, I exhaled sharply, shoving past him, storming toward the door.

As I reached for the handle, his voice stopped me.

"She deserves to be happy, Cain," Dante said, quieter this time. "Even if that means it's not with you."

I yanked the door open and stepped out, slamming it behind me.

Outside was quiet again, but my mind was anything but. My chest heaved as I made my way back to my room, the weight of Dante's words settling deep into my bones.

I didn't know what burned more—the whiskey, or the truth.

I left the room, the weight of whiskey and Dante's words pressing heavily on my chest. My steps were unsteady, but I didn't care. My head throbbed, my body burned with frustration, and the hallway stretched before me in a blur of flickering lantern light and deepening shadows.

As I turned the corner, movement caught my eye. A shadow glides silently toward Dante and Everly's room. I froze, my pulse hammering against my ribs. The figure moved with quiet certainty, a familiar grace.

Everly.

Of course, it was her. I would recognize her anywhere, even in darkness, even in a sea of fae. There was something about her presence that drew me in, something unspoken that stretched between us like an invisible tether. It was maddening, suffocating, intoxicating. She was halfway to the door now, her hand reaching for the handle, and I just stood there, rooted to the floor, watching.

Dante was right. I had put them in the same room. I had separated myself, given them space, pretending it was the logical thing to do. That it was just practicality. But was it? Or had I been punishing myself, driving a knife into my own ribs just to see if I would bleed?

Why had I done it?

To protect her? Or to hurt myself?

I forced myself to move, shoving open my door and stumbling inside. I didn't bother to light the lamp. The darkness suited me. I collapsed onto the bed, my limbs heavy, my mind tangled in thoughts I didn't want to acknowledge.

I was the blood of a royal line. My duty was to the crown, to my people, to responsibilities that weighed heavier than any personal desire. And she—she was a hybrid. A half-blood. Just like him.

Their union would be easier. It would make more sense.

I squeezed my eyes shut, but the ceiling still spun above me. A cruel reminder that no matter how much I drank, no matter how much I tried to force the thoughts away, she was still there.

Through the thin walls, I could hear the soft murmur of voices. I couldn't make out the words, but I knew the sound of her voice better than I should. It drifted through the space between us, slipping under my skin, lulling me into restless oblivion.

And for the first time in a long time, I hated sleep. Because I knew she would follow me there as well.

Chapter 20

Everly

The walk back to the room was quiet, my thoughts swirling with the encounter I'd just had with Dante's sister. When I opened the door, Dante was sitting on the edge of the bed, his shirt unbuttoned, revealing a sliver of his chest and the lazy, relaxed posture that always seemed to carry an undercurrent of energy.

"You're back," he said, glancing up with a small smile. "Where'd you wander off to?"

I leaned against the doorframe, watching him as I crossed my arms. "I met someone," I said, pausing just long enough to catch his interest. "Your sister."

That got his attention. His smile faded, replaced by a more guarded expression, his gaze narrowing as he straightened his posture. "My sister?" he repeated, his voice low and cautious. "What did she say?"

"Nothing bad," I assured him, though I couldn't help but raise a brow at his reaction. "She mentioned you, of course. Said you could be... complicated." I let the word hang in the air, teasingly.

Dante let out a dry laugh, running a hand through his dark hair. "That sounds about right. I was hoping to speak with her as soon as we got here, but..." He trailed off, his jaw tightening. "I got... distracted."

"Distracted?" I asked, tilting my head, the playful edge in my voice making him glance at me sharply.

"You have a way of keeping my attention," he replied with a smirk, but the guarded look never entirely left his eyes.

He stood, brushing past me as he moved toward the small washbasin in the corner. "Did she seem alright?" he asked, his voice quieter now.

"She seemed fine," I said, overseeing him. "But I think she wanted to talk to you, too."

He nodded, his back to me, and I decided not to push further. Whatever was going on between him and his sister, it wasn't my place to pry—at least not yet.

As the night wore on, we got ready for bed, the tension between us softening into something almost comfortable. I hesitated for a moment before pulling the pillows from the sofa bed and placing them down the center of the mattress.

"Okay, you can sleep in the bed," I said, gesturing to the other side. "But this," I pointed to the barrier of pillows, "stays."

Dante chuckled, his smirk returning. "What, afraid I'll invade your side of the bed?"

"I'm not afraid of anything," I shot back, climbing under the covers. "But if I wake up with you anywhere near me, you'll regret it."

He raised his hands in mock surrender, settling onto his side of the bed. "Noted, Angel Eyes."

The night passed quietly, the rhythmic sound of his breathing eventually lulling me to sleep. No dreams invaded my slumber. But when I woke the next morning, the pillows were gone. My heart skipped as I realized Dante's arms were wrapped around me, his chest warm and solid against my back. His breath tickled the back of my neck, steady and soft, and for a moment, I didn't want to move.

My body betrayed me, leaning into his warmth as a strange comfort settled over me. His scent—mint and musk—was intoxicating, and I felt a flicker of something profound in my core that I quickly tried to suppress.

And then, as if sensing my wakefulness, his hold on me tightened slightly, his voice groggy but low. "Morning," he murmured, the sound sending a shiver down my spine.

I swallowed hard, trying to muster my usual sass. "What happened to the barrier?"

His lips twitched against the back of my neck. "Guess it wasn't strong enough to keep me away."

I twisted around to face him, our faces mere inches apart. "You're lucky I didn't wake up swinging," I said, though my voice lacked its usual bite.

"Lucky," he agreed, his eyes darkening as they searched mine. For a second, the space between us seemed to shrink, and I wondered if he could feel the way my heart raced against his chest.

But before I could say anything else, he pulled back with a soft chuckle, running a hand through his disheveled hair. "Relax, Angel Eyes. I'll stay on my side tonight... if you insist."

The teasing glint in his eyes made my cheeks flush, and I rolled away from him, muttering something about never letting him share a bed with me again. But deep down, I wasn't entirely sure I meant it.

We packed our things and met Cain in the dimly lit lobby of the inn, the air still heavy with the faint scent of woodsmoke from the fireplace. As we stepped out, the chill morning air nipped at my skin, waking me more than the bitter coffee I held. A quick stop at a local shop provided us with fresh pastries, their buttery warmth a fleeting comfort as we made our way to the stables.

Dante's sister was already there, her pale gold wings catching the first rays of sunlight. Her presence was commanding yet casual, as though she belonged everywhere and nowhere all at once. Her sharp eyes landed on me, and she greeted Dante warmly before smirking in my direction. "Ah,

Spirra's rider," she said teasingly, her voice melodic and slightly mocking.

Dante cleared his throat and made the introductions, his tone more clipped than usual. "Everly, this is my sister, Lyssandra. Lyss, this is Everly."

Lyssandra tilted her head, her piercing gaze taking me in with a hint of amusement. "So, you're the rider," she said, her voice playful but sharp. "Did my brother give you any more grief last night after we talked?"

Her words hung in the air just long enough for Dante to pick up on them. His head snapped toward us, brows furrowed. "Wait—you two talked about me?"

Lyssandra's lips curved into a sly smile as she turned her attention to him. "Oh, come on, Dante. Don't act so surprised. Of course, we talked about you," she teased, her tone laced with just enough mischief to make Dante visibly uncomfortable.

"Having a big brother is as annoying as it sounds," she said with a wink. "You're lucky you don't have one."

I managed a smile, though a pang of longing hit me. "I wouldn't know. I've always wondered what it'd be like to have a sibling."

Cain, standing just behind us, raised a brow, his arms crossed over his broad chest. "A sister never came up in the background research we did back at the palace," he said, his tone even but his eyes sharp.

Dante stiffened, his jaw tightening. "It wasn't relevant," he replied tersely, avoiding Cain's piercing gaze.

The tension between them was palpable, but I couldn't bring myself to focus on it. Something about Lyssandra's presence unsettled me. Maybe it was the way she held herself, like she knew far more than she let on. As she handed us the reins, her hand brushed mine, and the world around me shifted.

Another vision hit me with the force of a storm.

Lyssandra and Dante stood side by side, their eyes void of pitch black, glowing faintly with an unholy energy. Behind them, the landscape was a barren wasteland, the ground cracked and scorched as far as the eye could see. And in the distance, a towering, shadowy figure loomed, its form shrouded in swirling black smoke. Tendrils of darkness twisted and stretched outward, corrupting everything in its path.

I gasped, stumbling back as the vision dissolved. My hand still tingled from the contact as I looked into Lyssandra's eyes. She held my gaze, her expression unreadable, but her knowing smirk was gone. For a fleeting moment, I swore she knew what I'd seen.

Cain's voice cut through the haze. "Everly, are you alright?"

I nodded quickly, my heart racing. "Fine," I lied, gripping Spirra's reins tightly. But Lyssandra's stare lingered, a faint flicker of something unspoken passing between us. Whatever it was, I knew it wasn't over.

The road stretched endlessly before us, the tension between the three of us as thick as the forest shadows that lined our path. The oppressive silence was gnawing at me, so I decided enough was enough. If we were going to survive this journey together, someone had to break the ice. Naturally, that someone would be me.

"Alright," I announced, turning in my saddle to face both Cain and Dante, "let's play a little game. What's your favorite color?"

Cain glanced at me out of the corner of his eye, his jaw tightening. "Why?"

"Because," I said, rolling my eyes, "we've been traveling together for days in silence. It's suffocating. I refuse to spend another minute surrounded by this... gloomy brooding energy. So, spill."

Dante chuckled, his voice warm and teasing. "A bonding exercise, huh? I'm in." His grin turned sly as his gaze lingered on me. "My favorite color? Green—like your eyes."

Heat crept up my neck, but I refused to give him the satisfaction of flustering me. "Smooth," I quipped. "And you?" I shot the question at Cain, who sighed as though I had just asked him to recite a sonnet.

"Black," he replied curtly, his voice devoid of enthusiasm.

"Shocking," I deadpanned, earning a smirk from Dante. "Alright, favorite meal?"

Dante didn't hesitate. "Anything with a face."

I burst out laughing, the memory of our awkward-but-fun friend date flashing through my mind. "Of course it is."

Cain's gaze flicked to me, his expression unreadable as he added, "Chicken pot pie."

I blinked, startled. For a moment, it wasn't the curt, untouchable Cain speaking, but the man who had teased me back in Ashmoor about my mother's cooking. Before I could comment, the conversation took an unexpected turn.

"Alright then," Dante said, his voice laced with mischief, "let's talk about her favorites. Your favorite color? Definitely green. Your favorite food? Chicken pot pie—but only if it's your mother's."

"Excuse me?" I said, raising a brow.

Cain leaned back slightly in his saddle, his lips twitching in what could almost be a smile. "And don't forget her favorite pastime—challenging authority."

"Oh, you're both hilarious," I shot back, though a smile tugged at my lips despite myself.

The tension between us eased as we continued down the path, the quiet now filled with laughter and teasing. It wasn't much, but it felt like a step forward.

The rest of the ride passed in heavy silence, the camaraderie we'd tried to build earlier slipping away with the setting sun. As the darkness deepened, so did my unease. Sleeping outside for the first time wasn't on my list of exciting new experiences. When Cain finally called for a stop in a small clearing within the dense woods north of Laseel, I felt a wave of relief mixed with apprehension. The trees loomed around us, their silvery leaves shimmering faintly in the dim light.

"This is as good as it's going to get," Cain announced gruffly, sliding off his massive black horse. "It's getting dark—darker than usual."

While Dante disappeared to gather kindling, Cain unrolled the bedrolls from the horses. He began arranging them in a tight cluster around the growing fire. My brows furrowed as I noticed just how close they were to each other. "Uh, do we not get, I don't know, personal space?"

Cain looked up, his grey-blue eyes glinting in the flickering firelight. "Unless you want to freeze tonight, you'll accept the arrangement. The temperature's going to drop fast out here. Trust me, you'll want to be in the middle."

The way he said it left no room for argument, and I could already feel the chill creeping into my bones. Still, I couldn't help but glance between the rolls, imagining the awkwardness of being squished between Dante and Cain all night. Somehow, I doubted they'd cozy up to each other, no matter how much progress they'd made as travel companions.

Dante returned, dumping a pile of kindling near the fire with a triumphant grin. "There. Fire problem solved. Now, who's hungry?"

I grimaced at my measly rations, realizing how unsatisfying they were compared to the hearty meals we'd enjoyed in Laseel and Ashmoor. Before I could even voice my complaint, Dante unsheathed his Starfire sword with a dramatic flourish. "I'll find us something better."

Cain snorted, the sound low and disbelieving. "You? Find something edible? Please."

Dante's grin widened, and he gave an exaggerated bow. "Challenge accepted, Corporal Killjoy." With that, he disappeared into the woods, leaving me alone with Cain.

The crackling fire filled the silence between us as I stared into the flames, unsure how to broach the topic that had been gnawing at me all day. Finally, I turned to Cain. "Do you still think Dante's hiding something?"

His gaze shifted to me, the flicker of firelight casting shadows across his sharp features. "It's not a matter of thinking," he said evenly. "Finding out he has a sister was concerning enough. The fact that it wasn't uncovered in the palace's background checks? That's a problem."

I hugged my knees, his words confirming my own suspicions. "Maybe it's just…family stuff. Complicated relationships. Not everyone likes airing out their dirty laundry."

Cain's jaw tightened as he stared into the flames. "Or he's hiding something much bigger. Either way, until we know more, we stay cautious."

His tone sent a shiver down my spine, and it wasn't just from the cold. Cain's guarded nature had always been frustrating, but tonight, it felt more like a shield—a way of protecting himself, and maybe even me.

The fire crackled softly between us, casting warm flickers of light across Cain's chiseled features. His sharp profile looked even more severe in the low light, his brows knit in thought as he stared into the flames.

"Cain," I began hesitantly, breaking the silence that had stretched between us. He glanced up at me, his gray eyes catching the firelight like molten steel.

"Yes?" His tone was even, guarded as always, though there was a trace of curiosity in his expression.

Taking a deep breath, I looked into the fire instead of his piercing gaze. "I know he rubs you the wrong way.

Honestly, he's not exactly easy to pin down, but… could you give him more of a chance?"

Cain leaned back against a log, crossing his arms over his broad chest. "You want me to trust him," he said flatly, his tone making it clear he wasn't sold on the idea.

"I want you to try," I said, my voice softening. "You don't have to be his best friend or anything. Just… be a little friendlier. He's trying, in his own way. And I know what it's like to be different, to not belong." My throat tightened as I spoke, but I pushed through it. "It's not easy being a hybrid. I didn't ask for this. I didn't ask to be born of two kinds of fae."

Cain's gaze softened slightly, though his lips pressed into a thin line. "Everly—"

"No, let me finish," I interrupted, my eyes finally meeting his. "You've seen what it's like for me, Cain. You've seen how people look at me, how they talk to me, even back at the palace. Do you think it's any different for Dante? He's a hybrid, just like me. He didn't choose this life either, but he's here, trying to make the best of it. Just like I am."

The tension in his shoulders eased a fraction, and for a moment, he looked almost… remorseful. "I don't dislike him because he's a hybrid," he said after a long pause. "I don't trust him because he's hiding something. There's more to him than he's letting on, and that makes him a liability."

"I get that," I admitted. "But we're all hiding something, aren't we? Even you."

His jaw tightened, but he didn't argue.

"I'm not saying you have to ignore your instincts," I added gently. "Just… try to see the person he is, not the one you're suspicious of. If anyone knows how it feels to be ostracized for something out of their control, it's me. I wouldn't wish that on anyone—not even Dante."

Cain sighed, dragging a hand through his blond hair. In the firelight, the strands shimmered like burnished gold. "You're relentless, you know that?"

I smirked, some of the tension easing from my chest. "It's one of my better qualities."

He shook his head, a hint of a smile playing at his lips. "Fine. I'll… try. But I'm not making any promises."

"That's all I'm asking," I said, my tone lighter now. "Thank you, Cain."

He held my gaze for a moment longer, something unreadable flickering in his eyes. Then he looked back at the fire, his profile shadowed yet undeniably handsome. "You're not as fragile as you look, you know," he murmured.

The quiet compliment caught me off guard, and I felt warmth creep into my cheeks. "Neither are you," I said softly.

The fire crackled again, and for a brief moment, the tension between us shifted into something else entirely—something unspoken, but undeniably there. The sound of crunching leaves signaled Dante's return.

"Dinner is served," he called, holding up two freshly caught rabbits. His grin was smug, his violet eyes glinting mischievously as he dropped them near the fire. "I told you I'd find something."

Cain's lips twitched, but he didn't say anything, his silence doing little to dim Dante's self-satisfied glow. As the smell of roasting meat filled the clearing, I couldn't help but feel the tension between us all. Secrets hung in the air like the smoke from the fire, curling and twisting, waiting to be unraveled.

We settled into our sleeping arrangements, just as Cain had insisted—with me sandwiched in the middle. Despite my initial protests, I had to admit that the extra body heat was a welcome relief against the biting chill of the forest night. The cold that had seeped into my bones from the ride slowly retreated, leaving me warm and cocooned between the two men. Still, I couldn't stop myself from briefly worrying about the horses.

“I packed a few extra blankets for them,” Cain murmured, his deep voice cutting through the darkness as if sensing my thoughts. “They’ll be fine.”

It was such a small thing, but something about it tugged at my heart. Sweet wasn't a word I typically associated with Cain. Still, moments like this made me wonder what else lay beneath his steely exterior. As I lay there, surrounded by the subtle scents of cedar and woodsmoke from Cain on one side, and mint and musk from Dante on the other, I tried—and failed—to keep my thoughts pure.

The tension from the day still lingered, amplified by our close proximity. I lay stiffly on my back, determined not to give either of them the impression that I was cozying up to one over the other. My arms were rigid at my sides, and my heart raced as if I were afraid to breathe too deeply and shatter the fragile boundary I'd drawn in my head.

Above me, the canopy of trees opened in patches, revealing glimpses of glittering stars. I focused on them, counting constellations in an attempt to calm the riot of thoughts in my mind. The nocturnal sounds of the forest—chirping insects, the rustle of leaves, the occasional hoot of an owl—blended with the steady breathing of the two men. I dared a glance to either side and noticed they both lay with their backs turned to me, their shoulders rising and falling in an unspoken rhythm.

Eventually, the soothing cadence of their breaths lulled me, the warmth from their bodies weaving a strange sense of security I hadn’t expected. As my eyelids grew heavy, I let the sounds of the forest carry me into sleep.

Once again, my sleep was invaded by a dream—no, a vision. The dark figure, cloaked in swirling shadow smoke, loomed larger than life, standing before Cain. His Starfire sword gleamed in his grip as he raised it, his expression fierce with determination. But the figure lifted a hand, and an eruption of Shadow blasted Cain off his feet, sending him skidding across the desolate ground.

Dante stood to the side, his face a mask of uncertainty. His hand hovered over the hilt of his sword, indecision flickering in his dark eyes. Suddenly, the earth trembled, and a creature—stitched together from pieces of the barren land itself—emerged with a guttural roar, charging straight at Cain. He pushed himself up, his face set with vengeance and an unrelenting fire. With a single, powerful strike, he cut the creature down. He turned, pointing his blade at Dante, his voice ringing with fury. "I will not let you destroy my kingdom!"

I jolted awake, my heart pounding so loudly it drowned out the quiet hum of the forest. The air around me felt stifling, too hot despite the chill of the night. It took me a moment to realize why—I wasn't alone. Dante's warm breath ghosted against the back of my neck, his arm heavy and possessive around my waist. His body pressed against mine, every inch of him radiating heat.

And then I became aware of something else—Cain. He had turned in his sleep, his body close enough to feel the steady rise and fall of his chest against mine. His leg had somehow wedged itself between mine, his warmth anchoring me in a way that felt both protective and far too intimate. My head rested just below his chin, and I could feel the soft tickle of his breath against my hair.

I was trapped between them, their warmth and presence cocooning me, stirring something low in my stomach. My breath hitched as I tried to adjust, but I quickly realized there was nowhere to go. Every slight movement brought me closer to one of them, and my heart raced at the sheer proximity.

The heat of their bodies, combined with the lingering haze of the dream, left me flustered and restless. But their steady breaths and the rhythm of the forest soon lulled me back into a restless sleep, though the fire within me refused to fully extinguish.

Chapter 21

Everly

The soft light of dawn barely pierced through the dense canopy above, casting long shadows across the forest floor. The quiet hum of the woods was broken by a sudden rustling sound. I blinked awake, disoriented, and caught sight of Cain groggily lifting his head; his expression quickly shifted from sleepy to alarmed.

"Shit!" he shouted, scrambling to his feet. His Starfire sword was in his hand before I could even process what was happening.

Around us, a dozen furry weasel-like creatures with elongated bodies and stubby legs scurried about in a frenzy. One darted past me, clutching a bag of rations in its tiny mouth. I sat up, propping myself on my elbows, trying to make sense of the chaos unfolding around me. Dante, looking like he'd just rolled out of bed, sprang to his feet with surprising agility and bolted after the little thief. His movements were smooth, but his muttered curses ruined the illusion of composure.

Cain, meanwhile, was kicking at a pair of the creatures rummaging through his discarded bag. "Get out of there!" he growled, his voice low and commanding, though it didn't seem to faze the mischievous beasts in the slightest. One zipped under Shadow's feet, causing the horse to rear slightly, attempting to stomp it into the dirt. The creature dodged with ease, darting between Spirra's legs and sending the horses into a restless frenzy.

I finally managed to drag myself out of the bedrolls, the morning chill biting through my clothes and making me shiver.

"What are these things?" I asked, my voice hoarse with sleep as I rubbed my eyes, still not entirely convinced I wasn't dreaming.

Cain shot me an exasperated look as he moved to calm the horses, his hand firm and steady against Shadow's neck. "They're packrats—forest scavengers. And they're way too smart for their own good."

One of the little devils bounded up onto Dante's back as he bent to retrieve the bag of rations. I couldn't help but laugh as it grabbed a strand of his dark hair and tugged. He swatted at it, cursing under his breath, his usual charm nowhere to be found in the face of the chaos.

"Not exactly the dignified morning I had in mind," I muttered, pulling my cloak tighter around me to fight the morning chill. Cain turned, a ghost of a smirk playing on his lips despite his annoyance.

"Welcome to life outside the capital, princess," he teased, his tone lighter than usual. "Better get used to it."

I yanked on one boot hastily, my other one already missing. My eyes darted around until I spotted the culprit—a packrat dragging it away by the laces. "Oh, no, you don't!" I lunged forward, grabbing the boot mid-escape. The creature froze, its large brown eyes wide and innocent, its little button nose twitching. My heart softened. It was adorable, almost painfully so, with its plush-looking fur and those soulful eyes. The overwhelming urge to scoop it up and cuddle it washed over me.

Then it hissed.

The sound sent a shiver down my spine, and its mouth opened to reveal rows of razor-sharp teeth that gleamed menacingly in the early light. I yelped and recoiled, clutching my boot to my chest. Around us, a dozen more of the packrats scampered through the campsite, leaving chaos in their wake.

A sharp cry caught my attention, and I whipped my head toward Cain just in time to see one of the creatures latched onto his arm. He snarled, shaking it off with a swing of his sword. Even in the midst of this madness, his movements were precise and calculated, the faint sunlight reflecting off his focused expression.

I turned to grab my Starfire sword and made the mistake of picking up the nearest one. The moment my fingers curled around the hilt, a jolt of electricity surged through me, sharp and unrelenting. It shot up my arm, into my shoulder, and exploded at the side of my head. I dropped the weapon instantly, gasping as my right ear rang and my vision blurred at the edges.

"What the—" I muttered, pressing my palm to my temple as I tried to steady myself. Before I could regain my bearings, Dante was suddenly at my side, his hand brushing my arm as he bent to retrieve the weapon.

"That one's mine," he said, his voice calm but firm, his violet eyes flicking to meet mine. "Yours is over there."

I followed his gaze to see two of the weasels valiantly attempting to drag my Starfire sword away, their tiny bodies straining under the weight of it. Growling under my breath, I sprinted toward them. They scattered, hissing indignantly as they disappeared into the shadows of the forest.

The chaos slowly died down as the last of the packrats fled, their rustling receding into the woods. The campsite fell silent—eerily so. Or maybe that was just my head still ringing from the jolt of Dante's sword. I bent down to pick up my own weapon, eyeing it warily.

"So that's what happens if someone else tries to use it," I murmured, more to myself than anyone else.

Dante chuckled softly beside me, his voice low and smooth. "Lesson learned, angel eyes."

I shot him a glare, though it lacked any real heat, still shaken by the morning's madness. Cain approached with his hand over the bite he sustained, a faint white glow emitting from his palm. He brushed off his tunic, his gaze assessing us both. "Let's pack up before they come back," he said brusquely, though I caught the subtle twitch of amusement at the corner of his lips.

As I gathered my things, I couldn't help but glance at Dante, who was now tightening the straps on his pack with an infuriating grin. His presence was somehow both comforting and terrifying, the details of last night's vision coming back to the forefront of my mind.

Back on the horses, the morning air was crisp, but the unease from our earlier encounter with the packrats lingered. Dante adjusted his reins, his sharp violet eyes flicking toward Cain.

"Why do you think those... ferrets, or whatever they were, are this close to Laseel?" he asked, his tone casual, though I could sense the underlying concern in his question.

Cain's jaw tightened as he guided ShadowShadow over a slight incline. His dark silhouette against the overcast sky gave him an air of quiet authority. "They're packrats," he corrected, his voice measured. "And they usually stick to the Eversleep Forest along the outer wall of Erynvale."

I glanced between them, the conversation tugging at my curiosity. "So why are they here?" I asked, pulling Spirra up alongside Cain's horse.

"The Blight," he said grimly, his gaze fixed on the path ahead. "It's pushing them inward, away from the desolation. Toward the cities."

The weight of his words settled heavily on my chest. My fingers tightened around Spirra's reins as I considered the implications. "If the packrats are seeking refuge within the walls," I murmured, more to myself than to them, "what else might be following?"

Dante let out a low whistle, breaking the tension with his usual irreverent charm. "Hopefully nothing with sharper teeth," he said, flashing me a grin, though the humor didn't quite reach his eyes.

Cain didn't respond, his focus still on the road ahead, but I caught the flicker of unease in the set of his shoulders.

We rode on in silence a little longer, the rhythmic clopping of the horses' hooves the only sound breaking the stillness of the morning. The tension was palpable, and I could feel the weight of unspoken words hanging in the air. Then, from behind me, Dante started to whistle a light, jaunty tune. At first, it was subtle, almost soothing, but as the seconds ticked by, it became louder and more persistent.

Cain, riding ahead, stiffened, his grip tightening on the reins. His head tilted slightly, and I could sense the irritation radiating off him even before he turned his sharp gaze back over his shoulder. "Can you not?" Cain's voice cut through the air, clipped and cold.

Dante grinned, entirely unbothered by the edge in Cain's tone. "What? It's too quiet. Thought I'd liven things up a bit."

"Well, don't," Cain snapped, his jaw tightening as he faced forward again. "We don't need to draw unnecessary attention to ourselves."

Dante rolled his eyes but complied, letting out an exaggerated sigh. "You know, Cain, sometimes I wonder if you've ever had a moment of fun in your entire life."

Cain didn't respond, his silence as cutting as his earlier words. I glanced back at Dante, whose grin lingered despite the tension. He caught my eye and gave me a playful wink, as if to say, *Well, I tried.* I shook my head, suppressing a small smile. The silence resumed, but this time it wasn't quite as heavy; Dante's rebellious energy somehow lightened the mood just enough.

Cain's sharp grey eyes locked onto mine for a long moment, his lips pressing into a thin line. Then, with a heavy sigh, he nodded, as though resigning himself to a task he'd much rather avoid. I knew it wasn't easy for him to let go of his reservations, but this small step meant more than he'd probably ever admit.

He turned in his saddle slightly, his gaze shifting to Dante, who rode behind us with his usual casual air. "What's your horse's name?" Cain asked, his tone gruff but noticeably less icy than usual.

Dante blinked, clearly taken off guard. "What?"

Cain rolled his eyes. "Your horse. Does it have a name? I'm trying to get to know you. Don't make it a thing."

For a split second, Dante just stared at him, his expression caught somewhere between shock and amusement. Then, a slow grin spread across his face. "Oh, uh… Midnight. Named him myself. Figured it suited his coat."

Cain nodded, his gaze flicking briefly to Midnight before returning to the road ahead. "Fitting," he said simply, his voice neutral but not unkind.

The atmosphere shifted, lightning just a touch. Dante seemed genuinely pleased, a warmth in his violet eyes that hadn't been there moments ago. He sat a little straighter in the saddle, his grin lingering.

I couldn't help but smile, my heart swelling with a quiet kind of satisfaction. Cain was trying, and Dante seemed to appreciate it.

"Did you have any pets growing up?" Cain asked, his tone carefully casual.

Dante blinked, clearly caught off guard for the second time that day. "Pets?" He tilted his head as though the word was foreign. "Uh, yeah. We had a dog. Big mutt named Jax. He followed my sister everywhere. Hated baths but loved stealing bread off the counter."

Cain gave a faint smile, nodding slightly. “Dogs are loyal. Good companions.”

“They are,” Dante said, his voice softer now. He seemed lost in the memory for a moment, then added, “Jax was probably the only reason Lyssandra stayed out of trouble as a kid.”

Cain hummed thoughtfully, then switched gears. “What’s your favorite thing to do on the weekends? Back when you had free time, I mean.”

Dante chuckled, rubbing the back of his neck. “Free time feels like a myth now, but... I used to play cards with some of the guys. Sometimes we’d sneak out to the coast and just sit on the rocks, talking about stupid things. What about you?”

Cain raised an eyebrow. “I didn’t say this was a two-way conversation.”

“Oh, come on. You’re prying into my life; the least you can do is throw me a bone,” Dante said, a playful grin spreading across his face.

Cain gave him a dry look but indulged. “I read,” he said simply. “History books, mostly.”

Dante groaned. “Of course you do.”

Cain seemed more willing to engage, though his questions had taken on a sharper edge.

“So,” Cain began, his tone measured but curious, “if your mother still lives in Laseel with Lyssandra, why the lie about her moving to Verdanis to live with your uncle?”

Dante stiffened in the saddle, his hands tightening on the reins. His usual carefree expression faltered, replaced by something heavier. "That's a complicated story," he said after a moment, his voice quieter than normal.

Cain pressed, his sharp gaze unwavering. “Complicated how? It’s a simple question, Dante. Why lie?”

Dante let out a slow breath, glancing toward the horizon as though searching for an escape route. When none appeared, he finally spoke. "After my father died, things got... hard. My mom was grieving, trying to keep things together for Lyssandra and me. But raising two kids on her own, especially one like me, wasn't something she could handle anymore."

Cain tilted his head, his expression unreadable. "One like you?"

Dante let out a humorless laugh. "Troublemaker. At least, that's how most people would have seen me. But the truth is, the trouble I got into wasn't about breaking rules for fun. I was trying to help someone, and things went wrong. Really wrong."

I looked over at him, my curiosity piqued. "What kind of trouble?"

His jaw tightened, and he didn't meet my gaze. "Let's just say someone was in a bad situation, and I stepped in to try to fix it. Took the fall for something I didn't do because it was easier that way. The whole thing blew up, and my mom... she couldn't handle it. She sent me to live with my uncle in Verdanis, hoping he could 'shape me up.'" He paused, his voice turning bitter. "And to give her some peace with Lyssandra."

Cain was silent for a moment, his sharp eyes narrowing slightly. "You sacrificed yourself for someone else. That doesn't sound like a troublemaker to me."

Dante shrugged, but there was no humor in his usual carefree posture. "Intentions don't matter much when the consequences are the same. People see what they want to see."

I couldn't help but feel a pang of sympathy for him. He'd been painted as the villain in his own story, forced to leave his family behind to spare them further pain. Cain, however, still seemed wary, though his expression softened ever so slightly.

"Your mother sent you away to protect you—or maybe to protect herself. But you left Lyssandra behind," Cain said, his voice low. "How does she feel about that?"

Dante sighed, running a hand through his hair. “She doesn’t blame me. She understands why things happened the way they did, even if I hate it. Lyssandra’s tougher than people give her credit for. She had to be.”

The conversation fell silent after that, the weight of Dante’s words hanging in the air. Cain didn’t push further, but I could see the wheels turning in his mind. I glanced at Dante, who looked ahead with a far-off expression, his usual bravado stripped away for the moment. It was a rare glimpse of vulnerability, and it made me see him in a new light.

I shot him an incredulous look, my eyebrows arching as if to say, "Really?" In response, Cain merely shrugged, the corners of his mouth twitching upward in an almost imperceptible smirk. His shrug was casual, nonchalant, but the gleam in his eyes betrayed him. It was as if he were silently saying, *'I did what you wanted, and it worked out exactly as I intended.'* The audacity of it made me want to laugh and roll my eyes simultaneously. Of course, Cain would find a way to turn my request into something that served him. Typical.

Chapter 22

Cain

The sun had barely risen by the time we broke camp, the tension between us thick enough to choke on. The incident with the pack rats had passed, but it left an unease in my chest that I couldn't quite shake.

Not because of the damn creatures. No, I'd dealt with far worse.

It was Everly.

It was Dante.

It was the way she laughed when he teased her, the way he looked at her like he knew something I didn't. It gnawed at me, relentless, a weight I couldn't set down no matter how much I tried.

We rode in tense silence, the rhythmic sound of hooves on dirt filling the space between us. I kept my eyes ahead, scanning the tree line for movement. The deeper we traveled into the wilds, the more exposed we became. My father's unit had been stationed somewhere beyond this stretch of land, and though I wouldn't admit it aloud, I knew what we were likely to find.

Bodies.

Or worse—nothing at all.

Everly rode beside me, her posture tense but composed. I knew she was trying. I had seen her progress firsthand, had pushed her harder than anyone else would have dared. And she never faltered, never backed down.

But she was still green.

Still too soft for what lay ahead.

Dante, of course, was unbothered. He was relaxed in his saddle, his gaze drifting between the trees, his lips curled into the ghost of a smirk. He had no right to be this comfortable, this at ease when we were heading straight into unknown danger.

"Something on your mind, Cain?" he asked suddenly, his voice cutting through the quiet like a blade.

I clenched my jaw. "Just stay focused."

He chuckled. "Oh, I'm plenty focused." His gaze flickered toward Everly. "Aren't you?"

She shot him a glare. "Don't start."

I exhaled sharply through my nose, gripping the reins tighter. "We're close to where my father's outpost," I said, steering the conversation back to what mattered. "We'll take stock of anything left behind that may point us in the direction of where he may be."

Everly nodded, determination flashing across her face. "And if we find something?"

My throat tightened. "Then we deal with it."

The rest of the ride passed in relative silence, the air growing heavier with each mile. The terrain shifted subtly, the trees thinning, the underbrush giving way to flattened grass and broken branches. Signs of movement. Signs of something unnatural.

I lifted a hand, signaling for them to stop. Dismounting, I stepped forward, my boots crunching against the ground as I knelt beside a patch of disturbed earth. Blood. Dried, but unmistakable.

My gut twisted, the unease settling deep. I had heard the whispers before we left the capital—rumors of renegades, groups of fae working in the shadows for Nightshade. The Defense Counsel had discussed them in hushed meetings, always brushing them off as unfounded myths, but the stories were spreading. Elementals from Laseel had allegedly been defecting, abandoning the city's laws to practice forbidden magic. It was said they weren't just hiding—they were taking out guards, recruiting in secret, spreading corruption through the ranks of the kingdom.

There was no proof. No tangible evidence. Just fear woven into speculation. But standing here now, staring at the bloodstained ground, I wasn't so sure it was just a myth anymore.

Everly and Dante joined me, their expressions turning grim.

"Someone was here recently," Everly murmured.

I nodded, rising to my feet. "Stay close. We move on foot from here."

As we moved deeper into the clearing, my pulse thrummed steadily in my ears. My father had been stationed here. If he wasn't among the dead, if he had somehow survived whatever happened to his unit, then there was still a chance.

A chance to find him.

A chance for answers.

But my instincts screamed at me that whatever we found ahead would change everything.

And I wasn't sure I was ready for it.

Everly, in her infuriating optimism, had decided somewhere along the way that Dante and I should be friends. That we should, at the very least, tolerate each other beyond strained civility. I saw it in the way she tried to include both of us in conversations, the way she glanced between us when we bickered, the way she lingered after an argument like she expected us to shake hands and laugh about it.

I wanted to tell her it wouldn't happen. That some people were simply meant to be at odds, and Dante and I were two of them. He grated on every nerve I had: his cocky smirks, his careless confidence, his way of always being in her orbit.

And yet, for her, I tried.

I bit my tongue when he provoked me. I tolerated his presence longer than I should have. I kept my hands to myself when he pressed every single one of my buttons. Because Everly wanted peace between us, and I would do anything to appease her—even if it meant burying every ounce of my dislike deep beneath the surface.

I didn't have to like Dante. But if making an effort kept her happy, I would force myself to endure it.

And yet, no matter how much effort I put into swallowing my irritation, it never stopped gnawing at me. Every time Dante leaned a little too close to her, every time he made her laugh, every time she looked at him with anything resembling admiration, I felt my control slip—just a little.

I told myself it was nothing. That my problem with Dante had nothing to do with Everly. That it was his arrogance, his unpredictability, the way he always seemed to know more than he let on. That was why I distrusted him. That was why I watched him so closely.

But the truth clawed at the back of my mind, refusing to be ignored.

It wasn't just about distrust.

I wanted her to look at me the way she sometimes looked at him. I wanted to be the one who made her laugh, the one she sought out when she needed comfort or reassurance. I wanted—

No.

I shoved the thought away before it could take root. Wanting her was dangerous. Letting myself feel anything more than duty and responsibility for her was a mistake.

But mistakes had a way of creeping up on you when you least expected them.

The forest thickened as we pressed on, the air shifting from crisp and open to dense and suffocating. The route to my father's cabin was familiar, but the energy around us felt wrong. Birds had stopped singing. The usual rustling of small animals had gone eerily still. My fingers flexed over the hilt of my sword, my senses sharpening with every step.

Dante, despite his usual nonchalance, had fallen silent, his gaze scanning the trees. Even Everly, ever determined to prove herself, moved with more caution.

Chapter 23

Everly

By the time nightfall came, rain was pouring steadily, the sound of it drumming against the trees and the mud squelching under our horses' hooves. There were no weather fae out here to dictate the skies as they did back in the cities. The rain was cold, cutting through the warmth of our cloaks, but it wasn't long before we reached the outpost—our final stop before the wall.

The first thing I noticed was how barren it felt compared to the others we'd stayed at. There were no women or children, only hardened men moving with purpose in the dim torchlight. Cain nodded toward a small path off to the side. "The families don't live here," he explained, his tone as clipped as ever.

"There's a village just up the road. The men stay here in shifts."

We led the horses toward a modest cabin tucked away at the edge of the outpost. It was small, barely visible in the rain until we were nearly on top of it. Cain opened the door, and a musty, earthy scent greeted us. The space inside was simple—a main room with a worn table and chairs, a fireplace stacked with logs, a bed pushed against the far wall, a cluttered desk, and a tiny kitchen area. A door led to what I assumed was the bathroom.

"This was my father's cabin," Cain said, setting his things down by the desk. There was something heavy in his voice as he looked around, like the memories of this place weighed on him.

Grateful for a chance to dry off, I claimed the shower first. The bathroom was cramped, but the hot water was a welcome relief after hours in the rain. When I emerged, I was dressed in the warm pajamas Matilda had given me back in Ashmoor and feeling slightly more fae. Cain was already rifling through his father's books and notes, his sharp eyes scanning the pages with an intensity that made me wonder just how much he hoped to find.

Dante grumbled something about needing the next turn in the shower and disappeared into the bathroom. Left alone with Cain, I picked up one of the books from the desk, flipping through its yellowed pages. I had no idea what I was looking for, but it felt better than standing around.

After a moment of silence, I glanced up at him. "The queen had two sons, right? Your father had a brother?"

Cain froze mid-page, his knuckles tightening around the book's spine. When he finally looked at me, there was a shadow in his eyes I hadn't seen before. "Yes," he said slowly. "But I've never met him. No one talks about him. He was cast out decades ago."

I wanted to ask more, but thought better of it. There was something raw in his expression, a glimpse of a deeper pain he wasn't ready to share. I nodded and turned back to the book, flipping through the pages until something caught my eye—a passage about ancient cities outside the borders of Erynvale. It described a forgotten temple, with notes scribbled in the margin about seers who supposedly lived there—seers who might hold answers to ending the Blight.

"Cain," I said, sliding the book across the table toward him. "Look at this."

He leaned over, his expression sharpening as he read the passage. "This… this could be something," he muttered, his voice more alive than I'd heard it all evening. His fingers traced the handwritten notes, his lips moving slightly as he committed the details to memory.

As he read, I gathered my courage. "Cain," I started, my voice hesitant. "What do you know about Nightshade?"

His head snapped up, his piercing gaze locking onto mine. "Where did you hear that name?" he asked, his tone edged with something close to anger.

I hesitated, fumbling for an excuse but knowing it wouldn't work. Finally, I sighed. "Dante told me. He said Nightshade is behind the Blight. That he uses dark magic to create those… things."

Cain's jaw tightened, his expression darkening. "Dante shouldn't know that," he said, his voice low. "That information isn't meant to leave the council."

"Well, he does," I said quietly. "And now I do too."

For a moment, Cain didn't say anything. Then he exhaled sharply, raking a hand through his hair. "Fine," he said. "If you're already this far in, you might as well know the truth. Yes, it's all true. Nightshade was once one of us—a fae. He was an Elemental, but his power grew twisted, corrupted. He's the reason the Blight exists, why the land beyond the walls is nothing but a wasteland. He takes what's dead—land, animals, even people—and turns them into weapons. Creatures made of ShadowShadow and despair."

A chill ran down my spine. "I've seen him," I whispered. "In my dreams. And the creatures. They feel so real… like warnings."

Cain's gaze softened, just slightly. "Dreams like that aren't uncommon for hybrids," he said quietly. "Especially when their magic is close to manifesting. If Nightshade is in your dreams, it's not a coincidence."

The weight of his words settled heavily over me, and I looked down at the book on the table. The mention of seers suddenly felt more urgent than ever.

Cain leaned back in his chair, studying me with a mixture of fascination and excitement as I recounted my past visions. "You might be a seer," he said, his voice low, almost reverent. The weight of his words made my stomach flip. "We need to test this. Exercise it. You could be crucial to this mission."

He gestured for me to sit in the chair closest to the fire. The warmth radiated across my skin as I settled in.

"Close your eyes," he instructed. "Think back to the train. You said you were meditating when you saw something. Let's try that again."

I sighed, closing my eyes as the flicker of flames danced against my lids. A few moments passed, and I let out an exasperated breath.

"It's hard to focus with you just sitting there watching me."

Cain chuckled softly, the sound warm and unexpected. "I'll stay quiet. Try again."

This time, I pushed the irritation aside and closed my eyes once more. His voice came softly, guiding me. "Focus on someone familiar. Start there. Picture them clearly."

I chose my mother, her face appearing in fragments behind my lids. Then, slowly, the vision sharpened. She was in the garden, tending to the delicate blooms that grew around our home. The image was faint but steady, and my heart swelled with emotion at the sight of it.

"I see her," I whispered, my voice shaking slightly.

"Good," Cain said, his tone encouraging. "Now try something closer. Me. I'm going to grab a book from the desk. Focus on me and tell me which one it is."

I hesitated but nodded, letting my mind shift to him. The sound of his footsteps shuffling toward the desk seemed to echo, and suddenly, the faint blur of a red leather-bound book came into focus. I could almost make out the embossed words on its cover.

"A red book," I said. "Leather-bound, with writing on the cover."

I heard him return, the weight of something settling in my lap. My eyes blinked open, and there it was—the exact book I'd seen in my vision. My heart soared with excitement. "I did it!" I exclaimed, jumping up in a burst of joy and wrapping my arms around him without thinking.

Cain stiffened for only a moment before his hands settled on my back. Embarrassed, I quickly stepped away, my cheeks burning as I tried to stammer out an apology. But when I looked up, his expression stopped me cold. His gray-blue eyes sparkled with something raw and unguarded, a rare vulnerability I hadn't seen before.

"You're amazing," he said, his voice barely above a whisper. His hand lifted, brushing a stray strand of hair from my face. "Your bravery, your adaptability, and now this… It's more than I ever expected. I owe you an apology, Everly."

"For what?" I asked, my voice unsteady under his gaze.

"For everything. For how I acted when we first met. For judging you unfairly," he said, his words thick with sincerity. "I've always had to keep my guard up. This mission has only made it worse, but that's no excuse. I said things that made it sound like I hated hybrids, but I didn't—" He paused, shaking his head slightly. "I don't. I misjudged you. You're extraordinary. And your eyes…" His lips quirked into the faintest of smiles. "They're beautiful."

The air between us grew thick; my heart was pounding so loudly that I was sure he could hear it. I felt an overwhelming urge to close the distance, to lean into him and let whatever this was take over. His eyes searched mine, and I saw a flicker of something that told me he felt it too.

Just as I moved slightly closer, the door to the bathroom creaked open, and Dante emerged, toweling off his damp hair. The moment shattered, and I stepped back, pretending to straighten my shirt as if nothing had happened. Cain cleared his throat, his mask of composure slipping back into place, but I didn't miss the flicker of frustration in his eyes.

Dante grinned, oblivious to the tension in the room. "What did I miss?"

"Nothing," I said quickly, the words feeling hollow as I glanced back at Cain. His gaze lingered for a moment longer before he turned his attention to the book in his hands, leaving me to wonder what might have happened if we hadn't been interrupted.

Cain leaned against the edge of the table, his arms crossed, as he addressed Dante, his tone measured but distant. "Everly found some information in one of my father's books," he began, his eyes flickering briefly to me. "It mentioned an old temple. Seers were said to reside there, offering… insight."

Dante arched a brow, clearly intrigued. "Insight? For what exactly?"

Cain shrugged, keeping his expression neutral, but I caught the faint flicker of guardedness in his gaze. "That's not relevant right now. What matters is that the temple could hold answers to what's happening beyond the wall."

I frowned at Cain, sensing his omission. He wasn't telling Dante everything—particularly about Nightshade. My stomach churned uneasily at the idea of the two of them at odds when we were all supposed to be on the same side.

Dante, for his part, didn't push further. Instead, he plopped down in the chair I vacated moments before, feigning indifference. "Well, if it's so important, we should get moving soon, yeah? Temples with all-knowing seers aren't exactly easy to come by."

I glanced at Cain, a question forming on my lips. "What was the temple for? I mean, who built it?"

Cain's expression softened slightly, though his tone remained practical.

"Fae used to worship old gods and goddesses—before the kingdom united. Some of the other kinds of fae still do, though their numbers are dwindling. Temples like this one were sacred spaces for their rituals and prayers. It's likely the temple belonged to one of those kinds of fae, the ones the Blight wiped out or forced out of their lands."

The weight of his words settled heavily in the room, and I couldn't help but feel the loss of those fae Cain spoke of. What had once been a thriving, diverse world was now scarred and fractured by the Blight's dark magic.

Dante, ever the optimist, leaned forward, his violet eyes gleaming with curiosity. "So, we're heading into ancient ruins that might be cursed or abandoned by gods? Sounds like a great idea."

Cain shot him a glare, his patience visibly thinning. "If you'd rather stay behind, feel free."

The tension between them was palpable, but I stepped in before it could escalate. "This could be a chance for answers," I said, glancing at both of them. "If there's even a slim chance this temple holds a clue, it's worth it."

Cain nodded, his expression softening as his gaze lingered on me. "We'll leave at first light."

Dante huffed out a laugh, running a hand through his dark hair. "Guess I'd better get some rest then. Wouldn't want to disappoint the gods."

As he walked back into the bathroom, Cain sighed, rubbing the back of his neck. "He has a point about the temple being dangerous. We'll have to tread carefully."

I hesitated before placing a hand on his arm. "You're not wrong to be cautious, but you don't have to keep everything to yourself. We're in this together."

Cain's eyes met mine, something unspoken passing between us. But before he could respond, he stepped back, retreating behind his usual guarded demeanor. "Get some rest. We'll need all the strength we can muster."

The final stretch to the wall passed quicker than I anticipated, the landscape blurring beneath Spirra's steady gait. Cain had set a brisker pace than usual, his focus unrelenting as if he were trying to outrun the tension that clung to our group. The silence between us was palpable, broken only by the rhythmic beat of hooves on the path. Though he didn't say it, I suspected Cain's urgency had more to do with avoiding any further exchanges with Dante than reaching the wall.

When we finally reached it, the wall loomed ahead, an imposing stretch of stone that seemed to blend seamlessly into the horizon. Its sheer height blocked the view of anything beyond, a testament to the kingdom's desire to keep the unknown out. The massive stone gate at its center bore intricate carvings of ancient fae runes, shimmering faintly with residual magic. It wasn't a gate that could be opened by mere strength or mechanics; it required the energy of those sworn to protect its secrets.

As we approached, Cain dismounted, his boots crunching on the gravel path. A pair of guards descended from the battlements, their faces stern but respectful as they raised their hands toward the carvings. The runes flared to life, glowing brighter until the gate groaned and rumbled. The earth trembled beneath us as the heavy slabs of stone parted, revealing the vast, untamed wilderness beyond.

I tightened my grip on Spirra's reins, a shiver running down my spine as the cool air of the outside world hit me. Dante whistled low under his breath. "Never thought I'd see the day I'd be on the other side of this thing."

Cain shot him a look, then swung back onto his horse. "Let's move. We don't have time to marvel."

The land beyond the gates was bleak at first, with sparse and brittle grass, dotted with blackened stumps of trees that had long since burned or decayed. But as we rode further, signs of life reemerged—a strange resilience that clung to the edges of desolation. By mid-afternoon, we reached the edge of the Eversleep Forest, its dark, menacing canopy blocking out most of the light.

The trees here were unlike anything I'd seen before, their trunks dark and twisted, their branches bristling with long, gleaming thorns. Even at a distance, I could feel the malevolent energy emanating from them. Cain pulled ShadowShadow to a halt and turned to us, his face grave.

"This is the Eversleep Forest," he said. "The thorns are coated with a poison that'll put you into an eternal sleep. There's no waking from it, and no cure. It's been weaponized in the past—arrows, swords, even traps. Be careful."

"Lovely," Dante muttered, his sarcasm failing to hide the unease in his voice.

We dismounted to lead the horses through the tangled pathways, weaving carefully between the thorny branches that seemed to reach for us. The air was thick and heavy, muffling even the sound of our footsteps. Shadows darted at the edges of my vision, and the occasional rustling of leaves hinted at creatures watching us.

Packrats, I thought with a shudder. Cain had said they frequented this forest, but our plan was to push straight through, avoiding any unnecessary distractions. As the last light of day faded, a low, mournful howl echoed through the trees, making my heart jump.

"Wolves," I whispered, glancing at Cain. "Do you think they're timber wolves?"

Cain's expression was unreadable, his eyes scanning the darkness. "Could be. Keep moving."

The howls grew louder, closer, as we pressed on. My hand drifted to the hilt of my Starfire sword, the cool metal grounding me as anxiety coiled in my chest. Every step felt like an eternity, the forest closing in around us. But then, as abruptly as it had begun, the oppressive weight of the Eversleep Forest lifted. We emerged onto an open plain, the sharp scent of mountain air filling my lungs.

I exhaled a breath I hadn't realized I'd been holding, glancing back at the dark silhouette of the forest. The wolves' howls had faded, but their haunting echoes remained in my ears. Ahead of us, the peaks of a mountain range rose like jagged teeth against the night sky. It was a daunting climb, and as the stars began to dot the heavens, Cain called for us to stop and make camp.

We slipped into our familiar routine: Dante wandered off to gather kindling, and Cain set to work arranging the sleeping rolls near the fire's future site. I busied myself with tending to the horses, tying their reins securely to a nearby tree. Carefully, I pulled out the blankets Cain had packed in his saddlebag and draped them over the horses' backs, brushing a hand over Spirra's spotted coat for reassurance. After laying out a small portion of hay from Cain's supplies, I stepped back, satisfied they'd be comfortable for the night. Once the horses were settled, I joined Cain and Dante by the fire.

"I'm keeping watch," Cain said firmly, his tone leaving no room for negotiation as he poked at the campfire with a stick, sending embers crackling into the sky.

Dante, seated on a fallen log with his arms crossed, arched a brow. "Why you? I'm perfectly capable."

Cain scoffed, his lips twisting into a smirk. "You're about as quiet as a packrat when you move. The last thing we need is for you to wake up every creature within a mile."

"I'm not the one who tripped over a root earlier," Dante shot back, his grin sharp and teasing.

I sat between them, my eyes darting from one to the other as the verbal sparring continued. The firelight danced across their faces, highlighting the deep furrow in Cain's brow and the mischievous gleam in Dante's eyes. The air was thick with unspoken challenges and grudging respect.

"Enough!" I finally blurted, throwing up my hands. "One of you decide before I pick someone myself."

Cain's eyes softened briefly as they flicked to me, but his voice remained firm. "I'll take the first watch," he said, standing and grabbing his Starfire sword. "You two get some rest. We've got a long day ahead."

Dante threw his hands up in mock surrender, though I caught the subtle clench of his jaw. "Fine, fine. Enjoy your alone time, Corporal."

Cain muttered something under his breath and moved to the edge of the camp, his silhouette a stark contrast against the velvety blackness of the forest beyond.

I sighed and settled into my bedroll, the tension still buzzing in the air. It took longer than usual for sleep to claim me.

When it did, it was no comfort.

In my dream, the shadows were alive, writhing and coiling like smoke. They formed into the ominous figure I now recognized from my visions—Nightshade. The air around him was suffocating, thick with menace. Cain stood before him, his Starfire sword raised defiantly. But Nightshade merely raised a hand, and with a surge of dark energy, Cain was thrown back.

"Cain!" I screamed, but my voice didn't carry. The forest around us twisted and died, the trees blackening and crumbling into ash.

Then I saw Dante. His eyes—once warm and teasing—were now pitch black, voids that sucked the light from the world around him. He stood motionless, his hand resting on the hilt of his sword. "It had to be done," he said, his voice cold and resonating in every direction, as if the forest itself spoke through him.

I jolted awake, my heart pounding so hard it felt as though it might burst from my chest. The fire had dimmed to glowing embers, and the faint sounds of the forest filled the air. Cain sat a few paces away, his back to me as he stared out into the valleys below. The weight of the dream still clung to me as I quietly stood and approached him.

He didn't acknowledge me at first, his focus distant, lost in the endless expanse of darkness. I sat down beside him, pulling my cloak tighter against the chill. For a long moment, neither of us spoke.

"Couldn't sleep?" he finally asked, his voice low but steady.

"Something like that," I admitted. "Nightmares again."

His eyes flicked toward me, a hint of concern softening his sharp features. "About Nightshade?"

I nodded, not trusting myself to elaborate. Instead, I changed the subject, the quiet intimacy of the moment emboldening me. "I was thinking about the capital…about growing up there." I hesitated, then pressed on. "Being a hybrid wasn't easy. People always stared, whispered behind my back. My mother tried to shield me from it, but I could see how it weighed on her too. She's the queen's seamstress, you know. I think they're best friends, though she'd never admit it. Still, I think even the queen couldn't protect her from everything."

Cain remained silent, listening intently as I spoke. "And then my father…" My voice faltered. "He was conscripted when I was just a child. Growing up without him…it was lonely. Being an only child, there wasn't anyone else to share it with."

Cain shifted, his gaze fixed on the valleys below. "Loneliness isn't unique to hybrids," he said quietly. "My father…he's not exactly the nurturing type. After the accident…" He trailed off, his jaw tightening.

"What accident?" I asked softly.

He exhaled a long breath, his shoulders sagging under the weight of the memory. "When I was a boy, my older brother and I were out riding. I pushed the horse too hard—it reared, and we both fell. My brother didn't survive, and I…my leg was crushed. The healers did what they could, but the damage was too severe, even for fae magic."

I swallowed hard, my chest tightening at the pain in his voice.

"My father never forgave me," Cain continued. "Not for the accident, not for surviving when my brother didn't. He renounced his title after that, withdrew from court entirely. My mother…" He paused, his voice heavy with emotion. "She's never been the same. It's like she mourns both of her sons."

I reached out, my hand brushing his arm in silent support. "That's not your fault."

He met my gaze then, his eyes shadowed but sincere. "It doesn't matter. My grandmother, the queen, stepped in after my father left. She's been grooming me to take the throne ever since. As soon as I marry, I'll be king." He let out a bitter laugh. "The idea of it terrifies me."

I studied him, the vulnerability in his expression a stark contrast to the stoic mask he usually wore. "You'll be a good king," I said firmly. "You care more than you let on. That's what makes the difference."

He smiled faintly, a flicker of something warmer breaking through. "You think so?"

"I know so," I replied.

For a moment, the weight of our respective burdens seemed a little lighter, shared between us under the vast, starlit sky.

As we sat near the fire, I tilted my head toward Cain and smirked. "So, about this marriage you're supposed to arrange… do you have your eye on anyone yet?"

He arched an eyebrow, his lips tugging into the faintest of smirks. "Planning to help me, are you?"

"Just curious," I teased, leaning back on my hands. "I mean, I'm pretty sure Amaya from combat class was eyeing you like a hawk during training. She practically drooled every time you walked by."

Cain snorted, his tone light but firm. "Not into blondes." He leaned forward slightly, his gaze catching mine, warm and unrelenting. "I've always preferred redheads."

The teasing edge in his voice sent a flush creeping up my neck and straight to my cheeks. I looked away quickly, pretending to be more interested in adjusting the straps of my boots than in the sudden, unmistakable tension between us.

Why did he have to say things like that? And why did it make my stomach twist in ways I didn't know how to unravel? My mind immediately wandered to Dante—his easy smiles, the way his hand felt when he helped me onto my horse, his voice when he spoke to me like I was the only one who mattered. But then there was Cain: quiet, guarded, powerful in ways that made my heart race when I least expected it. They were opposites, but somehow they both managed to pull at something deep inside me.

I didn't even know what I wanted. Could I ever be a part of Cain's life? His world of royalty, duty, and expectations seemed like another universe compared to mine. And then there was Dante, who made me laugh, made me feel… seen. How had I ended up in the middle of this impossible triangle?

I clenched my hands in my lap. What was so special about me, anyway? I wasn't the smartest, the strongest, or the most talented. Yet, here they were, both of them, each one pushing me in a direction I hadn't been prepared for. It was all too messy. Too complicated. And I wasn't sure I had the answers to any of it.

"Careful, you're blushing," Cain teased, his voice breaking through my spiraling thoughts.

"Am not," I shot back, glaring at him halfheartedly.

He chuckled softly, the sound low and rich, and leaned back, his sharp gaze still locked on me. "Whatever you say."

My heart hammered in my chest as I tried not to let his attention undo me completely. The quiet of the mountains wrapped around me, heavy and unyielding. The night sky stretched endlessly above, a canvas painted with a thousand glittering stars. For the first time since leaving the capital, the weight of it all came crashing down. No distractions. No new sights to marvel at or tasks to occupy my mind. Just silence, the rhythmic crunch of the fire's wood as it burned low, and my thoughts.

I pulled my knees to my chest, wrapping my arms around them. Home. My heart ached with the thought. I'd never been away from my mother for this long, and the realization hit me like a stone to the chest. She had always been my anchor, my safe haven, and the person who could make me laugh even when the world seemed like it was falling apart. Her absence was a void I hadn't dared acknowledge until now.

I thought of Ferra and Peris, my closest friends, and how much I wished they were here. I needed their advice, their laughter, their honesty. They would know what to say about this tangle of emotions—this impossible triangle of feelings I'd gotten myself into.

And Lyla. A pang of guilt hit me. Our friendship was still so new, so fragile, and I had vanished without a word. What did she think of my absence? Did she worry? Did she even notice? The loneliness coiled tighter around me, a heavy knot in my chest. A single tear slipped down my cheek before I could stop it.

A warm hand brushed against my face, startling me. I blinked up to find Cain leaning towards me, his thumb catching the stray tear before it could fall further. His expression was softer than I'd ever seen it, his sharp, stoic features tinged with concern.

"What are you thinking about?" he asked quietly, his voice low and grounded in the stillness.

I hesitated for a moment before letting out a shaky breath. "Home. I miss it. I've been using the mission and everything new around me to push it all aside, but now…" My voice wavered, and I gestured at the vast expanse of stars above us. "Now, it's all catching up to me. This view—it's breathtaking—but it makes me feel so small. And so far away."

He was quiet for a moment, as though weighing his words. "I didn't think about that," he admitted finally. "When the queen gave me the mission, my thoughts were consumed by my father and my duty. I didn't stop to consider what it might mean for you or Dante—what I was pulling you away from."

His honesty surprised me, and for a fleeting moment, I saw the man beneath the weight of his responsibilities. Not the soldier, not the heir to a kingdom, but someone who carried his own burdens and regrets.

"The stars make you feel far from home," he continued, his gaze lifting to the sky, "but they're the same ones your mother sees. The same ones your friends see. Maybe they're not so far away."

I smiled faintly at his words, the ache in my chest easing just a little. For the first time that night, the quiet didn't feel so lonely. His hand lingered on my cheek, the warmth of his touch grounding me even as my emotions swirled like a storm. His eyes held mine, steady and intent, and for a moment, I forgot the cold night, the distant stars, and the weight of the journey ahead.

"I meant what I said back at my father's cabin," Cain said, his voice low, a hint of vulnerability threading through it. "You are utterly remarkable. I'm sorry it took me so long to see it."

The sincerity in his words stole my breath, and before I could respond, he leaned in, brushing his lips softly against mine. It was tentative at first, like he was giving me a chance to pull away. But I didn't. A rush of heat started in my core, unfurling through my stomach and rising to the tips of my pointed ears. My lips parted instinctively, and he deepened the kiss, his tongue brushing against mine in a way that sent shivers down my spine.

The kiss turned fevered, an intensity that spoke of unspoken emotions and restrained desires. His hand slid into my hair, tilting my face closer as though he couldn't get enough. My hands found their way to his chest, the fabric of his tunic rough under my fingertips, but I could feel the warmth of his skin beneath it.

A sudden snap of a twig in the tree line shattered the moment. We both froze, his lips still hovering just above mine. For a breathless second, the only sound was the distant rustle of leaves. Then, Cain pulled back slightly, a quiet chuckle escaping him. "Guess the forest doesn't want to give us any privacy."

I smiled, though my heart still raced. I glanced over my shoulder, my gaze landing on Dante's still form, unmoving under his bedroll beside the fire. Relief flooded through me that he hadn't stirred. When I turned back to Cain, his eyes had softened, his usual guarded expression replaced by something warmer, more open.

"You should get some sleep," he murmured, his voice dipping into that commanding yet gentle tone he seemed to master so well. "It'll be light in a few hours."

I nodded, the weight of what had just happened settling over me as I stood. My heart still thrummed in my chest, but as I walked back to my bedroll, I couldn't stop the small smile that lingered on my lips. Cain returned to his spot, his gaze fixed once more on the valleys below, but I felt the connection between us—a thread that wasn't there before tonight. As I lay down, pulling the blanket over me, I closed my eyes, wondering if I was about to fall into dreams of him.

Breakfast was nothing more than a handful of berries foraged from the bushes lining the camp. Dante had gone off to hunt for meat, proving he could be helpful when it mattered. Our rations, even with careful refills at every outpost, felt more like a tease than sustenance, leaving us all hungry for something more.

As I busied myself brushing Spirra's coat to a gleaming sheen, I glanced up at Cain soaring high above the campsite. His wings were a masterpiece—black as MidnightMidnight yet shimmering with an iridescent sheen when caught by the sun, like the swirl of colors on an oil slick. Flying looked effortless for him, each sweep of his wings propelling him higher as if he belonged to the sky itself. The sight was mesmerizing, filling me with a deep yearning for my own wings to finally emerge. The freedom, the grace—it was almost tangible.

Dante, of course, kept his wings tucked away, using everyday magic to retract them. Always practical, never showing off. Still, I couldn't help but wonder how it felt for him to keep such a part of himself hidden. With the two of them occupied, the camp was quiet, and I took the moment of solitude to sit by the fire.

Spirra, now perfectly groomed, nuzzled my arm before wandering to graze.

I decided to use my sight, hoping to coax another vision into existence. Closing my eyes, I focused on the void behind my lids, letting my mind wander. At first, it was nothing but darkness, then colors began to shift and form. I saw Cain, his silhouette descending rapidly from the sky. He landed just in front of me, startling me. My eyes flew open instinctively, and not a heartbeat later, the vision came to life. Cain dropped down in front of me, his boots hitting the ground with a quiet thud. This time, he didn't startle me. Instead, I smiled up at him knowingly.

"Hello," I said, unable to hide the satisfaction in my tone. His eyes twinkled with curiosity, and a half-smile played on his lips.

"You don't look surprised," he remarked, tilting his head.

"I saw it before you did," I replied, brushing off invisible dust from my lap as I stood. His gaze lingered on me, his half-smile deepening.

"Impressive," he said softly, his voice carrying a warmth that made my stomach flutter. For a moment, I thought he might say more, but instead, he left me to my practice, giving me a slight nod before walking away.

I closed my eyes again, eager to see if my sight would grant me another glimpse. The world blurred and then sharpened, showing me Dante returning to the camp with a triumphant grin, six rabbits strung together on a stick slung over his shoulder.

I opened my eyes just as Cain returned to his seat near the fire. "Dante's back," I said with a small smile. "Looks like we're eating well today."

Cain glanced at me, an eyebrow raised in mild disbelief, but before he could question it, Dante strode into the clearing exactly as I'd seen. He held up his bounty proudly, the rabbits swaying with each step.

"Breakfast is served," Dante announced with a grin, and Cain shook his head, a faint smile tugging at the corner of his lips. He didn't say anything, but the way he looked at me lingered, almost as if he was starting to believe my abilities could truly be something extraordinary.

We sat around the fire, tearing into the rabbit Dante had hunted. The meat was tender, but it was the first authentic meal we'd had in days, and I was grateful for it. When I noticed Cain quietly finishing his portion, I offered him the second rabbit I had barely touched. "Take it," I said softly. "You'll need it more after all that flying."

He hesitated, his piercing gaze meeting mine before accepting with a slight nod. "Thanks," he murmured, tearing into the meat with a focus that betrayed just how hungry he really was.

Meanwhile, Dante knelt by the horses, his hands hovering over the canteens. His water magic flowed effortlessly, a steady stream of crystal-clear liquid replenishing their water supply and giving the horses a much-needed drink. It was mesmerizing to watch, even though he made it look so simple.

Cain brushed off his hands and spoke, his tone steady. "There's a worn path to the east. We'll take it across the mountains. On the other side is wasteland—I'm certain the temple we're looking for is nested somewhere within it."

I closed my eyes for a moment, the world around me blurring as I tried to focus. A vision flickered to life: us, following the path Cain described, the mountains giving way to desolation. I opened my eyes, my voice calm but sure. "He's right. That path will lead us to the wasteland."

Dante froze, his brow furrowing as he stared at me. "How do you know that?"

I hesitated, the weight of his gaze pressing down on me. Finally, I decided to tell him—part of it, anyway. "I have sight," I admitted cautiously. "Sometimes, I see things before they happen."

His expression shifted, a mixture of astonishment and something darker—fear, maybe. "Sight," he repeated, almost to himself. "Our kind hasn't had a seer in… decades."

Cain's sharp eyes flicked between us, but he said nothing, letting the tension hang in the air. Dante's voice dropped lower, suspicion coloring his words. "What else have you seen?"

My stomach twisted, and I fought to keep my face neutral. The visions of Dante with blackened eyes and his sister standing beside him loomed in the back of my mind, but I couldn't tell him that. Not yet. Instead, I forced a light laugh and shrugged. "Innocuous things," I lied. "My mother gardening, for instance. Oh, and I know who'll win the next ports ball tournament."

Dante arched a brow, his skepticism clear. "Sports ball?! That is not what it is called. Do you even know any sports?"

"I know what Battleball is," I shot back, feigning indignation. "And I know the Wingnuts are the best."

A smirk tugged at his lips, and for a moment, the tension eased. "The Wingnuts?" he repeated. "Really?"

I shrugged, trying to keep the conversation casual. Ferra loves attending events. She talks about them all the time." My voice softened at the mention of her name, a pang of homesickness sneaking up on me.

Dante chuckled, and even Cain cracked the faintest smile as he shook his head.

We packed up our camp in the early morning light, the crisp mountain air biting against my skin as we prepared to set off. Cain took the lead, his eyes scanning the horizon with practiced vigilance. The path he scouted the day before was narrow, winding through jagged cliffs and dense patches of trees. Spirra's hooves crunched against loose rocks as we descended further into the mountains.

Suddenly, a jolt of something unfamiliar gripped me—a flash of a vision. My breath hitched as I saw a bear lumbering across our path just ahead, its massive body silhouetted against the trail.

“Cain, stop!” I called out, my voice sharper than I intended.

He pulled ShadowShadow to a halt, glancing over his shoulder at me, his brow furrowing. "What is it?"

I didn't answer right away; my focus was still locked on the image in my mind. Moments later, the bear emerged just as I had seen, ambling across the trail down the slope, its enormous paws silent against the forest floor. It never even noticed us.

Cain turned back to me, his lips twitching into a rare smile. “Well done,” he said softly. The pride in his voice sent warmth coursing through me, and I couldn’t help the small smile that tugged at my lips in return.

Dante rode closer, his curiosity written plainly across his face. “Is it just people you see?” he asked, his voice low and intense. “Or is it events too? Could you—” He hesitated, but his eyes burned with determination. “Could you look for the temple? To see if there really is a seer who can help us?”

I sighed, glancing down at my hands on the reins. “I can try,” I offered hesitantly. “But it’s not controlled yet. I can focus on people, but I haven’t tried places. It also... it leaves my head foggy. And I’m not sure if—”

“For the good of the mission,” Dante interrupted, his voice insistent. “It’s worth the risk, isn’t it?”

His words sent a ripple of unease through me, but the determination in his tone left no room for argument. With a reluctant nod, I closed my eyes, willing my mind to focus on the temple. The image in my head was incomplete, vague. I tried to picture it—a place of old gods, of answers. But there was nothing. Only blackness.

I exhaled slowly, opening my eyes to find Dante’s gaze fixed on me, searching for answers I couldn’t give him. “I didn’t see anything,” I admitted. “Without knowing where it is or what it looks like... I can’t.”

Disappointment flashed across his face, but he said nothing. Instead, he nudged his horse forward, riding ahead to give me space. Cain's eyes lingered on me for a moment longer, his expression unreadable, before he followed.

The path stretched out before us, and the weight of Dante's disappointment pressed heavily against my chest. I tried to shake it off, focusing instead on the rhythm of Spirra's movements beneath me.

Chapter 24

Everly

Cresting over the ridge of yet another hill, we reined our horses to a stop, the chill of the wind carrying with it an eerie silence. The view below stretched out like a scar across the land, a city consumed by decay. The bottom of the mountain was barren, the dead earth dotted with skeletal trees that seemed to claw at the gray sky above. Patches of brown grass clung stubbornly to life, a futile attempt to mask the lifeless soil beneath.

"This must be Doren," Cain said, his voice low as if afraid to disturb the stillness. His gray eyes were fixed on the crumbling city below, unreadable in the fading light. "The notes said the temple is here."

The ruins of Doren sprawled across the wasteland, a ghostly echo of what once must have been a thriving place. Hundreds of buildings stood in disrepair, their structures leaning and cracked as though some vengeful force had swept through, leaving nothing but devastation in its wake. My breath caught in my throat, a sharp ache blooming in my chest as I took it all in.

The Blight. This was what it did. Not just stories whispered in court or dry accounts written in books—this was real. The actual weight of its destruction pressed down on me, cold and unforgiving.

We urged the horses forward, their hooves striking the stone streets with hollow echoes that carried too far in the emptiness. The air smelled of damp rot and ash, the memories of life here reduced to debris scattered on the ground. I could almost hear the laughter of children that must have once bounced off these walls, the clamor of market stalls, the bustle of everyday life now stolen.

A child's toy lay abandoned near the edge of the road, its faded colors dulled by time and exposure. I thought of the families who fled, desperate to escape the inevitable, leaving behind the lives they'd built. And of those who had refused to go—the stubborn, the hopeful—only to face a cruel fate as the Blight consumed them. My hands clenched the reins tighter, the ache in my chest deepening.

"The Veil took them too soon," I murmured, the words barely audible over the sound of our movement. Cain glanced back at me, something akin to understanding flickering in his eyes, but he said nothing.

Dante rode in silence at my side, for once, no teasing words on his lips. His jaw was set, his gaze scanning the broken city as if daring anything to come out of the shadows. He was stoic, but I could feel the tension radiating from him.

We wound our way deeper into the city, the eerie quiet enveloping us. Every step, every breath felt heavy, the weight of those who had lived here pressing against us. These streets had once been full of life, but now they were nothing more than a graveyard, a haunting reminder of what could happen if we failed to heed the warning.

"This is the cost of the Blight," Cain said finally, his voice rough as though the words themselves pained him. His knuckles whitened as he gripped the reins, and I could tell the sight had unsettled even him.

I nodded, unable to form words. As much as I had tried to prepare myself for what lay outside the safety of the kingdom, I hadn't been ready for this. I doubted anyone could be.

We rode on, the echo of hooves and the whispers of lost memories our only company as Doren loomed around us, a grim harbinger of the darkness still to come.

In the heart of the city's desolate expanse stood a building that seemed to defy the decay surrounding it. A towering structure crowned with a cracked, tarnished dome rose above the ruins like a sentinel of forgotten times. The once-brilliant white bricks were now dulled with age, their surfaces etched with ancient carvings that glinted faintly in the dying light. Pillars that had once held the weight of gods now bore the scars of time, many cracked or broken, their jagged edges reaching for the heavens. The wide stone steps leading up to the entrance were worn and uneven, an eerie path that spoke of countless feet that once climbed them in devotion.

The doorway yawned open, its arch jagged and dark. No door remained, only shadows and a silence that pressed against my ears. The black void inside seemed to swallow the light whole, beckoning us forward and warning us to stay away all at once.

"We're here," Cain said, his voice low, the weight of the moment thick in the air.

We dismounted; the clink of reins and soft thuds of hooves on the dead earth were the only sounds breaking the oppressive quiet. I felt the pulse of something—something ancient, alive, and potent—thrum beneath my feet. It wasn't audible, but I could feel it in my core, a rhythmic vibration that seemed to sync with my heartbeat. My breath caught, the sensation overwhelming, like the temple itself was aware of me.

"You feel that?" I asked, my voice barely above a whisper, unsure if I even wanted to draw their attention to it. I looked at Cain and Dante, expecting them to acknowledge it.

They both glanced at me in confusion. Cain shook his head. "Feel what?" His gray eyes flicked to the temple's looming silhouette, suspicion tightening his expression.

"It's…like a pulse. Below us. Beneath the ground." I placed my hand on the building's wall, as if the contact could clarify the strange sensation, but it only amplified it. Warmth coursed through my fingers, leaving a faint buzz in its wake.

"I don't feel anything," Dante said, adjusting his grip on his Starfire sword. "But then again, this place doesn't exactly scream 'relaxing day out.'"

Cain's eyes lingered on me, narrowing slightly as though trying to piece together my reaction. "Stay close," he said, his tone clipped but laced with an edge of concern. "And don't touch anything else."

We tied the horses to what remained of a carved stone post near the side of the temple, ensuring they were secure and out of harm's way. Spirra snorted nervously, her ears swiveling, as if she could sense something I couldn't name. Shadow stood perfectly still, his massive frame calm but watchful, and Dante's horse Midnight pawed the ground, mirroring my unease.

The moment we crossed the threshold into the temple's darkened interior, the air grew heavy, thick with a weight that pressed against my lungs. The floor beneath us was made of smooth stone, worn but remarkably intact. The carvings that adorned the building's exterior extended to the walls inside, intricate symbols and depictions that seemed to shimmer faintly, almost alive.

Cain took the lead, his movements deliberate as he scanned the area. Dante followed close behind, his sword drawn, the blade's faint glow casting a silvery light that danced along the walls. I stayed between them, unable to shake the feeling that the power I felt beneath my feet wasn't just some residual magic from the building—it was watching us. Waiting. For what, I didn't know.

"What do you think we'll find in here?" Dante asked, his voice breaking the eerie silence.

Cain didn't answer immediately, his eyes flickering over the cracks in the floor and the faint light emanating from further within. "Answers, hopefully," he finally said. "If the notes were right, this temple held seers who claimed to know how to find my father. If anything remains of them, we'll find it here."

His words should have reassured me, but they didn't. The pulsing sensation grew stronger with every step, as if the temple was drawing me in. I clenched my hands to stop them from trembling and tried to focus on my breathing.

The pull of the temple tugged at me like an invisible thread, guiding my steps away from Cain and Dante. They were absorbed in examining the central dome area, their attention on the towering statues of gods and the spiral staircase spiraling into shadow above. My feet carried me toward a long corridor, its ancient walls lined with faint carvings that seemed to shift in the flickering light. The deeper I ventured, the stronger the pull became, until I entered a room that felt alive with energy.

The space was shrouded in dimness, illuminated only by the soft, flickering glow of lanterns hanging along the walls. It was a worship area, its rows of pews facing a raised dais at the front. On the dais, candles burned in careful arrangement around a podium that commanded attention. Someone had lit those candles.

The thought sent a shiver down my spine, but I couldn't stop myself. My steps carried me forward, the faint hum of power thrumming beneath my feet growing louder with every step. I reached the podium and saw an open book resting upon it. The pages were blank, the ancient parchment unmarred. Yet, as my fingers brushed across the surface, a tingling sensation spread through me, sharp and electric.

"Didn't I tell you not to touch anything?" Cain's voice cut through the silence, sharp with authority. I turned to see him standing at the entrance to the room, his expression a mix of exasperation and concern. Dante followed close behind, his sword drawn and glowing faintly, casting silver light across the pews.

"I…" My words faltered, but I didn't step away from the podium. "I was just—"

Before I could explain, a low, resonant tone echoed through the room. It was the unmistakable sound of a singing bowl, the deep vibration reverberating through the air and settling into my chest. All three of us froze, the sound pulling our attention to a curtain at the side of the dais.

The fabric rippled, parting to reveal a man who stepped into the room with an otherworldly grace. His golden robe shimmered in the dim light, flowing around him as though it were alive. His dark skin glowed faintly, his long braid cascading down his back like a river of Midnight. A beard framed his sharp features, and his eyes—vivid, glowing green—seemed to pierce through me.

"Apologies," he said, his voice smooth and resonant, carrying an undercurrent of power that made my heart skip. "I did not mean to startle you."

Cain stepped closer, his protective instincts evident in the tension in his shoulders. "Who are you?" he demanded, his tone firm but wary.

The man smiled faintly, inclining his head in a gesture of peace. "I am Seran, keeper of this temple. And you…" His glowing eyes fixed on me, making my breath hitch. "You are the one I've been waiting for."

Seran gestured to the pews, his golden robe catching the flickering light of the lanterns. "Sit," he said, his tone both commanding and soothing. "I will answer your questions. The gods have a message for you, but only if you ask the right ones."

I exchanged a glance with Cain, who nodded warily before taking a seat. Dante hesitated, his gaze flickering between Seran and the dais before he joined us, his movements tense. I perched on the edge of a pew, my heart hammering in my chest.

Dante broke the silence first. “Why are you here?” he asked, his voice low. “Why no one else?”

Seran’s piercing green eyes shifted to him, and a faint smile curved his lips. “Because the gods protected me,” he replied simply. “They saw fit to keep me here, waiting for the moment when my purpose would intertwine with yours.”

Cain leaned forward, his elbows resting on his knees, tension radiating from him. “My father wrote of this temple,” he began, his voice edged with urgency. “He believed it might hold the answers to what happened to his unit. They were destroyed, and he… he’s missing.”

Seran’s gaze softened, and he inclined his head. “The gods know where your father is. He is alive.”

The words hung in the air like a lifeline, and I saw the flicker of hope that crossed Cain’s face, quickly shadowed by suspicion. “Then why hasn’t he returned?” he demanded. “Who has him?”

“The dark wielder,” Seran answered, his tone weighted with gravity. “Nightshade.”

Cain’s jaw clenched, his hands balling into fists. “What does Nightshade want with him?” he asked, his voice sharper now, as though he could will the truth into the open.

“Revenge,” Seran said, his answer cutting through the air like a blade.

“Revenge against who?” Cain pressed, his voice rising. His storm-gray eyes locked on Seran, desperate for clarity.

Seran’s gaze flickered to Dante briefly before settling back on Cain. “The people of Erynvale,” he said. “Specifically, the Mystics.”

Dante's silence was deafening. He sat rigid, his eyes fixed on the floor as if he were grappling with something he didn't want to reveal. The weight of his unspoken thoughts filled the room, and I couldn't shake the feeling that he already knew the answer to questions none of us had dared to ask yet.

"Why?" I blurted out, unable to hold back. "Why does Nightshade want revenge?"

Seran's expression darkened, the glow in his green eyes intensifying as his gaze swept over us. He exhaled deeply, his voice carrying a weight that felt centuries old.

"You ask why Nightshade wants revenge," he began, turning his focus to Cain and Dante. "But to understand, you must first understand who Nightshade truly is—and the legacy of betrayal that birthed him."

The room seemed still, the flickering lantern light casting shadows that danced ominously against the walls. I swallowed hard, the pull of Seran's words urging me to lean closer.

"Nightshade was the first of the hybrids," Seran said, his tone steady but laced with something between pity and anger. "Born of a Mystic mother and an Elemental father—a union that defied every rule, every unspoken law of our world. His existence alone terrified the Mystics. They feared what he represented—what he might become."

Cain stiffened, his hand resting on the hilt of his sword. "So they cast him out," he said, his voice low and tense.

Seran nodded, his eyes narrowing as though the memory was his own. "They did more than cast him out. The Mystics stripped him of his name, his place in society, even his magic, or so they believed. He was driven beyond the wall, left to fend for himself in a world that was already crumbling under prejudice. To them, Nightshade was a mistake—a stain on their lineage. The forbidden made flesh."

The words settled in my chest like a stone, pressing against memories I had tried to bury. I knew what it was like to be judged for something you couldn't control, to be made to feel less for simply existing. "But why punish him for something he didn't choose?" I asked, my voice trembling with anger.

Seran's gaze softened slightly as it landed on me. "Fear," he replied simply. "Fear of the unknown. Of a power that neither side could fully claim as their own. But fear breeds hatred. And hatred… breeds monsters."

Dante broke his silence, his voice tense. "If Nightshade was cast out by the Mystics, why destroy everything? Why target the Mystics and the Elementals?"

"Because rejection has no boundaries," Seran said, his voice bitter. "The Mystics exiled him, but the Elementals turned their backs on him as well. Neither side claimed him, neither side welcomed him. To him, all fae are guilty. The Blight is not just a weapon—it's his retribution."

The fire crackled softly, the sound almost deafening in the stillness of the room. Cain's jaw tightened, his hand twitching as if itching to grip his sword. "So what does Nightshade want now?" he demanded. "Why target my father? Why pull us into this?"

Seran studied Cain, his expression unreadable. "Your father is part of the past that shaped Nightshade. He is a symbol of what was lost—a reminder of a world that rejected him. Nightshade does not just seek vengeance. He seeks to unmake this world and rebuild it in his image. He believes that only through destruction can there be peace."

Seran's gaze lingered on Cain, the weight of his expression growing heavier with each passing second. Finally, he spoke, his voice like thunder in the stillness of the temple.

"Cain," he began, his tone measured, almost cautious. "You carry the weight of a legacy that runs deeper than you know. The roots of this story tie not just to Nightshade's revenge but to your very bloodline."

Cain straightened, his hand gripping the hilt of his sword. “What are you saying?” he asked, his voice sharp with suspicion.

Seran took a step closer, the green glow of his eyes fixed entirely on Cain. “Nightshade… is your uncle.”

The words hung in the air like a curse. I gasped, the realization hitting me like a blow to the chest. Dante stiffened beside me, his expression unreadable, though his eyes darkened with unease.

Cain frowned, his jaw tightening. “That’s impossible,” he said firmly. “My uncle—my father’s brother—was cast out centuries ago. He was never spoken of again.”

“Precisely,” Seran said, his tone steady. “Because the Mystics erased him from their history. Nightshade was born Eryndor—the first son of Queen Anastasia. Your grandmother. Your father, Alaric, is her second son, the one deemed worthy of carrying on her legacy. Eryndor, however… he was rejected. Not for his blood, but for what he represented.”

Cain’s grip on his sword faltered, his knuckles turning white. “You’re saying Nightshade is my father’s brother? The queen’s son?” His voice was cold, as if he didn’t want to believe it.

Seran nodded solemnly. “Yes. Nightshade, or Eryndor as he was once called, is the firstborn prince of Erynvale. But he was born of an Elemental father—a man Queen Anastasia fell deeply in love with before she ever met Prince Aldren.”

The revelation left Cain visibly shaken, his shoulders stiffening as Seran continued to speak.

“Anastasia and the Elemental man shared a love that defied borders and kingdoms. But their union was never meant to be. Her parents, nobles from across the Saffron Sea, arranged her marriage to Prince Aldren, a political alliance designed to secure peace between their kingdom and

Erynvale. At the time, Erynvale was ruled by Aldren's parents, who eagerly agreed to the treaty but closed the kingdom's borders to outsiders once the wedding was complete."

Seran's voice softened, though his words carried a cutting weight. "Anastasia was already with child when the wedding took place. Aldren knew this and chose to keep her secret. Their marriage was one of duty, not love. He protected her because it was expected of him. But the king and queen of that time saw Eryndor's birth as a threat to the purity of the Mystic bloodline. When Alaric was born, pure in every way the royals demanded, they had the perfect heir. Eryndor was cast out, erased, and condemned to the wastelands."

Cain's breathing grew uneven, his usual composed demeanor cracking under the weight of the revelation. "Why would my grandmother—why would the queen—allow this to happen?" he asked, his voice shaking. "She's always spoken of duty, of unity. And yet she abandoned her own son?"

Seran's expression softened, though it didn't lose its gravity. "The queen is not without guilt, Cain. She was young and bound by the expectations of a kingdom she had only just entered. The council of Mystics deemed Eryndor too dangerous and too unstable to rule. They feared what his existence might mean for their people. She chose the kingdom over her son. And in doing so, she sowed the seeds of Nightshade's wrath."

I placed a hand on Cain's arm, but he barely seemed to register it. His shoulders were tense, his gaze fixed on Seran as though trying to see through the layers of deception and history. "And my father?" he asked, his voice quieter now. "What does he have to do with this? Why does Nightshade want him?"

"Alaric was everything Eryndor could never be in the eyes of the Mystics," Seran explained. "Pure, obedient, chosen. But he was also the one who benefited most from

Eryndor's exile. Your father ascended as the heir to the throne, taking the place that should have been Eryndor's. Nightshade sees your father as the ultimate symbol of his rejection and betrayal."

I tilted my head, unable to hold back the question bubbling in my chest. "I understand why Cain was put on this mission," I said, glancing briefly at him, "but why me? I'm no soldier. No hero. So why am I here?"

Seran's glowing green eyes settled on me with an intensity that made my breath hitch. It wasn't judgment or disapproval—just a weight that felt impossibly ancient, as though he could see every thought I'd ever had.

"You have been chosen," Seran said, his voice calm but heavy with meaning. "Not by me, not by Cain, and certainly not by chance. The gods and goddesses themselves have set their eyes upon you, Everly. You were born to harness a power they do not grant haphazardly."

My brow furrowed, and I shook my head slightly. "A power? I… I don't understand. I can't even fully control the sight I have now. How am I supposed to wield something more?"

Seran's lips quirked in a small, almost fatherly smile. "The power you possess now is but a fraction of what lies within you. You are destined to hold the same power I was entrusted with. But more than that…" He paused, and I swore I felt the ground beneath my feet hum faintly. "The gods have chosen you to bear a power even greater than mine. A power capable of stopping Nightshade and the Blight he has wrought."

The weight of his words settled over me, pressing against my chest. I glanced at Cain, who looked as confused as I felt, though his expression quickly hardened into one of concern. Dante was silent, his brows drawn together as if trying to piece together a puzzle he didn't like.

Seran stepped closer, his eyes never leaving mine. "You will face a trial, Everly. A challenge unlike anything you've ever experienced. Only through it will you obtain this power."

I swallowed hard, my mouth dry. "What kind of trial?"

"That," he said, his voice softening slightly, "I cannot tell you. The gods guard their will closely, and I am only a vessel for their guidance. What I can tell you is this—when the time comes, you must face it with an unshaken heart. It will ask much of you, but the reward will be worth the cost."

My hands trembled slightly, and I clasped them together to still the shaking. "What if I fail?" I whispered.

Seran's gaze didn't waver. "Then Nightshade will succeed."

The room seemed to grow colder at his words, and I fought the urge to take a step back. My mind raced with questions, doubts, and fears. Why me? Why not someone stronger, someone more capable? What made the gods think I was the right choice?

But deep down, beneath the fear, a small ember of determination flickered. I couldn't let the Blight continue. I couldn't let Nightshade destroy everything and everyone I cared about. If this were my path, I had no choice but to walk it.

Cain stepped closer to me, his presence grounding. "Whatever this trial is," he said firmly, "you won't face it alone."

Seran's smile returned, faint but knowing. "You have more strength than you realize, Everly. The gods do not make mistakes. Trust in them… and in yourself."

Cain's gaze hardened as he stood tall, his voice low but commanding. "And him?" he asked, gesturing toward Dante with a tilt of his head.

The room seemed to hold its breath as Seran turned his glowing green eyes on Dante. The air grew heavy, and even the faint crackle of the torches seemed to fade into silence. Dante sat unnaturally still, his shoulders rigid, but his face was carefully blank—except for his eyes. They bored into Seran's with an intensity that sent a shiver down my spine.

Seran's expression softened, almost pitying. "The boy already knows," he said evenly, the words hanging in the air like a storm cloud. "He has the choice now to tell you himself… or I can elaborate."

The tension between them was palpable. Cain's hand twitched near the hilt of his Starfire sword, his suspicion all but radiating off him. I looked at Dante, my heart hammering in my chest. His silence was louder than anything he could have said. Finally, he shifted, his jaw tightening.

"I'll say it," Dante said, his voice devoid of its usual teasing lilt. It was flat, almost hollow, as though he were resigned to the weight of the truth he was about to reveal. His gaze never left Seran's. "Nightshade is my father."

My breath caught in my throat, and Cain's sharp intake of air matched my own. I couldn't believe what I was hearing. The words echoed in my mind, refusing to settle. Nightshade—Dante's father? It didn't make sense. How could he be…?

Cain's reaction was immediate. His hand gripped the hilt of his sword, and he took a step toward Dante. "What the hell are you saying?" he demanded, his voice a mix of anger and disbelief. "You've known this entire time?"

Dante stood, his movements deliberate and slow. "Of course I've known," he said, his tone sharp now, cutting through the thick air. "You think I didn't figure it out when my so-called elemental blood didn't align with the rest of my family? Or when my mother couldn't even look at me without breaking into tears?"

I felt a pang of sympathy for him, but it was quickly overshadowed by the shock of the revelation. Dante turned to Cain, his jaw clenched. "I didn't ask for this," he said, his voice quieter now but no less intense. “You think I wanted to be the son of a monster? You think I didn’t spend years hating myself because of it?”

“Why didn’t you say anything?” Cain shot back, his voice hard. “You should have told us before we left Verdanis. We could’ve prepared—”

“Prepared for what?” Dante snapped, his frustration boiling over. “For you to look at me like you’re doing right now? Like I’m him? Like I’m about to turn into some dark creature and destroy everything in my path?”

Cain opened his mouth to respond, but I stepped between them, my hands raised in a placating gesture. “Stop,” I said, my voice trembling slightly but firm enough to draw their attention. “This isn’t helping.”

They both glared at each other for a moment longer before Cain reluctantly stepped back, his grip on his sword loosening but not releasing entirely. Dante crossed his arms over his chest, his expression closed off.

Seran watched the exchange with quiet patience, his hands clasped in front of him. "The blood of Nightshade runs through him," he said, his voice breaking the silence. "But it does not define him. Choices do."

Dante's gaze flicked to Seran, his expression unreadable. I reached out and lightly touched his arm, hoping to offer some kind of comfort. "Why didn't you tell us?" I asked softly.

He looked down at me, his shoulders sagging slightly. “Because I didn’t want to give anyone another reason to doubt me,” he admitted, his voice tinged with exhaustion. “I’m not him, Everly. I’m not like him.”

“I know,” I said, my voice firm. And I meant it. Whatever darkness Nightshade wielded, I couldn’t see it in Dante. Not in the boy who joked about my favorite fruit or tried to cheer me up when I missed home.

Cain, however, was not as easily convinced. His eyes bore into Dante's, as if he were trying to see through him. "If you're not like him," Cain said, his voice low, "then prove it."

The room fell silent again, and I could feel the weight of Seran's gaze on all of us. This mission had become infinitely more complicated, and I was wondering if we'd all make it to the end intact.

Before I could gather my racing thoughts, Cain stormed out of the room, his footsteps echoing through the ancient halls. The heavy door slammed shut behind him, leaving an almost oppressive silence in his wake. I glanced at Seran, his serene expression unwavering despite the chaos that had just unfolded.

"Thank you… for everything," I said, my voice quieter than I intended.

Seran inclined his head, a slight bow that made me feel oddly out of place.

"Practice your sight," he said, his voice calm but insistent. "It will guide you to the answers you seek. Trust it."

Chapter 25

Cain

The moment the door shut behind me, I felt like I was suffocating. The walls of that cursed temple had been closing in on me, trapping me in a nightmare I never saw coming. My boots struck the stone floor in sharp, echoing beats as I stormed down the hall, my heart pounding against my ribs, my breath uneven. The cool night air slapped against my face as I stepped outside, but it did nothing to quiet the storm raging inside me.

I paced, unable to stand still, my hands clenched into fists so tight my knuckles ached. My mind reeled, trying to piece together the fractured reality that had just been thrust upon me.

Dante. My cousin.

A lie buried so deep that even I, someone trained to see deception, had never seen it coming. The betrayal stung worse than any wound I had ever taken in battle. Did my grandmother know? Had she kept this from me, too? How many more secrets had been woven into the very fabric of my bloodline?

I gritted my teeth, my chest rising and falling with sharp, shallow breaths. My father was missing, my uncle was the infamous Nightshade, and now I was saddled with a family connection I never wanted. Every time I thought I had control, that I understood the rules of the game, the board would be flipped, and I would be left grasping at pieces I no longer recognized.

The door creaked open behind me, and I didn't need to turn around to know who it was. Everly. Of course, it was her. She had followed me, like she always did, like she always would. I was wondering if that made it better or worse.

"Cain—" she started, her voice soft, cautious.

"I knew it!" I cut her off, my voice raw with emotion. I turned to face her, my expression twisted with anger, with hurt, with something I couldn't name. I threw my arms up, pacing faster. "I knew Dante was lying to us! From the beginning, something felt off. But this—" I laughed bitterly, shaking my head. "A cousin? A cousin I never knew existed?"

Everly watched me, her green eyes filled with concern, but she said nothing. She knew me well enough to let me vent, to let the fire burn before trying to douse it.

I raked a hand through my hair, tugging at the strands. "And Nightshade? My uncle? What the hell am I supposed to do with that? How am I supposed to process that the very man we're meant to stop is my blood?"

Silence stretched between us, thick and suffocating.

Then, the door behind us groaned again, and I stiffened. Dante stepped out, his face unreadable, his body tense. He was cautious, slow, as if he were approaching a cornered animal.

"Cain," Dante said, his voice low. "Stop pacing and listen to me."

I froze mid-step and turned to him, my blood boiling at the sound of his voice. "Listen to you?" I sneered, my rage laced in every syllable. "You've done nothing but lie to us! Why the hell should I listen to anything you have to say?"

"I lied because I didn't have a choice!" Dante snapped, his own composure cracking. "You think I wanted this? You think I wanted to be part of this mess?"

Before I could think, before I could even reason with myself, my fist connected with his face. The impact was solid, satisfying for half a second before he stumbled back, wiping the blood from his nose.

He barely hesitated. He lunged.

We hit the ground hard, fists flying, rage spilling out in the only way it knew how. I felt my knuckles split against his cheekbone, felt his knee slam into my ribs. Dirt and gravel scraped against my skin, but I didn't care. I wanted to hurt him, to make him feel the betrayal that was searing through my veins like wildfire.

"Stop it!" Everly's voice cut through the chaos, but I barely heard her.

Dante grunted as he landed a punch to my jaw, sending a sharp burst of pain through my skull. I responded in kind, driving my elbow into his ribs. He gasped but didn't stop. We rolled, locked in a battle neither of us was willing to end.

Then the ground shook beneath us.

A deep, guttural vibration spread out from where Everly stood, her fists clenched, her eyes wide with something almost… primal. Loose stones rolled across the ground, and the horses tied nearby neighed in alarm. The force of it was enough to make us pause, just for a moment.

Dante and I froze, still gripping each other, chests heaving, fists poised to strike. We both turned to look at Everly.

Her expression was wild, her breathing ragged. "Enough," she said, her voice shaking, but not with fear—with power.

Dante slowly rolled off me, wiping his mouth with the back of his hand. I shoved myself to my feet, the anger still thick in my veins but tempered now by something else. Something close to disbelief.

"What… was that?" Dante asked, his voice quieter now, less confident.

Everly looked down at her hands, as if she didn't recognize them. "I—I don't know," she admitted.

I wiped the blood from my own mouth, still glaring at Dante, still feeling the weight of everything crashing down on me. I extended a hand to him, hesitating only a fraction before he took it and pulled himself up.

The tension between us hadn't vanished, but for now, it had settled, simmering beneath the surface instead of boiling over.

"We can't do this," Everly said, her voice stronger now, more certain. "We can't fight each other. We won't survive if we keep tearing each other apart."

She was right. I knew she was right. But it didn't make it any easier to accept.

I turned away, inhaling sharply, swallowing down the pain, the anger, the betrayal.

I had lost control. And that was the one thing I could never afford to do.

Chapter 26

Everly

The sun was dipping low, casting long shadows across the abandoned streets of Doren. I glanced at the darkening sky, my voice cutting through the heavy silence. "It's going to be dark soon. We should find somewhere to shelter for the night… figure out our next move."

Cain and Dante exchanged a glance, tension still simmering between them from the fight, but neither objected. With a nod from Cain, we began scouting the nearest houses for one that was still intact. The air felt thick, the stillness pressing down on me as we passed crumbling walls and shattered windows. Each step felt like an intrusion, a violation of lives that had been lived and lost here.

Finally, we found a small house at the edge of the city. The roof sagged slightly, but it was whole. The front door hung crookedly on its hinges, but the interior mainly appeared untouched by time. I hesitated on the threshold, peering into the dim space beyond. It was eerie, standing in a place that had once been someone's home. Faded family portraits lined the walls, their faces smiling in frozen moments of joy. A forgotten toy lay in the corner of the room, covered in dust. It felt wrong, stepping into this space as if it were ours, but we had no choice.

Inside, Cain immediately got to work. He knelt by the hearth, striking flint to light the brittle logs still stacked nearby. Soon, the room glowed with the warmth of the fire. The flickering flames cast dancing shadows against the cracked walls, easing some of the oppressive chill that had clung to me since we entered the city.

Dante remained quiet, moving wordlessly into the kitchen. I watched as he used his water magic to fill the cracked sink basin. The liquid shimmered unnaturally in the faint light, a reminder of just how powerful he was despite the rift between us. He found an old bucket near the back door and filled it, setting it near the fire to warm for washing. When he turned to me, his eyes softened for just a moment.

"Here," he said simply.

"Thank you," I murmured, my voice barely audible over the crackling fire. He nodded, not meeting my gaze, and returned to sorting through what remained in the house.

I watched him go, my chest tightening with emotions I couldn't untangle. Anger, hurt, and betrayal warred inside me. I wanted to confront him, to demand an explanation that felt more personal, more real, but the words stuck in my throat. What could he say to make this right? To erase the knowledge of who his father was? Of what he had kept from us?

Cain moved through the small abode, lighting old candles and lanterns with the fire. Their golden glow illuminated the room in patches, but the flickering light only made the house feel more ghostly. I wrapped my arms around myself, trying to shake the unease that had settled over me since we stepped into this city.

They hadn't spoken a word to each other since the fight. The silence between them was louder than any argument could have been. I wanted to bridge the gap, to say something that would ease the tension, but I didn't know where to start. The rift between them wasn't just about the fight—it was about trust, about betrayal, and about truths too big to ignore.

I sat near the fire, staring into the flames as they devoured the dry wood. My heart felt as fragile as the glass scattered in the streets outside, ready to shatter under the weight of everything that had happened. I let the heat of the fire warm my hands, but it did little to ease the cold ache in my chest.

I glanced at Cain, who was methodically checking the room for anything useful, his movements precise and detached. And then at Dante, whose face was set in a mask of calm that I knew hid far more turmoil than he'd ever admit. We were all pretending to be fine, but the truth was, we were hanging on by threads—threads that felt like they could snap at any moment.

I wandered into the larger bedroom, where I found a wardrobe tucked into the dimly lit corner of the space. Its wood was worn, the edges softened by time, but when I opened it, I found clothes still neatly folded inside. The faint scent of lavender lingered, as if whoever had lived here had left not so long ago. I sifted through the garments, pulling out a pair of soft, worn pajamas. My own clothes were still damp from washing in the sink, and I welcomed the dry fabric against my skin as I changed.

The room was quiet except for the faint crackle of the fire from the other room. I heard footsteps, and Cain appeared in the doorway. He paused, his dark eyes meeting mine, and then walked inside, his shoulders heavy with the weight of everything that had happened. Without a word, he sat down on the edge of the bed, his elbows resting on his knees, his hands clasped together.

I stood there for a moment, unsure of what to say or do. My heart ached for him. The betrayal, the secrets, the burden his family had placed on him—it was all too much. Slowly, I crossed the room and sat beside him. The mattress dipped slightly under our combined weight, but he didn't acknowledge me at first, his gaze fixed on the floor.

"He took the smaller room," Cain said finally, his voice low and rough. "Said I could take the couch."

I hesitated before speaking. "You should take this room. You need the rest."

He shook his head, his jaw tightening. "I'll be fine. You should stay here. Get some sleep."

There was a vulnerability in his posture, in the way his broad shoulders seemed to curve inward as if shielding himself from the world. I reached out and rested a hand on his arm, squeezing gently. "Cain… I'm so sorry. For all of this."

He laughed softly, but there was no humor in it. "I don't even know what 'this' is anymore. My father… my uncle… Dante." He exhaled sharply, running a hand through his dark hair. "Everything I thought I knew about my family, about who I am, is unraveling right in front of me."

His voice cracked on the last word, and my chest tightened. Seeing him like this—always so composed, so strong—made the hurt feel even sharper. "It's not fair," I whispered. "They've put you in the middle of all of this without even giving you a chance to prepare. You didn't deserve that."

He turned his head slightly, his eyes meeting mine. There was something raw in his gaze, something unguarded that he usually kept hidden. "I don't know what I'm supposed to do," he admitted, his voice barely above a whisper. "How am I supposed to lead a mission like this when I can't even make sense of my own bloodline?"

"You're not alone in this," I said softly. "You have me… and even Dante, whether you want to admit it or not. We're here to figure it out together."

Cain let out a shaky breath, his head dipping forward. "You shouldn't have to be."

"I'm choosing to be," I replied, my tone firm. "You don't have to carry all of this on your own."

For a long moment, we sat in silence, the room holding nothing but the quiet sounds of our breathing. I could feel the tension in him, the war waging behind his calm exterior. Finally, he looked up, his gaze heavy with unshed emotion.

“Thank you,” he said, his voice still cracked but sincere.

I wanted to say something more, to offer him comfort, but the words wouldn't come to mind.

Before I could think better of it, I found myself standing in front of him. My heart pounded in my chest as I closed the space between us, standing between his knees. Cain’s silvery eyes, flecked with storms of deep blue, met mine with a vulnerability I’d never seen before. The pain swirling in his gaze made my chest ache, and I couldn’t bear to leave him in that darkness.

Slowly, I reached up and combed my fingers through his dark hair, the strands soft under my touch. He exhaled sharply, his hands instinctively winding around the backs of my thighs. It wasn’t calculated—it wasn’t planned. It was raw, a reaction to the unspoken weight between us.

I leaned down, brushing my lips lightly over his. The kiss was tentative, fleeting, but it felt like the beginning of something neither of us could name. His grip on me tightened, his hands sliding higher until they rested firmly on my waist. My heart stuttered as I kissed him again, this time with more urgency.

His lips parted under mine, and the slow, deliberate brush of his tongue against my own sent a surge of heat racing through me. It pooled low in my stomach, spreading warmth through my entire body. My breath caught as he pulled me into his lap, his strong arms anchoring me against him.

My nipples brushed against his chest, the contact sending a sharp jolt of heat through me as they hardened into sensitive peaks. My hand slid down the hard planes of his chest, pausing at the hem of his tunic. Slowly, I pulled the fabric up, my fingers grazing the taut muscles of his stomach before tugging it over his head.

He leaned back for a moment, his stormy eyes studying me with an intensity that made my breath hitch.

Then, with one hand sliding behind my neck, he pulled me into another kiss—this one deeper, hungrier.

I shifted my hips, grinding against him, feeling his growing cock press firmly against the confines of his pants. I moaned softly, and his chest rumbled with a growl in response. Desire coiled low in my stomach, pooling between my thighs. His hands roamed my body, warm and insistent, tugging at the hem of my tunic. I barely had time to pull it off before he flipped me onto my back, the bed beneath us bouncing softly with the movement.

Cain hooked his fingers into the waistband of my pants, sliding them down and off in one fluid motion. His gaze roamed over me, lingering on the thin fabric of my bra and underwear. The cool air kissed my skin, raising goosebumps. Still, the heat of his stare ignited something deeper, something raw and unrelenting. His eyes burned with an intensity that made me feel as though I might catch fire beneath his touch.

Cain's breath was hot against my ear as his lips brushed along the curve of my neck, each kiss sending a shiver down my spine. His hands roamed from my arms to my stomach and my thighs, the heat of his palms searing me. The room seemed to narrow, the world beyond its walls fading into irrelevance as his mouth moved lower, tracing a path along my collarbone.

I tilted my head back, surrendering to the pull of him. My hands threaded through his dark hair, tugging gently, encouraging him closer. His silvery eyes flicked up to meet mine, stormy and filled with a hunger that stole the air from my lungs. "Tell me if you want me to stop," he murmured, his voice low and rough, a promise and a question all at once.

Instead of answering, I guided his face back to mine, capturing his lips in a kiss that left no room for hesitation. It was a clash of need and tenderness, his mouth exploring mine with an urgency that matched the rapid beat of my heart. His hands slid under the edge of my bra, fingertips grazing the bare skin of my nipples and igniting a fire that spread through me like wildfire.

The bed shifted beneath us as he explored, pressing into me against the soft covers. His weight was comforting, grounding, yet the sparks of energy between us felt like they might lift me right off the mattress. He paused, his gaze searching mine as though asking for permission once more, and I answered by pulling him closer.

His lips trailed lower, leaving a path of warmth across my skin. Each kiss was slower, more deliberate, as if he wanted to memorize every inch of me. His hand skimmed along my thigh, his touch both reverent and possessive. His fingers trailed to the apex of my thighs, finding my underwear and skimming a finger once over me. I arched into him, my body moving of its own accord, desperate for more of the connection that seemed to tether us to each other in this moment.

He moved my underwear aside, using his finger to circle the bundle of nerves of my clit. My legs trembled with the sensation, my breathing turning into moans of pleasure. The tension that coiled in my stomach is now directing tension between my legs, a pressure building.

His other hand brushed the edge of my bra, hesitating for the barest second before continuing its exploration. He slid his hand to my back and unhooked the strap, releasing my breasts into the chilly air. I reached for him, my fingers finding the firmness of his chest, the strength beneath his skin, and I marveled at how perfectly we seemed to fit together.

The room was quiet except for the sound of my breathy moans, mingling in the space between us. Cain moved his finger lower and found the wetness of my desire for him.

"You're incredible," he growled, his voice filled with awe that made my heart ache and my skin flush.

With one smooth motion, he slid a finger into me, making my hips buck. Slowly, he pulled it out, then back in again. My breaths came faster as the pressure built even further. My hands roamed his body with one still gripping his hair, the other on his back. I was sure I was leaving marks where my fingernails dug into him. He kissed little kisses down my body. Starting below my ear, he made his way between my breasts. His tongue lightly traced the valley between them before he took one of my nipples into his mouth.

The sensations he left on my skin were a symphony of fire and electricity, building an unbearable tension within me. Just when I thought the pressure would break and send me spiraling, he pulled his fingers away. The sudden absence of his touch sent a jolt of frustration through me, and I couldn't stop the pout that tugged at my lips.

Cain's low chuckle filled the space between us, warm and teasing, yet steeped in admiration. "Impatient, are we?" he murmured, his voice like velvet and smoke. The intensity in his stormy eyes held me captive as he stood, towering over me. With deliberate slowness, he unbuckled his belt, each motion precise, as if savoring the moment.

My breath hitched as his gaze swept over me, taking in every inch of my body. It wasn't just the heat in his stare—it was the reverence, the way his silvery, blue-flecked eyes seemed to map every curve, every scar, every piece of me as if committing it to memory. The air between us grew heavier, charged with unspoken desire and anticipation.

"You're breathtaking," he said, his words a low rasp that sent a shiver down my spine. His hands moved with purpose, discarding the last of his clothing. For a moment, he just stood there, the firelight dancing over the planes of his muscular form, his wings faintly visible in the flickering glow.

I gazed at his rigid cock with eagerness and longing.

As he knelt back down, his touch returned, more deliberate this time—reverent, almost worshipful. The rough callouses of his fingers grazed over my skin, reigniting the heat that had pooled low in my stomach. His lips brushed against mine, soft and slow, teasing me into surrender before deepening the kiss. The connection between us was raw, electric, a firestorm I never wanted to extinguish.

"Are you sure?" he asked softly, his voice a whisper that settled over me like a blanket. The question wasn't about whether I wanted this moment—it was deeper, asking if I trusted him, if I believed in whatever it was we were building between us.

I nodded, my hand sliding up to cup his face. "I've never been more sure."

I saw his rigid cock at my entrance as he pushed himself inside me slowly. The stretching sensation nearly catapulted me over the edge. He eased in at an agonizingly delicious pace, making sure I felt every inch of him. I lifted my pelvis to meet his as he buried himself in me to the hilt. Between the rapid pulse of my heart and my pussy pulsing in need, I felt lightheaded. Letting me get used to the fullness, he waited there.

Once I caught my breath and relaxed a little, he started moving back slowly. The pace was tantalizing as that pressure low in my body built with a crescendo. My body reacted to his light moans every time he bottomed out again. Each trust sent an electric pulse through me. The world faded completely, leaving only us and the tangled mess of emotions and desires that burned between us like an unquenchable flame.

My nails bit into his back as I lifted to meet his thrusts; they became more complicated and faster. With a loud moan, I felt the snap of the tension that built, and my whole body convulsed, stars of white light dancing across my vision. The spasms deep inside me, wrapped around his cock, drove him to his release. He thrusted one last time, deep and hard, before going still. I watched his face of pure ecstasy while he rode out his release.

He gazed down at me, his silver eyes softened with a tenderness that made my heart ache. His lips brushed mine in a gentle kiss, one that lingered as though he wasn't quite ready to let go of the moment. Slowly, he rolled onto his side, pulling me with him until we lay tangled together. Our breaths mingled in the stillness as the weight of what had just happened settled between us.

Cain reached down, tugging the blanket over us with one hand while his other found its place on my waist, anchoring me to him. I adjusted, nestling into the curve of his body, my back pressed to his chest. His warmth wrapped around me like a shield from the outside world. Just as my breathing began to slow, I felt the softest kiss against the shell of my ear, his lips brushing a promise I wasn't sure I was ready for.

"If there's anything I'm certain of in this world right now, Everly," he murmured, his voice low and vulnerable, "it's that I'm falling for you."

The words unraveled me in ways I didn't expect. I lay there in silence, my thoughts spiraling. Only nights ago, this could have been Dante lying beside me. The weight of that truth gnawed at my chest, making it hard to sort through the chaos of my feelings. How had things shifted so quickly?

The answer was easy. We let the emotions of betrayal from Dante's lies get the best of us. I am sure by tomorrow morning, Cain will be back to his usual broody self and leave me in a tangle of confusion yet again.

Cain's arms tightened around my waist, drawing me back into the present. His steady breaths tickled the back of my neck, and I felt his body relax, his breathing evening out. His warmth and the constant rhythm of his heartbeat against my back began to soothe the storm in my mind. Slowly, despite the tangle of emotions, I drifted into sleep, cocooned in his embrace.

Chapter 27

Cain

The first rays of sunlight filtered through the cracked shutters, casting faint beams of light across the room. I stirred, feeling the warmth of Everly's bare skin against mine, my arm draped heavily over her waist as if, even in sleep, I wasn't ready to let go.

The air still carried the remnants of last night—the heat of it, the way she had moved beneath me, the soft gasps and whispered curses against my lips. A lingering scent of sweat and satisfaction mixed with her natural sweetness, making it impossible to pretend this was anything but what it was—something that had crossed a line, something that would make everything more complicated than it already was.

But I wasn't a man of regret.

I knew this was a mistake, knew that by morning she would be picking apart everything we had done, searching for the parts she wanted to keep and the ones she would try to bury. It was written in the tension of her body even now, in the way she lay still, her breathing slow and measured, as if she were trying to delay the moment when we had to acknowledge it.

I wasn't going to make it easy for her.

I tightened my arm briefly around her waist, a lazy smirk tugging at my lips as I buried my face in the crook of her neck. She stiffened slightly before relaxing, her fingers brushing absently over mine where they rested against her stomach.

For a moment, I allowed myself this—this rare moment of quiet, of something that wasn't war or duty or the constant battle to prove my worth to people who would never be satisfied. But it was fleeting, always fleeting, because the world didn't let me have nice things.

A light knock sounded at the door, followed by the creak of it opening before either of us could move.

Everly turned her head sharply, but I didn't have to follow her gaze to know who it was. The way the air in the room shifted, the barely muffled intake of breath, the sudden rigidity in Everly's posture—I already knew.

Dante.

I cracked one eye open, just in time to see him freeze in the doorway, his gaze darting between Everly's wide-eyed expression and my arm still wrapped possessively around her waist.

I expected a reaction. Anger. Jealousy. Something explosive.

Instead, I saw something much worse.

For a fleeting second, his expression was blank—completely unreadable. Then his jaw tightened, his shoulders squared, and that mask he always wore slipped perfectly into place, smooth and detached.

"I, uh..." He cleared his throat, his voice unusually stiff. "I was going to see if you wanted me to scout for breakfast, but..." His lips twitched into something that wasn't quite a smirk, wasn't quite a frown. "Clearly, you're... occupied."

Everly let out a slight, frustrated noise, like she wanted to disappear into the mattress. I, however, was far more entertained. If Dante was going to pretend this wasn't getting to him, I wasn't about to let him off that easily.

I propped myself up on one elbow, raking a hand through my disheveled hair with a deliberately slow, lazy motion. "Morning, Dante," I greeted, my voice still rough with sleep but undeniably smug.

His jaw ticked, and I saw the way his fingers curled slightly at his sides before he forced himself to unclench them. He leveled his gaze at Everly instead of me, his voice cooling. "Everly, I'll be outside when you're… ready."

There was something in his tone, something that wasn't just irritation or discomfort. I recognized it because I had seen it before—the sharp edge of disappointment, of realization. It was the look of a man who had just figured out he'd lost before he even knew he was playing the game.

I didn't care.

Dante's feelings weren't my problem. He could stand there all morning, fuming or sulking or pretending this didn't gut him, and it wouldn't change a damn thing. Everly wasn't his. Maybe he thought she had been once, maybe he still thought he had a chance, but that was his mistake. His miscalculation.

Because I wasn't the kind of man who lost what I wanted.

Everly turned toward him. "Dante—" she started, but he was already gone, stepping back into the hall with a click of his boots.

The moment the door shut behind him, Everly let out a groan, rubbing a hand over her face as she collapsed back against the pillow.

"Well, that wasn't awkward at all," I drawled, stretching leisurely.

She shot me a glare before sitting up, pulling the blanket tighter around her bare body. "He didn't deserve to find out like that."

"No, he didn't," I agreed, my smirk fading slightly. I shifted onto my side, resting my head in my hand as I watched her. "But it was bound to happen sooner or later. You can't keep tiptoeing around him forever, Everly."

She sighed, looking away, her fingers gripping the blanket so tightly her knuckles turned white. "This isn't about tiptoeing. I just… I didn't mean for any of this to happen."

Something cold twisted in my chest, sharp and immediate, cutting through the heat of the moment with the precision of a blade. I sat up, the muscles in my back tightening, my voice steady but edged with something darker. "What did you mean by that?"

I already knew I wasn't going to like the answer. The way she wouldn't meet my eyes, the tension in her shoulders, the hesitation thick in the air—I'd seen it before. I'd heard it before. It was the kind of thing people said when they wished they could take something back, when regret was creeping in like a slow poison, poisoning what had been undeniable just hours before.

But this wasn't just some meaningless moment for me. I wasn't the type to let emotions rule me, wasn't the type to make reckless choices, to indulge in things that didn't matter.

Everly mattered.

That was the problem.

I wasn't an idiot. I knew she and Dante had danced around something before this mission. There was tension between them, unspoken and unresolved. And I hadn't given a damn about it. Because it didn't matter. Because she was here, now, with me. Because I wasn't some uncertain boy circling around a woman, waiting for her to make a choice.

And yet, hearing those words from her lips, seeing the way she shrank from the weight of what we had done—it felt like a fucking gut punch. Like she was already pulling away, already rewriting the story in her head into something it wasn't.

I refused to let her.

My fingers flexed against the sheets as I fought the surge of something I wasn't ready to name. Anger? No. Not quite. Something heavier. Something colder. I wasn't the type to plead, and I sure as hell wasn't going to start now.

She was either in this or she wasn't.

And if she wasn't, I needed to hear her say it.

She sighed, looking away, her fingers gripping the blanket tightly. "This isn't about tiptoeing. I just… I didn't mean for any of this to happen."

Something cold twisted in my chest. I sat up, my voice steady but sharp. "What did you mean by that?"

She froze mid-motion, clutching the blanket even tighter before turning her head slightly, just enough to meet my gaze over her shoulder. "I didn't mean for this mission to get any more complicated than it already is."

I stared at her, something slow and dark curling through me. "Do you regret what happened last night?"

Her breath hitched slightly, her lips parting like she hadn't expected the question. "No," she said, firm and quick, but there was hesitation there, just beneath the surface. "Of course I don't. But…" Her throat bobbed as she swallowed, her next words coming out softer. "I can't deny that Dante and I had… chemistry, back in Ashmoor."

A muscle jumped in my jaw.

Chemistry.

That was a polite way of saying she had been considering him before she ended up in my bed.

I exhaled slowly, my fingers pressing into the mattress beside me. "So, that's it?" My voice was quiet, but there was a weight to it. "You're torn between him and me?"

Everly turned away fully now, standing to grab her tunic, her movements sharp and tense. "It's not that simple, Cain," she muttered, pulling the fabric over her head. "Nothing about this situation is simple."

The room was silent as we dressed, the air thick with things left unsaid. When she finally moved toward the door, my voice stopped her.

“But he lied, Everly.” My tone was sharper now, edged with something close to anger. “Lied about everything. Who he is, why he moved to the capital. We don’t even know what else he’s lying about. And what about those visions you keep having about him?”

Her shoulders stiffened, and for a moment, I thought she might deny it, brush it off like she always did when things got too close to the truth.

Then, before she could answer, the door opened.

Dante stood there, arms crossed, his expression carefully blank. Like he was trying to act unaffected, like he wasn't standing in the doorway, realizing he'd already lost. "What visions about me?" he asked, his voice steady, but I heard the crack beneath it—laced with suspicion, with something bitter and biting.

Everly hesitated, shifting between us, her stomach clearly twisting. She could feel it too—the weight of what she had done, of what we had done. And yet, she still tried to defuse the situation. “It’s nothing,” she said quickly, attempting to brush past him, to escape before this turned into something worse.

Dante didn’t let her.

He stepped into her path, his violet eyes locking onto her like he had some kind of right to the truth. Like she owed him something. Like he was entitled to her.

It made my blood boil.

“Don’t give me that,” he pressed, voice sharper now, frustration seeping through his carefully crafted mask. “If it’s nothing, then why not just tell me?”

I stepped forward, closing the space between us, making my presence unmistakably dominant. “Back off, Dante.”

He barely spared me a glance. The fucking audacity of it.

His focus was still on her, still clinging to whatever delusion he had about what they were, about what she might still be to him. "Are you two… together or something?"

The question should have been pathetic. It should have been funny. It should have made me laugh in his face.

Instead, I met his gaze head-on, refusing to waver, refusing to let him even think he had ground to stand on. I let the truth cut through him like a blade. "We were last night," I said flatly. "And we're already more together than you and Everly ever were."

His jaw clenched so tightly I thought he might snap his own teeth.

"Cain," he said through gritted teeth, his voice low, simmering with something close to rage. Good. Let him stew in it. Let him choke on it.

Everly groaned, exasperated. "This isn't going to turn into some ridiculous dick-measuring contest."

Dante scoffed, tilting his head, his lips curling into a lazy, mocking smirk. "Well, I haven't gotten to show mine yet."

That was it.

I took a step forward, my entire body coiled with tension, ready to remind him exactly who he was dealing with. But before I could move, Everly's hand was on my chest, stopping me.

"Enough," she snapped, her voice cutting through the air like a blade. "We're supposed to be a team. I'm not some prize for you two to fight over."

Dante's smirk faltered.

I caught it. The flash of something real beneath his mask. It wasn't just jealousy—it was realization. That no matter what had happened between them before, no matter what he thought he was owed, she had chosen me. And that killed him more than anything.

Without another word, Everly turned on her heel and walked out the door.

Dante didn't move, his gaze lingering on the empty space where she had been, as if he stood there long enough, she might come back.

She wouldn't.

I exhaled through my nose, slow and measured, but the rage in my chest still burned, still clawed at the inside of my ribs, demanding to be let loose.

Dante's fingers curled into fists at his sides before he spoke, his voice quieter now, but no less sharp. "This isn't over."

I smirked, rolling my shoulders, letting the weight of the moment settle. "No, it's not."

And we both knew it.

I turned, walking away without another glance back. Because I had already won.

Chapter 28

Everly

The cool morning air nipped at my cheeks as I walked through the crumbled streets of Doren. My boots kicked up dust from the desolation, my thoughts swirling like the wind whispering through the abandoned buildings. I should be able to flirt with whoever I want, sleep with whoever I choose, without feeling like it ties me to them for life. Why is it that just because I share a bed with someone—or even a kiss—they suddenly feel entitled to a piece of me?

I stopped in the middle of the road, staring at a broken signpost leaning against the remains of a shop. My hands clenched into fists as I took a deep breath. It wasn't just Cain or Dante. It was this whole situation. The road was lonely. The nights were colder than I wanted to admit. The tension between them was suffocating. And I was stuck in the middle, navigating their bruised egos and unspoken feelings while trying to figure out my own.

I am a person. A woman. A fae. Not some toy to be fought over or claimed. I deserved more than this. More respect, more understanding, more space to figure out what I wanted without someone else dictating my choices.

And yet, here I was, pulled in two directions by their intensity, their desires, and the raw connection I felt with each of them in different ways. It wasn't fair to them or to me.

I walked past a toppled bench, the silence of the city pressing in. The thought of staying here another minute, of dealing with their brooding gazes and sharp words, made my skin crawl. I needed answers. Needed to feel some semblance of control in this chaos.

The temple loomed ahead, its cracked white dome stark against the pale morning sky. It called to me, just as it had when we first arrived. I made my way up the broken steps, my resolve hardening with each step. If anyone could give me clarity, it was Seran.

When I pushed through the heavy door, the cold, sacred air of the temple wrapped around me like a cloak. I found Seran exactly where we'd left him, seated cross-legged near the dais, his hands resting on his knees as though he'd been waiting for me. His green eyes lifted to mine, glowing faintly in the dim light.

"You've come back," he said softly, his voice carrying the weight of ages. "I suspected you would."

I stepped forward, crossing the threshold of the sacred space. "I have questions," I said firmly. "And I think you might have the answers."

Seran gestured for me to sit, his expression calm but knowing. "Then ask, Everly," he said, his tone soothing and enigmatic. "The gods have brought you here for a reason. Let us find what that is."

I sat cross-legged on the floor across from Seran, the ancient temple's air cool and still around us. The glow of the candles flickered softly, casting shadows on the walls, as I hesitated, chewing over the words I wanted to say.

"I've had visions about Dante," I began, my voice quieter than I intended. "And his sister, Lyssandra. There's something… dark in them. His eyes, hers too. They're black, like they've been consumed by something." I looked down, tracing a crack in the floor with my finger. "What do these visions mean? What are they showing me?"

Seran's luminous green eyes studied me for a moment, the weight of his wisdom pressing against me like an unseen force. Finally, he spoke, his voice calm yet laced with a gravity that made the hairs on my arms rise.

"The story of Dante and his sister," Seran began, "is one deeply entwined with the very darkness that threatens our world. What you see in your visions is not a fabrication but the truth of their heritage. Their father—Eryndor, once known as a prince of this kingdom—has ensured that darkness follows them wherever they go."

"Eryndor," I whispered. The name hung heavy in the air.

Seran nodded. "When Eryndor was cast out by the Mystics, shunned for being the first hybrid among their ranks, his resentment festered like a wound. He sought solace and revenge in forbidden knowledge. He found it in an ancient book, one that spoke of rituals using dark magic. It led him beyond our borders, to a cave deep within the mountains of another kingdom. There, he discovered onyx crystals said to hold the power of death itself. Using these crystals, Eryndor performed the ritual, tethering himself to the magic of decay and the shadows."

The weight of Seran's words settled over me, but he continued before I could ask any questions. "When he returned, cloaked in disguise, he infiltrated Verdanis. There, he encountered Dante's mother—a pure-hearted woman. He seduced her, not initially as part of some grand scheme, but because, for a moment, Eryndor's thirst for power gave way to the desire for normalcy. For a life he had lost."

My hands tightened into fists. "So, Dante… he didn't ask for this. He was born into it."

Seran nodded solemnly. "Indeed. Dante's mother became pregnant, and Eryndor's ambitions reignited. He saw Dante as a vessel—a means to extend his power and secure his vengeance. He intended to raise Dante steeped in dark magic, to mold him into an ally for his plans to overthrow the kingdom of Erynvale. After Lyssandra was born, Eryndor repeated the ritual, binding her to the same shadows that gave him his strength."

My stomach churned. "But… his mother? Did she know?"

"She did," Seran said grimly. "When she discovered what Eryndor had done to Lyssandra, she threatened to take the matter to the Imperial Counsel. Eryndor couldn't allow that. He cast a spell upon her, one that twisted her mind and forced her into submission. Under his command, they fled to Laseel, a place far from the capital's eyes."

"And then?" I pressed, my voice trembling.

"Eryndor left them," Seran said, his gaze darkening. "He abandoned his family, choosing to continue the Blight in other kingdoms to amass an army of the dead. He knew that with each kingdom consumed, his strength grew. All of it has been in preparation for his ultimate goal—to strike at the kingdom of Erynvale. To take back what he believes was stolen from him."

My breath hitched as I tried to process everything. The visions, Dante's lies, the betrayal—none of it felt real, and yet, it explained so much.

"Dante…" I whispered. "Does he know all of this?"

Seran tilted his head. "Parts of it, perhaps. But the rest? That remains to be seen. He is a complicated man, burdened by a legacy not of his choosing. His struggle between the darkness within him and the person he wishes to be will determine his role in what is to come."

I sat back, feeling the chill of the temple seep into my bones. "And what about me?" I asked quietly. "What am I supposed to do with this?"

"You are the tether," Seran said, his voice soft but firm. "To him, to Cain, and to the fate of this kingdom. The gods have chosen you to face these trials, to wield the power to stop Eryndor, should you rise to the challenge. But you must decide what role you wish to play. Your choice will shape the future."

His words left me silent. A choice. It all came down to a choice—one I wasn't sure I was ready to make.

I shifted in my seat, the air of the temple pressing heavier on me now. The dim flicker of candlelight cast shadows across Seran's face, and his gaze softened as if he knew the weight of my next question.

"What about Cain's father?" I asked, my voice barely above a whisper. "How do we find him?"

Seran regarded me for a moment, his expression unreadable. "You have a gift, Everly," he said, his voice low and steady. "The Sight has shown you glimpses of the past and the future. It is time you tried to wield it with purpose. Focus on Cain's father—let the gods guide you."

I hesitated, doubt creeping into my thoughts. "I don't know if I can," I admitted. "It doesn't always work. What if I see nothing?"

Seran leaned forward, his luminous green eyes locking onto mine. "The Sight chooses what to reveal, but your heart must remain open. Trust it, Everly. Trust yourself."

Taking a deep breath, I closed my eyes and tried to focus. The world around me faded as I called Cain's father to my mind—a man I'd never met, but one whose life hung in the balance of this mission. The temple's air seemed to still, and for a moment, I felt the pull of something greater, deeper.

Then, it came.

A vision rippled through my mind like a stone dropped into still water. I saw a dim, damp cell lit by a faint, eerie glow. The walls were carved from jagged stone, and the floor was slick with moisture. A man sat slumped in the corner, his frame gaunt and shivering with cold. His hair was disheveled, and his hollow cheeks spoke of starvation. My heart clenched—it had to be him.

Outside the cell, a figure loomed, draped in black. Shadows curled around him like living things, licking at his boots and whispering secrets I couldn't hear. His presence felt suffocating, as though the darkness emanating from him reached through the vision to press against my chest.

Then another man approached, stepping into the faint light. His features were sharper, his stance poised with authority. He leaned toward the man cloaked in shadows and said something, his words muffled and distant, as though I were listening through water. I strained to hear, my heart racing.

One word reached me, cutting through the haze like a blade: Merewick.

The name of a city.

The vision began to waver, and I fought to hold on, to see more. But the pull receded, and the scene dissolved into darkness.

I gasped as I opened my eyes, my chest heaving. The temple was utterly silent. The candles that had illuminated the room moments ago were snuffed out, leaving me in near-complete darkness.

"Seran?" I called, my voice echoing against the ancient stone walls. But there was no response. The air felt colder, heavier, as if the power that had drawn me here had left.

He was gone.

I sat for a moment, trembling, the weight of the vision pressing down on me. Cain's father was alive, but he was in danger—deep underground, held captive by the very darkness we sought to destroy. And Merewick... a name, a clue. But it was also a threat.

I stood slowly, the silence of the temple filling my ears as I made my way back toward the entrance. The vision still swirled in my mind, and with every step, I felt the urgency mounting.

Cain needed to know what I'd seen. And we needed to move—before it was too late.

Chapter 29

Everly

The deserted streets of Doren felt even more desolate as I made my way back to the house where I'd left Cain and Dante. The sky above had darkened to a bruised gray, the clouds hanging low and heavy. Each step I took echoed faintly, the only sound in a city where no life stirred. The vision still lingered in my mind, vivid and raw—the man in the cell, the suffocating darkness of the figure in black, and the name: Merewick.

My breath hitched as I reached the doorway of the small house. I hesitated, my hand hovering over the weathered frame. Cain's father was alive, but the image of his hollow cheeks and trembling body was burned into my mind. How would Cain react to this news? The answers I had were few, but they were crucial, and they would only deepen the weight he already carried.

With a deep breath, I pushed open the door.

The warmth from the fire Cain had built earlier greeted me, but it didn't reach me. My hands were cold, my fingers trembling. Inside, the house was quiet except for the faint crackle of the fire and the occasional creak of the wooden floorboards. Cain sat at the table, his head resting in one hand, his eyes staring into the flickering flames. Dante was nowhere to be seen, and for that, I was grateful. The tension between them had been unbearable earlier, and I didn't have the energy to referee again.

Cain glanced up as the door creaked open, his silver-blue eyes meeting mine. The storm of emotions in them—anger, hurt, and exhaustion—was palpable. He straightened, the chair scraping against the floor as he rose to his feet.

"You were gone a while," he said, his voice even, though there was a sharp edge to it. "Did you find anything?"

I nodded, closing the door behind me. The weight of the vision pressed harder on my chest, and I struggled to find the right words. "I... I used the Sight," I began, stepping further into the room. "I saw him."

Cain's posture stiffened. "My father?" His voice was low, cautious, as though daring to hope.

"Yes," I said softly, crossing the room to stand near him. "He's alive, Cain. But... he's not in a good place."

His eyes narrowed, and he reached for the back of the chair, gripping it tightly. "Where is he? What did you see?"

I swallowed hard, my throat dry as I relived the vision. "He's in a cell—underground, I think. He looks... he looks weak, Cain. Starved and cold. But he's alive."

Cain's grip on the chair tightened, his knuckles whitening. "And who's holding him?"

"There were two men," I said, closing my eyes briefly to recall the details. "One of them... he was cloaked in shadows, like they were alive and curling around him. The darkness was... it was suffocating." My voice faltered, but I forced myself to continue. "And there was another man, standing next to him. He said something, but I couldn't hear most of it. I only caught one word."

Cain's gaze bore into me, intense and unyielding. "What word?"

"Merewick," I said, my voice barely above a whisper.

Cain stepped back, his eyes widening as the name sank in. "Merewick," he repeated, the word heavy with recognition.

"That's... it's a city near the border of the Blight. I've read about it. It was one of the first places to fall when the Blight started spreading."

I nodded. "Then that's where we need to go. That's where he is."

He turned away, his hands gripping the edge of the table now, his head bowed. The tension in his shoulders was evident, and I could feel the weight of his turmoil. "You're sure? You're absolutely sure?" His voice cracked with emotion.

"Yes," I said firmly. "I'm sure."

For a long moment, he didn't say anything. The room was silent except for the fire, and I could see the wheels turning in his mind. Finally, he turned back to me, his expression a mix of determination and fear.

"We need to prepare," he said, his voice steadier now. "Merewick isn't just a city—it's a death trap. If he's there, it's for a reason. Nightshade is there too, isn't he?"

I hesitated, then nodded. "The man cloaked in shadows—it has to be him."

Cain exhaled sharply, running a hand through his dark hair. "Damn it," he muttered. "He's using my father as bait. He knows someone would come for him."

"That doesn't mean we can leave him there," I said quickly, stepping closer. "He's your father, Cain. We have to try."

He looked at me then, his eyes filled with something I couldn't quite place—gratitude, fear, and something more profound. "I know," he said softly. "And we will. I'm not leaving him behind. Not again."

I placed a hand on his arm, grounding him. "We'll figure it out," I said. "Together."

At that moment, the door opened, and Dante stepped in, his expression cautious as his gaze shifted between us.

"Did I interrupt something?" he asked, his voice carefully neutral.

Cain shook his head, stepping away from me. "We have a lead," he said curtly. "My father's alive. He's in Merewick."

Dante's eyebrows shot up. "Merewick?" He glanced at me, then back at Cain. "And you trust this vision?"

Cain's jaw tightened, and I quickly stepped in. "It's not about trust, Dante. It's about taking action. If Cain's father is there, we can't waste time doubting it."

Dante nodded slowly, though his expression was unreadable. "Then we should start planning."

Cain's gaze lingered on me for a moment longer before he turned to Dante. "Agreed. We leave at first light."

The conversation between Cain and Dante shifted into strategies and logistics, their voices low but firm as they hashed out the plan. I stood by the fireplace, running my fingers absently along the edge of the mantel. The tension between us all was palpable, though the temporary ceasefire seemed to hold for now. But I could feel the storm brewing just beneath the surface.

"I'm going to check on the horses," Cain said suddenly, his tone clipped. He stood, adjusting his coat before heading for the door. He paused for a moment, his silver-blue eyes flicking to mine, then back to Dante, before pulling the door open and stepping outside. The sound of it shutting behind him felt louder than it should have, leaving me alone with Dante.

The silence that followed was thick and uncomfortable. Dante's eyes turned to me almost immediately, his brow furrowing in thought. "So, is that it then?" he asked, his voice quieter than usual but heavy with an edge. "You're choosing Cain?"

I blinked, taken aback by the question. "It's not like that," I said quickly, shaking my head. "Dante, you lied to me."

His jaw tightened, and his shoulders stiffened as though bracing for a blow. "I know," he admitted, his voice low, almost a whisper. "But I had my reasons."

"Reasons?" I scoffed, crossing my arms. "You lied to me in a way that cut me to my core. I opened up to you. I trusted you, Dante, and you couldn't even be honest with me. About who you are, about what you've done."

He flinched, his eyes darting away from mine. "I didn't want to hurt you," he said finally. "But it wasn't just about me."

"And the dark magic?" I pressed, my tone softer but no less firm. "I know about it, Dante. I know what you're capable of."

His head snapped up at that, his dark eyes narrowing. "Who told you?"

"It doesn't matter who," I said. "The point is, I know. And it scares me, Dante. It scares me because I don't know where your loyalties lie, and I don't know what you're capable of doing—to me, to Cain."

His expression shifted, softening, as he took a hesitant step toward me. "I would never hurt you," he said, his voice steady and earnest. "Or Cain, for that matter."

I wanted to believe him. I wanted to believe the boy I'd gotten to know back in Ashmoor, the one who made me laugh and who felt like an escape from the pressures of this journey. But the pieces weren't adding up, and the cracks in his story left room for doubt.

"Then what's your plan, Dante?" I asked. "What are you even doing here if it's not to hurt us?"

He hesitated, his gaze dropping to the floor as though searching for the right words. "My father," he said finally, his voice almost breaking. "He had plans for me. Plans I wanted no part of."

"What kind of plans?" I asked, taking a step closer.

He sighed heavily, dragging a hand through his dark hair. "He was going to use me," he said, bitterness lacing his tone. "When he sent me to Verdanis, it wasn't so I could start a new life or learn about the Mystics. It was to put me in the palace guard. Once I was there, he planned to compel me—use his dark magic to control me—and make me... kill the queen."

My breath hitched, the weight of his words settling like a stone in my chest. "Kill the queen?" I whispered.

Dante nodded, his expression grim. "He wanted revenge, Everly. Revenge against the Mystics, against everyone who cast him out. And I was supposed to be his weapon. His way back into Erynvale."

"Then why are you here?" I asked. "Why not just stay with him if that's what he wanted?"

His gaze met mine, and for the first time, I saw something raw and vulnerable in his eyes. "Because I didn't want that life," he said simply. "I wanted to stop him. To stop all of this."

"And Cain?" I asked softly. "Where does he fit into this?"

"I wanted to get to know him," Dante admitted. "To understand what it's like to have family—real family. I wanted to try, Everly. But everything went wrong when my father kidnapped Cain's father. He forced my hand, made me choose between him and... this." He gestured around us, his voice breaking on the last word.

I stared at him, my heart torn between anger and pity. His story was complicated and messy, just like everything else on this journey. But there was something in his eyes, something earnest and desperate, that made me believe him. At least, I wanted to.

"This mission was never supposed to be about me," he said finally, his voice low. "But now it is. And I'm trying to make it right, Everly. I swear to you, I'm trying."

I didn't respond, my thoughts swirling too fast to form words. The sound of the door creaking open made us both turn, and Cain stepped back into the room. His eyes flicked between us, suspicion clear on his face.

"What's going on?" he asked, his voice sharp.

"Nothing," I said quickly, stepping back from Dante. "We were just... talking."

Cain strode toward the wooden table in the center of the room and unrolled a large, weathered map, its edges curling with age. The firelight flickered over the parchment, casting shifting shadows over the drawn mountains and winding rivers. His finger traced a path past Doren, beyond the hills that bordered the kingdom's farthest reaches.

"There," he said, his voice firm, tapping a spot at the very edge of the map. "Merewick."

I stepped closer, my breath catching as I took in the distance. Merewick wasn't just far—it was beyond the kingdom's final strongholds, past lands that had long been abandoned to wilderness and ruin. "That's weeks away," I murmured.

"At least two, if the weather holds and we travel light," Cain confirmed, his expression unreadable. "The mountains, Valthorne Ridge, will be our first obstacle. There's a pass here—" he pointed to a narrow gap between jagged peaks "—but it's slow-going, and we'll need to be prepared for unpredictable conditions."

Dante exhaled sharply, shaking his head. "This is a suicide mission."

Cain's gaze snapped to him. "Then stay here," he said flatly. "No one's forcing you."

Dante rolled his eyes but didn't argue. I could feel the tension between them tightening again, but my focus remained on the map. Merewick. The name still sent a shiver down my spine.

"We'll need supplies," I said, straightening. "Everything we can carry. Food, medical kits, weapons."

Cain nodded. "We'll take whatever's left here in Doren, but it won't be enough. There are small villages along the way—we'll have to barter or hunt."

"Then we should get moving," I said, trying to quell the nervous energy building inside me.

We spent the next few hours gathering what we could from the remains of Doren. Canned goods, preserved meats, spare blankets—anything useful was packed into sturdy leather satchels. From the abandoned houses, we scavenged extra cloaks, a few serviceable weapons, and old maps that might help once we left known roads.

As we stood in the hollowed-out ruins of the town square, the wind howling through empty streets, I glanced back at the place that had been our temporary refuge. A town emptied of its people, a ghost of what once was. And now, we were leaving it behind for something even more uncertain.

Cain adjusted the strap of his pack and swung up onto his horse, glancing down at us. "This isn't just a rescue mission," he reminded us. "Whatever's happening in Merewick… It's bigger than my father. It's bigger than all of us."

I met his gaze, gripping the reins of my own horse. "Then we'd better not fail."

Dante sighed dramatically, climbing into his own saddle. "Great. Another impossible quest with terrible odds. You sure you two aren't just making this up for the thrill of it?"

Cain didn't dignify that with a response. Instead, he turned his horse toward the dark horizon. With one last glance at Doren, I followed.

We rode into the unknown, the mountains looming ahead like silent sentinels of whatever awaited us beyond.

Chapter 30

Cain

The road to Valthorne Ridge was treacherous, a twisting artery of rock and ice carving its way through the spine of the land. These mountains had once been a natural boundary, a fortress of jagged cliffs and sheer drops that separated Erynvale from the Blighted Lands beyond. Now, they were little more than a gauntlet, a place where the wind howled like a dying beast and the air grew thinner with every step upward.

The ridge itself loomed ahead, its peaks rising like broken teeth against the storm-heavy sky. Gray stone jutted out at sharp angles, fractured by time and weather, with patches of snow clinging stubbornly to the crags. The higher we climbed, the more the trees thinned, their gnarled branches reaching out like skeletal fingers toward the clouds. What little vegetation remained was hardy—tufts of dark moss clinging to boulders, wind-bent shrubs twisting from the cracks in the stone.

The trail was barely a trail at all, just a worn path carved by time and the passage of desperate travelers. It zigzagged up the ridge in narrow, uneven steps, lined with loose shale that threatened to give way beneath our horses' hooves. Even the animals seemed tense, their ears flicking at every gust of wind, muscles coiled as though expecting the earth to drop away beneath them.

I adjusted the straps of the saddle bags, feeling the familiar weight of supplies shifting as my horse navigated the uneven path. We carried only what we could afford—nothing more, nothing less. The journey ahead would demand every resource we had, and the mountains would not be forgiving.

Each of us bore our Starfire sword, its hilt warm to the touch, bound to us by magic older than the kingdom itself. The blade rested against my hip, a constant presence, its power humming faintly beneath my fingers. I also carried a pair of daggers, sheathed at my belt—small, fast weapons, their edges honed to cut more than just flesh if the need arose.

Our rations were packed into sturdy leather satchels strapped behind our saddles—dried meats, hard cheese, oatcakes, and a handful of root vegetables scavenged from the ruins of Doren. It wasn't much, but it would keep us moving. Water was the greater concern. Streams in these parts were scarce, and we had only what we carried in our flasks, filled from the last clean source we'd passed. Every drop had to be rationed.

Tucked within my saddle bag was a small but essential healing kit in case neither Dante nor I would be able to use our healing magic —bandages, salves, and two vials of concentrated fae elixir. The potion was powerful enough to mend a wound, but it came with a price—energy drained, magic taxed. It wasn't a solution; it was a last resort.

The mountain air cut through our layers, sharp as a blade. We wore thick woolen cloaks, fastened with the insignia of the royal guard, but they only did so much against the biting wind. Beneath them, our black combat tunics and reinforced leather armor offered protection but little warmth. By nightfall, we'd need fire, or the cold would seep into our bones.

Our camping gear was minimal—a flint and steel, a single iron pot, and tightly rolled bedrolls secured to our saddles. We would sleep when we could, wherever we could, though stopping too long in unknown territory was a risk in itself. This was no leisurely journey. Every step forward took us deeper into the unknown, into a place where the map became little more than a guess.

Dante shifted in his saddle beside me, rolling his shoulders. "I hate this silence," he muttered, voice barely audible over the wind.

I agreed, though I didn't say it. Silence meant something was wrong. A place like this should have been alive with the sounds of wind in the trees, the scurry of small animals, and the distant cries of birds. But there was nothing. Just the steady crunch of hooves on frost-hardened earth and the low creak of leather saddles.

Everly rode ahead, her fingers tight on Spirra's reins. She hadn't spoken much since we left Doren, and I knew the journey was wearing her down. Her form was stiff in the saddle, every shift in her seat a sign of growing discomfort. But she hadn't complained. Not once.

I nudged my horse forward, closing the space between us. "You need to adjust your weight," I said, my voice carrying over the wind. "Let the horse move beneath you. You're fighting her every step."

She glanced at me, her green eyes catching the faint light that struggled through the storm-heavy clouds. "I'm trying," she muttered.

I reached across, adjusting the way her foot sat in the stirrup. "Loosen here. Keep your knees steady, but don't lock them. The ridge is worse ahead."

Everly exhaled, adjusting her grip. "Thanks," she murmured, barely audible.

Dante, of course, wasn't about to let a moment pass without comment. "Look at that. Cain, the master of horse riding and tender encouragement. What's next? You gonna read her bedtime stories, too?"

I shot him a warning look, but Everly beat me to it. "If you'd like to switch horses, Dante, be my guest," she snapped. "I'd love to watch you get thrown into the mud."

Dante grinned. "Tempting, Angel Eyes. But I think I'll stay right here."

Everly muttered something under her breath, but I didn't catch it.

Ahead, the ridge sharpened into an even steeper ascent, the path narrowing to a thread of earth between two sheer drops. The wind howled through the gaps in the rock, carrying with it a whispering sound that prickled at the edges of my senses. Not words, but something close.

I reined in my horse and raised a hand, signaling for a halt. Dante and Everly obeyed without question, their hands instinctively drifting toward their weapons.

The air felt wrong. Heavy.

I turned my head slightly, listening. The wind had carried something unnatural, something I couldn't quite place. Not a voice. Not an animal.

Something else.

Everly's breath was shallow beside me, her fingers tightening around her reins. "Cain," she whispered. "Do you hear that?"

I nodded once.

Ahead, beyond the subsequent rise, something waited. Something that did not belong in the world we knew.

I slid my hand to the hilt of my sword, feeling the pulse of its magic against my palm.

We had reached Valthorne Ridge. And we were not alone.

The path had become too steep for the horses to climb. Loose shale slid beneath their hooves, and the narrow trail ahead wound upward into a jagged incline, bordered by sheer drops on either side. The air had grown colder, and the wind cut through the pass like a blade, howling between the craggy peaks. I pulled my horse to a stop and glanced back at Everly and Dante.

"We go on foot from here," I ordered, dismounting. "The horses can make it, but not with our weight on their backs. We lead them the rest of the way."

Dante groaned but obeyed, swinging off his saddle with a bit too much ease. Everly followed suit, adjusting Spirra's reins as she landed lightly on her feet. Her breath was visible now, small clouds forming in the thin, icy air.

The ridge ahead was barely a trail—more of a crumbling edge carved into the mountainside. It twisted alongside the cliffs in uneven steps, portions of it eroded away by years of wind and rain. Just beyond it, I could see the first entrance to a cave system. The dark maw of stone yawned open like a waiting beast, and though I couldn't yet see inside, I knew it would provide shelter—and possibly a way through. If the caves were connected, we could use them to navigate the mountain instead of braving the highest, most treacherous peaks.

But something was wrong.

The feeling had been gnawing at me for miles, a presence lingering just out of Sight. The air carried more than just cold and wind—it carried weight, an unnatural stillness between gusts. The silence felt... occupied. As if something moved when we weren't looking. Something just beyond reach, its steps quiet, its breath hidden beneath the howling wind.

I clenched my jaw, keeping my senses sharp as I gestured toward the ridge. "Stay close to the rock wall and watch your footing. One wrong step and you won't be getting back up."

Dante muttered something under his breath, but I ignored him, adjusting my hold on my horse's reins before starting forward. The animals were tense, their ears flicking, their movements hesitant. They felt it too.

The trail narrowed almost immediately. We had to walk single file, pressing close to the rough stone of the mountainside while carefully guiding the horses behind us. Below, the valley stretched into misty darkness, a sheer drop of nothingness that disappeared into the unseen depths. The wind carried loose pebbles over the edge, and I watched them vanish, swallowed by the abyss below.

Everly kept her focus on the path, her jaw tight as she moved carefully along the uneven ground. Dante, despite his usual arrogance, was taking it seriously as well—until the path crumbled beneath his feet.

It happened in a split second. The loose rock gave way, and suddenly, Dante was falling.

I reacted before I could think.

My hand shot out, seizing his wrist as he plunged over the edge. His weight nearly pulled me down with him, my boots skidding against the unstable trail. My muscles burned as I gritted my teeth, using every ounce of strength to hold him.

Dante's fingers dug into my forearm, his violet eyes wide with something I hadn't seen in him before—fear. He wasn't smirking now. He wasn't making jokes. He was holding on for his life.

Everly scrambled forward, gripping the back of my cloak to anchor me as I pulled Dante up inch by inch. The wind roared around us, cold and merciless, but I didn't let go. With a final heave, I dragged him back onto the ridge, and we collapsed against the stone, breathless.

Dante let out a ragged laugh, rolling onto his back, staring up at the sky. "Well... that was fun."

I shot him a glare. "You're an idiot."

He sat up, shaking dust from his hands. “And yet, you saved me.” I didn’t answer. I just stood, dusted off my coat, and pressed forward.

We had bigger problems.

The cave entrance loomed ahead, its dark depths stretching beyond Sight. Whatever was following us was still out there, watching. Waiting.

Chapter 31

Everly

My hands were still shaking. No matter how many times I flexed them, how hard I squeezed the leather of Spirra's reins, the adrenaline wouldn't drain from my system. The moment Dante's foot slipped, time had collapsed into something sharp and unrelenting. The image of him dangling over the edge, fingers barely clinging to Cain's wrist, was burned into my mind. The drop beneath him had been endless—a dark abyss swallowing the valley far below. If Cain hadn't reacted as fast as he did, Dante would be dead. Just like that. Gone.

And yet, somehow, despite having almost plummeted to his death, Dante had laughed it off. Like it was just another stupid mistake, another joke in his endless arsenal of deflections. I wanted to punch him for being so reckless or hug him just to confirm that he was still solid, still here.

But beneath the residual panic from the near fall, something else had settled into my chest, cold and persistent. Something was following us. I didn't know how I knew it—only that I did. It wasn't just paranoia. It wasn't my nerves playing tricks on me. The feeling had started long before Dante slipped, but now it was worse, pressing against the edges of my senses like an itch I couldn't reach.

It was the silence. The way the wind howled through the crags but carried no echoes of life. No birds, no insects, no distant rustling of unseen creatures. Just emptiness. Watching. Waiting.

I pulled my cloak tighter around me, trying to shake the feeling as we reached the entrance of the cave. The yawning mouth of stone was impossibly dark, stretching into the mountain like the throat of some slumbering beast. I swallowed hard, forcing myself to focus on the present. I had bigger problems than the unsettling feeling of being watched.

Like the tension crackling between Cain and Dante.

I'd noticed it before—Cain's clipped tone when addressing him, the way his eyes would narrow just slightly whenever Dante spoke. But after what just happened, that tension had morphed into something heavier, something more personal. Cain had saved him, but it hadn't softened anything between them. If anything, it had sharpened whatever lay beneath the surface.

I stole a glance at Cain as he adjusted his cloak, his movements precise and controlled. His jaw was tight, his mouth set in a grim line as he led his horse toward the cave's entrance. His emotions were locked down like a fortress, but there was something there—something simmering just beneath his skin.

Dante, for his part, wasn't making it easier. If anything, he was pushing Cain on purpose, flashing that cocky, infuriating grin despite everything. It could be his way of coping, or he simply enjoyed pushing buttons. Either way, Cain wasn't rising to the bait. He was ignoring him entirely, and somehow, that was worse.

I exhaled slowly, my breath misting in the cold air. How much longer can they keep this tension between them from boiling over? And then there was Cain and me.

My stomach twisted as the memory of last night flickered through my mind.

The firelight danced across the walls of our shared room. The moment my robe slipped open. The way his gaze had darkened, lingering just long enough to make my pulse stutter. The air had felt different then—charged with something neither of us had acknowledged. Something I wasn't ready to accept.

But I couldn’t deny it anymore.

I felt something for Cain.

I didn't know what it was—not really. Attraction? Definitely. Something deeper? Maybe. It was confusing, infuriating, and so much more dangerous than I wanted to admit. Because Cain was not the kind of man who let people in. He was a wall of steel and discipline, and I had no business trying to break through it.

And yet, I wanted to.

I shook my head, as if the motion could dislodge the thoughts completely. This is not the time. I had too much to worry about already—surviving this mission, figuring out my magic, avoiding whatever lurked in the shadows of the mountains. The last thing I needed was to get tangled up in my feelings for a man who probably saw me as nothing more than a burden.

And then there was Dante.

Dante, who had lied to me. Who had betrayed my trust? And yet, somehow, I still couldn't bring myself to hate him.

I had tried. I wanted to. I wanted to shove him into a box labeled traitor and never look back. But the problem with Dante was that, despite everything, he was still Dante—the same man who had made me laugh when I wanted to scream, the same man who had shown me kindness when no one else had.

And now, after seeing the fear in his eyes when he almost fell, after watching Cain pull him back from the brink, I felt something else for him. Something I didn’t expect.

Pity.

He had no one. Not really. His father was… well, his father. His mother never mentally recovered from his father's dark magic, and even his place in the royal guard had been a favor, not an earned position. He acted like the world was a game, like nothing could touch him, but I had seen the cracks in that act before. Now, after nearly losing him, those cracks were impossible to ignore.

I sighed, rubbing my temples. This was too much.

Too much to process. Too much to feel all at once.

All I knew was that, at some point, I was going to have to face these feelings—these tangled, messy emotions that had somehow woven themselves into my mind like a net.

But not now.

Now, I had to survive the night.

Cain had already stepped into the cave, his sword drawn, the blade gleaming faintly in the dim light. Dante followed, unusually quiet, his usual bravado muted by something unreadable in his expression.

I took a steadying breath, forcing my thoughts into order, and followed them inside.

The cave swallowed us whole.

The moment we stepped inside, the wind died. The outside world—the endless sky, the howling air, the towering peaks—vanished behind a curtain of darkness. The silence was immediate, absolute. Even our footsteps felt muted, absorbed by the cold, damp stone beneath us.

The entrance had opened into a vast chamber, its ceiling arching high above us, hidden in shadows too thick for our eyes to pierce. The walls glistened with faint traces of mineral deposits, slick with condensation, giving the cave an eerie shimmer when the light from the entrance still touched it. But the deeper we went, the more that light faded, swallowed by the labyrinth of tunnels stretching before us like the veins of a slumbering beast.

Cain took the lead, as always, his posture tense, his head tilted slightly as if he were listening for something beyond our hearing. Dante walked a few steps behind him, his fingers occasionally grazing the damp stone, his violet eyes flicking between the tunnels as if mapping every turn in his head. I lingered closer to Dante than Cain, overseeing both of them, trying to absorb the confidence in their movements while fighting the claustrophobic sensation crawling up my spine.

The walls narrowed as we moved further in. The tunnels twisted and wove around each other, some dropping sharply downward into unseen depths, others curving into shadowed passages that led deeper into the belly of the mountain. The air was thick, damp, and tinged with something earthy—moss, stone, and the metallic bite of mineral-rich water.

It felt ancient. Unmapped. Alive.

My breath came shallow, my pulse quickening with every step. "How do we even know where we're going?" I finally asked, my voice hushed against the weight of the cave.

Cain reached into his saddlebag and pulled out three fist-sized quartz crystals. Their pale surfaces caught the dim light, smooth and slightly cloudy, yet untouched by time. He held one up in his palm and exhaled slowly, flexing his fingers as a faint glow began to emanate from his skin.

Then, magic happened.

A soft, golden light pulsed from Cain's hand, weaving into the crystal like threads of sunlight sinking into glass. The quartz flared to life, its interior filling with a warm, steady glow that cast soft, flickering light across the cave walls.

I inhaled sharply, completely captivated. "That's… incredible," I breathed.

Cain ignored me, already reaching for the next crystal. One by one, he repeated the process, infusing each stone with his magic, until three luminous orbs of quartz floated in his hands, their golden light pushing back the oppressive darkness.

But he wasn't done.

"Dante," he said, his voice steady but expectant. "Pull the moisture from the walls."

Dante blinked, then smirked. "Finally, I get to show off." He stepped forward, rolling his shoulders before holding out both hands, palms facing the stone. A moment passed, then another, before the first shimmer of movement stirred in the air.

Droplets of water beaded on the cave walls, trembling before peeling away in thin, rippling streams. The moisture gathered, weaving together like silver threads, until it merged into the air, forming three distinct orbs of water that hovered between us.

I stared.

It was mesmerizing—watching water bend to his will, the way it swirled and pulsed as though alive, catching and refracting the glow of the quartz like tiny captured stars.

Cain, unfazed, reached out and placed each glowing crystal inside the three floating spheres of water. The moment the quartz touched the liquid, the light diffused through them, casting refracted patterns across the cave walls like rippling sunlight through a pool.

Then, with a flick of his fingers, Cain levitated them.

The orbs lifted, rising to hover in the air around us, their glow bobbing gently as though obeying some silent command. Suspended in liquid, the quartz shimmered, its light dancing through the tunnels, illuminating our path in golden waves.

I had never seen anything like it.

"You—" I turned to Cain, completely breathless. "You just—"

He glanced at me, unimpressed. "Basic spell work," he said flatly, as if he hadn't just bent the laws of nature to his will.

"Basic? That's basic?" I sputtered. I turned to Dante, who was clearly enjoying my reaction, his smirk deepening.

“I’d call it a bit more than basic,” Dante admitted, though he shot Cain a playful glare. “But I suppose when you’re the royal golden boy, even levitating enchanted orbs of water is mundane.”

Cain ignored him, his focus already back on the tunnels. “They’ll stay with us,” he said, nodding to the floating lights. “They’ll move when I move. We have our path.”

I was awestruck.

Not just at the magic, but at him—the way he carried it so easily, like it was second nature. I had known Cain was skilled, but I had never seen him wield magic like this before. I had assumed he was just another hardened warrior, all steel and strategy, but this? This was something else entirely.

Something powerful.

Something… beautiful.

I swallowed hard, forcing my attention back to the cave. “Right,” I muttered. “Let’s—uh, let’s keep moving.”

Cain strode forward, the glowing orbs drifting alongside him, casting our shadows long against the cavern walls. Dante walked beside me, smirking as if he knew exactly what was going through my head.

I shoved my thoughts aside.

The magic, the tension between them, the unspoken things lingering in my chest—none of it mattered.

Not yet.

As we progressed, the feeling of being watched grew stronger.

The cave opened into a massive cavern, its ceiling vanishing into the darkness above. The walls were lined with jagged rock formations, glistening with moisture, and the air carried a faint metallic tang—like iron and damp earth. But what made my stomach twist wasn’t the sheer scale of the space.

It was the five tunnels stretching ahead of us.

Each one was tall enough for us and the horses to walk through comfortably, their openings gaping like open mouths, waiting. Each one led somewhere different. And we had no idea which one would lead us forward—or to our deaths.

Cain stopped, his jaw tightening as he studied the pathways. He glanced back at me, his silver-blue eyes sharp and expectant. "Which way?"

I blinked, gripping Spirra's reins tighter. "You're asking me?"

He nodded. "Use your Sight."

My stomach lurched. "I don't—I mean, I'm not—" I exhaled sharply, shaking my head. "Cain, I don't even know if I can do that. I don't have control over it. What if I get it wrong?"

"You won't," he said, firm as ever. "You're the only one who can do this. So do it."

I swallowed hard.

Dante must have noticed my hesitation because he stepped closer, his voice gentler than usual. "Everly, you don't have to—"

Cain cut him off. "She does. This is what the queen saw in her. If she doesn't start trusting herself now, when will she?"

I clenched my fists, my breath unsteady. He was right. And I hated that he was right.

Slowly, I closed my eyes and focused on the deep, thrumming pull inside my chest—the strange, invisible thread that had always led me toward moments of knowledge I shouldn't have had. I reached for it, even though I wasn't sure what I was doing, willing myself to see.

At first, nothing.

Then, like ink spilling across a blank page, the visions came.

I focused on the path to the far left of where we stood. The moment my mind touched this path, a suffocating pressure closed around my throat. I saw us moving forward, deeper into the tunnel, only for the air to grow thicker—a gray, swirling mist rising from the ground. At first, it seemed harmless. But then Dante gasped, clutching his throat, his eyes widening in terror. Cain reached for his sword, but his movements were sluggish, like he was sinking into deep water.

The fog seeped into our lungs.

I watched, helpless, as our bodies collapsed, one by one, vanishing into the mist. There was no fight. No chance for escape. Just… silence.

With a shiver down my spine, I switched my focus to the second path to the middle left. A flash of heat scorched my vision, and suddenly, we were running. This tunnel led into a chasm, and something was down there—something huge.

I saw fire burst from the darkness, lighting up the cavern like a forge. Massive, reptilian eyes glowed through the smoke, and a low, guttural growl reverberated through the stone. A wyrm—a creature from legend, its body coiled through the tunnels, its scales like molten obsidian, its mouth opening to unleash fire hotter than the sun.

Cain grabbed my arm, shouting something, but I barely heard him over the roar as the flames swallowed us whole.

The third path I focused on came into view. Cold. Endless cold.

This path led deep into the mountain, where the walls shimmered with ice, an unnatural perfection. At first, it seemed safe. We walked carefully, our breath fogging in the frigid air.

Then the ice moved.

From the frozen walls, figures emerged—translucent, ethereal, wraiths with hollow eyes. Their whispers filled the tunnel, clawing at my mind, pulling me down into a sea of memories that weren't my own.

Dante screamed.

I turned and saw him sinking into the ice, his body frozen mid-motion, his eyes wide with horror. Cain swung his sword, but the blade passed through the wraiths like smoke.

I tried to run, but my legs wouldn't move.

The ice claimed us.

The fourth path to the middle right was darkness. Pure, impenetrable darkness. We stepped forward, and suddenly, there was no light. Not even the faintest glimmer of our magic. The orbs Cain had created? Gone.

I reached for Dante, but my hands grasped nothing.

Cain's voice called out, sharp and commanding—but distant. Too distant. I spun, my heart hammering in my chest, but I couldn't see. I couldn't hear them anymore.

I was alone.

And then, something breathed against my neck.

Finally, focusing on the fifth and last path. This one was different.

At first, the vision was unclear—just shadows shifting along the tunnel walls. Then, I saw ourselves walking forward, the floating quartz orbs still intact, their glow uninterrupted. The air remained cold, but not freezing. The tunnel twisted but did not narrow.

And nothing waited for us in the dark.

It wasn't safe, but it was the best choice.

I gasped, snapping back into the present. My legs were shaking, my heart slamming against my ribs. The cave was exactly as we had left it, but now, I felt the weight of the wrong choices pressing against me.

Cain's voice cut through my haze. "What did you see?"

I took a deep breath, steadying myself. "The first path will kill us with poison. The second leads to a wyrm—one that breathes fire. The third… the third is worse. The ice there isn't just ice. It's alive." I swallowed hard. "The fourth path… it swallows the light. And once you enter, you never find your way back."

Cain's expression remained unreadable, but I could see the calculation behind his eyes. "And the last?"

I hesitated, glancing toward the far-right tunnel. "It's not safe. But it's the only path that doesn't guarantee death."

He studied me for a long moment before nodding. Without another word, he turned toward the far-right tunnel, leading his horse forward.

I let out a breath I hadn't realized I was holding.

Dante placed a hand on my shoulder, squeezing lightly. "That was incredible," he murmured.

I wasn't sure if I agreed. It had felt like drowning, like peeling back something inside me that I wasn't sure I could close again. But when I looked at Cain, at the quiet trust in his eyes, something inside me settled.

I had chosen right.

And now, all we had to do was survive.

Dante let out a low whistle, shaking his head as he glanced toward the second tunnel—the one where I had seen the wyrm. "Hold on a second," he said, folding his arms. "A wyrm? As in, actual wyrms? You're telling me those things still exist?"

Cain adjusted his grip on his horse's reins, his expression grim. "If it's in these mountains, it never left."

Dante scoffed. "I thought they were myths. You know—scary stories for kids, relics from the old world, things that were supposed to be long dead." He gestured vaguely toward the tunnel. "You're saying they're real?"

Cain exhaled sharply, his eyes flicking to me for the briefest moment before settling back on Dante. "They were never myths."

Something in his voice made me pause. I had never heard him talk about something with that much certainty before—not just as fact, but as if he had always known, as if it was ingrained in him.

Dante noticed too. His smirk faded, his brows pulling together. “You’re serious.”

Cain nodded, gesturing toward the walls of the cavern. “These mountains weren’t just a natural barrier. They were a designed one. A fortress of stone and magic, built to protect the gods of old—the ones who once resided in our kingdom, long before men ruled these lands.”

A chill ran through me. I had heard of the old gods before—whispers of names lost to time, deities that had once been revered but had long since faded into obscurity. But Cain spoke as if it wasn't just a legend. As if it were true.

Dante frowned. “The gods? The same ones they were still worshiping back in Doren?”

Cain gave a short nod. “Some cities still hold on to the old faith, even though most of the kingdom has long forgotten them. But those temples, those relics—they weren’t built for nothing.” His voice darkened. “The gods were real. They lived, they ruled, and then, they died.”

I swallowed. “What happened to them?”

Cain’s gaze flicked toward the tunnel where the wyrm waited, his expression unreadable. “No one knows for sure. Some say they were betrayed, others say they simply faded, their power drained until they became nothing but echoes in the stones. But whatever the truth is, these mountains were meant to deter outside fae from entering the land of the gods uninvited. This was their final barrier.”

A heavy silence settled between us. The idea that the mountains themselves had once been constructed defenses, not just land shaped by nature, sent a shiver through me.

Dante let out a low, thoughtful hum. “So, what you’re saying is... something’s still here.”

Cain's jaw tightened. "Something was left behind."

I felt a slow dread creep up my spine. If these tunnels had once been the last line of defense for the gods, then whatever lingered in the shadows... was never meant to let anything through.

Chapter 32

Cain

The path was cold, damp, and endless.

Everly had chosen the safest route, but that didn't mean it was welcoming. The tunnel stretched deep into the mountain, its ceiling narrowing in places, forcing us to walk single file. The stone walls were slick with moisture, beads of water gathering in thin rivulets that dripped from the uneven ceiling. The air was thick and heavy, the kind that settled in your lungs like a weight.

There was no way to tell how long we had been walking. No light from the outside, no shifting shadows to gauge the time. Just the steady drip… drip… drip of water against stone and the quiet shuffling of hooves as our horses carefully picked their way forward. The glowing quartz orbs still hovered above us, their golden light reflecting off the wet cavern walls and casting shimmering patterns across the rock.

It should have been silent. Instead, Dante started whistling. The sharp, careless tune bounced off the walls, filling the tunnel with sound where there should have been none. It was almost mocking in its lightness, a casual defiance of the weight pressing down on us. My teeth clenched.

"Would you stop that?" I snapped, my voice cutting through the narrow space.

Dante didn't even turn around. He just smirked, continuing to lead his horse along the path like he hadn't heard me. "What? Too much for your royal ears?"

I exhaled slowly through my nose, forcing myself to keep my temper in check. "We don't know what else is in these caves. Making unnecessary noise is asking for trouble."

Dante let out an exaggerated sigh. "Right. Because if something is lurking in here, they definitely weren't going to notice us before I whistled." He waved a hand toward the floating orbs of literal magic glowing above us. "You're walking around with floating lights, Cain. We're not exactly subtle."

"That's different," I growled.

"Oh, of course," he drawled. "Your magic lights are necessary. But my whistling? Unacceptable."

The tension between us was thick enough to choke on. I hadn't forgotten how close he had come to falling off the ridge earlier. Hadn't forgotten how, in that one fleeting moment, I had grabbed his wrist and saved him from plummeting into the abyss. And I knew he hadn't forgotten either. Because Dante had barely acknowledged it.

No gratitude. No admission of how close he had come to death. Just another joke, another smirk, like it hadn't mattered. Like I hadn't mattered. That irritated me more than it should have.

"You don't take anything seriously, do you?" I muttered.

Dante turned slightly, his violet eyes glinting in the dim light. "And you take everything too seriously."

I clenched my jaw. I knew this wouldn't end well. It never did with him. There was too much history between us, too many things left unsaid. We could tolerate each other when we had to, but it was always a thin, fragile thing—one wrong step, and it snapped. And I was already at my limit. Everly's voice cut through the tension before it could get worse.

"Would you two stop?" she said, her tone tired. "We're in the middle of a mountain, in a dark, ancient tunnel, following a path that I saw could still kill us if we make one wrong turn. So maybe, just maybe, can we not do this right now?"

Dante shrugged. "I wasn't the one who started it."

I stared at him, resisting the urge to grab him by the collar and shake the smugness right out of him. But Everly had a point. We had bigger things to worry about than our personal grudges. I exhaled sharply and turned away, focusing on the path ahead of me.

The tunnel sloped downward now, the air growing cooler with every step. The sound of dripping water echoed ahead, but there was something off about it. The way it hit the stone didn't sound random. It was too rhythmic, almost patterned. I didn't like it.

But for now, I kept moving. Because one thing was sure—this cave wasn't just empty stone and forgotten history.

The tunnel finally widened into an open space, a hollow carved into the mountain like a natural refuge. The walls curved around three sides, shielding us from the ever-present draft, and the ceiling stretched high enough that our voices didn't feel like they were pressing back down on us. It wasn't much, but it was enough.

I turned to the others. "We make camp here."

No one argued. We had been walking for hours—maybe longer. Without the sun or sky, there was no telling how much time had passed. The weight of exhaustion clung to all of us, sinking into our bones. Even I felt it, a dull ache settling in my legs and shoulders. And if I thought it, Everly definitely thought it.

She didn't say anything, but I caught the subtle signs—how she leaned against the cavern wall for a breath longer than necessary, how her fingers trembled slightly when she unbuckled her bedroll. She was exhausted, but she wouldn't admit it.

I wouldn't call her out on it. But I would make sure she rested. We set up camp quickly. I gathered a small circle of stones for a fire pit, arranging them in the center of our clearing while Dante spread out the bedrolls. Everly pulled her pack apart, shifting through supplies while Spirra and the other horses nudged at the stone floor, their tired huffs filling the quiet space.

Once the fire was lit, I pulled a small pot from my saddlebag and placed it over the flames. From another bag, I pulled out a few unlabeled cans and pried one open with the small knife at my hip. The scent of beef stew hit me almost immediately—rich, meaty, and just enough spice to remind me of old meals cooked over real kitchen hearths.

Dante leaned over, eyeing the contents as I dumped the stew into the pot. "Lucky pull," he commented.

I frowned, grabbing another can and popping the lid. Same stew. A third one—identical. I exhaled through my nose. "Looks like all the cans are the same."

Dante let out a low laugh. "Well, at least we won't have to fight over favorites."

I stirred the stew as it warmed, the thick broth bubbling gently. At least it was something warm. Something filling.

Dante took that as his cue to work, moving to the far side of the cavern. He rolled his shoulders, stretched his fingers, and then lifted his hands, palms upward. The air shifted, cool and damp, as moisture peeled away from the cavern walls, drawn toward his open fingers. The droplets wove together, twisting and merging until he had gathered enough to fill several canteens.

He handed me mine without a word, then walked over to the horses. From his own supplies, he pulled a second pot, setting it before the animals before filling it with another stream of purified water. Spirra drank first, her ears flicking toward Everly, who had settled onto her bedroll and was slowly peeling off her boots.

She sighed as she set them aside, pressing her fingers into the sore arches of her feet. I glanced at her, watching how her brow furrowed in relief, how she flexed her toes and rubbed away the aches from the long trek. I didn't let myself stare—not for long, anyway.

Dante, however, had no such restraint.

"You know," he said casually, running a damp hand through his own dark hair, letting the remaining water drip down his arms and soak into his clothes. "I could help with that."

Everly blinked up at him. "With what?"

Dante smirked. "Washing off the dirt and grime." He stretched his fingers, droplets forming at his fingertips. "It's an easy trick. Quick. Cleans better than cold cavern water."

Something in my chest tightened. Everly hesitated, glancing at her own hands, her palms still streaked with dust from gripping the reins all day. I could see the temptation flicker across her face.

No.

I didn't know why the thought was so immediate, so visceral, but I hated the idea of Dante touching her like that. The image of his magic, cool and smooth, running over her skin—his hands skimming over her arms, her face, undoing the exhaustion in slow, practiced motions—it made my blood heat in a way I didn't like.

Because I knew exactly how Dante worked. How he charmed his way into people's trust. How he could get too close, too fast, with nothing more than a grin and a well-placed offer.

I forced my voice to stay even. "She can wash herself just fine."

Everly turned to me, blinking at the sharpness in my tone. I even heard it.

Dante arched a brow, not missing a thing. “Relax, Cain,” he drawled, his grin widening just enough to piss me off further. “It was just an offer.”

I scoffed. “Right.”

Everly, clearly picking up on the tension, exhaled and shook her head. “I’m fine, really.” She shot a look at Dante before rolling her shoulders. “Thanks, but I’d rather not be drenched in the middle of a freezing cave.”

Dante put a hand over his chest, mock-wounded. "Suit yourself."

I exhaled slowly, letting the moment pass, focusing back on the stew instead of the way my pulse had picked up. The food was ready. I ladled portions into tin bowls and handed them out. Dante took his first, then Everly, then me.

We ate in silence for a while; the only sounds were the occasional crackle of the fire and the quiet shifting of the horses as they settled. The warmth of the stew spread through me, loosening the worst of the stiffness in my limbs. But I was still wound too tight.

I stole a glance at Everly as she slowly sipped at her meal, strands of hair falling loose from her braid, her shoulders finally relaxing as the warmth from the fire settled into her skin. I looked away just as quickly.

She wasn't mine. And Dante was a fool if he thought he could get to her. But what bothered me more was I.

The fire flickered low, casting warm, uneven light over the cavern walls. The tension between me and Dante had finally settled into something tolerable, if not entirely gone. The stew was filling enough, and though my body still ached from the endless walking, I could feel the warmth of the food working against the exhaustion.

We ate in relative silence, the occasional scrape of metal against tin echoing through the cavern. Everly, sitting across from me, twirled her spoon absently between her fingers, clearly lost in thought.

Then, she looked at me directly. "Cain," she said, tilting her head, "your magic… how much can you actually do?"

I swallowed my bite of food, setting my bowl on my knee. "What do you mean?"

She shrugged. "I mean, back in the tunnel, when you used the quartz and the water orbs, that was…" She exhaled, clearly struggling to find the words. "That wasn't just basic magic—not to me, at least. I thought everyone only had small amounts of magic, but you seem to have more than just a little."

Dante smirked. "Oh, he definitely has more than a little."

I shot him a look before turning my attention back to Everly. "Everyone has common magic," I explained. "Things like light manipulation, slight enhancements to speed and strength, small tricks with energy flow. That's why people can do simple enchantments—like sealing letters or warding their homes against small disturbances. But not everyone knows how to use it properly."

Everly nodded slowly, absorbing my words. "And you?"

I exhaled, setting my bowl aside. "Yes. Since I come from a royal line, it's always been assumed that my magic would be more advanced. But it's not because I can do more—it's because I can do it differently."

She frowned slightly. "What do you mean?"

I extended my hand and focused, feeling the familiar shift in the air. The small tin bowl I had just been eating from trembled slightly before lifting off the ground, hovering between us. It didn't just float—it shifted weightlessly, drifting as if it had lost all connection to gravity itself.

Everly's eyes widened as she watched it hover.

"I'm not lifting it," I explained. "I'm not grabbing it with magic and holding it in place. That's not how my ability works." I rotated my hand slightly, and the bowl slowly began to turn midair, as if caught in a gentle, unseen current. "I manipulate the weight of an object, its connection to the force that pulls it down. I remove that force so that it can float freely."

Dante leaned forward, watching with mild interest. "So, what? You can just make anything weightless?"

"To an extent," I admitted, lowering my hand. The bowl slowly drifted back to the ground, settling onto the stone floor without a sound. "It works best on non-living things—objects, weapons, sometimes structures. But it doesn't just make things weightless. I can redirect movement, shift momentum, and alter how force interacts with them."

Everly's gaze flicked back to the bowl. "That's... incredible."

I let out a slow breath. "It has its uses. But it's not perfect. The heavier something is, the harder it is to remove its weight completely. And I can't just suspend something forever—it takes energy, and the bigger the object, the more it drains me."

Dante let out a low whistle. "Still, that's one hell of a trump card."

Everly nodded. "What else can you do?"

I hesitated before answering. "I can manipulate spatial forces in small ways—like controlling the balance of an object midair, adjusting a thrown weapon's trajectory, or redirecting kinetic force. If someone swings a blade at me, I can shift its momentum just enough to make it miss."

Dante snorted. "That explains why no one can seem to land a hit on you."

Everly's expression was still one of wonder. "And you consider this common magic?"

I gave her a slight nod. "It's just an advanced version of it. Magic isn't always about elements—fire, water, wind, and so on. The foundation of magic is in energy and force. That's what I manipulate."

She seemed to consider that for a long moment before glancing at Dante. "What about you?"

Dante, who had been finishing the last of his stew, paused, then sighed heavily. "Guess now's as good a time as any."

I frowned. "For what?"

He set his bowl down and straightened, rolling his shoulders as if bracing himself. "I said I wanted to be completely honest with you both," he said carefully. His usual smirk was gone, replaced with something more serious. "That means telling you the whole truth."

Everly tensed slightly. "About your magic?"

He nodded. "About the dark magic I was forced to take."

I felt my muscles stiffen. I had suspected as much, but hearing him say it outright made something cold settle in my chest. Dante stretched out his hand, fingers slightly curled, and slowly, the shadows around us began to move.

The flickering fire cast long, shifting forms against the cavern walls, but instead of staying still, those shadows drew inward. Like smoke being pulled toward him, the darkness condensed, twisting and curling around his fingers.

Everly sucked in a sharp breath.

"This is what my father did to me," Dante murmured. "What he forced me to take." He flexed his fingers, and the shadows stretched, spiraling up his arm like ink sinking into his skin. "But unlike him, I learned how to manipulate it."

The darkness pulsed, then vanished, as if it had never been there.

Everly let out a slow breath, her voice quiet. "What… what exactly does it let you do?"

Dante's violet eyes glowed faintly in the firelight. "I can pull shadows in. Absorb them, bend them to my will. I can also manipulate them physically—change their shapes, make them solid for brief moments." He smirked slightly, though it didn't reach his eyes. "I'm not saying I can make myself disappear entirely, but I can blend into darkness easier than most."

I crossed my arms. "And you think that's a good thing?"

Dante's smirk faded. "No," he said simply. "But it's what I have."

Everly was still watching him, her eyes sharp but unreadable. I couldn't tell if she was impressed or wary.

I was both.

Dante sighed, rubbing the back of his neck. "Look, I don't expect you two to trust me overnight. But I'm not hiding anything anymore. I don't want to be like my father. That's why I'm telling you this."

Everly exhaled, glancing at me. I could see the question in her eyes. Do we believe him?

I wasn't sure.

But one thing was sure—Dante had always been a wildcard. And knowing what he was truly capable of only made that more dangerous.

Later, I woke to the flickering glow of dying embers and the quiet sound of breathing.

For a moment, I didn't move. The cavern walls loomed around us, the firelight barely stretching to the corners of the hollow where we had made camp. Dante was still asleep, his bedroll undisturbed, his breathing slow and even. The horses rested nearby, their quiet huffs the only other noise in the vast stillness.

But Everly was awake.

She sat a few feet away from the fire, knees drawn up, arms wrapped around herself. Her gaze was distant, fixed on something unseen in the dark tunnels beyond. The way the firelight flickered over her face made her look smaller somehow, more fragile. But Everly wasn't delicate.

And yet… There was something in her posture that made my chest tighten.

I pushed myself up, rolling my shoulders to shake off the stiffness from the cold stone beneath me. My boots made the slightest scuff against the cavern floor as I moved toward her, but she didn't turn, didn't react.

"You should be sleeping," I murmured, lowering myself beside her.

She let out a quiet breath, not quite a sigh, but close. "So should you."

We sat in silence for a long moment. The fire crackled softly, the warmth barely touching the chill of the cave. I studied her profile, the delicate slope of her nose, the curve of her lips, the way a stray lock of hair had slipped free from her braid.

Finally, I spoke. "Everly… about what happened between us."

She tensed. I saw it in the way her fingers curled slightly against her knee, in the way her shoulders lifted just a fraction before she exhaled and turned to face me.

"What about it?" Her voice was careful, measured.

I clenched my jaw, trying to find the right words. "It wasn't just—" I hesitated, shifting slightly, feeling the weight of what I was about to say settle deep in my chest. "It wasn't just about needing a distraction. Or a release. Or any of the other reasons you're probably telling yourself."

Her brows pulled together, uncertainty flickering in her expression. "Cain…"

"I mean it," I cut in, my voice firm. "I know there's a lot happening. I know my entire life has been ripped apart in the last few weeks, but this—you—it's not just something I grabbed onto because I needed comfort." I exhaled, dragging a hand through my hair. "I'm falling for you, Everly."

She froze. For a long moment, she didn't say anything, just stared at me, her green eyes wide, caught between shock and something I couldn't quite place. Then, she laughed. It wasn't a joyful laugh. It wasn't even a real laugh. It was sharp, hollow, pained.

"You're falling for me," she repeated, shaking her head like the words were impossible.

I frowned. "Why is that so hard for you to believe?"

She scoffed, looking away, her gaze flicking back to the fire. "Because, Cain, I'm nothing special. I've spent my entire life being treated like an abomination, like I shouldn't even exist. People have hated me just for being." She swallowed hard, her fingers tightening against her arms. "I don't know how to be anything other than a mistake."

Her words hit deep. Because I understood them in a way I hadn't before.

I thought of my grandmother, Queen Anastasia, and the life she must have lived. How she had fallen in love with an elemental man, how she had defied everything to be with him, to have a child with him. And how the kingdom—her own people—had turned on her for it.

She had created something that the world told her wasn't meant to exist.

And instead of fighting, instead of burning down the world for what was hers, she had been forced to make an impossible choice. She had cast her own son away to protect him, to save herself, to keep the peace. And I had judged her for it.

But now? Sitting here, looking at Everly, seeing the raw ache in her eyes—the years of being unwanted, of being shunned, of believing that she had no right to be loved…

I understood.

My grandmother must have lived the rest of her life with a broken heart. A heart that had been shattered when she had to let her son go, when she had to watch the world erase him.

I felt something crack inside me. My fingers curled into fists against my thighs as I exhaled sharply. "I was wrong," I muttered.

Everly glanced at me, frowning slightly. "What?"

"I was wrong," I said again, shaking my head. "About my grandmother. About Dante. About… everything."

She didn't say anything, but I could feel her watching me, waiting.

"My grandmother… Anastasia," I started, my voice lower now, rougher. "She was a princess betrothed out of contract. She had power, she had a kingdom at her feet. But she loved someone she wasn't supposed to. And for that, my grandfather's parents took it out on my uncle." I swallowed, my throat tight. "And instead of fighting for him, she let them take him away."

Everly's lips parted slightly, but she stayed quiet.

I let out a bitter breath. "When we found out at the ruins, I thought she was weak for that. I thought she should have done more. Should have burned the whole damn kingdom down to keep what was hers." I exhaled sharply. "But I get it now."

Everly's fingers twitched against her knee. "Because of me?"

I hesitated, then nodded. "Because of you."

She stared at me, something shifting in her expression, something unreadable.

I shook my head. "She must have felt this same anger. This helplessness. She must have loved her son more than her own life, but it didn't matter. The world my grandfather's parents were building still told her it was wrong." I let out a slow breath. "And I took out that anger on Dante. Not even thinking about how it affected him as it did my grandmother. Leaving her… broken."

Everly's voice was soft when she finally spoke. "Like me."

I turned to her, my chest tight. I wanted to tell her no. That she wasn't broken, that she was stronger than she realized. That everything about her—the way she fought, the way she refused to back down, the way she survived—was precisely why I had fallen for her in the first place. But I knew she wouldn't believe me. Not yet. So instead, I took her hand.

She stiffened slightly, but she didn't pull away.

"You're not a mistake, Everly," I said quietly. "And you're not an abomination. The world has been wrong about you. About a lot of things. I now see my grandmother's vision of bringing the kingdom together once again. And when I take the throne, I will ensure her vision stays."

She looked down at our hands, staring at where my fingers curled around hers.

For a second, I thought she might pull away. But she didn't.

Instead, she tightened her grip. Just slightly. Just enough.

And for now, that was enough.

Chapter 33

Everly

If sleep had come at all, it had been restless, dreamless, and timeless.

When I opened my eyes, the fire had burned low, flickering weakly in the circle of stones Cain had built. The cavern looked the same as it had when I first sat awake beside it—silent, unmoving, endless. There was no morning light creeping through the cracks of a tent, no birdsong to mark the passage of time. Just the same damp, cold air pressing down on us and the flickering glow of the quartz orbs still hovering around the cave.

I sat up slowly, stretching my arms, my muscles sore from the endless walking. How long had we been down here? A day? Two? More? It was impossible to tell. The concept of time had started to unravel, twisting into something meaningless in the depths of the mountain.

Cain was already awake, of course. He sat near the dying fire, adjusting the straps on his pack, his face unreadable as always. If last night's conversation had shaken him, he didn't show it now. Dante stirred a few feet away, groaning as he pulled his blanket over his face.

"Ugh. Still here?" he muttered.

Cain snorted. "Unfortunately."

I rubbed the sleep from my eyes. "If we don't start moving soon, we'll be here forever."

That got Dante up. He pushed himself up with a yawn, running a hand through his already-messy hair. "Right. More walking in circles through dark, endless tunnels of doom. Can't wait."

We packed quickly, gathering our supplies with a quiet efficiency that had come from days—weeks?—of travel together. I rolled up my bedroll and strapped it to the back of my pack, adjusted my cloak, and checked my sword at my hip.

Cain's glowing orbs still hovered nearby, casting long shadows against the uneven walls. They had been our only source of light since we entered this forsaken cave, and I couldn't imagine trying to navigate this place without them.

We set off in silence, the only sounds our footsteps echoing against the stone. The tunnels sloped upward and downward interchangeably, twisting through the mountain in ways that made no sense at all. Were we at the top now? Or were we even deeper than before? There was no way to know.

My legs burned from the strain of constantly adjusting to the incline, and my boots scuffed against loose stones, sending small rocks tumbling into the darkness. It was disorienting—like the mountain itself was shifting around us.

Every few hours, Cain would stop at a split path, glancing back at me. No words were needed—I already knew what he was asking. I closed my eyes, reaching. Each time, the visions came easier, less like an attack and more like a door creaking open. I saw what lay ahead—some tunnels collapsed, others led to dead ends or worse. Each time, I guided us down the right path.

Dante watched with mild fascination as I blinked away the remnants of a vision, shaking off the phantom sensations of paths not taken.

"You're getting better at that," he noted.

I exhaled. "It still feels like drowning."

Cain, who had been watching me closely, gave a slight nod. "But you haven't been wrong yet."

It wasn't meant as praise, but something about it still settled in my chest like a quiet weight. He trusted me. And trust in a place like this? It meant everything.

Hours passed. Or longer. We walked until our legs ached, until the caves all started to look the same, until the silence became too much. Dante broke it first.

"Not to bring down the mood," he said, adjusting his pack, "but what if we never actually get out of here?"

Cain gave him an unamused look. "We will."

Dante huffed. "Sure. But when? I'm starting to think we've been here so long that when we finally emerge, the kingdom will have fallen, the Blight will have consumed the land, and we'll step outside to find an entirely new civilization thriving on the ruins of our failure."

I shot him a look. "Not helpful."

"I'm just saying," he continued, undeterred, "what if these caves don't end? What if we've been going in circles? What if we're already—"

Cain stopped walking.

Dante nearly ran into him. "Hey, what—"

"Quiet."

Cain's eyes narrowed as he turned his head slightly, listening. I held my breath, trying to pick up on whatever he had heard. The drip of water. The shuffle of our own movement. The distant sound of… something else.

A slow, deliberate scrape. Like stone against stone. Or something moving in the dark.

Dante exhaled. "Okay. Yeah. I don't like that."

Neither did I, because I had seen too many paths in my visions where we didn't make it out of these tunnels alive. And I had a sinking feeling that whatever had been watching us before…

It was finally ready to make itself known.

The sound came again—a low, dragging scrape, followed by a deep, guttural growl. I went still, every instinct screaming danger.

The tunnel stretched ahead, sloping downward into shadows that the floating quartz orbs couldn't quite reach. And just beyond the bend—a figure loomed. A shadow, taller than any man, hulking, with thick limbs and the distinct outline of clawed hands. The air around it shifted, as if the space itself was warping under its presence.

The growling deepened, vibrating through the stone beneath my boots. Cain immediately stepped in front of me, his sword whispering free from its sheath in a single, practiced motion. His stance was sharp, controlled, ready to strike. Dante, for once, didn't have a sarcastic remark. His hand hovered near his own weapon, his violet eyes locked on the shifting shadow ahead.

I swallowed hard. This was it. The thing that had been following us—the thing I had felt watching us for hours, maybe days. And now, it had finally decided to show itself.

The shadow moved. It rounded the bend, stepping into the light. Cain lunged.

"STOP!"

I grabbed his arm before the blade could connect. Cain froze, his breath sharp, his muscles locked with the force of barely restrained momentum.

Because the thing standing before us was not a monster. It was a dog.

A black dog, knee-high, its coat dark and sleek as midnight. Its stance was tense, ears perked, hackles raised, muscles coiled as if it were preparing to bolt or fight.

But that wasn't what made my breath catch.

It had three heads.

Three sets of glowing amber eyes locked onto us, three pairs of ears flicking toward the sound of Cain's sword. Its mouth curled back slightly, revealing sharp, gleaming teeth, but the growl wasn't a snarl of aggression. It was fear. It was defensive.

And as I stared at it—really looked at it—I realized something else. It was alone. My fingers loosened on Cain's arm, but I didn't let go completely.

"Wait," I whispered. "Cain, don't."

His eyes didn't leave the creature, but his grip on the sword adjusted, shifting slightly away from an attack position. He wasn't lowering his guard—but he wasn't striking, either. The dog let out another growl, its middle head staring at Cain, unblinking. I took a slow, careful step forward. The dog's heads turned toward me in eerie unison, muscles rippling under its dark coat.

Dante let out a low breath beside me. "Well. That's new."

Cain didn't respond, his grip still tight on his sword. I could feel the tension rolling off of him, every part of him still prepared for a fight. But something about the dog—it didn't feel wrong. It wasn't attacking. It wasn't charging us.

The three-headed dog stood utterly still, its six glowing amber eyes locked onto me as I took another cautious step forward. Its black fur was sleek, but there was an untamed wildness to it—something ancient, something forgotten.

I slowly crouched, keeping my movements measured. "Hey there," I murmured, holding out a hand. The dog sniffed the air, then—to my absolute surprise—it wagged its tail.

Dante made a choked sound. "Oh, you've got to be kidding me."

Before I could react, the middle head nosed my palm, warm breath puffing against my skin. Then the other two followed, each of them nuzzling me, bumping my arms, my shoulders, my face. One even licked my cheek, and I couldn't help but laugh.

It was warm. Much warmer than a normal dog. Like standing near a fire—its body radiated heat enough that I could feel it through my clothes. Then, just as I ran my fingers through its fur, it shrank. The massive, knee-high form compressed, its shape rippling like a liquid shadow until it was half its size. Then half again. By the time I blinked, it was the size of a house cat.

I let out a breath of amazement. "I knew it."

Cain, still holding his sword, glared at me. "Knew what?"

I grinned, scratching behind the ears of the middle head as all three tails wagged furiously in unison. "I've read about these before. It's a Cerberus."

Dante tilted his head. "A what-now?"

"A Cerberus," I repeated, gently lifting the now small, wiggling creature into my arms. It licked my chin, its warmth seeping into my skin. "They're extremely rare. Supposedly bred as guardians for the gods. They can control their size, shifting from something as small as a mouse to as big as a horse—or larger."

Cain pinched the bridge of his nose. "Everly—"

"It likes me," I interrupted, rubbing my cheek against the soft fur of the middle head as its side heads nuzzled into my hands. It adored me.

Cain sighed, exasperated. "You cannot keep it."

I blinked up at him. "Why not?"

Cain gave me an incredulous look. "Because it's not a pet."

Dante, for once, nodded in agreement. "Yeah, I'm with him on this one. You can't just pick up a three-headed stray in the middle of a death tunnel and decide it's yours."

The Cerberus let out a soft, trilling whine, pushing all three heads into my arms like it was trying to bury itself against me. My heart melted.

I looked between the two of them. "But it likes me."

Cain groaned. "That is not a reason."

Dante crossed his arms. "It's exactly the reason women always give."

Cain let out a sharp breath, rubbing his temples. "It really is. I don't understand it. Why do women see an obviously dangerous stray animal and immediately decide they have to take it home?"

Dante threw up a hand. "Right? It's like some ancient female instinct. 'Oh, look, a feral beast that could kill me—better pet it.'"

I narrowed my eyes. "You two are just jealous because it chose me."

Cain looked physically pained. "Everly. That's not the point."

I turned back to my new companion, who had now settled comfortably in my lap, panting happily. "He's staying."

Cain exhaled through his nose, muttering something about how he had lost control of this situation entirely. Dante ran a hand down his face.

"Of course. Of course we're keeping the death dog." He said.

The Cerberus wagged its tails so hard that its whole body shook. The dog shrank even more, its sleek black form compressing until it was no bigger than a rabbit. It curled up in my hands, letting out a contented sigh, all three heads nuzzling against my fingers. I was keeping it. End of story.

I reached for my saddlebag, opened the flap, and carefully placed the tiny creature inside. It wriggled into the soft fabric, nestled between some supplies, and settled in like it had been there all along. Its tail curled around its body, and its middle head peeked out, blinking up at me sleepily.

"You're really doing this." Cain looked exhausted just watching me.

I met his gaze, completely unrepentant. "Yes."

His expression hardened. “And what exactly are you going to feed it?”

I froze.

Dante snorted. “Yeah, good question. Do you even know what Cerberuses eat? Because if it’s something like, oh, I don’t know—souls, I’m not sharing mine.” I shot him a glare.

“I’ll figure it out.”

Cain crossed his arms, unimpressed. “So you have no idea.”

I huffed, adjusting my saddlebag so the pup was more securely in place. "I just know I'm not leaving it here. It's been alone in the dark long enough."

Cain’s expression faltered for just a second, something unreadable flickering across his face. I softened my voice.

I couldn't put my finger on the feeling, but I just felt in my soul that I was meant to cross paths with the creature. Who knows how long he has been wandering these cave tunnels, alone. I related to feeling alone.

“I feel like… I was meant to find him.” I ran a gentle hand over the Cerberus’s fur, feeling the way its body radiated warmth, as if trying to mimic my own. “Look at him. He was just waiting here, in the dark, with no one. How could I just walk away?”

For once, Dante didn’t have a snarky response. He looked at the tiny creature, then at me, and sighed dramatically, shaking his head. Cain pinched the bridge of his nose.

“This is going to be a disaster.” He whispered to himself.

I smiled, rubbing the Cerberus’s middle head with my thumb as it licked my hand in response. “No, it’s going to be perfect.”

Cain muttered something under his breath that sounded a lot like “unbelievable.”

Dante just sighed again. “You’re lucky I actually like dogs.”

I grinned, scratching behind the Cerberus’s ears. “See? He’s already part of the group.”

Cain looked toward the ceiling of the cave like he was praying for patience. But I didn’t care. Because for the first time in a while, something in this dark, endless place felt right.

Chapter 34

Everly

The air changed.

It was subtle at first, a barely there shift that made me inhale deeper, my lungs filling with something crisper and cleaner than the thick, heavy dampness of the caves. The scent of stone and earth faded, replaced by something cold—the sharp bite of high-altitude wind.

And then, after what felt like a lifetime in darkness, we saw it.

The tunnel walls widened, and ahead, framed by jagged rock, was an opening. The last few steps felt unreal, my legs moving forward even as my mind refused to believe it. And then—

We stepped outside.

The cold wind hit me like a wave, sending a shiver straight through my bones. I pulled my cloak tighter around me, stepping forward onto the uneven rock of a mountaintop ledge. The sky stretched out vast and endless, its deep, dark blue hue littered with stars. The wind carried the distant scent of pine and snow, crisp and untouched, a stark contrast to the stale, stagnant air we had been breathing for what felt like days.

I turned, and sure enough, the three horses followed, their hooves carefully picking their way out of the cave behind us. Spirra huffed as she adjusted to the open air again, shaking her mane as if she too was relieved to be free of that endless tunnel.

And then, of course, there was the Cerberus.

The tiny black creature poked its head out of my saddlebag, three sets of glowing amber eyes blinking at the open world as if seeing it for the first time. It let out a tiny snuffling sound, as if testing the wind, before shaking itself and curling deeper into my bag, content to stay where it was safe and warm.

Dante stretched, rolling his shoulders dramatically. "Finally. I was starting to think we were just going to wander in there forever."

I stepped past Cain and Dante, my breath catching as I took in the view.

A vast valley stretched out below, cradled between the mountains. On the far side, two towering peaks stood side by side, rising like ancient sentinels guarding the land beyond. But it wasn't the mountains that held my gaze.

It was the valley itself.

Lush and green, it was alive in a way the caves never could be. Dense trees blanketed the slopes, and in the center, a river wound through the heart of it, glinting like a silver thread under the twilight sky.

It was beautiful. Breathtaking. For a long moment, I forgot how tired I was, how sore my feet were, how hungry I had been for more than cave-stale air.

"It's stunning," I whispered.

Behind me, Dante let out a groan. "More mountains. Of course." He slumped forward, dragging a hand down his face. "Just when I thought I'd left every cursed stone and winding tunnel behind, the mountains decide to breed."

Cain moved to stand beside me, his eyes scanning the valley with purpose. "That river," he said, pointing, "runs between the final ridge—the last of the mountain wall separating this region from Merewick."

Dante grunted. "So we're going over those too?"

"No. We'll follow the river through the valley. There's no need for more tunnels or climbing. It'll lead us to the low pass between the twin peaks. It'll be a longer journey on foot, but it's safer—and the terrain will be easier on the horses. We'll travel at first light," he said, voice steady.

I sighed, my legs aching at just the thought of more walking. "So, another camp?"

Cain nodded. "We set up here for the night."

"Another night outside in the freezing cold? Wonderful." Groaned Dante.

Cain shot him a pointed look. "Would you rather go back into the cave?"

Dante glared but didn't argue.

We moved quickly, securing the horses near the rock wall where they'd have some shelter from the wind. I pulled out my bedroll and spread it beside the firepit Cain was already building, watching as he pulled a flint from his pack and struck it against stone, sparking flames to life.

The warmth was immediate, the fire casting flickering light across the uneven ground.

The Cerberus stretched lazily in my lap, yawning with three mouths before curling up again, its tiny body radiating heat like a living furnace.

Dante sat cross-legged beside the fire, rubbing his hands together. "Alright, Everly," he said, eyeing my new companion. "Since we're stuck here for the night, how about you finally tell us what you're naming the death dog?"

Cain, who had been adjusting the firewood, paused and gave me a warning look. "You're not naming it."

I raised a brow. "Of course I'm naming him."

Cain exhaled sharply, clearly losing the battle against his own patience. "It's not a pet."

"It's mine, so yes, it is." I grinned, rubbing the Cerberus's middle head, which thumped its tiny tail in excitement.

Dante smirked. "Alright then, let's hear it. What's the name?"

I thought for a moment, running my fingers through the Cerberus's sleek fur. Then, I smiled.

"Nyx."

Dante hummed. "Nyx. Like the old god of night?"

I nodded, glancing up at the star-scattered sky above us. "Yeah. He was waiting for me in the dark… so I think it fits."

Cain shook his head, standing and brushing the dirt off his hands. "Great. Now we have a three-headed monster with a name."

Nyx yipped in response, wagging his tail again.

Dante grinned. "I like it."

Cain sighed. "Of course you do."

I smiled, curling up beside the fire, my new stray Cerberus snuggled into my side. The cold wind howled through the mountains, but for the first time since we entered those damn caves, I felt warm.

The world was made of soft darkness and the quiet crackle of fire. Sleep clung to me like fog, my body heavy and aching from the endless walking. Even the cold mountain air couldn't quite pierce the exhaustion weighing down my limbs.

I stirred slightly, my cheek pressed against the rough fabric of my bedroll, my eyes half-lidded as I glanced around the camp. The fire had dwindled to embers, its glow barely enough to chase away the shadows.

Cain slept just across the fire, his back propped against the stone wall, his arms folded over his chest. His face was drawn, even in sleep, lines of tension etched into his features as if he expected danger even in his dreams.

Dante lay sprawled on the other side, one arm slung over his eyes, his mouth slightly open in a way that would have been comical if the situation weren't so relentlessly bleak.

And then I heard it. A rustling sound—quiet, deliberate, wrong.

My eyes snapped open, my body tensing as I tried to pinpoint the noise. There, just beyond the firelight, a shadow moved. I wanted to call out, to warn Cain, but the words caught in my throat. My pulse thundered in my ears.

I saw the shape behind him, something low and sleek, the darkness itself seeming to ripple around it. A figure, humanoid but not quite right, standing just beyond Cain's shoulder.

My mouth opened. I tried to shout. But before a sound could escape, a hand clamped down over my mouth. I inhaled sharply, the bitter, sickly-sweet scent of something soaked into a rag filling my nose and throat. My vision blurred, panic flaring hot and frantic through my veins. I tried to struggle, to twist away, but the grip on me was iron-hard.

The world swayed, tilted. Then, everything went black.

I came to with a throbbing ache in my head and the sharp, uncomfortable pressure of ropes digging into my wrists. The air was colder here, the chill creeping into my skin even beneath my cloak. I shifted, wincing as the ropes bit deeper into my skin.

My eyes fluttered open, the darkness gradually giving way to the dim, flickering light of a lantern swaying from the ceiling of… a wagon? I was on the floor of a covered wagon, rough planks creaking beneath me as it lurched forward.

Cain was bound and seated to my right, his arms tied behind his back, his shoulders tense, and his expression thunderous. Dante was on my left, still groggy but very much awake, his brows drawn together in equal parts confusion and irritation.

"What…?" I croaked, my voice rough.

Dante snorted. "Welcome back to the land of the living, Angel Eyes."

"Shut up, Dante," Cain snapped, his voice low and laced with fury. His silver-blue eyes flicked toward me. "Are you alright?"

I nodded slowly, the motion making my head throb. "I think so. What… happened?"

"We were ambushed," Cain growled. "Whoever took us made sure we wouldn't fight back."

I wriggled my fingers experimentally. The ropes were tight, cutting off circulation, but not impossible to break if I had the time to spare.

"How long have we been out?" I asked.

"No idea," Dante said, shifting awkwardly against his restraints. "But we're moving. And the worst part? I'm pretty sure I just figured out who's taking us for a ride."

Cain frowned. "What do you mean?"

Dante twisted his neck, craning to peer through the tiny window at the front of the wagon. His eyes narrowed, his mouth pulling into a tight line. "Yeah. That's what I thought."

"What?" I demanded.

Dante looked at me, his expression torn between annoyance and genuine worry. "The wagon's being pulled by a giant panther."

"What?" I blurted, straining against my bonds to try and see for myself.

Cain shifted beside me, his own gaze narrowing as he looked through the tiny window. His jaw tightened. "He's right. Duskravens."

The name sent a shiver down my spine. "Duskravens?"

"Night Prowlers," Cain explained, his voice low and urgent. "Fae who can transform into massive, shadowy feline creatures. They're territorial, highly intelligent, and they don't take kindly to trespassers."

"So, what, they just decided to kidnap us because we were passing through their mountain?" Dante grumbled. "I feel like that's a little extreme."

"It's not just that," Cain said, his expression darkening. "They're suspicious of everyone. They watch, they observe, and if they think you're a threat, they remove you before you can prove them right or wrong."

Great. As if things weren't bad enough.

"And now we're tied up in their wagon being taken… where exactly?" I asked, my voice tight.

Cain shook his head. "If they haven't killed us yet, it means they want something. Or they're trying to figure out if we're a threat."

"Well, I vote for not pissing them off any more than we already have," Dante muttered. "Anyone have any bright ideas on how to get us out of here?"

I glanced down at my hands, my fingers already working against the rope. The knots were tight, but not impossible to untie. My Sight can show me something, a way out, a way to talk to them, anything. But deep down, I knew we were already at their mercy. And with creatures like Duskravens, that wasn't a comfortable place to be.

The wagon creaked and swayed as it descended the mountain path, flanked on all sides by the Duskraven. I couldn't see all of them through the slats in the wood. Still, I could hear them—the soft padding of enormous paws, the occasional scrape of claws against stone, the low growls that rumbled like distant thunder. Shadows moved in tandem with the wagon, too fast, too fluid to be anything natural. They were keeping us surrounded. Herding us.

The descent grew smoother, and I could tell we were nearing the valley floor. The light outside had dimmed to the soft gray-blue of early dusk, and through the thin window at the front of the cart, I caught glimpses of trees, river glints, and open sky.

And then—we passed through something.

A strange pressure pressed against my chest, like walking through a thick curtain of invisible fog. The air shifted; it hummed against my skin and filled my lungs like cold smoke. A low, vibrating tingle ran down my spine, not painful, but deeply uncomfortable—like the sensation you get when someone brushes too close behind you. You know they're still there, even if you can't see them.

A magical ward.

Cain stiffened immediately beside me. "My magic," he muttered, voice sharp with unease. "It's locked. I can feel it—sealed off like someone slammed a door in my chest."

Dante cursed under his breath. "Yeah. Same here."

I frowned, instinctively reaching for that tangled thread inside me, the one that led to my Sight. It had never been reliable, not when I wanted it, and certainly not when I needed it. But something about the way the magic shifted around me made me try anyway.

I closed my eyes and pulled inward, reaching past the static hum of the ward, past the dull ache of fatigue, toward that flickering thing inside me that had always existed just at the edge of sense.

Something answered. A flash of light. A ripple of movement. Images slammed into my mind—but they were wrong. Blurred. Twisting like reflections in broken glass.

I saw movement—people? Beasts? I couldn't tell. The edges of everything shimmered like heat waves, and the colors bled together like smeared paint. A low whining sound rang in my ears, building until it became a piercing throb that dug into my temples.

I gasped and flinched, my head snapping back against the wagon wall. Pain bloomed behind my eyes, sharp and pulsing.

Cain turned toward me immediately, brows furrowed. "Everly?"

"I saw something," I whispered, pressing my wrists against my forehead, "but it's off. Like… interference. Static.

Everything's distorted. I think the ward is scrambling my Sight."

Dante leaned forward as much as the ropes would allow. "Well, that's great. We're blind and helpless. Love that for us."

Before I could respond, the wagon lurched to a stop.

The sudden silence outside was suffocating. No wind, no footsteps. Just the heavy presence of waiting.

Then came the thump of latches, and the back of the wagon dropped open, slamming into the ground with a dull echo. A ramp.

And standing at the bottom—not a beast. Not a Duskraven panther. But two men.

They were massive, easily half a foot taller than Cain, and broad in a way that felt deliberately intimidating. Their chests were bare, covered in intricate tribal tattoos that curled over their arms and down their sides like living vines inked in deep black. Their skin was bronze-dark, gleaming faintly with sweat.

And that was it. That was all they wore.

My breath caught in my throat. They were naked. Completely. Utterly.

I was yanked to my feet by one of them, his grip firm but not cruel, and pulled down the ramp. Cain and Dante followed, dragged in turn, the three of us pushed to our knees side by side at the base of the wagon.

The air outside was warmer, thick with the scent of river water and pine. Still, the awkwardness of our position made it impossible to appreciate. Because from this angle, kneeling on the ground, my gaze level with the… situation, I was very aware of the fact that I was eye-level with a row of very naked men.

I swallowed hard and very purposefully stared at the ground.

This was not how I imagined dying.

Beside me, Dante gave a strangled cough that sounded dangerously close to a laugh.

Cain muttered, "You've got to be kidding me," under his breath.

The silence that followed was uncomfortable at best, unbearable at worst. The bare-chested men loomed over us, their gazes unreadable, their size alone making us feel small and vulnerable. Still on our knees, bound and unarmed, there wasn't much we could do but wait and try not to look too closely at... anything.

Dante shifted uncomfortably beside me. "For the love of the old gods," he muttered under his breath, "could they at least put pants on? One wrong breeze and I swear his junk is going to touch my shoulder."

I bit the inside of my cheek, unsure whether to laugh or vomit.

Cain said nothing, his expression carved from stone, but I could see the muscle twitching in his jaw. He was alert—watching, listening, waiting for the shift.

It came quickly.

From beyond the clearing, movement stirred in the trees. The sound of padded steps on soft earth. The low growl of something massive.

And then the Duskraven emerged.

They came from the brush, from between tree trunks, from shadowed dips in the ground—at least two dozen of them, sleek and massive and terrifying. Each one the size of a horse, their bodies rippling with muscle beneath coats of deep indigo-black fur.

Their eyes glowed a piercing amber-yellow, unblinking and intelligent. Their elongated fangs jutted from powerful jaws, sabretooth-like and glistening with saliva. They moved in silence, forming a half-circle behind the men who had dragged us out of the wagon, each one settling into place like it had been choreographed.

Not a single one blinked.

Not a single one looked away.

We were surrounded.

One of the fae in front of us stepped forward and said something low and guttural, the language curling strange and sharp across his tongue.

"Zarn vek tora ven'al."

What the hell are we supposed to do with that? There's no way any of us are going to make it out of this if we don't even know how to explain ourselves.

Until Cain answered.

Without hesitation, his voice rolled out in a calm, authoritative tone, "Taran ven Erynvale. Nel'ka vara solan."

The shift was immediate. A ripple of stillness passed through the clearing. The two fae men exchanged glances, and the one who had spoken cocked his head slightly, almost intrigued.

Dante turned to Cain, wide-eyed. "Okay, what the hell was that?"

Cain kept his eyes forward. "I told you—I'm an heir of Erynvale. I studied the old languages. Duskrani was one of them."

"You speak Duskrani?" I gaped at him.

He shrugged. "Better than I speak sarcasm, apparently."

"Of course the prince speaks ancient cat." Dante muttered.

And then the fae leader let out a sound that cut through all our thoughts. A roar. Low, guttural, and building until it echoed across the clearing—a sound that raked through my bones like claws. Behind him, the panther-like Duskraven tensed, their glowing eyes locked on us, their muscles rippling beneath fur the color of midnight.

The air grew impossibly still, the roar still echoing faintly in my bones. The Duskraven pack behind us remained poised, watchful, glowing eyes never blinking. And then—movement from the trees.

A woman stepped forward from the shadows.

And gods, what a woman she was.

She was completely naked, like the men before her, but somehow more regal than obscene. Her skin was a warm, sun-kissed bronze, and long dark brown hair fell in neat braids, some woven with beads and feathers, cascading down her back and over her chest with just enough coverage to make her nudity feel more ceremonial than crude.

Tattoos in thin, elegant lines stretched across her cheekbones, curling down her forehead from her hairline in symmetrical arcs that gave her an almost divine appearance. Atop her head sat a small tiara, delicate and wild-looking—gilded ivy, leaves twisted into elegant, sharp points like a crown of nature itself.

But that wasn't what made my heart stutter. No. That was the tail swaying slowly behind her. The way her hips rolled with a predator's grace. The tapered cat ears that poked out from her hair, twitching subtly with every sound. And those eyes— not human, slitted and gleaming gold in the growing light, watching everything like she could see more than just flesh and bone.

She walked with silent authority, right up to Cain.

Still kneeling, hands bound behind his back, he looked up at her with that unshakable, unreadable calm of his. But my chest tightened when her fingers reached forward and grasped his chin, lifting it gently so his face tilted up to meet hers.

My breath caught. It wasn't threatening. Not exactly. But the intimacy of the gesture made something hot and cold twist in my stomach. She studied him with those feline eyes, as if she were considering whether to eat him or worship him. And there I was, helpless, watching another woman—a stunning, exotic, probably half-shifted shapeshifter queen or goddess or something—cup Cain's face like she had every right to.

My heart thudded hard, not from fear. Or—not just from fear. Jealousy? No. That's ridiculous. That's stupid. But also... maybe not.

Because there she stood—beautiful and wild, radiant in her power, naked in every sense of the word, while Cain knelt before her like something out of a storybook. My mind flicked—unwanted and uninvited—to the image of her leaning down, her lips brushing his, the fire between them catching like dry tinder…

Nope. Nope. What the hell, brain?

I shook my head sharply, dragging myself back to reality.

She let go of his chin and straightened, her posture commanding but not cruel. The male fae Cain had spoken to murmured something else in Duskrani—this time softer, a tone that felt more reverent than confrontational. Something changed in her eyes. Recognition? Understanding, maybe?

She turned her gaze from Cain to the rest of us and, for the first time, spoke in our language, her voice smooth and firm, threaded with an accent like warm stone and wind.

"I am Princess Ilyrana of Vareth'Telan," her accent heavy with something wild and unrefined—each word rounded in a low, rolling cadence that made them sound older, more profound than they should've. There was a purring undertone to her voice, a subtle growl hidden beneath polished speech. "You walk through the heart of my valley."

Her tail twitched once behind her, slow and deliberate. And suddenly, the snarling cats behind her felt more like soldiers than beasts. And we—bound and kneeling—were guests in the court of a very dangerous, very naked princess.

Cain's voice was calm, steady, full of quiet power.

"I am Cain Jarethorne, heir to the throne of Erynvale. I speak to you as a sovereign equal, not as a trespasser."

The name hung in the air like a drawn blade.

Jarethorne.

I have never heard him use the royal name before. It makes sense, given our situation, so I'm not sure why it surprised me. But he said it here, in front of the Duskraven princess, without flinching. My heart twisted. Not hurt, exactly—but something close. Why was he giving pieces of himself to her and not me?

Wait, why am I jealous again?

Dante, of course, didn't seem fazed by any of it.

"Dante Verris," he offered with his usual wry tone. "Not royal. Not polite. Not planning to be executed today, if that's still on the table."

Cain shot him a look, sharp as a blade. Dante just gave a slight shrug, as if to say *I'm being reasonable, for once.*

Then they were all looking at me. I straightened my spine.

"Everly Walker," I said. "I'm not royalty either. I'm just here."

It sounded too simple. Too small. But it was all I had.

As I spoke, my gaze flicked again—unintentionally—toward the male fae who had first talked to Cain. The smirk on his face made me feel uneasy.

Princess Ilyrana said something sharp and decisive in Duskrani, her voice cutting through the stillness like a whip.

"Teshka var'an. Cut them loose."

The male fae who'd spoken with Cain moved behind us. With a flick of something I couldn't see, the ropes binding our wrists loosened and fell away. I rubbed at the angry marks around my wrists, grateful to feel blood returning to my fingers.

Cain stood first, then Dante. I followed, unsteady on my legs at first, and immediately began checking for my things.

That's when I noticed it—our weapons were gone.

My heart leapt into my throat. "Where are our swords?" I asked, trying not to sound panicked.

As if summoned by my words, another naked man—honestly, at this point, I didn't know where to look—approached, carrying a large roll of leather bundled in his arms. He unfurled it smoothly on the ground before us.

Inside lay our weapons—our swords—wrapped with care, polished and intact.

Dante crouched and reached for one of the blades without hesitation. "How did they disarm us without the swords electrocuting them or whatever they do?" he muttered, more to himself than anyone else.

As soon as his fingers curled around the hilt, Cain's hand snapped out and grabbed it from him.

"That one's mine," Cain said coolly. He turned the sword over and held it up to show us the etched rune near the pommel—an ancient symbol, carved with precision and glowing faintly now that it was back in his grip.

"They're marked," he explained. "Old royal protocol. Just in case we're ever… separated from them. Each rune is unique. Watch."

He picked through the rest, finding Dante's by tracing the shape of a lightning-shaped mark along the hilt. Then mine, its symbol more delicate but unmistakably familiar—a spiral set within a crescent moon. How have I never noticed that before?

He handed it to me, and the moment my fingers closed around the hilt, something inside me settled. The sword had become an extension of me. Having it back was like remembering I had a voice.

With our weapons reclaimed, we were led into the forest again, this time not as prisoners. The Duskraven, still partially in their feline forms, slinked around us, silent sentinels in the shadows.

Eventually, the trees thinned and the ground leveled out into a clearing. And there it was—a village.

Dozens of Duskraven fae walked the worn paths between thatched-roof huts, their manner casual but sharp-eyed. Some were fully clothed in layered woven wraps and light armor; others remained in partial shift or, yes, still entirely naked. Children darted between homes. A woman stirred something over a fire pit. Laughter echoed in bursts across the clearing.

We followed Ilyrana to a larger structure at the center of the village, its woven roof supported by dark wooden beams and vines trained around its frame. Inside, the air was surprisingly calm and fragrant, with a scent reminiscent of citrus and pine.

Spacious, with patterned rugs covering the floor and carved bowls resting on low tables. Women moved gracefully around Ilyrana, tending to her like a queen. One wiped the sweat from her brow, another offered a tray of bright fruits, and two more were adjusting and brushing off what looked like a bamboo throne, now being prepared for her arrival.

She lowered herself into it with practiced ease.

I couldn't help but glance around in awe. "It's… warm here. But it was cold outside. How is that possible?"

Ilyrana looked at me with something between amusement and pride. "The wards. This valley is hidden within an intricate web of magic passed down through generations. The climate here is of our own design—controlled, tailored to what we prefer."

My brow furrowed. "You mean… you created your own weather?"

"Yes," she said simply. "And more. The wards not only shape the climate, but they keep the valley invisible to all who don't belong. Anyone approaching is repelled—turned away by suggestions and diversions that lead them around, not through. The Blight has passed us by more than once, unaware of what lies here."

I stared at her, stunned. They hadn't just survived the Blight. They had thrived. Safe. Protected. Untouched. The Duskraven had built a kingdom in silence—and somehow, it was more alive than anything I'd seen in months.

Princess Ilyrana reclined in her bamboo throne like it had been grown around her body—her posture effortless, regal, and undeniably feline. Her tail curled around the leg of the chair, flicking with a slow, calculated rhythm as she watched us with unreadable golden eyes.

With a flick of her fingers, she gestured toward the far side of the room.

Three men emerged from behind a woven curtain, each carrying a low, backless stool carved from dark wood and smoothed by age. They placed them in a half-circle across from the princess's seat, and we were wordlessly guided toward them.

I lowered myself onto the stool, trying to keep my posture as composed as possible despite the tension twisting in my spine. Cain and Dante sat beside me, silent, watchful.

A small wooden table was placed between us, no higher than our knees. And then came the food.

Women moved gracefully around the room, setting down bowls of vibrant fruit, smoked meat wrapped in dark leaves, flatbread dusted with herbs, and clay vessels filled with a scent that smelled like spiced wine. The scents hit me all at once—sweet, savory, unfamiliar, and intoxicating.

My stomach tightened, reminding me just how long it had been since we'd eaten anything that wasn't stew from a dented can. But Ilyrana didn't move. She remained completely still in her throne, eyes half-lidded, her expression unreadable. She didn't reach for the food or acknowledge it.

The silence grew heavier. I glanced at Cain, unsure.

He noticed immediately and leaned toward me just slightly, his voice low and steady. "It's customary," he said. "Guests eat or drink first. It's a sign of trust. If we don't, it's considered an insult. If she doesn't eat, it's because she's waiting for us to prove ourselves."

I looked at the table again—at the carefully arranged dishes, the elegant display of generosity wrapped in quiet scrutiny. A test of trust. Of nerve. I reached forward and picked up a piece of fruit—something round and golden-orange, the skin soft and fragrant. I bit into it.

It was sweet and tart, tasting like sunshine after a long storm. Cain followed next, lifting a piece of flatbread. Dante, predictably, reached for the wine. Across from us, Princess Ilyrana finally smiled. It seems we passed.

The moment Cain placed his flatbread back on the table, Princess Ilyrana leaned slightly forward, her gaze finally flicking from the table to his face.

"We thank you for your hospitality," Cain said, his tone formal but not cold. "We didn't come here with violence in mind. Since you've seen that for yourself, we'd ask to stay the night. Just until morning. We've traveled far, and the valley is... not easy to reach."

Ilyrana regarded him in silence, one hand draped over the carved arm of her throne. Her fingers tapped lazily, rhythmically, like a thought pulsing through her body.

As the quiet stretched, I became very aware of the women still lingering near the walls—Duskraven, dressed in little more than sheer fabric and feathers. Some of them whispered behind their hands. One of them—tall, elegant, and smiling—was watching Cain with blatant interest.

I felt something sharp and strange twist in my stomach.

My eyes narrowed slightly without me meaning to. Why did they have to look at him like that?

Yes, he was… fine. More than acceptable, even. But still.

I crossed one leg over the other, trying to shake the irrational buzz crawling beneath my skin.

Dante, on the other hand, seemed to notice the attention too—and he wasn't bothered. In fact, he leaned slightly to one side, elbow propped on his knee, and gave one of the women a wink. She giggled and quickly turned away, hiding her smile behind a carved tray.

"Seems friendly," Dante muttered under his breath. "Maybe we stay two nights."

I shot him a look.

The nudity, the attention, the way everyone moved so comfortably in their own skin—it was getting to me. I didn't know if it was the magic, the culture, or just my own insecurities, but I felt strange, off-balance in my own body.

And then, I saw him again.

The male Duskraven who had spoken to Cain, the one who had smirked at me during introductions. He now stood at Ilyrana's right, guarding the throne like a statue carved from shadow and gold. He hadn't spoken since we arrived, but he watched everything. Especially me. Our eyes met again.

His eyes were too knowing, too calm. Like he was waiting for something from me. I narrowed my eyes at him in warning, the tension coiling again in my gut.

Ilyrana's voice cut through the air like a blade. "Norvas, stop making my guests feel like prey."

His gaze shifted—slowly, deliberately—back to the room, but he said nothing.

Ilyrana looked at me then, eyes softer. "Forgive him. It's not personal."

"What is it then?" Cain's brow furrowed.

She tilted her head slightly, her voice silk over stone. "All Duskraven are born with magic—unique to our bloodlines. Norvas's gift is emotional manipulation. It's unconscious unless focused, but even in rest, he can stir… sensations. Doubt. Lust. Fear. Insecurity."

That twisting jealousy. The discomfort. The sudden, irrational fear that I didn't belong, that I wasn't enough— it hadn't been mine.

A wave of relief washed through me, sudden and profound. But it left a hollow ache, too. Because if those feelings were false, what did that say about the ones I'd had before?

Still, I sat straighter. "That would've been useful to know earlier."

Ilyrana gave a slow, feline smile.

"Perhaps. But how else would I know who you are beneath your armor?"

I glanced around the room again, suddenly more aware than ever that every Duskraven here could be hiding something under their skin—not just fangs and claws, but magic that could bend minds, twist emotions, shape reality.

What else could they do?

"You are more than welcome to stay," she said smoothly, her voice curling like smoke through the open room. "One night, two, however long you need to recover your strength. We've already brought your horses into the valley. They're safe—grazing near the eastern riverbend and enjoying the fresh water."

I let out a breath I hadn't realized I was holding. The thought of Spirra in some hidden stable had gnawed at me more than I wanted to admit.

"But," Ilyrana continued, her tone brightening, "you've arrived on a most fortunate evening. Tonight, we celebrate Vareth'Sul."

Cain tilted his head. "That's a holiday?"

"A sacred one," she confirmed. "It marks the first moon after the mid-harvest, when we honor the harmony of our magic and the protection of the valley. There will be ceremony and celebration once the sun sets."

Dante perked up, already looking interested. "Do these celebrations involve more wine and fewer clothes?"

Ilyrana only smirked.

"Until then," she continued, "you'll be set up in my personal abode. I have two guest rooms, though I must apologize—there are not more."

She glanced between the three of us. "I assumed the men would be comfortable sharing."

Cain's posture tightened. "No."

Dante snorted. "Yeah, hard pass. That guy will murder me in my sleep."

Ilyrana's brows lifted in surprise, her cat-like gaze drifting from Cain to Dante, then back again.

"I see," she said slowly, and then—unexpectedly—offered a solution. "Then, Everly, you may stay in my chambers. There's more than enough space. The guest rooms will go to each of them separately."

That earned a blink from all three of us.

Before anyone could object, Ilyrana clapped once, and women moved forward from the edges of the room—each of them tall, graceful, and barely dressed.

"Please," she said. "Get settled. You've traveled long and hard."

One of the women, eyes sparkling, reached for Dante's arm. He took it with enthusiasm, casting a smirk over his shoulder. "Finally, some hospitality I can appreciate."

The woman giggled as she led him away. "Don't wait up," he added with a wink.

Cain hadn't moved.

He stood with his hands behind his back, his jaw tight, his eyes fixed solely on me. There was a question in them. Not one he could ask out loud, not here. But it was written in every line of his face.

Do you want to stay with her? Or… with me?

I felt the weight of that question hit somewhere deeper than I wanted it to.

I gave him a soft, reassuring nod. “It’s okay,” I said quietly. “Go.”

His shoulders tensed, but he nodded once, turning only when one of the women gestured for him to follow.

Then it was my turn.

Another woman approached, her steps silent on the woven mats, her expression gentle as she gestured for me to come with her.

I looked back once—just once. Cain was still glancing over his shoulder, his expression full of unspoken things.

Chapter 35

Everly

The path we followed twisted through low-hanging trees and lantern-lit clearings, the soft glow casting Sylra's silhouette in gold and shadow. She walked gracefully beside me, bare feet making no sound as they touched the forest floor.

After a few quiet steps, she glanced at me. "I speak your tongue… not perfect. But enough?"

"Yes. You're doing great." I said as I smiled at her.

She gave a pleased nod. "I am called Sylra."

"Everly," I replied.

Sylra gestured ahead toward a raised wooden structure partially hidden by trees. "That is Princess Ilyrana's place. You stay there. I find something… to wear."

I raised a brow. "So… you *do* wear clothes?"

She laughed, a sound soft and warm. "Yes, yes. Just… not much. Easier for us. Clothes tear when we shift. Most prefer skin."

That made sense, even if it still left me blushing more than I'd admit.

I glanced over. "Can everyone do what the Princess does? You know… the half-form?"

Sylra shook her head. "No. Only royalty. Born with it. They can shift *between*—stay part-feline, part-fae. It is how we see… um…" She paused, searching for the right word. "Line. Legacy. Yes?"

"It's how you recognize the royal family."

"Yes. That. And… looks good." She grinned playfully. "Very cool."

"It really does." I laughed lightly.

We walked in silence for a moment. Then Sylra tilted her head, golden eyes sharp with curiosity.

"Cain or Dante… are they your…" she struggled for a word, her brow furrowed. "Your… bond? Partner? Mate?"

I nearly stumbled. "What? Oh—no. I mean… it's complicated."

Her ears twitched as she waited, clearly interested.

"I thought I liked Dante first," I admitted. "He's like me—different. Out of place. He made me feel like I wasn't alone."

"And Cain?" she asked gently.

I hesitated. "Cain was… authority. Distant. Someone I respected but didn't think I could reach. But that changed."

My voice grew quieter.

"There was a night. Back in Doren. After everything that happened…"

The memory flashed like heat under my skin—Cain's hands on my body, the way he touched me like he knew exactly where all the broken pieces were and didn't want to fix them—just hold them. The way he looked at me was as if I wasn't something to resist but something to choose. It had been raw. Real. And far more than just physical, though I didn't say that part out loud.

Sylra's head tilted slightly. "You shared warmth."

"That's one way to put it."

She gave a slow, knowing smile. "Mmm. That explains the varenya."

My brows drew together. "The what?"

"Varenya," she said again. "A flower. We give it to someone when we choose. It means commitment. Devotion." She sniffed lightly in my direction. "You carry the scent of it. Very strong."

My mouth went dry. "So… you're saying I smell like a love flower?"

"Yes," Sylra said simply. "But only when the feelings are real."

"It must be hard to be around someone like Norvas with your ability." I say, trying to change the subject.

Sylra chuckled, the sound low and pleasant. "Yes," she said without hesitation. "He is… loud. Even when silent."

She looked at me, her eyes shining with subtle warmth. "But you—your emotions are different. Bright. Like a torch in still water. You're not hard to sense. Just… honest."

Something about the way she said it made my chest tighten, like being seen in a way that had nothing to do with what I looked like—and everything to do with what I carried inside.

"You are beautiful. You should embrace the ceremony tonight. Let them see you."

My cheeks flushed at the compliment, and I looked away as we rounded the bend that led to Ilyrana's abode. The place was massive—larger than I expected—woven walls and bamboo supports blending with the natural surroundings, as if it had grown here instead of being built. Sylra led me up a wide set of stairs into a space that was open, airy, and shockingly elegant.

The room she guided me into took my breath for a moment. A canopy bed stood in the center, the sheer fabric draping from its frame billowing slightly in the breeze that moved through the open slats of the walls. A full-length mirror, polished and tall, rested in the corner beside a low vanity table topped with small glass jars and carved wooden brushes. A rack of clothing—if you could call it that—stood by the wall, all of it sheer, light, and entirely unlike anything I'd ever worn.

Sylra moved with purpose, immediately turning toward me. Without hesitation, she began tugging gently at the strap of my tunic.

I stepped back instinctively. “Wait—what are you doing?”

She tilted her head, curious. “Helping you change. You are tense. I can smell it.” She smiled. “You can trust me, Everly Walker.”

It was strange how those words settled over me like a balm. And against my better judgment, I nodded. She moved more slowly this time, reverently unbuckling my sword sheath and lifting it from my shoulders. She carried it to the door and hung it carefully on a wooden peg, as if it were something sacred. Then she knelt, unlacing my boots and sliding them off one at a time. I watched her fingers move to the braid in my hair, and when she gently unraveled it, I didn't stop her.

It felt… weird. Intimate. But not romantic. Not invasive.

“Do you always touch people like this?”

She smiled as she stood. “It is our way. We are… open. Intimacy is shared. Bodies are not secrets.”

I blinked. “You mean like… everyone is just okay with—sharing each other?”

Sylra nodded as if this were the most natural thing in the world. "Yes. We are one tribe. We comfort, we connect. There are no rules around touch. Around love. All is given freely, and taken with respect.”

My face went hot. The idea of a whole village living like that—sharing everything—being that open—was almost too much to comprehend. I glanced at Sylra’s body—sleek, lithe, effortlessly perfect. And couldn’t help comparing it to my own—softer, curvier, every inch of me wrapped in awkwardness.

But Sylra didn’t seem to notice. She reached for my hand, wordless now, and led me toward a door on the far side of the room. I expected a washroom. A private bath, maybe. Instead, we stepped outside.

A small wooden deck led to a bubbling hot spring, its surface steaming beneath the midmorning sun. The world was quiet out here, wrapped in birdsong and the rustling of leaves. Sylra let go of my hand, pointed to a woven basket filled with soaps and oils, and turned with a graceful nod. “Take your time. I return soon.”

And just like that, she vanished back inside. I stood there, naked under the open sky, the warm air brushing across my skin. Everything in me screamed to cover up. But the spring beckoned.

I stepped in slowly, letting the heat seep into my aching muscles. The moment I was submerged to my shoulders, a long sigh escaped me. The journey. The cold. The weight of everything—it melted, inch by inch.

I leaned back against the smooth stone edge of the spring, tilting my head to the sky, now glowing a perfect, cloudless blue. My eyes drifted closed, the warmth lulling me into stillness. For the first time in what felt like days… my body began to truly relax.

How much time has passed? The water was so warm, so comforting, that the minutes had melted away like steam rising from the surface.

I was halfway through rinsing soap from my hair, tilting my head back and smoothing my fingers through the tangled strands, when I heard someone clear their throat behind me.

I jumped, nearly slipping, and instinctively ducked lower beneath the water, arms coming up to cover my chest. Spinning halfway in the spring, I looked up—

and froze.

Cain was standing a few feet away at the edge of the stone, and… he was naked. My brain stuttered. My mouth opened. Nothing came out. He didn't seem even remotely embarrassed. If anything, he looked amused. Calm. Completely in control, he asked, "Mind if I join you?"

His tone was casual, confident, like we'd done this a thousand times before.

"Uh—sure. Yeah. It's… it's just water," I stammered, and immediately cursed myself for how dumb that sounded.

I quickly moved to the far side of the spring, putting about ten feet between us. Not that it helped. I could still see every inch of him when he slid into the water with effortless grace, steam curling around his shoulders like the valley itself welcomed him. I focused hard on washing my arms, refusing to look.

Don't look. You'll regret it. Don't—

I looked. And regretted it. But also didn't.

Cain was watching me. Quiet. Still. Not leering, not smug—just… watching.

I ducked under the water, rinsing the last of the soap from my hair. The heat clung to my skin, making me feel both relaxed and entirely on edge. When I surfaced, pushing my wet hair back, he was still watching.

He moved slowly, reaching for the soap I'd set near the edge. "Want me to wash your back?" he asked, voice low.

For a second, I forgot how to breathe. I hesitated, then turned my back to him, moving closer until I could feel the shift in the water behind me.

"Okay," I said quietly.

Cain didn't rush. He lathered the soap in his hands first, then gently touched my shoulders, slick palms gliding across my skin.

"The soap smells like jasmine and honey," he murmured. "Sweet. But grounded."

His voice was close to my ear, a little lower than usual. I tried not to shiver, but his hands were firm, slow, moving over the planes of my back, down my spine, then back up to the sensitive space between my shoulders. The place where my wings were supposed to emerge. That spot had always felt… strange. Bare. Exposed. But his touch didn't feel invasive. It felt reverent. Like he was memorizing something sacred. His fingers gently brushed my wet hair to the side, and a moment later, his lips brushed the skin just between my neck and shoulder blade. Every nerve in my body lit up like it had just remembered exactly who was touching me.

And worse, that I wanted him. Badly.

The warmth of his lips lingered on my skin, seeping in deeper than the heat of the spring itself. But I couldn't let myself drown in it—not again.

I pulled away slowly, the water rippling around us, and turned to face him. My arms instinctively crossed over my chest beneath the surface, just enough to preserve some illusion of modesty. Cain didn't move, but his eyes stayed locked on mine, steady and unreadable.

"We should talk about it," I said quietly. "About Doren. That night."

His expression didn't change. "What is there to discuss?"

I swallowed hard. "We haven't said more than two words about it since we left. It just… happened. You had just found out about your father—about all those lies. I figured you were looking for comfort. Something to take the edge off the pain."

Cain's jaw flexed, but he didn't look away. "You really think that's all it was?"

"I don't know," I admitted, voice softening. "Maybe?"

I hope not.

"You don't see clearly, Everly," he said, voice firm but not unkind. "You never have—not when it comes to how I see you."

My breath caught.

"I've been drawn to you from the start. Not because I was grieving. Not because I was broken. But because you are… you. Strong. Stubborn. Brave enough to stand beside me when everyone else steps back." He paused, eyes searching mine. "And after everything we've been through out here, after all the things I've seen you survive… I'm not afraid of how I feel anymore."

My heart fluttered with a hope I didn't know I could have.

"How do you feel?"

His voice dropped, low and certain. "I've fallen for you."

Oh gods.

"Cain…" I shook my head, pushing wet hair behind my ear. "You're going to be the prince someday. Your father's never going to take the throne, and you've been raised to lead. To rule. You'll have a kingdom to worry about."

I looked away, focusing on the shifting water around my fingers. "What am I supposed to do? Go back to Verdanis and… what? Be your Princess?"

He said nothing, so I kept going, the words spilling out. "The people there would never accept me. I'm not—I'm not royalty. I'm not graceful or proper or *worthy.* I'm just the half-fae girl with a Sight she barely understands. I don't belong in a castle."

Cain moved closer, just enough for his voice to drop into something warmer. Closer. Real.

"That's just it," he said. "Out here, you don't treat me like they do. At the palace, the ones who know my name treat me like a prince. The ones who don't treat me like the war general's son. Either way, I'm just a title to them. A future. A set of expectations."

His eyes softened. "But you… you treat me like a man. Just Cain."

My heart pounded as I stared at him, still not quite able to believe the words he'd just said. Cain… the prince, the soldier, the man who carried the kingdom on his back… was standing in front of me, saying he had fallen for *me.* And meaning every word of it.

I leaned in slowly, eyes never leaving his. My hand rose almost of its own accord, brushing over the curve of his broad shoulder, then tracing down his chest—warm, solid, genuine—until I was close enough to feel the soft exhale of his breath against my lips.

His eyes searched mine, unwavering, and then he whispered, voice low and

steady,

"I choose you. If they can't accept you… I can't sit on that throne."

That was it. The wall between us cracked and shattered. I closed the space between us and pressed my lips to his. At first, the kiss was slow, deliberate—like we were finally tasting something we'd both been craving but hadn't dared reach for. But it didn't stay that way.

All the emotion we'd been holding back—the grief, the fear, the longing, the tension—ignited. The kiss deepened, rougher now, urgent, like we were both afraid it would be our last. Our tongues brushing past each other. I pulled his bottom lip between my teeth, and his breath hitched. Cain's arms wrapped around me, pulling me against him until there was nothing but heat and breath and skin. His hands explored my back, fingertips skating across the sensitive space where wings should be, and the contact made me shudder against him. His other hand runs its way down my side, past my hip, and around to the bottom of my ass cheek.

My hands moved of their own accord, exploring the contours of his body, memorizing the shape of the man I hadn't let myself fall for—until now. He kissed me like he'd been starving. And I kissed him like I didn't care if I ever came up for air again. I could feel his hard length press against my thigh as I pressed against him. I started to open my legs just a little bit more.

Just as Cain's mouth brushed the corner of mine again, a voice called out—bright and innocent as a bell.

"Everly! I have clothes for you!"

I froze. Cain pulled back only slightly, just enough for us both to look up and see Sylra standing at the edge of the hot spring, holding a folded bundle of deep red fabric in her arms.

I immediately pushed away from Cain and stood, water cascading around me as I moved toward the stone ledge, trying to hide the ridiculous smile on my face—and the bright heat coloring my cheeks.

"Th-thanks, Sylra," I said, clearing my throat as I climbed out, keeping my eyes anywhere but on her or Cain.

She gave a sly grin but said nothing as she handed me a soft towel. Cain didn't seem even remotely phased. He simply leaned back in the water, arms stretched behind him, eyes glinting with satisfaction. "See you at the ceremony," he said, his voice laced with amusement.

Sylra, ever composed, turned to him with a lifted brow. "You were supposed to have escort. Woman to show you around."

Cain smirked. "She found her way to Dante's room. Along with *his* escort."

Sylra rolled her eyes with a huff and muttered something in Duskrani under her breath.

She followed me back into the Princess's private quarters, where a thin red robe had been laid out across the bed. I slipped it on quickly, grateful for the thin layer of fabric, even if it still left very little to the imagination. My skin was still warm, and my heart hadn't settled from the water… or Cain.

Sylra stepped behind me, holding the outfit she had brought. It was beautiful. And daring. A sheer red skirt, silky and soft, that wrapped around my hips and tied at the waist, parting open along one leg to reveal nearly everything. The top was like a bikini, also sheer, but adorned with tiny rubies sewn into the edges in curling patterns. It shimmered every time it caught the light. I didn't notice there was no underwear.

"Red matches your hair," Sylra said, adjusting the knot at my waist. "And is color of power. Very strong." Her English was still halting, but the message came through clear as day.

I felt… powerful. A little exposed, yes, but there was something in the fabric, in the way it moved against my skin, that made me hold my shoulders a little higher. She guided me to the mirror and began weaving my damp hair into a crown of braids across the top of my head, leaving the rest down in long, soft waves. I barely recognized myself when she finished.

When we stepped outside, the sun had dipped low, casting everything in golden-pink light. The center of the village had come alive with color and movement. Duskraven fae in every form—half-shifted, feline, and fully fae—danced in the open space, laughter echoing between the huts, music pulsing from hand drums and wooden flutes. Bright lanterns hung from trees and beams, glowing in soft blues, oranges, and greens.

It was more than a celebration. It was a festival of life. As we walked, I noticed many of the fae wore flower leis made of woven blossoms—some simple, some intricate, glowing faintly with inner magic.

I turned to Sylra and nodded toward one. "What do those mean?"

She smiled. "The leis… are for first Vareth'Sul. When one is new… mated half. First ceremony as bonded."

I blinked. "Like… newly chosen mates?"

She nodded. "Yes. It is symbol. Of love… and acceptance."

I glanced around again, heart thudding. Everywhere I looked was warmth. Joy. Connection. And now, walking among them in crimson and gold, I wasn't sure I'd ever felt more seen.

Across the village's center, beyond the fire flickering high into the twilight sky, I caught sight of Dante. He was lounging on a bamboo couch nestled beneath a curtain of low-hanging tree branches, the shadows of the leaves playing across his bare chest like dancing ink. Two women sat on either side of him, practically in his lap, laughing at something he'd said, their hands lazily tracing the lines of his arms.

The grin on his face stretched wide—almost too wide. The kind that looked like it belonged to someone living their best life. But I knew better.

For a moment, I was taken back to the beginning. To the classrooms where he sat behind me, flicking paper at my hair until I finally snapped and threw my pen at his head. The wry smiles. The way he referred to everything we did as a "mission." The friend date he dragged me on, where he insisted it wasn't romantic and then paid for my tea anyway.

We used to joke. Laugh. Bicker like we were made of equal parts tension and comfort. We still bicker… but now it cuts deeper. The jokes are sharper. Meaner. Laced with bitterness, we both pretend it's not there. There's a chasm now—this vast, unspoken rift between us that I'm not sure can ever be crossed again.

My heart pulled tight at the thought.

Betrayal hurts. But guilt might hurt more. Especially when it wasn't just my heart that was caught in the fallout. Cain…

I shifted my weight, looking down at my hands.

Then back at Dante.

He was still smiling, still charming the women beside him with that roguish sparkle in his eye. But I saw it—just beneath the surface—the weariness, the ache, the shadow in his gaze that no amount of attention or praise could erase. He had been through so much. Shaped by people who saw him as a weapon, not a person.

And maybe he hadn't always made the right choices. Perhaps he had lied. But he had been a friend once. Even now, even when he tried so hard to look untouchable… I still felt bad for him.

Sylra gently took my arm, guiding me through the crowd with soft, knowing smiles. We wove between dancers and drummers, laughter and music swirling like smoke. The scent of spiced fruit and burning oils clung to the air.

She led me toward a clearing near the heart of the village, where a throne had been placed beneath a newly constructed canopy of silk and woven vines. Lanterns floated overhead, casting the space in golden light. There, seated beside the throne in conversation with Princess Ilyrana, was Cain.

His back was to me at first, head tilted toward the Princess, his posture relaxed. But the moment he turned and saw me, his body stilled—and his eyes, gods, the look in them made my breath catch. They burned with hunger, sharp and focused. He stood slowly, like he couldn't help himself. Only then did I realize why he looked at me that way.

I was… practically naked.

The sheer red fabric clung to my curves, the slit in the skirt offering more leg than it concealed, the ruby-lined top shimmering against the soft lantern light. I suddenly felt overexposed, vulnerable beneath his gaze, even though I'd walked with confidence just moments ago. I swallowed down the heat climbing up my neck and forced myself not to fold inward. Cain, for his part, was not helping.

He was shirtless, his chest bare and sculpted, the muscles of his arms flexing as he moved. His pants were white, loose-fitting, and nearly sheer, clinging just enough to make my mouth go dry.

But it was the tattoos and scars that drew my attention—the intricate black markings that twisted along his side, across his shoulder, and ribs. And then there was the angry scar—deep purple-red—slashing from his left hip down to just beneath his knee, barely visible under the fabric. A reminder of the weight he carried. Of everything he'd endured.

He stepped toward me, slow and deliberate, and when he reached me, he leaned in and brushed a kiss against the corner of my mouth. His lips barely touched my skin, but it sent a pulse down my spine.

"You look ravishing," he whispered into my ear.

I felt my face flush, but managed to keep a calm expression as we turned to face the Princess.

"Everly," Ilyrana said with a warm smile, eyes flicking over my attire approvingly. "Radiant. The color suits you."

"Thank you," I said, glancing over at Sylra, who still stood beside me. "Would it be alright if she stayed? She's been… amazing. I really like being around her."

The Princess gave Sylra a knowing glance, lips curving. "Of course. You may keep your shadow, Everly Walker."

Sylra dipped her head and stepped back silently into the space just behind me. Cain and I sat beside the Princess beneath the canopy, cushions arranged around a low table. Ilyrana reached for a carafe, its surface etched with vines and runes, and poured a glowing liquid into two cups.

"To new friends and new bonds," Ilyrana raises her glass.

Cain raised a brow but accepted a glass. I took mine more cautiously, unsure what the evening still held. As our glasses clinked softly in the golden light, I couldn't help the flutter in my chest.

Princess Ilyrana sipped delicately from her own goblet and turned her golden gaze toward Cain.

"You come from Erynvale," she said. "From the city of Verdanis, yes? Tell me… how fares the kingdom?"

Cain shifted beside me, keeping his voice measured. “The capital still stands. Strong, though not without unrest. The Blight edges closer every season.”

“And the people?” she asked, swirling her drink. “Do they still follow tradition, or has the fear made them forget their gods?”

Cain tilted his head. “Some traditions hold, others fade. The court worships peace now more than power. At least, outwardly.”

The Princess's eyes sparkled knowingly. "Peace is a lovely illusion. But it makes a poor shield." Then she glanced toward me, then back to Cain.

“And your companion—the shadow-eyed one with the charming grin. Who is he?”

Cain took a slow breath. “His name is Dante Verris. A companion on our journey. Capable… but complicated.”

Ilyrana chuckled. “Aren’t we all?”

She leaned forward, resting her elbow on the carved arm of the throne. “But this is not a night for complications. Tonight, we honor Vareth’Sul, the day of forgiveness, and the god of love. Perhaps you can all find your way into his spirit… and make this a night to remember.”

I smiled politely, but before I could respond, I felt… strange.

It started in my stomach—a slow, pleasant warmth that wasn’t like anything I’d ever felt before. It spread outward like honey in tea, thick and lazy, wrapping around my ribs, down my arms, through my thighs.

My fingers tingled. My skin buzzed. The world seemed brighter somehow, like the edges of everything had been traced in light. Then my limbs started to feel heavy, like my body had remembered gravity all at once. I turned slowly to Cain, and his expression matched mine—wide-eyed, disoriented, and slow.

He raised his hand, brushing my cheek with his knuckles. His voice was deep, low, slurred like velvet. "Do you feel heavy?"

I let out a laugh, light and tinged with surprise. "I do. What—what is this?"

That's when I felt the soft pressure of a hand on my opposite shoulder. I turned my head to find Princess Ilyrana, now standing beside me, a faint smile on her lips.

"You drank the varenye flower juice," she said calmly. "As is custom for our ceremonies. It opens the body… and the heart."

Varenye. My memory flashed—Sylra telling me it was the flower used in bonds. In choosing. The love flower. Sylra appeared as if summoned by the thought, stepping lightly from the shadows with a grin that said she'd known this would happen all along.

She reached for me and gently tugged my hand. "Come," she said, her voice warm and sweet.

I barely thought about it—I turned, still buzzing with warmth, and grabbed Cain's hand as I followed Sylra. His fingers wrapped around mine without hesitation. Together, the three of us moved back into the heart of the festival, where the central fire blazed tall and wild, throwing golden sparks into the night. Music poured from instruments that looked like they'd grown from the trees themselves—flutes carved from bone, drums made from vines stretched tight over wooden bowls. The fae danced in patterns around the fire, laughter rising into the stars.

Sylra pulled us into a long, weaving line of dancers. I had no idea what I was doing. But the steps were simple. Right foot, hop, hop. Spin. Left foot, hop. Spin again. Clap. Grab hands. Repeat.

We moved in unison, our fingers clasped with strangers, spinning and laughing and rolling like we were all part of something older than time. I caught Cain's eyes through the whirl of movement—he was grinning, the purest I'd ever seen it. And I was laughing too, my face flushed, my heart light, my body humming with joy and magic and something so close to belonging it made my throat ache.

After what felt like hours of dancing, the warmth in my limbs began to fade—not gone, just… settled. I peeled myself gently from the rhythm of the circle, slipping between laughing fae and flickering shadows until I felt the night air cool against my overheated skin.

The further I moved from the fire, the more the breeze kissed my arms and legs. My lungs expanded fully for the first time in what felt like forever. I found the bamboo couch Dante had claimed earlier—now empty—and sank into it with a sigh, fanning myself with my hands. My heart still raced with the echo of the dance, and my cheeks burned—not from embarrassment, but from too much smiling. Moments later, Sylra appeared, her steps light, her expression soft as moonlight. She sat beside me, her bare shoulder brushing mine lightly.

"You danced beautifully," she said, voice low and pleased.

I laughed. "I doubt that. But thank you."

Sylra looked at me with something tender in her eyes. "I want to thank you. For asking Princess Ilyrana to let me stay with you tonight."

I tilted my head, smiling. "Of course. I liked having you with me."

She hesitated, then added, "But I cannot. I have… important roles to play tonight. I am one of the Princess's consorts."

It took me a beat to process what she meant. Then my eyes widened slightly.

"Oh—oh! I didn't mean to, um…" I trailed off, flushing. "Of course. You can go to her. I wasn't trying to—keep you or… interfere."

Sylra laughed gently. "You did nothing wrong."

I nodded quickly, brushing hair from my face. "Still. Sorry if I stepped on any—royal toes."

She leaned closer, her voice warm. "You have a kind heart, Everly. I see it clearly."

Then she stood, smoothing the sides of her sheer, glittering skirt. As she turned to leave, she paused and looked back at me.

"You radiate beauty tonight," she said, eyes bright with something that felt like truth. "Embrace it. Let the night claim you. It may be the best night of your life."

With a playful wink, she disappeared into the shadows beyond the firelight, leaving the scent of jasmine and something wild in her wake.

And for a moment, I just sat there, hand resting on my chest, wondering if maybe… she was right.

My brain felt like it had been wrapped in silk and spun too fast. The stars above danced in swirls, and even though I was sitting still, everything around me swayed like a boat drifting on lazy waves. I'd had wine before—plenty, in fact—but this… this wasn't wine. This was a spell in a bottle. That flower, the *varenye*, really knew how to sink its claws in.

I sank deeper into the cushion, eyes fluttering closed. The world was soft, hazy. Warm. It wasn't until I felt the cushion next to me shift that I realized someone had sat down. I cracked one eye open. Dante's face greeted me—grinning like he'd just heard the funniest joke in the world. His teeth looked impossibly white. Had his mouth always been that big?

"How you feelin', Ever?" he asked, voice lazy and bright.

I blinked at him slowly, then looked around like the trees might answer instead. "Everything's… weird," I muttered. "Like my arms are full of honey and my brain is on… velvet? Or maybe clouds?"

Dante laughed. “Yeah. That sounds about right. Closest I’ve ever been to this was the time I took street acid and ended up at a firelight concert in Northwatch. Danced with a tree for an hour.”

I snorted. That sounded about right. But then the haze lifted just a little, just enough for something else to slip through—the guilt I’d been keeping locked behind my ribs.

“I’m sorry,” I blurted.

He blinked. “For what?”

“All of it,” I said, waving a hand vaguely. “The lying. The yelling. The way you look sad even when you smile. I feel bad. I know you didn’t have a… a good start. And you deserved better.”

My words spilled out in a slurry mess, my mouth clearly disconnected from any filter my brain might have had left. Dante gave a small, crooked smile—a real one this time.

“Don’t worry about me, Angel Eyes. I’ve got work to do. Always do. But I spent my whole damn life trying to find family, and I’m not about to let a few bruises keep me down.”

He leaned back, arms resting lazily on the back of the couch. “I’ve got a plan. I’ll win Cain over eventually.”

Just then, a chorus of giggles rang through the night. A few naked women came racing over, calling Dante’s name in Duskrani, their voices playful and musical. He laughed as they piled onto the couch beside him—on him, really—pressing kisses to his cheeks, his neck, their bodies draped over his like vines.

I started to rise, prepared to make a graceful… well, sort of… exit, when Dante winked and said, “Or maybe I’ll just stay here the rest of my life.”

That’s when I saw it. He was completely naked. My eyes widened, and I immediately looked away, a panicked noise catching in my throat.

By the gods.

I silently thanked every celestial being above that I hadn't noticed earlier.

And with that, I got up and walked very, very fast in the other direction—trying to pretend my brain wasn't still buzzing and that my "sort of" best friend wasn't currently being smothered in kisses by naked fae women on a couch.

I wandered back toward the sound of laughter and drums, the music spilling like smoke through the trees. My skin still hummed from the wine—or the flower, or both—and my mind floated somewhere between clarity and heat.

Just as I stepped past the edge of the light, a hand grabbed my wrist. I spun, breath caught in my throat—ready to scream— Until I felt him.

Cain.

His chest pressed to my back, his breath warm against my ear.

"I was looking for you," he whispered.

My whole body melted into his. His hands moved slowly, one settling at my hip, the other wrapping around my waist, pulling me closer. My back pressed flush to his chest, and I could feel every inch of him through the thin fabric between us. The air disappeared from my lungs as I leaned into him—deliberate, teasing. His body responded instantly, and I felt him growing hard as I pressed my ass back into him.

My head tipped back onto his shoulder, and he took that silent invitation with a hunger I felt all the way to my core.

His mouth found the Line of my throat, then the curve of my neck. Kisses—soft, then open-mouthed—burned against my skin. He lifted his hand from my waist to my other shoulder, running his fingers lightly over my collarbone and then down the valley between my breasts. My nipples peaked to a painful point, aching for his touch.

A soft moan escaped me, unbidden. The heat between my thighs flared so hot I had to press my legs together, using the friction to ground the building ache. But it only made it worse. I squirmed slightly, needing something—anything—to soothe the growing fire that was pulsing through my blood like the rhythm of the drums. Cain's hand, still on my hip, gripped more firmly, as if he could feel exactly what I needed.

And gods, I wanted to let go.

Cain's mouth moved down the side of my neck, but I managed to gather just enough breath to whisper, "Not here."

He paused, lips hovering above my skin. "Where then?"

I turned slowly in his arms, grabbing his hand and guiding him with me through the trees, away from the music and the glow of the firelight. "Come on," I said, glancing back with a grin. "I have a better idea."

The path curved in gentle shadows until the steam of the hot spring appeared ahead, curling upward like it had been waiting for us all night. I stepped to the edge, turning back to face him. Cain's eyes locked on mine, every bit of him hungry and heated—and still, he waited.

I reached back, my fingers finding the knots at the back of my top. One by one, I untied them slowly, the fabric loosening with every breath. The top slid down my arms and fell to the grass with a quiet whisper. Then my fingers moved to the tie at my waist. I released it with a gentle tug, letting the red skirt drift down to pool around my ankles. His breath hitched audibly.

I stepped back into the spring, the heat enveloping me, and glanced over my shoulder. "You coming or just going to stare?"

Cain's hands were already at his waistband, and he looked undone entirely—like a starving man watching his first meal. He practically stumbled out of his pants, the sheer fabric catching briefly around his calves before he kicked them off.

I watched him as he climbed in—every inch of him—admiring the length and strength of the man I had somehow come to crave. He reached me, and I pushed his back gently against the stone wall, just like I had imagined since earlier that night. My legs wrapped around his waist, anchoring us together, and I pulled him into a kiss that stole the breath from both of us. It was heated. Desperate. Like our mouths couldn't decide whether to devour or worship. When we finally broke for air, he rested his forehead to mine, still panting.

"I absolutely love you naked," he murmured, voice rough and reverent. "But it's a shame that outfit didn't last the night."

I laughed breathlessly. He lifted my chin, his eyes burning through the shadows and steam.

"You looked like a princess," he said. Then quieter, more certain—"My princess."

And in that moment… with his hands on my skin and the stars watching above… I almost believed it could be true.

Hearing that word made me feel feral. I ground myself on his rigid cock. The head of it glides over my clit, the pressure sending sparks through my nerves, shattering any lingering thoughts. Every pass of his against me lit my body with static—bright, electric. Cain's breathing grew shallow as his mouth trailed heat down my neck. When his lips found my breast, he captured my nipple gently between his teeth, while his hand explored the other with slow, deliberate care. A surge of sensation shot through me, connecting every nerve from my chest to the ache between my thighs.

I could feel the energy low in my belly stirring wild abandon. Every place his skin touched mine felt like an epicenter of an earthquake within my body. The sounds of my moans drown out the little sound we could hear of the party still going on beyond the abode. I slid myself down his shaft a little more so the tip of his dick was lined perfectly with my entrance. Cain leaned his head back.

"Your pussy is so fucking hot for me, princess."

Without warning, he picked me up and spun us around. I was sitting at the edge of the spring. He looked up at me and forced my knees apart, and I grabbed him by his hair and started pushing him down. At first, he resisted—Cain always liked to be in control—but the moment passed, and he surrendered. His mouth found me with reverence. First, it was just a flick of his tongue across my clit. Once. Twice. Each time, my body arched, and a breathless cry escaped my lips. The third time was slow and from clit to my hole. He sighed when he tasted how much I desired him. When he groaned softly against me, I shivered.

"You taste like sin," he murmured.

And then he gave in completely. His tongue pushed into me, and his fingers followed. The world blurred, and I gave myself over to it—every nerve, every sound, every heartbeat. He pumps in and out, causing me to tighten around his fingers.

A muffled "Princess" was all it took for my body to convulse. My pussy clamped down on his fingers while lightning flashed behind my eyelids. He kissed his way back up my body as I rode out the storm in me, pulling his fingers out after the last of the spasms.

Cain pulls me into the spring in his arms. I wrap my legs around him once again, but this time he doesn't let me tease him. He pushes me so that my back is now against the edge of the spring. I felt his stiff cock push into me. He started off slowly, letting me get used to his thickness.

Oh gods, I forgot how big he is.

The more he pushed in, the more my walls tightened around him. Once he was buried in me to the hilt, he stopped to look me in the eyes.

"Gods, Everly…" His voice was a whisper and a vow. "I swore I wouldn't do this again. But maybe it's not just the flower-wine. Maybe it's you. All of you. Because I love you."

I could barely breathe, much less speak. But I managed, through the haze of sensation, to answer.

"I can't say I love you yet… I need to be sure. But what I do know?" I leaned in, kissing the corner of his mouth. "You're mine, Cain."

The smile on his face says it all as he grabs my face and pulls me in for another scorching kiss. I started moving my hips to match his as the pace began to get more punishing. His cock was hitting a deliciously sensitive spot that left me screaming with each thrust. The hot water surrounding us feels like it's being heated by our passion.

I opened my eyes and noticed we weren't alone. In fact, there were more than a few couples, and thruples, and multiples getting intimate in the hot springs. I tapped Cain on the shoulder, and he stopped to look as well. My face turned bright red. The heat is no longer from arousal, but embarrassment. Cain laughed lightly. He turned to me and asked, "Do you want to stop?"

Curiosity got the best of me as I watched a pair of women across the spring. One's head was between the other's legs, while the woman receiving played with her nipples. But she was looking. Right. At. Me. We locked eyes, but instead of embarrassment, it turned me on. I turned back to Cain.

"No." I said, "I think this is part of their custom and I would hate to be rude."

He chuckled, voice rough with desire. "Ah. Yes. Respecting tradition."

Without another word, he thrust back into me and started fucking me with a newfound fervor. I grabbed his hair by the back of his head and pulled him down to my chest. He took my nipple into his mouth immediately, eliciting a moan from me. All the while, my eyes were still locked with the woman's. Moans of ecstasy and pleasure could be heard everywhere. More than once, I thought someone was going to ask to join in with me and Cain or invite us in with them. I stopped making eye contact but still watched as much as I could.

Our thrusts were hard, like we were both struggling for power over the situation. Struggling to be the alpha. I lifted my leg a little higher, allowing for Cain to push in just a little bit more. I felt his whole body tense as his cock started to twitch. My walls locked around it as I came at the same time he spilled into me. I rode out the waves, staying grounded as he caught his breath.

His hand wrapped around the back of my neck, and he kissed me lightly. When he pulled back, his eyes were half hooded, and one side of his mouth quirked up in a crooked smile.

"Well, I don't know about you, but I could use a drink," he says as he pulls himself out of the water and holds out his hand for me.

We walked back toward the center of the village, the path bathed in warm, flickering light from hanging lanterns and scattered flame bowls. Our clothes were long forgotten, but for once, I didn't feel exposed.

I felt free.

And Cain's eyes on me only fed that fire. Every glance, every lingering look down my body like I was a sunrise he couldn't stop watching—it gave me a strange, electric confidence I'd never known before.

As we stepped into the clearing around the central firepit, the music quieted. A hush had settled over the village, a kind of reverent silence. Something ceremonial was happening. Figures surrounded the flames, some seated, others standing in a loose half-circle. I could hear words being spoken, rhythmic and unfamiliar—Duskrani, no doubt. It flowed like water, beautiful and otherworldly, but I couldn't catch a single meaning.

I stayed still, holding Cain's hand, as we watched. A woman approached us quietly, barefoot and graceful, carrying a tray with two cups of glowing liquid. The same flower-wine from earlier. Cain took one and handed the other to me, his thumb brushing over my fingers as I accepted it.

The woman gave a soft nod, then turned to a small bowl that was being passed around. Inside was a thick, glossy black paste. She dipped her fingers into it and stepped closer to me. I didn't move—just watched, breath held, as she began to paint me.

With delicate precision, she drew dark streaks and flowing patterns across my chest, over my shoulders, down my arms. Her touch was warm but grounding. The marks looked like warrior sigils but interspersed with shapes that felt older—like runes, maybe blessings in a tongue I couldn't understand.

She moved around me, fingers gliding across my back, up along my cheekbones, and across the bridge of my nose. When she stepped back, I didn't feel painted. I felt marked. Seen. Chosen. She turned and did the same for Cain. He knelt so she could reach his chest and shoulders, and the sight of him—bare, powerful, and reverent in the firelight—made my chest ache.

I caught a glimpse of the Princess, seated beside the fire in her own half-shifted form. Her eyes found mine, and she smiled—not politely, but with warmth and approval. I smiled back, heart thundering in my chest.

The Princess rose slowly, raising both hands as her voice rang out in the native language, loud and clear. The crowd responded in unison—a cheer, vibrant and wild. Not knowing what was said, I still cheered with them, my voice joining the chorus.

The night air felt heavy—sticky with heat and magic, the sounds of laughter and passion drifting like music through the trees. The village pulsed with life and movement, yet all I yearned for was stillness.

I leaned against Cain, my head resting on his shoulder. "I'm really tired," I murmured. "Can I sleep in your room with you tonight?"

"Of course." He said, wrapping his arm around my waist and kissing the top of my head.

His voice held a warmth that made my chest flutter. Not desire this time—something quieter. Safer. We made our way back to the guest hut where he'd been staying, the light of the fire behind us casting long shadows through the trees. Inside, the air was cooler. Softer. The hum of the village faded slightly behind thick walls and woven curtains. I spotted them first—two neatly folded outfits at the end of the bed. If you could call them outfits. They were barely more than thin silk wraps.

I couldn't help but giggle. "Princess Ilyrana must've known we'd end up here together."

"She does have a talent for prediction," Cain said with a smirk.

We changed—turning around for modesty at first, then laughing at ourselves when we realized modesty had left us long ago tonight. When we finally crawled beneath the light, airy sheets, the mattress dipped under our weight, and I curled instinctively into him, my back against his chest, his arm draped easily over my side.

The haze from the flower-wine still lingered, making the room spin gently like the world had slowed to a lullaby. I let out a long breath, the warmth of Cain's skin grounding me.

"We still need to figure out this whole… princess thing," I whispered.

He didn't answer right away. Just pressed a kiss to the back of my shoulder, right where one of the painted runes still tingled against my skin.

"But for now," I added, closing my eyes, "I'll settle for just being us. Outside the walls."

His arm tightened slightly, and I heard the soft hum of agreement against my neck.

For now… it was enough.

Chapter 36

Cain

Morning came softly. The dusky light filtered through woven curtains, and somewhere nearby, songbirds chirped their greeting to the rising sun. But the only thing I cared about was the warmth in my arms.

Everly.

Her back pressed perfectly to my chest; our legs tangled under the light blanket. One of my arms was draped around her waist, the other tucked beneath her head, and I wasn't sure where she ended and I began.

I never thought I'd have the courage to tell her how I felt, to actually say the words. But I had, and somehow… impossibly… she wanted me, too. That feeling alone was enough to make my chest feel too full, like I couldn't contain it. I'd do anything to keep this—to keep her.

When we returned home, I would make her my Princess, no matter what anyone said. After all, my grandmother—the queen herself—had broken traditions to open the borders, to welcome unity. She would stand behind us. She had to.

Everly stirred against me, and I kissed the slope of her shoulder, soft as a breeze. Her eyes fluttered open—those impossibly bright green eyes—and just like that, my heart skipped a beat.

Gods, she looked like a goddess in the morning light. She smiled, and I smiled back, brushing a piece of hair behind her ear.

"I have a meeting this morning," I murmured, "with some of the Duskraven. They may know how to get into Merewick without getting us killed."

She nodded, yawning softly, and we both climbed out of bed. In our travel packs, we found clean clothes—extra uniforms we had packed away for a moment just like this. Once dressed, we stepped outside, the village slowly waking around us. Sylra was waiting. She wore a mischievous, knowing smile as she fell into step beside us.

"Sleep well?" she asked, the glint in her eye needing no translation.

Everly laughed softly. I just rolled my eyes and shook my head. "Lead the way."

She brought us back to the same large hut where we'd first met with Princess Ilyrana. The Princess was already there, lounging like a queen on her bamboo throne, her catlike eyes bright and sharp as ever. As soon as she saw us, her lips curled.

"Well," she said with a purr in her voice, "I suppose congratulations are in order."

Everly and I exchanged a look. I arched an eyebrow and turned back toward the Princess. "For what?"

Ilyrana laughed softly, standing tall. "You two participated in the marriage ceremony last night."

The color drained from my face.

"Wait. What?" Everly blurted, blinking rapidly. "What do you mean *marriage ceremony*?"

Then she turned to me, eyebrows raised high. "I thought you spoke their language!"

"I do!" I said, defensively. "I just… might've been a little inebriated last night. I wasn't exactly… focused on the vocabulary."

Before either of us could say anything else, the door curtain swished open and in strolled Dante, shirtless, beaming like he had just won the gods' lottery.

"Morning, lovebirds," he grinned. "I had the best night of my life. What did
I miss?"

I opened my mouth to respond, but for once… I was utterly speechless.

Married. To Everly. And I hadn't even asked.

Gods help me, I couldn't decide if I wanted to laugh… or panic.

"Apparently this dumbass got us married last night!" Everly snapped.

I didn't even get a chance to defend myself before Dante stared at me… went silent… and then exploded into laughter.

He stumbled back a step, then dropped into a woven stool, clutching his stomach. "You—*you two*—you got accidentally married? At a naked flower ceremony?" He was laughing so hard I half-expected him to choke on his own air. "This place is incredible."

Everly looked ready to throw something at him. I just dragged a hand down my face and stared blankly at the floor like it might open up and swallow me.

Ilyrana, calm as ever, didn't miss a beat. "I do apologize if this was not clear," she said, her voice as soft as silk. "But your prince seemed to understand our customs well enough."

I looked up, trying not to glare. "I studied the diplomatic dialect. I wasn't prepared for… flower-wine-induced orgy-vows in a language full of metaphors."

Just then, a man stepped into the room—bare-chested, with black cat ears poking through his hair and a long, twitching tail swaying behind him. He had the same sharp eyes as Ilyrana, golden tattoos glinting along his collarbones.

"Cain," Ilyrana said, glancing between us, "this is my brother, Prince Rhivane. He's agreed to share his knowledge of Merewick. You may speak privately, if you'd like."

I gave Everly a quick look—she was trying to kill Dante with her eyes—and followed Ilyrana's gesture toward a curtained room to the left. Finally, a reprieve. Behind me, I heard Dante's voice rise again.

"So! How was the wedding night? Did the flower-wine spice things up? Was the hot spring the honeymoon suite?"

Everly groaned. "Shut up, Dante."

"I'm just saying, for a guy who can't say 'I love you,' you sure skipped a few chapters!"

The curtain fell behind me, and I exhaled slowly. Married. I had no idea how I was going to explain this to my grandmother.

But first, I had to figure out how the hell we were going to make it to Merewick alive.

The room Rhivane led me into was cooler than the main chamber, the air still and shadowed. Maps hung from the curved walls, hand-drawn and aging, with newer ink added where fresh borders and hazards were marked. The scent of parchment, stone, and old ash lingered.

He moved to the center of the room and gestured for me to sit at the low table scattered with scrolls and jagged stones for weights.

"Merewick," he began without preamble, "is not what it once was. The ruins are mostly buried now, overrun by time and war. Nightshade has taken what's left and turned it into a stronghold."

I folded my arms. "That tracks. We're not expecting a welcome mat and flowers."

Rhivane's eyes met mine—sharp and intelligent. "The last we heard, he's built an army from defectors. Men and women who abandoned their kingdoms. Some are mercenaries, others desperate. They believe his promises. Others… don't get a choice."

He leaned over the table, tapping one long finger on a spot marked with crude lines.

"He takes prisoners," he said. "If he doesn't kill them on the land he destroys, he keeps them. Bends them. Mind control. Not like the old blood-spells. It's darker. Subtle. Like a fog that never lifts. It's the shadows that he infects people with."

I frowned. "How does anyone even get close without being turned?"

"Few do," he admitted. "Our warriors rarely make it far beyond the outer ridges. The ones who do… if they come back, they're not the same." He paused. "We gather what we can from survivors. Whispers. Names."

He reached into a folded cloth and pulled out a small strip of worn leather. Sewn into it was a symbol. I didn't need to look closely to know what it was. My chest tightened.

"The last name we heard," Rhivane said carefully, "was *Walker*. A man wearing this."

He placed it gently in front of me. The royal crest. My crest. The one sewn into my own tunic, the one I wore into every council meeting and battle plan. I stared at it.

"Do you know him?" Rhivane asked.

I didn't answer right away. My thoughts raced, caught between disbelief and sickening clarity. *Walker*. My mind is only on the woman in the next room, with whom I just shared a bed.

"That's her father," I said quietly. "Everly's." I ran a hand over my face. "Fuck! Of course he's alive. Of course, he's a prisoner in the one place we're walking into blind."

Rhivane watched me for a long moment but said nothing.

I leaned back, exhaling through my teeth. "So let me get this straight. I just accidentally married Everly—haven't even told her I love her properly—and now I'm sitting here debating whether to start this 'marriage' with a lie or tell her father might be a mind-controlled prisoner of war."

I laughed, but it came out humorless. "Real strong start for a husband."

Rhivane raised a brow. "She doesn't know?"

"No." I shook my head. "Not yet obviously."

"Then tell her," He said simply. "If she's strong enough to walk into Merewick, she's strong enough to know who's waiting inside."

I nodded slowly, the weight of the leather patch sitting between us like a curse. "Yeah. I know."

But that didn't make it any easier.

Chapter 37

Everly

Dante's voice cut through the haze in my mind. "So… are we going to talk about last night, or are you just going to pretend it didn't happen?"

I blinked at him, shifting uncomfortably where I sat. The morning air was warm, but it felt heavy, like my skin wasn't sure if it wanted to settle over my bones just yet.

"I have no idea what I'm going to do," I admitted, voice low.

He tilted his head, studying me the way he always did when he knew I was unraveling from the inside out. Princess Ilyrana had been silent for a while, sipping something that smelled sweet and potent. When a woman approached and whispered in her ear, the Princess nodded and stood.

"We will speak again soon," she told me gently, her amber eyes lingering on mine. "I will try to ease your worry."

Then she was gone, leaving me alone with Dante.

He waited until the curtain fell behind her before speaking again, his voice gentler now. "Are you really okay?"

I let out a long, slow breath. "I don't know."

And then, slowly, I told him everything. About the night. The touch of Cain's hands. The way he kissed me was as if I were something sacred. The way he looked at me when he said he loved me. How my whole body felt like it had turned inside out under the stars and yet… I was still afraid. I was scared that I would wake up today and find Cain back to his broody self, ignoring me.

Dante didn't interrupt. He just listened. The way only someone who had once known your heart intimately could.

When I finally fell quiet, I turned to him. "Is this weird? Us talking about it?" He smiled—not the sharp, flirtatious smirk I was used to, but something softer. Sadder.

"No. Not weird." He shrugged. "Because now I see it. You were never meant for me."

His words didn't sting.

"You were the push I needed. The catalyst," he said. "Whatever we were… it got me here. It got me to people who see me. It got me to fight for something real."

I swallowed hard. "I'm still your friend, you know."

"I know."

His hand brushed mine briefly, a flicker of comfort in all the uncertainty.

"Always," he added.

And for the first time in a while, I believed him.

"I need to go for a walk," I say as I stand and walk out of the hut.

The village buzzed with life, humming with the rhythm of another sunlit morning. I wandered aimlessly, letting the warm breeze guide me past huts and stands, through shaded paths and bursts of laughter.

Children darted around, half-shifted and carefree. Their little tails swished as they played tag, their bare feet quick over the packed dirt. It made me smile—how easy it was for them to find joy in a world that felt so fragile to the rest of us.

A loud rustling came from the tree line along with a cacophony of small voices. A now pony-sized Cerberus barreled through the path ahead, three heads barking in playful harmony as a half-dozen children chased after him, shrieking with delight. His tail wagged furiously, occasionally knocking over baskets or scattering flower petals in his wake. Two little ones clung to his back, giggling wildly as he galloped in wide loops like a parade float with paws. One of the children waved a ribbon high in the air, as if leading a cavalry charge.

"Nyx!" I called, laughing.

He skidded to a stop in front of me, all three tongues lolling happily as he trotted over to nuzzle my hand, still panting from his impromptu joyride. The children slid off his back, breathless with laughter, while the rest caught up and immediately began clambering to be next in line for a ride.

The most minor child tugged at my sleeve, her cat ears twitching from the exertion of the chase.

"He say you his person," she said solemnly, her tiny voice full of pride. "All heads agree."

Nyx gave an affirming chuff and licked my cheek with one of his side heads. At the same time, the center one stared at the children, already calculating the next step in their chaotic adventure. One of the boys climbed onto his back with a squeal. Before I could say anything, Nyx took off again, now three kids riding, three chasing, the whole mob vanishing around the corner like a stampede of joy.

I watched them go, smiling like I hadn't in days. Somehow, in the middle of everything—war, magic, grief—Nyx had become something whole and pure. A protector, a companion, and apparently… a playground on legs.

As I watched my new puppy with his playmates, a small girl with a braided crown of hair and twitching cat ears broke from the group. She came straight up to me, holding a flower in both hands—a white bloom streaked with deep violet veins. She looked up at me with golden eyes and placed it gently in my hand.

"Thank you," I said softly.

The girl giggled and ran off again, her tail flicking behind her.

"She name Jerika," a voice said beside me. "She give flower only when she feel… good heart." I turned to find Sylra walking toward me, a knowing smile on her lips.

"Well… that's sweet of her," I laughed. We fell into step together, the sounds of the village trailing behind us.

I glanced over. "So… how many of you are actually royal?"

Sylra chuckled, brushing her hair over one shoulder. "Mmm, many. Princess Ilyrana is first child. She… oldest of twenty-two."

My eyes widened. "Twenty-two?"

"Yes." She nodded. "Queen… still have babies. One more soon. Very soon." She tapped her stomach lightly and gave me a playful look. "That's why Queen and King not here for ceremony last night. Queen is with babies. King help when child grow… uh, how you say…?"

"Age up?" I offered.

"Yes, yes. Reach age of royalty. Then King teach—fighting, politics, speak to other kingdoms."

We walked in comfortable silence, a moment before Sylra suddenly turned toward a shaded structure. "Come. Do you like Java? I'll get us some. It's been a long time since I gossiped with new friend."

I smiled. "Coffee and gossip? You're speaking my language."

The shop was more of a stand, nestled under a large canopy with scattered seats and low tables. The scent of roasted beans met me like a warm blanket.

We took a seat, and a man with snow-spotted fur on his arms and a long, twitching tail brought over two cups. One sip and I nearly melted. It was smooth, bold, and impossibly rich.

"Oh gods," I sighed. "I missed this."

Sylra grinned. "Our warriors bring from low mountains. Very good, yes?"

"The best I've ever had," I said honestly, letting it warm me all the way down.

"So…" I looked at her. "What exactly are you to the princess?"

Sylra tilted her head, smiling. "I am… consort. One of them. But not only. I fight too. I train with Princess. With Rhivane. I go outside village and explore wastelands."

"You've been beyond the wards?" I asked, eyes widening.

"Yes. Not many do. I see what is out. I fight with Rhivane. We… learn much."

"What kind of things?" I asked, lowering my voice.

Sylra leaned closer. "The Blight. It not natural. Not sickness. It is… magic. Dark magic."

"Nightshade?" I whispered.

"Yes," she said, her tone more serious now. "Many here… they do not know. Do not want to know. They live happy, safe. But me? Rhivane? We see. We know he is real."

I looked down at the flower Jerika had given me, white and violet and fragile in my hand.

Sylra leaned back on the bench, legs folded beneath her as she took another long sip of her coffee. "Mmm. You drink fast. You like very much, yes?"

I laughed, wiping a drip from my lip. "Like? Sylra, if I could marry this coffee, I would've said 'I do' last night instead of Cain."

Sylra snorted into her cup, nearly choking. "Ha! Maybe I make you flower-wedding with cup next time."

We both laughed, the air between us lighter now. I leaned my elbow on the table and smiled at her. "You know, I kind of forgot what it felt like to just… sit and talk with someone. Back home, I had a couple close friends. Peris and Ferra."

Sylra tilted her head. "Mmm. Pretty names. They… like sisters?"

I nodded. "Yeah, honestly. Peris is the smart one—always correcting my grammar, always rolling his eyes when

I'd get distracted. He pretends he's annoyed with everything, but he's the first one to show up if I ever need him."

"Ah," Sylra said with a knowing grin. "The grumpy one who have heart like marshmallow?"

"Exactly!" I laughed. "Then there's Ferra. She's loud, blunt, and terrifying if you cross her. But she's also the one who'll braid your hair when you're crying and tell you that you're the most beautiful badass the world's ever seen."

Sylra leaned forward, intrigued. "She sound like someone I want to fight. Then hug."

"That's pretty much Ferra's entire personality."

"You miss them." It wasn't a question, but a statement.

"Yeah," I said, eyes softening. "Every day. I used to think I was just… surviving, back in Verdanis. It felt like my life didn't start until I left. But now that I've been gone this long, I realize they were my life. My grounding. And now..." I looked around at the colorful banners flapping gently in the breeze and the sound of children laughing in the distance. "This place feels… different. But in a good way."

Sylra reached across the table and tapped the back of my hand. "You strong. Even when you not sure. That what I see. Maybe this place not forever… but maybe it give you piece of your forever."

Her words sank in deeper than I expected.

"Thanks, Sylra."

She winked. "You are my first real gossip friend in long time. I not let you go easy."

I grinned. "Well, then you're stuck with me."

She raised her cup, and I clinked mine against it.

"Good," she said. "You fun. And I need more fun."

Sylra and I finished the last sips of our coffee, the warmth lingering in my chest as we stood and stretched beneath the leafy canopy. It had been too long since I laughed like that with someone new, someone who didn't expect anything from me except honesty and good company.

The village was quieter now as we made our way toward the hut that acted as a town hall. We slipped through the curtained entrance, the room already humming with conversation. Cain stood beside Prince Rhivane, while Princess Ilyrana sat cross-legged on a mat of woven reed, her head tilted as she listened.

Dante leaned against the wall near a map, arms crossed, looking like he hadn't slept but was still riding a high from last night's debauchery.

Cain's eyes lit up when he saw me, and he waved us over. "There you are," he said. "We were just talking about reinforcements."

Rhivane gave me a nod. "We're sending warriors with you," he said. "Ilyrana and I have agreed. I will be one of them. Sylra as well."

Sylra just grinned, sliding into the circle and plopping down beside the prince. "I like fight," she said casually. "Is good way to say hello and goodbye."

Ilyrana's expression was more serious. "There are few we can spare, but the ones we give you will be strong. One of them—Varon—can use his magic to make your group undetectable for a short time. Enough to get close."

My eyes widened. "That's… amazing."

Cain nodded. "We'll need it."

Sylra added, "I know way back to Doren. Much faster but must cross wasteland. Very hot. Very dry. But we go fast. Not stop."

Rhivane unrolled a map and pointed to a winding blue line. "This is the Rynmere River. Follow it and Merewick is—"

"We won't need the river," said a new voice from the doorway.

Everyone turned. A tall woman stepped inside, her presence immediately shifting the air. Her skin was the shade of midnight velvet, her lengthy hair woven with silver threads that glinted in the lamplight. Like Rhivane and Ilyrana, her eyes were gold and unreadable.

"Vaelora," Rhivane said, rising to his feet. "You're back."

She gave a slight nod. "I felt the veil stirring. I knew it was time."

Ilyrana stood as well. "My sister, Princess Vaelora. She walks between places."

"You mean she can teleport?" Dante asked, skeptical.

"In a way," Vaelora replied calmly. "I can create portals but only to lands I've walked. Doren is the farthest edge I've seen beyond the Blight."

Sylra leaned in, impressed. "She rarely leaves the groves. This… is not usual."

Cain crossed his arms. "And from Doren?"

"You should have no problem getting to Erynvale from Doren given the day's worth of head start the portal will give you."

Ilyrana stepped forward. "Then it's settled. Vaelora will open the portal as soon as you procure the captive."

There was a beat of silence. We were really doing this.

We stepped out to the stables, where Spira greeted me with a familiar snort and a gentle nudge.

"Oh, I missed you," I whispered, rubbing her nose.

The children had woven flowers into the horses' manes—white and red blossoms braided into strands of hair, their petals soft and fragrant.

"Luck," Sylra said behind me. "They believe flowers bring courage and hide you from bad eyes."

I smiled, heart squeezing. "We'll need both."

As we mounted up, Nyx padded over with a proud little bounce in his step, currently no bigger than a housecat. His three heads moved in unison—one yawning, one sniffing the air, and the middle one staring expectantly at the satchel strapped across my saddle.

Cain caught sight of him and crouched down, resting a hand on Nyx's back. "You should stay, little guy," he said gently. "I think you would be happier here."

Nyx let out a sharp huff—all three heads—and took a stubborn step forward, planting himself at my feet.

I crossed my arms. "He's coming."

Cain stood slowly, giving me a skeptical look. "Everly—"

"I'm not leaving him behind," I said, more firmly this time. "He's come this far with us. He's smart, quiet when he needs to be, and he fits in the satchel."

Nyx gave a self-satisfied growl and hopped lightly into my open satchel as if to say *See? I fit.*

Cain exhaled but didn't argue. He looked at Nyx, then at me, and finally gave a resigned nod. "Alright. But if he starts barking in the middle of a stealth run, you're carrying him."

Dante swung up onto his horse with a smirk. "So, what I'm hearing is—we're officially adopting the three-headed demon dog."

"He's not a demon," I said, adjusting the satchel so Nyx could peek out.

Dante tilted his head. "He breathes fire, glows in the dark, and eats undead skeletons for fun. If that's not a demon, I've got a few apologies to make to my exes."

"None of those things is true." I side-eyed him sternly.

"Exactly, we have no clue what he's capable of. How do we know if he is a liability?"

"Well, until that happens, he's mine. Even you were given a chance once you know." I said as we turned our horses toward the horizon and set off.

Chapter 38

Cain

The wind changed the closer we got to Merewick. It carried no scent of life—just dry dust and ash, the faint metallic tinge of old blood in the air. I pulled ahead slightly, signaling Dante with a glance. He slowed and dropped back next to me. Sylra, in her sleek black feline form, padded up silently to my other side, her yellow eyes flicking to me with quiet awareness.

"Keep your voices low," I said under my breath.

Dante nodded once. "What's going on?"

I hesitated for half a beat, then said it. "Everly's father is alive."

"What?" Dante asked in disbelief.

"He's in Merewick," I said, jaw clenched. "Nightshade has him. Mind-controlled, from what Rhivane told me."

Sylra made a low huffing sound from her throat, ears twitching.

"We can't let Everly see him," I continued. "Not yet. We came for my father. He's the priority. If she sees hers…" I shook my head. "It'll ruin her. She'll run in without thinking. She'll die."

Dante looked down, jaw tightening. "You really think she won't find out?"

"She might," I admitted. "But not from us. Not now. When the time is right—when we're safe—I'll tell her everything. I promise."

Sylra let out a soft growl of agreement and flicked her tail against my leg.

"We'll come back for him," I said firmly. "I swear it. But not today."

We rode in silence after that, the weight of what we were heading toward thickening with every step.

By the time we reached the final ridge overlooking Merewick, the sun was beginning to dip, casting the landscape in a bruised gold light.

We crested a hill, and then I saw it.

Merewick.

What was once a city now looked like a scar carved into the earth—half-collapsed stone walls, crooked towers of broken marble overtaken by creeping vines, blackened trees twisted like claws stretching skyward. But the worst part? The people. They moved in lines. Silent. Blank-eyed. Slaves.

Not bound by chains—bound by darkness. Their eyes glimmered black with shadow, their faces slack, stripped of identity. The magic clinging to them was suffocating, oily, and old. Among them walked others. Armed, alert. Defectors. Traitors from every kingdom, wearing mismatched armor and the insignias of fallen regimes. They looked proud. Fed. Alive. It made my stomach twist.

Rhivane came up beside me, his expression grim. He pointed to a squat, stone building near the inner edge of the city—partially sunken into the earth, half-covered in moss and shadows.

"There," he said. "That is where they keep the war general. If your father is still alive… he's in that building."

I stared at it, heart hammering. He was down there. So was Everly's father. I just prayed to the gods she wouldn't see him first.

We moved in calculated silence, the fading light casting long shadows over our cloaked figures. Rhivane took the lead, his movements sure, feline even in his fae form.

Dante and I flanked him, while the Duskraven warriors spread out in the terrain around us—each using their specific skills to weave protection and deception into our path.

Varon, the one Rhivane had spoken of, knelt near the ground at intervals, whispering in the duskraven tongue. A veil of mist shimmered into being around us with each breath of his spell—bending light and cloaking sound. We could move in daylight and not be seen, though we were warned not to speak unless absolutely necessary. His magic was thin, held together by concentration and sheer will.

From behind us, I could feel Everly and Sylra holding the rear—a silent, shadow-born partnership. Sylra moved effortlessly in her panther form, large and sleek, with eyes that missed nothing. Everly, though she didn't know everything, was focused. I felt her presence like a tether at my back, grounding me even as everything inside me pushed forward.

We slipped through cracked walls and collapsed corridors, ducking beneath exposed beams and ivy-choked arches. The air smelled of mildew and old magic, like spells that had bled into the stone and never faded.

Ahead, the building Rhivane had pointed to came into view. It was squat, circular, and partially sunken into the earth, like the gods had tried to bury it but failed. Two guards stood outside the entrance—defectors, judging by their ragtag armor and bored stances. Rhivane raised a hand. Two of the Duskraven peeled off into the shadows, disappearing without a sound.

A heartbeat later, both guards dropped—silent and swift, no cries of alarm, just the dull thud of bodies hitting the stone. The Duskraven had moved like whispers in the dark, never seen, only felt. Their blades were already sheathed by the time we crept toward the entrance, breath held tight in our chests.

We rushed forward, keeping low, feet quick but quiet. Every second counted now. The building's entrance loomed before us, half-sunken and worn by time, its stones slick with moss and old blood. The door was massive, framed by ancient runes worn smooth but still pulsing faintly with magical residue. Thick iron bars crisscrossed the front, sealing it shut. There was no visible handle, no latch, no hinges—just solid, unyielding steel.

I stepped forward and raised my hand, summoning the familiar warmth of magic into my palm. It flared to life beneath my skin, flickering gold across my fingertips. As I pressed my hand flat against the bars, I felt the resistance instantly. The iron hissed at my touch, reacting to the foreign energy, but didn't give.

I pushed harder, calling the spell deeper from within, letting it build in my veins. Still, the metal held fast. The bars quivered, almost flexed—but didn't move. Sweat beaded at my temple, frustration biting at the edges of my concentration.

It was awarded. Not just locked by mundane means but protected by layered enchantments. Strong ones. Old ones.

"Come on," I muttered through gritted teeth, magic flaring again, golden tendrils curling over the iron.

Still nothing. The door refused me. My magic wasn't enough.

Behind me, Rhivane stepped closer, eyes scanning the runes with a furrowed brow. "It's rune-locked," he said, voice low. "Not just any spell. This door—it was meant to keep things in. You need shadow or blood to undo it."

I withdrew my hand, chest heaving slightly. The metal smoked where my palm had been, but it hadn't so much as dented.

"I have shadows," Dante said, and he stepped forward. Our eyes met, and for a brief moment, I felt a real kinship with the guy. I almost felt bad for icing him out after everything.

He didn't wait for permission. He raised his hand and spread his fingers wide. The shadows from the walls bent toward him, coiling around his arm like smoke drawn to flame. They hissed and slithered down toward the seam of the door, pouring into the lock like living oil. The metal creaked, then groaned. With a final crack, the lock fell open.

Dante stepped back, his face pale but determined. "Go."

I didn't wait. Inside, the air was damp and reeking of sweat, mold, and rot. The corridor led to a single chamber lit by one flickering torch. My father lay on the floor.

The sight of him nearly shattered me. He looked like a ghost in a soldier's shell—a man who had once been indomitable, now reduced to frail limbs and sunken skin. I dropped to my knees beside him, the cold of the stone floor biting through my clothes, but I barely noticed.

His body was thin—too thin. Every rib stood out; his muscles wasted away to nothing. His once-proud uniform, the colors of Erynvale faded beyond recognition, hung off of him like a forgotten memory, torn in places and soaked with old blood and filth. His boots were missing. One foot was raw and swollen, the other wrapped in cloth so dirty it blended into the shadows.

His beard was long and ragged, threaded with gray and matted like he hadn't seen a proper bed in months. Cheeks sunken, eyes ringed with bruised hollows. His skin was waxen, almost translucent in the dim light. There was a fresh bruise on his jaw. And one of his wrists was still shackled to the stone wall, the iron biting into his skin so deeply it left an angry red welt.

I reached for him. "Father?"

For a moment, nothing. Then his eyes cracked open, dry and dull—but not lifeless. There was a flicker there. Faint. Fading. But there.

Recognition came like embers catching in ash—slow at first, then burning bright.

"Cain," he rasped. His voice was barely more than air, hoarse and broken.

My chest tightened, throat closing around a breath I didn't remember taking. I swallowed hard. "We're getting you out of here."

He coughed, the sound dry and raw. It shook his whole frame. He tried to sit up, but the effort nearly made him collapse again. I caught him before he hit the ground, his weight like that of a child.

"Not... safe," he whispered, eyes darting to the doorway. Fear flickered in them. Fear of what still waited.

I glanced up, nodding to Dante and Rhivane. "We're ready for anything," I said with a confidence I didn't feel. "Help me with the shackle."

Rhivane moved to cover the entrance, blade drawn, every muscle taut. Dante stepped forward without hesitation, raising his hand.

The shadows answered.

Dark tendrils crept up the wall, swirling around the rusted iron cuff. The lock hissed as if it were alive, resisting, but then—with a final pull and a sharp click—it snapped open.

My father collapsed into me, freed at last. He groaned as the weight shifted off his arm, and I wrapped mine around him, holding him steady, steadying myself. His breath came in shallow gulps, but he was still with me.

We moved fast after that.

Rhivane took the lead, scanning ahead for any sign of movement while Dante helped me support my father. The Duskraven warriors reappeared from the shadows like ghosts, guiding our path with soft clicks and hand signals. Every step away from that prison felt like a miracle, but I knew it wouldn't be over until we crossed the veil of trees back into the forest.

Sylra and Everly were waiting for us at the agreed-upon rendezvous point, just beyond the jagged edge of the city, where the crumbling bones of Merewick gave way to the sparse beginnings of green.

The covered wagon stood ready, shielded beneath a makeshift canopy of branches and cloth, hidden from prying eyes.

Everly rushed forward when she saw us, but stopped cold the moment her eyes fell on the bundle of frail limbs between us. Her expression crumpled.

"Is he—"

“He’s alive,” I said before she could finish, my voice tight. “But barely. We have to move.”

Everly didn’t speak, but the way she looked at me—shoulders trembling, jaw clenched—said everything. Grief, relief, and restrained panic danced behind her eyes. She blinked twice, then nodded, slipping her sword back into its sheath with mechanical precision.

Together, we laid my father in the covered wagon. Varon approached silently with a satchel of furs and something herbal-smelling in a small cloth pouch. He handed it to Everly, who opened it and blinked at the bitter-sweet scent.

“For pain,” he murmured. “He won’t wake yet. Body is too broken.”

I wrapped the furs tightly around my father, brushing the grime from his forehead with a gentler hand than I thought myself capable of. Every breath he took was shallow, but it was breath, nonetheless.

And then—movement.

A hush fell over the group as the trees behind us parted. A shadow emerged, graceful and fluid, her silhouette backlit by the dying sun. Long braids, laced with silver threads, swayed as she walked—each step measured, like she was in conversation with the earth.

Vaelora.

She was unlike her siblings—more distant, more solemn. Where Rhivane prowled and Ilyrana prowled with purpose, Vaelora moved like a drifting melody, soft and haunting. The Duskraven warriors bowed slightly at her approach. Even Sylra lowered her head in acknowledgment.

Vaelora's voice, when it came, was velvet and cool water.

"The veil is thin. If we are to leave, it must be now."

No one questioned her. The tension that had coiled in my chest like a drawn bowstring began to ease—not wholly, but enough to breathe. She stepped forward and reached into the air with both hands. No chants, no flourish. Just stillness. Then, the light fractured.

The air cracked open like glass, catching sunlight and revealing a portal rimmed with shimmering starlight. On the other side, a field stretched into forest, the land rising gently in a distant green swell. The ruins of Doren loomed in the background, ancient and forgotten.

Sylra, back in her fae form, gave a low whistle. "Even the trees look calmer there."

Dante stared, wide-eyed. "I don't know if I'll ever get used to that."

"Good," Vaelora said with a ghost of a smile. "Magic should never feel ordinary."

We moved quickly and efficiently. Dante and I lifted my father together—he was heavier than before. However, I knew it was only because my body had gone numb from grief and exhaustion.

The moment I stepped through the portal, something in me shifted. The pain, the rage, the guilt—they were still there. But the air felt different on the other side. Cleaner. Not just in scent, but in soul. Like the land itself hadn't been touched by Nightshade's rot.

Behind me, the others emerged one by one, hooves striking soft grass, armor glinting in the twilight. Everly came last, the portal light washing over her features like moonlight on marble. As she stepped through, the shimmer faded. The portal sealed behind us with a whisper, like a sigh escaping the gods.

We were in Doren now. No longer hunted—but far from free.

Chapter 39

Everly

Vaelora's portal dropped us just beyond the edge of the desolate city, where the forest rolled down into soft hills and the air smelled alive again. It was strange, feeling safe. Stranger still to realize how tightly I'd been clenching every muscle until now.

We found shelter beneath a canopy of leaning pines and sun-bleached stone. Rhivane scouted the perimeter while Sylra and two others arranged a lean-to with military precision. The others moved like shadows through the trees, vanishing to keep watch.

Most of the Duskravens didn't follow us through the portal. A small part of me felt sadness at not being able to say goodbye or even thank you to the ones who risked their lives. Only Sylra and Rhivane remained.

"This place will do," Rhivane said, breath visible in the cooling air. She had a way of speaking that made you feel like she was stating a fact, not offering an opinion.

Cain's boots crunched against the dry ground as he went straight to the wagon and climbed in without a word. I watched his back as he leaned over his father, brushing a strand of silver hair away from the man's face with such care it made my chest ache. Whatever fire burned inside Cain, it softened around Alaric. Rhivane and Sylra busied themselves pulling on heavy clothes from a bag they stowed in the covered wagon. I admired their preparedness.

Dante tied off the horses and checked the perimeter, his sword still slung across his back, but his hand never straying too far. Ever alert. Ever watching. I slid down from my horse last. My legs wobbled beneath me—not from the ride, but from the weight of everything I hadn't yet let myself feel. The adrenaline was wearing off, and beneath it, the exhaustion crept in like ice water. I stumbled a little, and Sylra was at my side in an instant.

"You alright?" she asked, her tone light but her eyes sharp. She had the kind of beauty that was sharp around the edges, like it dared you to look too long.

"Yeah," I said, though my voice cracked. "Just... catching up with myself."

She gave a slight nod and clapped me gently on the shoulder. "You did well back there."

I didn't know how to respond to that, so I just nodded. The camp came together slowly—just enough to keep us warm and hidden. A small fire, carefully built in a natural dip in the rocks. Bedrolls unrolled. The wagon shifted so Alaric could be partially propped up. He still hadn't stirred.

Cain sat beside him, unmoving. The firelight cast shadows under his eyes that made him look older. Worn. I sat down across from them and stared into the flames. For a while, no one spoke. The silence didn't feel awkward. It felt earned. Eventually, Dante joined us, settling beside me without a word. His knee brushed mine, and I didn't pull away.

"You think they'll follow us?" I asked, voice low.

"No," Rhivane said from where she perched on the rock above, her voice steady but low. "I cloaked us with Duskravian magic—they shouldn't be able to track us. But..." She paused, eyes narrowing as she gazed toward the horizon. "Something else is stirring. I can feel it in the wind."

That wasn't exactly comforting. I wrapped my arms around my knees and leaned in closer to the fire.

Cain finally looked up, his voice hoarse. "He's breathing steady. No fever. But he hasn't woken up."

"He will," I said, before I even realized I was going to speak. He looked at me then, and I forced a small, shaky smile. "He's strong. Like you."

Cain held my gaze a moment longer, then gave a slow nod and turned back to his father. The wind howled low around us, threading through the rocks like a ghost that had forgotten it was dead. The stars came out one by one, brilliant and cold above the wasteland. We were halfway to Doren. Just a few more days and we'd be out of this place. We could breathe. Maybe then I'd stop hearing the echo of those whispers from Merewick.

But for now, we were alive.

The fire had burned down to glowing embers by the time we settled for the night. The faint orange light flickered off the stone walls around us, throwing shadows long and strange across the cracked ground. The horses were tied, the Duskravens curled up near the wagon, and Alaric still lay silent in his blankets, unmoving except for the rise and fall of his chest.

Cain volunteered for the first watch. Rhivane joined him, perched atop one of the taller rocks like a sentinel. Her silver eyes glinted in the dark, unmoving as the wind stirred her braid. I was grateful for the quiet hum of her presence. If anything crept close, she'd know before the rest of us even stirred.

Dante paced near the fire, arms crossed tight over his chest. His brows were furrowed, and he kept glancing back toward the open desert.

"You alright?" I asked, voice low.

He looked over his shoulder at me, then shook his head. "I don't know. I just... feel weird. Like something's watching. Or… remembering me."

I stood up and stepped closer, trying to shake the feeling that his words had teeth. "You think it's just nerves? We've been through a lot."

"No." His answer was too quick, too specific. "It's not nerves. It's something else. Like there's a shadow still clinging to me."

Cain looked over at us from his post but didn't say anything. Rhivane's gaze flicked our way, sharp and quiet. I didn't press Dante further. We were all shaken. A few hours of sleep might help clear his head. I offered him my blanket, which he declined, and lay back down on my own. The wind sang low and mournful across the stone, and exhaustion finally dragged me into sleep.

That was when the nightmare came.

I stood alone in a field of ash. The world was gray—sky, soil, the broken bones scattered at my feet. And in the center stood a figure cloaked in smoke and shadow, his eyes glowing like twin coals.

Nightshade.

He didn't speak, didn't move. But I felt him. Felt the hunger in him. The darkness is pouring off him like ink in water. Around him, the ground writhed. Trees—dead and twisted—ripped themselves from the earth, dragging roots behind them like limbs. Their bark was splintered, their branches reaching like claws. Beside them, shapes moved: lumbering monsters born from crumbling stone and broken buildings. These twisted forms barely resembled what they once were. And skeletons—dozens, maybe hundreds—clacked and scraped, empty-eyed and endless.

They were all looking at me. Nightshade lifted a hand. From the shadows behind him, something moved.

It was Dante. But he wasn't… him. Not fully. His eyes were black, hollowed. And he was smiling. I tried to scream, but the sound caught in my throat.

Then the nightmare shattered into pieces, and I bolted upright, sweat slicking my skin despite the cold. My heart hammered in my chest, breath coming in short gasps.

“Everly.” Cain’s voice was sharp. Urgent.

I turned. He was already moving toward the others, waking them. Rhivane leapt down from her perch, her blade drawn.

"What is it?" I asked, still trying to shake the dream.

"Look." Cain pointed toward the horizon.

And then I saw it.

A shadow—massive and slow—rolling across the land like a wave of ink. It devoured the stars as it came, blotting out the moonlight. The earth trembled beneath us, and the wind went still, as if the world itself was holding its breath. The Duskravens shifted into their panther forms without hesitation. Dante was already on his feet, his face pale but set.

"He found us," Rhivane murmured. "He *followed.*"

The shadow stopped just before reaching the edge of our camp. And then, from the darkness, stepped a figure.

He was tall, draped in robes that seemed made from the void itself. His face was pale, almost inhumanly so, and his hair fell in black strands around sharp cheekbones. But it was his eyes that held me—bottomless pits of voidlight, swirling with something ancient and wrong.

Nightshade.

Behind him, the horde spread across the land—Timberwolves snarling, their bodies made from the mangled trunks of trees twisted and killed by his magic. Monstrous golems of shattered stone and debris lumbered behind them, their eyes glowing faintly. And in between, skeletons marched in perfect silence, weapons clutched in decaying fingers.

"You've led me quite the chase," Nightshade said, his voice a low, rumbling thing that seemed to vibrate in my bones. "But I must thank you for making it so easy."

No one moved. No one breathed. Cain stood in front of Alaric, sword drawn.

"What do you want?" he asked.

Nightshade chuckled. “Oh, come now. You must have guessed by now.” His eyes flicked toward Dante. “It’s thanks to my son that I found you.”

Dante stiffened beside me.

“I saw you, back in Merewick,” Nightshade continued. “Saw everything through the shadows still tangled in him. You think you freed my brother? You only fell into my trap.”

He smiled like it was all some grand joke.

“I let you take the old man,” Nightshade said, nodding toward the wagon. “A little bait. You played your part perfectly.”

“You used him,” Cain snarled.

Nightshade’s grin widened. “Of course I did. What’s a pawn, if not to be moved?”

He turned his gaze back to Dante.

“And you, my boy. Still clinging to the light? Still pretending you aren’t mine?”

Dante stepped forward. I could see the rage boiling beneath his skin, but his voice was steady.

“I’ll never be like you.”

Nightshade’s face darkened. “You already are.”

“No.” Dante’s voice cut the air like a blade. “You gave in. You let the darkness *define* you. But I’ve seen what it does. What it takes. And I won’t be part of it.”

Nightshade tilted his head, almost curious. “You think that defiance makes you strong?”

“I think it makes me *free*.”

Silence. The army stood behind him, unmoving.

Then Nightshade laughed. A terrible sound—cracked and bitter and hollow.

“So be it,” he said. “You’ve made your choice.”

He raised a hand, and the Timberwolves snarled, claws digging into the ground. The earth trembled as the golems stepped forward. Cain stepped to Dante’s side. Rhivane drew his second blade. Sylra, back in her shifted form, growled low in her throat. And I moved beside them, hands shaking but ready.

Nightshade looked at us all, his eyes gleaming with the promise of ruin.

"Let's see how long you last."

I could barely breathe. The air itself seemed to pulse with Nightshade's darkness, so thick it clung to my lungs like tar. My fingers tightened around the hilt of my sword, the leather-wrapped grip slick with sweat. Dante stepped forward, shadows dancing across his face. Cain moved to flank him, eyes locked on his father with a calm that felt like it might shatter any second.

Nightshade's army began to stir—Timberwolves snarling low and scraping clawed roots against stone, earthen golems lurching forward, skeletons rattling in anticipation like they remembered how to hunger.

There was no more time.

With a yell that tore from my chest, I drew my sword. Dante raised his hand, and a surge of water exploded from his palm. Cain whispered something under his breath—a language I didn't know but felt in my bones—and a wind unlike any I'd known whipped outward, sending the front ranks of Nightshade's monsters stumbling.

And then it was chaos.

I charged the nearest skeleton, blade flashing silver in the firelight. It raised a rusted sword, but I was faster. My strike cleaved through its spine, sending its upper body tumbling to the ground. I spun, slashing low to drop another one. They were fast, but brittle—bones clattered to dust if you hit them right. But they just kept coming.

To my left, Dante unleashed another blast of water. It curled and twisted like a living thing, knocking down two Timberwolves mid-leap. The spray of it brushed my cheek even from where I stood. Cain shouted something and lifted his sword—light exploded from the blade, lancing through the air and splitting a golem clean in half.

Still, they came.

I fought with everything I had. My muscles burned, my lungs begged for air, but I didn't stop. Couldn't stop. My sword sang through the night, slick with dark ichor and bone dust. One, two, three more fell.

But for every monster that hit the ground, two more surged forward.

Just as the Timberwolves breached our flank, a roar split the night—high-pitched, echoed in triplicate.

Nyx crashed into the battlefield from the left, now towering over the enemy, each of his heads snapping and snarling. He bit clean through the neck of a Timberwolf made of twisted bark, then leapt, pinning a skeletal knight beneath a paw the size of a barrel.

One head barked commands, another growled low, while the third scanned the field for threats near me. He was everywhere—teeth, shadow, fire.

Dante shouted something I couldn't hear over the roar of the Timberwolves. A massive creature made from blackened stone charged him, swinging a fist the size of my torso. He ducked and rolled, flames bursting from his outstretched palm, but the blow grazed his leg. He stumbled. Cain turned, yelling Dante's name, and that split-second of distraction nearly cost him—one of the wolves lunged, catching Cain in the side with a jagged root-claw.

"Cain!" I screamed.

He staggered, blood blooming across his shirt. Rage flared through me like a wildfire, so sudden it almost buckled my knees. No. Not him. Not now. I gripped my sword tighter and surged forward, cutting through two skeletons as I made my way toward him.

Then I saw Nightshade move.

He reached behind him, into the darkness, and pulled a bow made of twisted shadow and bone. An arrow materialized in his hand, the tip black and gleaming like obsidian.

I looked to Sylra.

She was mid-pounce, her feline form graceful and deadly, her fangs bared as she leapt for one of the remaining Timberwolves.

The arrow flew.

"Sylra!" I screamed.

The impact made a sickening sound—like something wet and final. She crumpled mid-air, crashing to the ground in a heap of dark fur and stillness.

Everything inside me shattered.

"No."

The word came out broken, more breath than sound. And then—light. A radiant white burst exploded from my hands. For a heartbeat, everything froze. Then the blast rushed outward like a tidal wave. The Timberwolves closest to me collapsed instantly, their forms turning to ash mid-snarling breath. The golems cracked and crumbled, their bodies splitting apart. Skeletons dropped in perfect silence, lifeless again.

Whatever force I unleashed—whatever last flicker of power had burst from my soul—it had devoured everything within reach. But Nightshade stood far beyond the blast, untouched. The battlefield went quiet. So quiet I could hear my heart pounding. Everyone turned to look at me.

I looked down—white light pulsed faintly from the center of my chest. No... not my chest. From somewhere deeper.

Nightshade raised another arrow. Aimed it directly at me. Time slowed. Cain turned, shouting something I couldn't understand. Dante lifted his hand to cast, but he was too far. The arrow hit.

Pain, unlike anything I'd ever known, bloomed in my shoulder. It burned cold—so cold—and spread like a poison through my veins. I collapsed to my knees, the sword slipping from my hand and clattering uselessly beside me. Cain was suddenly there, catching me before I hit the ground completely.

"Everly—no. No, no, no—please—"

I couldn't speak. Could barely see him. Everything was spinning. The edges of the world darkened.

Nightshade's voice echoed over the silence, distant and cruel.

"This isn't over," he said. "I'll return—for my family. For my kingdom."

He turned, cloak billowing, and vanished into a receding storm of shadow. His army—what remained—fled with him, swallowed by the night.

Cain cradled me in his arms, trembling.

"Poison," Dante whispered, dropping to his knees beside me. "Eversleep. That arrow was dipped in Eversleep."

"No—no, she'll fight it," Cain said, voice cracking. "She'll fight it. Just stay with me, Everly. Please—just—stay with me."

I want to. Gods, I want to.

But my limbs are so heavy. My blood feels like ice. My breath is shallow and thin. The poison is working fast.

Around us, the others gathered. Rhivane's face was pale, her jaw clenched. Dante looked stricken, lost. I couldn't see Sylra. My chest ached with the thought of her.

Gone. Just like that. I reach out blindly until my fingers find Cain's. He took them in both of his, holding on like he could will me to stay.

His face blurred in and out of focus.

"I'm sorry," I whispered. "For everything."

"Don't. Don't say goodbye," he begged. "We still have time. We'll find a healer. We'll fix this—"

I gave him a weak smile. “Cain... I love you.”

The words tasted like sunlight and sorrow. I saw his tears fall, felt his fingers tighten on mine.

Then the darkness took me.

Acknowledgments

This book would not exist without the unwavering support and encouragement of the people around me.

To my beta readers—thank you for your time, your honesty, and your faith in this story. Your feedback helped shape *Oath of Starfire* into something sharper, deeper, and more alive.

To my husband, Chris—your unending support, love, and patience have been my anchor through every chapter. Thank you for reminding me that even when I doubt myself, you never do.

To my Aunt Jill—your wisdom has guided me through more than just storytelling. Your insight helped me see the bigger picture, both on the page and off.

To my Nerd Herd at work—your endless banter about dice rolls, campaign chaos, and character arcs reignited my love for fantasy. It gave me the spark I needed to build this world. You may not have realized it, but your geeky joy helped create something magical.

This book is for all of you.

A Note from the Author

If you enjoyed *Oath of Starfire*, the best way to support this indie author is with a quick rating and review. It helps new readers find the story.

Review on:

- Amazon • Barnes & Noble • (and if you're there) Goodreads
-

Let's connect!

- Facebook & Instagram: Author Rikki Starbuck-Smith
- Website: wordsmithhollow.com